. . . and it is us.

W9-BOM-242

Resounding praise
for the Rachel Morgan novels
by *New York Times* bestselling author
KIM HARRISON

"Allow me to introduce you to Rachel Morgan,
witch, bounty-hunter and bad-ass."
Miami Herald

"The world of the Hollows is fast-moving,
funny, harrowing and scary, and—the greatest
compliment to a fantasy—absolutely real."
Diana Gabaldon

"Like a smoldering combination of Alice
Waters and Ozzy Osbourne."
New York Times Book Review

"A consistently delightful urban fantasy series."
Tulsa World

"Fascinating and unique. . . . Kim
Harrison carries it off with style."
Jim Butcher

"Harrison is the reigning queen of urban fantasy."
Sacramento Bee

"A very successful dark urban fantasy
series. . . . Fantasy with a capital F."
Charlotte News and Observer

"The Rachel Morgan series is fast becoming one of
the hottest tickets in the urban-fantasy subgenre."
Booklist (*Starred Review*)

By Kim Harrison

Books of the Hollows

PALE DEMON
BLACK MAGIC SANCTION
WHITE WITCH, BLACK CURSE
THE OUTLAW DEMON WAILS
FOR A FEW DEMONS MORE
A FISTFUL OF CHARMS
EVERY WHICH WAY BUT DEAD
THE GOOD, THE BAD, AND THE UNDEAD
DEAD WITCH WALKING

And Forthcoming in Hardcover

A PERFECT BLOOD

And Don't Miss

UNBOUND
ONCE DEAD, TWICE SHY
HOLIDAYS ARE HELL
DATES FROM HELL
HOTTER THAN HELL

KIM HARRISON

PALE DEMON

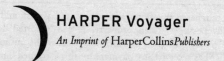

HARPER Voyager

An Imprint of HarperCollinsPublishers

This book is a work of fiction. The characters, incidents, and dialogue are drawn from the author's imagination and are not to be construed as real. Any resemblance to actual events or persons, living or dead, is entirely coincidental.

HARPER Voyager
An Imprint of HarperCollins*Publishers*
10 East 53rd Street
New York, New York 10022-5299

First Harper Voyager mass market printing: December 2011
First Harper Voyager hardcover printing: March 2011

Harper Voyager and) is a trademark of HCP LLC.

Printed in the U.S.A.

10 9 8 7 6 5 4 3 2

To the guy who knows how I take my tea . . .

Acknowledgments

I'd like to thank my agent, Richard Curtis, for everything he does so I can do what I love, and my editor, Diana Gill, who makes what I love to do look good.

PALE DEMON

One

Brown or green for the drapes, Rache?"

Jenks's voice slid into my dozing state, and I opened an eyelid a crack to find him hovering inches from my nose. The sun was hot, and I didn't want to move, even if his wings provided a cold draft. "Too close. I can't see," I said as I shifted in the webbed lounge chair, and he drifted back, his dragonfly-like wings humming fast enough to spill a red-tinted pixy dust over my bare middle. June, sunbathing, and Cincinnati normally didn't go together, but today was my last day to get a tan before I headed west for my brother's wedding.

Two bundles of fabric were draped over Jenks's arms, spider silk most likely dyed and woven by one of his daughters. His shoulder-length curly blond hair—uncut since his wife's death—was tied back with a bit of twine to show his angular, pinched features. I thought it odd that a pixy able to fend off an entire team of assassins was worried about the color of his drapes.

"Well," I hedged, not more confident in this than he was, "the green goes with the floor, but I'd go with the taupe. You need some visual warmth down there."

"Brown?" he said, looking at it doubtfully. "I thought you liked the green tile."

"I do," I explained, thinking that breaking up a pop bottle for floor tile was ingenious. "But if you make everything the same color, you'll wind up back in the seventies."

Jenks's wings dropped in pitch, and his shoulders slumped. "I'm not good at this," he whispered, becoming melancholy as he remembered Matalina. "Tell me which one."

I cringed inside. I wanted to give him a hug, but he was only four inches tall. Small, yes, but the pixy had saved my life more times than I had spell pots in my kitchen. Sometimes, though, I felt as if we were worlds apart. "Taupe," I said.

"Thanks." Trailing dull gold dust, Jenks flew in a downward arc to the knee-high wall that separated my backyard from the graveyard. The high-walled graveyard was mine, too, or Jenks's, actually, seeing that he owned the deed, but I was the one who mowed the lawn.

Heartache took me, and the sun seemed a little cooler as I watched Jenks's dust trail vanish under the sprouting bluebells and moss, and into his new bachelor-size home. The last few months had been hard on him as he learned to live without Matalina. My being able to become small enough to help him through that first difficult day had gone a long way in convincing me that demon magic wasn't bad unless you used it for a dark purpose.

The breeze cooled the corner of my eye, and I smiled even as I dabbed the almost tear away. I could smell the newly cut grass, and the noise of a nearby mower rose high over the distant hum of Cincinnati, across the river. There was a stack of decorating magazines beside my suntan oil and a glass of melted iced tea—the lull before the storm. Tomorrow would be the beginning of my personal hell, and it was going to last the entire week, through the annual witches' conference. What happened after that was anyone's guess.

Nervous, I shifted the straps of my bikini so there wouldn't be any tan lines showing in my bridesmaid's dress, already packed and hanging in a garment bag in my closet. The witches' annual meeting had started yesterday on the other side of the continent. I was the last on the docket—like saving the biggest circus act for the end.

The coven of moral and ethical standards had already shunned me, tried to incarcerate me without a trial in Alcatraz, sent assassins when I'd escaped, and finally accepted a stalemate only when I threatened to go public with the fact that witches had their beginnings in demons and I was the proof. The rescindment would become permanent after they replaced the missing member of the council and pardoned me for using black magic. At least that was the theory.

As much as I needed to do this, I was so-o-o-o not looking forward to it. I mean, I'd been accused of being a black witch—of doing black magic and consorting with demons, both of which I did. Do. Whatever. That wasn't going to change, but if I couldn't pull this off, I'd be hiding out in the ever-after for the rest of my life. Not only did I not particularly like demons, but I'd miss my brother's wedding and he'd never let me live it down.

I looked up, squinting into the oak tree as the familiar, almost ultrasonic whistle of a pixy cut through the drone of a mower. It was no surprise when Jenks darted out from behind the knee-high wall, going to meet Jumoke, one of his kids, coming in from sentry duty at the front of the church.

"What's up, Jenks?" I called out as I grabbed my sunglasses, and the pixies angled toward me, still talking.

"Black car at the curb," Jenks said, his hand on the hilt of his garden sword. "It's Trent."

My adrenaline pulsed, and I almost jabbed the earpiece of my sunglasses into my eye as I put them on. "He's early!" I exclaimed, sitting up. Trent and I had an appointment for me to annul his familiar mark, but that wasn't until five. The curse wasn't ready yet, and the kitchen was a mess. Maybe he wanted to see the prep, afraid of what might be in it.

Jumoke's wings hit a higher pitch when the front bell rang, and we all turned to the back of the church as if we could see through it to where Trent was standing on the front porch. The bell was one of those big farm bells with a pull, and the entire sleepy neighborhood could hear it. "Maybe he'll go away if we don't answer," I said, and Jenks rose—sixty feet in a mere second. In another second, he dropped back down.

"He's coming around back," he said, his gold dust looking black through my sunglasses.

Damn it back to the Turn. "Pix the sucker," I said, then waved my hand in negation when Jumoke clearly thought I was serious. The small pixy looked about six, and he took everything literally.

Jenks flew backward as I twisted, yanking on the back of the chair until it slid forward and I could sit more upright. Maybe this was a last-ditch effort to get me to sign that lame-ass paper of his, guaranteeing my safety from the coven but making me Trent's virtual slave in the process. Tomorrow I'd be on the West Coast, clearing my name and sliding completely out of his clutches. Either that or he was avoiding Ivy— a distinct possibility. He knew she'd be here tonight, and his spies had probably told him she was out now.

Jenks's wings clattered, and I flicked my gaze to his. "What do you want me to do, Rache?" he asked. "He's almost at the gate. My kids are mobbing him."

My jaw clenched, and I forced it to relax. I had a nice silk blouse picked out to wear tonight. Something professional and classy. And here I was in a bikini and with a dirty kitchen. "Let him come back," I finally said. "If this is about that paper of his, he can suck my toes and die."

With a nod and a wing chirp for Jumoke to accompany him, Jenks and his son darted to the side of the church and the slate path there. I settled back, tilting my head so I could see the gate without looking obvious about it. Trent's voice—his beautiful, resonant, soothing, political voice—slipped over me even before he got to the gate, and I touched the braid that Jenks's kids had put my curly red flyaway hair in this morning. I hated that I liked his voice, but it was a familiar hatred, one that had lost its fire long ago.

The wooden latch to the tall gate lifted, and my heart

thumped as I took my sunglasses off. Eyes half closed, I pretended to be sleeping.

Wreathed in pixy kids, Trent came into my garden, his motions both slow and irate; clearly he was not liking the noisy, winged escort. Keeping my expression bland, I took in his slim form. In the months since I'd last seen him, Trent had deepened his tan, and his baby-fine, almost translucent hair caught the dappled sun. Instead of his usual thousand-dollar suit, he had on a lightweight gray short-sleeved shirt, dress slacks, and shiny dress shoes. It made him look harmless, but Trent was anything but. And what was he doing here alone? Quen never let him out by himself.

Trent made his way down the fern-laced slate path with the pixies chatting at him, his innocent businessman facade hiding his true demeanor as the head of an illegal bio-drugs and Brimstone distribution. *Why am I helping him again?*

I am helping myself, I thought, suddenly feeling almost naked. If I didn't annul the familiar bond between us before I left for the witches' meeting, Trent would start trying to kill me again, and as much as I detested the man, I liked him rather more when he wasn't trying to put me in the ground.

Feeling like a big fat hypocrite, I closed my eyes entirely, listening to Trent murmur something to one of Jenks's kids as his steps scraped on the broken patio tile. My heart beat faster. If it had been anyone other than Trent, someone might think I liked the man. In reality, I was trying hard not to look like the crazy witch living in a church with a gargoyle in the belfry, pixies in the garden, and a cat on the fence—even if I was. No way was he getting into my kitchen. Not with candles all over the place and half-crushed herbs and magnetic chalk everywhere.

"You'll never guess who I found digging through our trash, Rache," Jenks said snidely, and I stretched, shivering as a cold shadow slipped over me.

"I thought we got rid of those raccoons," I said, opening my eyes to find Trent looming over me, nothing more than a black silhouette with the sun behind him. The scent of cinnamon and wine hit me, and I squinted up. *Trent was on edge? Curious* . . . If Trent was uncomfortable, then maybe I could keep the upper hand even if I was only half dressed. That would be a nice switch. He was good at putting me on the defensive.

"Oh! Hi, Trent," I said when the man said nothing, the half shadows of pixy wings making dappled patterns over both of us, their noise almost as loud as their chiming voices. "What the Turn are you doing here already? Avoiding Ivy, are we?"

He backed up, and the sun blinded me—just as he had planned. "Good afternoon, Rachel," Trent said dryly. "You're looking well."

"Thanks." I reached for my sunglasses and put them on as he moved to stand next to the chair with my robe draped over it, effectively stalling me from taking it. "It's amazing what two months of not being on anyone's hit list will do for a person." I hesitated, realizing his hair was in a more trendy style than usual. "You're not looking bad yourself, for a murdering drug lord."

At that, Trent's smile became real. I think he enjoyed our verbal banter—everyone else was too awed by his bank account to stand up to him. "I apologize for surprising you like this, but I have something I want to discuss with you." He glanced up at Jenks. "Alone, if possible?"

He *was* avoiding Ivy then, I mused, thinking it was funny. Jenks snorted, his hands going to his hips. His fingers just brushed the hilt of his garden sword, giving him a mischievous, dangerous look, like Puck with an attitude and penchant for killing. Amused, I beamed at Trent, pulling up a knee so I didn't feel so exposed.

"Actually, I am kind of busy right now," I drawled as I settled back into the chair and closed my eyes. "You have to make melanin while the sun shines." I opened my eyes, smil-
͟ ͟at him with bland insincerity, but a small ache of warning
͟ ͟d my brow. *He's here alone.*

͟ ͟iggle in the trees drew Trent's attention up, and he

made a quick step to the right, getting out of the way of one of last year's acorns. It pinged on the broken slate of the patio, bouncing and rolling under my lawn chair as a chorus of disappointment grew.

"Excuse me," Jenks said sourly, darting up into the tree. There was a noisy complaint, quickly hushed, and the pixies started to drop down one by one to leave an acorn, a stick, and even a marble on the table beside my glass of iced tea before they apologized and flew mournfully into the graveyard, all under Jenks's watchful eye.

"I have four hours to try to get this pasty skin a shade away from death-pallor white for my brother's wedding," I said, uneasy and trying to ignore the little drama, "and I'm not spending it in my kitchen twisting your spell. Come back at five. Or you can sit and wait until the sun goes down. I don't care. Is Quen in the car? He's welcome to come back. I've got more iced tea in the fridge. Or a beer. You guys drink beer, don't you?"

"I don't have a babysitter today," Trent said as if it was a victory, and I cleared my throat. I knew how he felt. My babysitter was either a four-inch man or an annoying ex-ghost, depending on how much trouble I was currently in and which reality I was occupying.

Jenks's youngest daughter, Jrixibell, dipped forward and back, twisting the hem of her brown silk dress. Apparently it had been her acorn. Under Jenks's stern gaze, the sweet-looking little girl mumbled a shamefaced "Sorry" and flew to where three of her sisters waited, and together, they darted into a nearby bush to plot further mischief.

Trent smiled, half-turned, and shocked the peas out of me when he brushed the nearby chair free of imaginary dust and sat down, moving gingerly, as if he'd never had to trust plastic webbing before. Staring at him, I took off my glasses.

He's staying? Sure, I'd offered, but I hadn't expected him to take me up on it! Suddenly I felt twice as exposed, and I could do nothing as Trent crossed his legs and leaned forward, taking the top magazine off the stack. "Doing some redecorating?" he asked idly.

"Uh, Jenks is," I said, heart thumping. Crap on toast, I couldn't just lie here and pretend he wasn't there. I'd thought he'd get huffy, spout some nonsense about his time being more important than mine, and leave. "You're, ah, going to wait? Don't you have something else more important to do?"

"Yes, I do, actually," he said as he turned a page, his green eyes darting over the images of tiles and artwork. "But I want to talk to you. Alone." His eyes lifted from the magazine, fixing on Jenks.

"Now just a fairy-farting minute . . ." Jenks rose up on a column of indignant silver.

My brow furrowed. Trent had come early, stinking of cinnamon and wine, to talk to me alone. So-o-o-o not good. "It's okay, Jenks," I said softly, but he didn't hear me.

"The day I leave you alone with Rachel is the day I wear a dress and dance the polka!" Jenks was saying, and I sat up, putting my feet to either side of the lounge chair.

"Jenks, I've got this."

"We are a team!" Jenks shouted, his hand on the hilt of his sheathed garden sword. "You talk to all of us or none of us!"

There were about a dozen pairs of eyes watching from the edges of the garden and graveyard, and I heard a rustle of leaves overhead. I glanced at Trent. His lips pressed together for an instant, and then his expression eased, hiding his irritation.

"Jenks," I said softly, "it's okay. I'll tell you what he says." Trent's eyes squinted, and I lifted my chin. "Promise."

Immediately Jenks calmed down, his wings clattering as he landed next to my iced tea in a huff. Trent got that little worry wrinkle, but it was true. I'd tell Jenks just about anything, and Trent needed to know that.

"Why don't you get your kids and check out the blackberries at the far end of the graveyard," I said, and there was another rustle in the tree overhead. "All of them."

"Yeah, okay," Jenks said sullenly. He rose up, pointing two

fingers at himself, then at Trent—the unmistakable gesture of "I'm watching you"—before he flew off, yelling at his kids to clear out and give us some space. Trent watched them leave from their hidden nooks and hidey-holes, his tension becoming more obvious as he laced and unlaced his fingers.

A wind blew across the graveyard, smelling of cut grass and warm stone, and I shivered. "Well, what is it?" I said, leaning back in my chair with my eyes closed, pretending indifference. "You going to tell me what you can't say in front of my partners and your office help, or are you just going to sit there ogling my bikini."

That didn't get the expected chuckle. I heard him take a breath and let it out. The soft, sliding sound of the magazine being replaced made me shiver again. "Your upcoming meeting with the coven?" he said softly. "I don't think you realize what's going to happen."

My eyes opened, and I turned to him. He'd leaned forward to put his elbows on his knees, hands laced between them. Bowed over, a worried slant to his brow, he looked up as he felt my gaze on him.

He was worried about the coven? "The witches' annual meeting?" I said. "Not a problem. I can handle it." The webbing was cutting into me, and I shifted uncomfortably.

"You're begging forgiveness for using black magic," he said, and my gut tightened at the reminder. "It's a little more than dodging drunk witches at the beach."

I shifted the strap of my top to hide my unease. Trent looked scrumptious sitting on that cheap chair, even if he was worried. "Tell me something I don't know," I grumbled.

"Rachel . . ."

Nervousness twisted in me, and I grimaced. "The coven called off their assassins," I said, but I couldn't look at him. Sure, they'd quit trying to kill me, but they could start up again in a demon minute. *Let me live in my dream world a day longer, okay, Trent?*

"You're leaving tomorrow for the coast?" he asked, and I

rubbed a hand under my nose, nodding. He knew that. I'd told him last week.

"What about Jenks and Ivy?"

My gaze slid to Jenks, standing on the knee-high wall between the garden and the graveyard. True to his word, he was keeping his kids corralled. He was pissed, though, his feet spread wide and his hands on his hips. His wings were going full tilt into invisibility, but his feet stayed nailed to the sun-warmed stone. I lifted a shoulder, then let it fall, trying to look nonchalant. "Ivy's staying to watch the firm. Jenks is coming with me. If he's human-size, he'll be able to handle the pressure shifts." *I hope.* Suddenly suspicious, I turned to Trent. "Why?"

He sighed. "You'll never make it. Even with Jenks."

My heart gave a thump, and I forced myself not to move. The slight breeze became chilly, and goose bumps ran down my arms. "Oh, really?"

"Really," he said, and I flushed as I saw him notice my gooseflesh. "Which do you think more likely: that the coven is going to let you come before them with that story of how they shunned you as part of an elaborate plan to test my security systems, or that they will simply make everything go away by killing you en route?"

It was hard to keep my head in the sand when he kept yanking my tail feathers like that. "I'm not stupid," I said as I grabbed the suntan oil. "You don't think I've thought about that? Where's my choice here? They said they'd pardon me if I kept my mouth shut."

"They never said whether or not the pardon would come while you were alive."

True. "That's so unfair." Peeved, I flipped the bottle top open and squirted some oil onto my palm.

"You can't afford to be stupid anymore," Trent said, and I frowned, smacking the bottle on the table. "The same qualities that make you an attractive employee—loyalty, honesty, passion, diligence . . . trust—will get you killed until you realize how few people play by your rules."

That last one, *trust,* had been hard for him to say, and I frowned, rubbing out the goose bumps under the guise of putting on suntan oil. "I'm not naive," I grumbled as I found the red marks from the webbing. Yes, I worked with demons, studied with them, and was one of only two witches capable of invoking their magic, but I'd been good. I'd *never* hurt anyone who hadn't hurt me first, and I'd *always* shown more restraint than those who'd tried to kill me. Even the fairies.

"The coven will never let you on a commercial plane, and the only way you're going to make it to the coast is if we go together," Trent said quickly. "The coven won't dare attempt anything if I'm with you."

Together? I blinked, then stared at him. *This* was why he'd come in my garden stinking of cinnamon and wine. He wanted to go out to the coast together and was afraid I'd say no. "Are you offering me a ride on your private jet?" I said, incredulous. I was almost free of him and the coven both, almost my own person again. If I got on his plane, it could land anywhere.

"You have to trust me," he said as if reading my mind, but his body language said I shouldn't.

I settled back, uncomfortable and feeling cold. "Yeah, like I believe you'd help me out of the goodness of your little elf heart. Don't think so."

"Would you believe I'm trying sugar instead of vinegar?"

He sounded amused, and I squinted at him. "Yeah," I blurted out. "I'd believe that, but I'm not getting on your jet. You are a drug-running, tax-evading, irritating . . . murdering man, and there hasn't been a month in the last two years that I've not worried about your trying to off me."

"Irritating?" Trent leaned back against my robe, seeming to like being irritating, his fingers laced and his ankle on one knee. The position would have made me look unsure, but on him it was confident. The scent of coconut oil mixed with cinnamon, and he dropped his eyes. Silent, I waited.

"The truth of the matter is I'd rather have you alive and free of the coven than dead," Trent said softly, glancing up as a torn leaf drifted down. "If you leave for the coast without me, you won't make it. I still harbor the hope that you'll someday work with me, Ms. Morgan."

We were back on familiar ground. Work *with* me was better than work *for* me, but how many times did I have to say no? "No—you're lying," I said, waving my glasses at him when he began to protest, green eyes looking innocently at me from under his wispy blond hair. "You walked in here all strung out about asking *me* to go with *you* to the coast, not the other way around. You want my trust? Try buying it with the truth. Until then, we've got nothing to talk about. Bye-bye, Trent. See you at five. Don't let the graveyard door hit you on the way out."

I jammed the glasses back on my face and reclined in a huff, ignoring him as he shuffled his feet. For a moment, I thought he was going to stick to his lame claim of city-power benevolence, but then he whispered, "I need to get to the West Coast. I have to have an escort, and Quen won't leave Ceri. She's three weeks from her due date."

Ceri? My jaw clenched, my eyes opening as I looked into the amber-tinted world. I sat up, eying Trent to see if he was lying. There was a hint of compassion there, but most of his expression was peeved, probably because Ceri liked his security officer instead of him.

"Quen won't allow me to leave Cincinnati unless you come with me," Trent said, clearly bothered. "He says you're raw but enthusiastic."

I laughed. I couldn't help it. "Okay," I said, swinging my legs to the broken patio again. "I think I've got it now. You say you want to join forces to help me—poor little me—but it's only because Quen won't let you go by yourself. How come? You planning on speaking out against me if I don't sign your lame-ass paper? I knew there was a reason I liked Quen."

"Will you forget about that contract?" he said, starting to look cross. "It was a mistake to try to bully you, and I'm sorry.

My need to get to the coast is a private matter. You're simply a means to get me there. An escort."

He was sorry? I thought, shocked by the admission. From the wall, Jenks flew up in a burst of orange. Clearly, he'd heard it, too.

"Please," Trent said, scooting to the edge of his chair. "Rachel, I need your help."

From the gate came the faint, familiar sound of a metallic click and a puff of air. Behind Trent, a little blue ball at chest height flew right where he would have been had he not leaned forward. It hit the tree, exploding in a familiar splat of sound as a piercing whistle echoed through the garden.

Trent stared at me, then the wet mark, his eyes wide.

Shit, we are under attack.

Two

Trent rose to his feet, stupidly staring at the tree and the foaming yellow mass of magic.

"Get down!" I shouted as I yanked him off balance. He started to fall, and still sitting, I pulled him toward me, bracing myself and levering his weight over me and to the patio on my far side. He hit the hard pavers with a gasp, eyes wide and hair askew. I was already reaching a quick thought out to the ley line in the backyard. Power flowed in, familiar but painful in my rush, and before Trent had tossed the hair from his eyes, the word *rhombus* whispered through my mind. In an instant, I relived the five-minute process to make a protection circle.

The semi-invisible barrier sprang up around us, me at its center as in all undrawn circles. Trent sat up, his head even with my shoulder. "Stay down!" I hissed, and we both jerked as two more splats hit my circle, their magic making little dimples of color on my black-and-gold aura. Beyond it, the pixies were moving in the graveyard, and I cursed my stupidity. I'd told Jenks to keep his kids centralized, effectively shutting down our first line of defense.

"Jenks!" I shouted as I stood, my circle inches from the top of my head, and reached for my robe, jamming my arms into the sleeves.

Jenks was gone, but his gold-dust trail still glittered, showing that he had flown straight up, getting the sitch. A shrill pixy chirp drew my attention to the front gate. My eyes met the would-be assassin's, and the attacker ducked.

"There!" I shouted, and more pixies arrowed toward the attacker.

Frowning, I fumed as I tied my robe. "Get in the church," I all but growled at Trent. "Put yourself in a circle."

"Rachel."

I turned, angry as I took in his tightly pressed lips and angry green eyes as he managed to be ticked that I'd pulled him to safety even as the attacker fled. "They were aiming at you, not me!" I said. "Get in the church!"

Not waiting to see if he did as I'd told him, I ran for the gate, gasping as I broke my circle and took the energy into myself. My bare feet were almost silent on the slate path, and my jaw clenched. My splat gun would have been handy right about now, but Al had melted it two months ago and no one would sell me a replacement.

Heart pounding, I shoved on the worn, rough wood of the gate, adrenaline sending it crashing into the bushes.

"Ms. Morgan, look out!" shrilled a pixy, and I jerked back at the puff of air.

"Crap!" I exclaimed as I fell against the fence and the gate smacked back into the door frame. Looking the way I'd come, I saw there was a new splat on the ground between me and the empty lounge chair. Miracle of miracles—Trent had actually listened to me and gone inside. The slightly itchy feeling in the back of my mind might have been him setting a circle. Or it might have been the assassin setting up a trap.

A dark-haired pixy landed on the fence, his hands in fists as they rested on his hips. "He's running now, Ms. Morgan," Jumoke said, and I gave him a quick, grateful smile.

I smacked the gate open again and ran through it, Jumoke flying just over my head. A passel of pixies trailed behind, shouting encouragement. The man who'd shot at me was indeed running, and a wicked grin spread across my face.

He was fast. I was faster, and I raced after his slim, dark

form as he headed for the street. My fingertips grazed the man's shirt as we reached the sidewalk, and heart pounding, I fell on him. He had time for one yelp of surprise, and I clenched my eyes against the coming cement.

We hit with a jar that knocked my breath away, and I scrambled for a new grip, sunglasses falling off. "You tap a line . . . and you won't . . . wake up . . . until next week!" I panted when I caught my breath. Oh God. My elbow was vibrating all the way up to my skull, but he'd taken most of the impact. Scrambling, I put my knee in the small of his back and twisted his arm around his own neck, ready to snap his wrist if he moved. The pixies were everywhere, talking so fast I couldn't understand them, but I caught the words "intruder" and "Papa." Just where was Jenks, anyway?

The man wasn't moving, and after some vigorous "encouragement" he let go of his splat gun and the pixies worked as a team to drag it out of his reach. It looked like mine, right down to the cherry red color. And the blue splat balls? They were almost my trademark.

"You trying to frame me for assaulting Trent?" I exclaimed, and he only grunted. "What you got in your splat balls, Jack? Maybe we should find out together? Real personal like?"

Breathing hard, the man tried to look at me, the anger obvious in his green eyes. Green eyes, blond hair, lanky build, tan: Was he an elf? An elven assassin? Not a very good one, though. And where the hell was Jenks?

The sound of running feet pulled my head up. There was a second man, and I could do nothing. Damn it, he was getting away!

"Are you after Trent or me?" I shouted at the guy under me and, furious, I thunked his forehead into the cement.

The man's eyes showed his pain. "Why do you even care?"

Huh?

There was a squeal of ultrasonic sound, and Jenks's kids dropped back to make room for their dad. "Two of them!" Jenks exclaimed, dropping silver sparkles and a zip strip from

my charm cupboard to hit the man's back.
kitchen. You want me to get her?"

Her? I slipped the zip strip around the man's
ratcheted it tight, immediately feeling better. "Jack   't
move as his maybe-contact with a ley line was severed, telling
me he hadn't been prepared to use one to begin with, but better
safe than sorry. I was spared the decision of what to do by the
sound of Ivy's cycle at the far end of the street. Jenks darted
away with a second zip strip, leaving his kids to sweetly tell
me what I ought to do to the man under me. He moved when
the subject of wasps entered the conversation, and I yanked on
his arm.

Ivy's bike slowed as Jenks's dust glittered over her, then she
gunned it, roaring past me and aiming for the woman fleeing
over the lawns. Ivy was a tad more protective of me than
Jenks, and with a silent fury she ran the woman down, using
her foot like a jousting pole. Wincing, I watched the woman
take a mouthful of grass as she slid to a front-face halt. Jenks's
children left me, and the woman slowly sat up, her hands in
fists over her head as they surrounded her, bright sparkling
spots of potential death in the sunshine.

"Kids!" Jenks's voice was shrill. "We've talked about this!
Lunkers are a no-kill species! How come you never listen to
me like you listened to your mom!"

It looked like it might be over. "Get up," I said, breathing
hard as I eased up on my grip.

The man spun under me, foot and fist lashing out. Jerking
up and away, I stood, grabbing for his foot. It smacked into me
with a bone-jarring thump, but I caught it. Determined green
eyes met mine, and when I went to snap his ankle, he side-
swiped me with the other foot.

I gasped and went with it, trying to keep my presence of
mind as I fell on the concrete walk, trying to turn it into something graceful. There was a sickening crunch under me. My
glasses. *Damn it!* I'd let go, though, and when I again found
my feet, he had stood and was coming at me with a knife.

"Rachel, quit playing with him," Ivy said loudly, her cycle idling back to us, the zip-stripped woman meekly walking before her with an escort of exuberant pixies holding swords.

"He's got a knife!" I exclaimed, teeth clenched as I did an X block, then dove under his arm to make him twist his own knife into his side. And there I stopped, breathing hard as I pressed the blade, still in his grip, into him, but not yet breaking the skin. He didn't move, knowing it was right over his kidney. Jeez Louise, the curtains of the house across the street were moving. We had to take this inside before someone called Inderland Security. The last thing I needed was the I.S. out here.

"You've lost, Jack!" I shouted as I pinched his wrist until he let go of the knife, then wrenched his arm up and pressed him into the nearby light pole. "We got Jill," I said as he grunted, "and no way are you getting that bucket of water in my garden. If you don't relax, I'm going to bust your crown! We clear?"

The guy nodded, but I didn't ease up. Spitting my hair out of my mouth, I realized that Ivy had parked her cycle and was coming up the walk with the woman. The female assassin's hands were in fists, high over her head. Jenks's kids were working together to shift the knife to the sidelines. Slowly I started to smile. We'd gotten them. Hot damn!

"Hi, Ivy," I said as she scuffed her booted feet to a halt. "Get the errands done?"

The slightly Asian-looking woman quirked her lips at my robe, smiling as she held up her pharmacy bag. The unmistakable shadow of a second splat gun and several knives showed through the thin plastic. Her lips were closed to hide her small, sharp canines, but her mood was good.

"You want to take this inside or bag them up and leave them here for big-trash pickup?" she asked, her black eyes going to the deceptively empty street. Her pupils were fully dilated despite the bright sun, evidence that she was working to maintain control of her instincts. Being in the sun would help; so would the wind now carrying away the scent of sweat and fear.

"Inside," I panted. I was out of breath, but ⸱ was six feet of lean, athletic living vampire, dreᵥ jeans, boots, and a tight black T-shirt. It would take n̤ running down a fleeing assassin on her bike to make her ⸱ ⸱k into a sweat.

"You going to be good, Jack?" I asked the man pressed against the light pole, and when he nodded, I let up. He grimaced as Ivy patted him down, adding another knife and more blue splat pellets in a clear, crush-proof plastic vial to her bag. I held my hand out for the splat balls and I refilled his hopper, fast enough to make Jack's eyes widen in appreciation.

Clicking the magazine away, I hefted the splat gun, thinking it felt good in my hand. "This is my house," I said as I indicated the church. "If you do something I don't like, you're going to get whatever's in the hopper, and the law will be on my side. Clear?"

They didn't nod, but they didn't spout threats, either.

"Move," I said, and with an obedience that told me the potions were nasty, the two of them started up the cement stairs and toward the double wooden doors. Slowly I began to relax.

Ivy looked at the gun, her brow furrowed. "It looks like yours," she said.

"You noticed that, too?" Eying the attackers, I pulled one side of the door open. Jenks's kids entered the church first— three of them carrying my broken sunglasses—then the bad guys, then us. "Are you okay?" I asked Ivy.

She smiled to show her fangs, small until she died and became a true undead, and I stifled a shiver. Ivy was great at maintaining a grip on her instincts, but fight, flight, or food brought out the worst in her, and this was all three. "Not a problem," she said as the dark foyer took us. One of these days, we were going to invest in a new light fixture, but the sanctuary beyond it was a bright wash of light, the sun coming in the tall stained-glass windows to make colored patterns on the new set of living room furniture, my unused desk, Ivy's exercise mats, and Kisten's burned pool table. I still hadn't had it refelted. My bare feet squeaked over the old oak, and I shoved Jack toward the small hallway at the back of the sanctuary.

"Trent is here already?" Ivy asked, clearly having smelled him. "He's still alive, right?"

I nodded, wiping the grit from the sidewalk off my feet. Good Lord, I had tagged an assassin in my bare feet and a bikini. If this showed up on the Internet, I was going to be peeved. "Last I knew, he was. I told him to go into the kitchen and wait." Assassins usually traveled in threes, but these were elven. I didn't know their traditions.

"He's in there," Jenks said derisively as he dropped down to us. "I don't think they're real assassins. They didn't know any ley-line magic."

"You don't need magic to be deadly, Jenks. You of all people should know that."

Jenks snorted. "I don't think they know any. They stink like elves, but they've got so much human in them, they might not *have* any magic."

I shrugged, guessing as much by the almost indifference Jenks's kids had shown the two attackers. The man in front of us glanced back as we entered the dark hallway, and I smiled mockingly. "All the way to the end," I directed as we passed the his and her bathrooms and twin bedrooms and headed to the huge, industrial-size kitchen. I cleared my throat in warning as Jack and Jill whispered between themselves, and they shut up.

The pixies were singing about blood and daisies as we entered the sunlit kitchen to find Trent safe within a circle of his own making between the cluttered center counter and the sink, full of dirty spell pots. The bright, cheerful gold of his circle was free of any demon smut, making me uncomfortable. He'd just been under my aura and had seen the mess I'd made of it. Demon smut. Ugly. Black. Permanent—mostly.

The kitchen was hands down my favorite room in the entire church, with its expansive stainless-steel countertops, fluorescent lighting, and center island counter with my spelling equipment hanging above it and in the open cabinets below it. There were two stoves, so I didn't have to stir spells and cook on the same surface. My mom's new fridge took up a wall. Bis, perched atop it, was asleep next to the skull-shaped cookie jar. The little gargoyle had probably been trying to stay awake after sunup and misjudged. He'd be down until sunset no matter how noisy we were, and it was getting noisy. Pixies were flitting in and out through the one small window over the sink. Ivy's computer was set up on the big farm-kitchen table against the inside wall, but the space felt like mine. That Trent had been in here alone sort of bothered me.

Jenks's kids were flitting everywhere, too excited to perch in one place, and they were starting to give me a headache. Trent, too, looked like he was hurting. "Look, Ivy! Elf under glass!" Jenks said, and I sighed, even as a small twinge on my awareness went through me and Trent dropped his circle.

Like one entity, Jenks's kids swarmed Trent. He stiffened, but did little other than grimace when Jrixibell asked if she could make a dandelion necklace for him. Yeah, Jack and Jill might be elves, but they weren't full-blooded like Trent. The pixies were almost ignoring them.

"Jenks . . . ," I prompted, my own head splitting from their noise as I glanced at Bis. How the cat-size, gray-skinned kid could sleep through this was a wonder, but he was, his leathery wings lying close to his back, his black-fringed ears drooping, and his lionlike tail wrapped around his clawed feet in slumber.

Jenks clattered his wings for their attention. "Okay, you lot!" he shouted. "Jumoke, Jack, Jixy, Jhan can stay if you're quiet! The rest of you, hit the garden. Evens take cleanup. Odds on perimeter. Not a butterfly crosses the lines without someone knowing! And watch the splat-ball marks. Stay back until we have a chance to get out there with salt water. And no dropping moths into the puddles to see what the charms do! Clear?"

In a chorus of affirmation and disappointment, they dispersed, the eldest children Jenks had asked to remain retreating to the overhead rack. I exhaled in relief, and realizing that I was standing like Jenks with my bare feet spaced wide and my hands on my hips, I dropped my arms.

"Sit," I said to the would-be assassins, pointing at the floor beside the fridge, and they gingerly lowered themselves. With a languorous stretch, Ivy shoved the magazines off her chair with a booted foot. They hit the floor with a thump and slid into a long pile against the wall. Deceptively calm and relaxed, she drifted back to the doorway, standing to look aggressive as she took her hair out of its ponytail and let the strands fall where they might. Unless the assassins went through the window, they were stuck.

A breath of self-preservation made me toss a roll of paper towels to the woman. Not only was her chin bleeding, but the man's forehead was scraped where I'd thunked him into the sidewalk. Ivy would appreciate it, if nothing else. The harsh ripping of the paper sounded loud, and folding up a sheet, Jill dabbed at her jaw and passed the roll to Jack.

"Move, and I'll be on you like a demon," Ivy said. "Do, please."

Jack and Jill looked at each other. Together they shook their heads. I kept one eye on them as I unloaded Ivy's bag next to my broken sunglasses, setting the two splat guns and five knives on the counter, looking right at home among my magnetic chalk and scrying mirror. The knives had an elaborate, intricately raised design on the handles to help with the grip. I didn't like that one of the guns looked like mine. I wondered what was in them. That first shot had been aimed at Trent, making me wonder about his story of Quen not letting him leave Cincinnati without me. He could've gotten himself on someone's hit list, but these guys weren't good enough to be taken seriously. And why would elves want me dead? No, I was betting they were here for Trent.

"Did they tell you who sent them?" Trent prompted, and I tightened my robe again.

"Not yet." Turning to them, I smiled. "Who wants to go first?"

No one said anything. Big surprise. I flicked a glance at Trent. It was a no-win situation. If I was tough, he'd think I was a thug. If I was too nice, I'd be a pushover. Why I even cared what he thought was beyond me.

Jenks dropped down to the man. "Who sent you?" he barked, sword angled at the man's eye.

Jack remained silent, and Jenks's wings began slipping an eerie black dust. In a whisper of sound, Jenks darted close and then away. The intruding elf yelped, his hand smacking his head where Jenks had been. I frowned when I saw the wad of hair in Jenks's grip. I didn't like this. Jenks was usually easy-going, more inclined to plant seeds in the ground than people, but his land had been violated, and that brought out the worst in him.

"Ease up, Jenks," Ivy said as she came forward to touch Jill's face. "You need more finesse with the big ones." She made a little trill of sound as the woman drew back in fear, and I sighed as Ivy started to vamp out.

Think, Rachel, I mused silently. *Don't just react, think.* "Guys," I said, conscious of Trent watching. "We need to find out what's going on without leaving any traces."

"I won't leave a mark," Ivy whispered, and Jill paled. "Not where you can find one."

"They might be a test from the coven," I said, and Ivy's finger, tracing the woman's jawline, curled under and she straightened in disappointment.

"We can't simply let them go," Ivy said. "Even if it wasn't much of an attack."

I winced. "Maybe we should call the I.S.?"

Jenks snorted, and from the overhead rack came a peal of high-pitched laughter. Yeah, bad idea.

"Mind if I hurry this along? I have an idea."

It had been Trent, and, as one, we all turned to look at him.

"*You* have an *idea*?" Jenks said sarcastically, hovering before him in his best Peter Pan pose, his hands on his hips and his red bandanna tucked into his waistband. "The day you have a good idea will be the day I eat fairy toe jam."

"He said it was an idea. He never said it was a good one," I scoffed. But my lips parted at the sudden prickling of magic. Like a blanket rubbing the wrong way, wild, elven magic scraped across my aura, both an irritant and an enticement, pulling at my pores as if trying to draw my soul from my body.

"Hey!" I shouted, knowing it was Trent. Elves were the only species that dared to use wild magic. Even demons shunned the art. It had a horrible unpredictability along with the horrible power. It couldn't be the two elves on the floor. They had zip strips on. "Trent, no!" I did not have a clue as to what he was doing, and with a satisfied glint in his eyes, he clapped his hands.

"Volo te hoc facere!" he exclaimed, the sound pinging through me, making me both cower and jump as the force I felt him drawing from the line abruptly fell to nothing.

I will you to do this? I thought, clutching my robe around me. An enthrallment spell?

But I think it was, and I stood at the table and stared at Trent, aghast. The rims of his ears were red, and his jaw was clenched in determination. "That was a *black* spell," I whispered, stepping forward and out of Ivy's reach. "That was a black spell!" I yelled, and he retreated to the table, his eyes falling from Jack and Jill. They were motionless, almost slack-jawed, eyes unfocused and hands limp, unable to do anything apart from the most basic things to survive unless told. "You enthralled them, didn't you!" I exclaimed, and he bowed his head. When it came back up, his eyes met mine with a fervent gleam, unrepentant.

"What did he do to them?" Ivy said, sidling up next to me. Jenks wasn't happy either, buzzing over them as they blinked vacantly.

"He enthralled them," I said, sure of it when Trent's lips

pursed. "And it's black." Damn it, I hadn't known he could do something that sophisticated. It changed everything.

"Black?" Jenks yelped, darting up in a wash of yellow dust.

"Go ahead, ask them who sent them," Trent said, standing stiffly as he gestured to them. "I know who did, but you wouldn't believe me if I told you. Not in time, anyway. Go on. It doesn't last long."

Well, that was one bit of good news. "And then what?" I said harshly. "Do you know how illegal those are? This is *my* kitchen, and *I'm* the one who's going to be blamed for this. Or is that your idea?" I said with a sneer, and Ivy caught my arm, thinking I was going to cross the room and smack him.

"You need to hurry up," he said, tossing his hair back in a rare show of nervousness. "I have this under control. I'll hit them with another charm so they don't remember."

I shoved Ivy's hand from me, shaking as I stood there. "Is that your plan? Make them forget? God, Trent. This is, like, six times illegal!"

Trent tugged his sleeves down as if unbothered, but his eyes were squinting. "True, but no one gets hurt this way. And I'd think you'd be the last person worrying about what's legal. You've got thirty seconds. Tick tock, Rachel."

As I stood there fuming, Jack started to blink. Ivy took my arm again, this time in encouragement, but I couldn't do it. It was wrong!

"Oh for Tink's little red shoes," Jenks said suddenly, and he darted down to hover before the man. "Who paid you to attack Rachel?" he barked, his hand on his sword hilt.

"No one," Jack said, and I turned to Trent, my brow furrowed.

Jenks's dust turned green. "You mean you don't know, or you weren't paid for it?"

Trent shifted his weight to his other foot. "They weren't attacking Rachel, they were attacking me. Try again."

Giving me an apologetic shrug, Ivy slipped past me and crouched before Jill, lifting her chin to force her to look at her.

"Who told you to attack Trent?" she asked calmly, and I crossed my arms over my chest. I wanted to know, but I'd rather scare it out of them than use black magic.

"Walter Withon," they said together, and a knot tightened in my gut.

"This was a warning," Trent said with a sigh, his shoulder easing to make him look somewhat embarrassed. No, guarded.

"Ellasbeth's dad?" I dropped back a step, my anger fizzling. Crap on toast. Ellasbeth was the woman Trent had been going to marry—until I'd arrested Trent at his own wedding. It was something Trent thanked me for later in a weird bit of honesty when we thought we were both going to die. Yeah, the Withons had the means for a hit, and they might be a little mad. But enough to take potshots at him?

"Now will you help me?" Trent said, and I took a breath, snapping myself out of my funk. Seeing my eyes on his, Trent smiled wickedly, hands moving in a ley-line charm.

"Trent, wait . . . ," I said.

But it was too late, and I could do nothing when I felt the line he was connected to give a lurch and he whispered, *"Memoria cadere."*

Again, I jerked back, setting up a protection circle around myself since I didn't know *what* the man was capable of anymore. Seeing its creation, Ivy flung herself almost under the table, and Jenks darted to the ceiling. I stood tall, heart pounding as a wash of my gold-tinted aura lapped over the circle with all the subtleties of a shadowy pearlescence. Bis, on the fridge, stirred, his bright red eye cracking open to find me before it slid shut again with a little sigh.

"Damn it, Trent!" I exclaimed, furious as the assassins sat, wide-eyed, and stared at me, bewildered but clearly no longer enthralled. "What in hell are you doing?"

"You're kidding," he said in disbelief. "You weren't going to ask them anything, worried it might be ille-e-e-e-gal."

He drawled it, mocking me, and I squinted at him, fear of the Withons mixing with the worry of what the assassins could have told us before but now couldn't. "You did that on purpose!" I shouted.

His head bowed slightly, and his lips quirked as he eyed me, looking both mischievous and polished. "I told you I was going to."

Anger grew in me, but I stayed where I was beside the table, sullen. It couldn't be undone. Not easily, anyway. "Dr. Anders teach you that?" I muttered. Memory charms weren't black; they were simply illegal as all hell. It didn't make me feel any better, though.

On the floor, the woman felt her chin, shocked when her fingertips came back wet with blood. "Um. Whoa," she said, looking tense but harmless. "I guess that explains why I have no idea who you people are or how I got here."

Her companion nudged her to be quiet, clearly not remembering anything, either, but knowing enough to keep his mouth shut. Bad. This was so bad. Two illegal charms, and if Trent got to the West Coast, he'd probably try to pin them on me if I didn't become his indentured servant. Damn it back to the Turn! I wasn't going to play this game!

Jenks dropped from where he'd been checking on his kids. His hand was on the butt of his sword, and he looked ready to give Trent a lobotomy. "I had more to ask them, even if she didn't."

"You wanted to know who sent them. Now you do. It was wearing off," Trent insisted, but I could see a hint of unease in him. "Our only other option was to kill them."

"Our?" I barked sarcastically. "There is no 'our.' This is your doing, not mine." I spun as Jill started to get up, her alarm obvious. "Park it, Jill!" I said, but it wasn't until Ivy cleared her throat that both of them checked their upward motion and slid back down.

"My name isn't Jill . . ." the woman started.

"It is today. So sit down and shut up until I tell you that you can leave. Got it?"

"Shit," the man said sourly as he thumped his head back

against the fridge and eyed me in mistrust. "I don't know who was supposed to pay us. Do you?" Jill shook her head. She looked too confused for it to be an act. "Awww, man!" the guy added. "I don't even know where I left my stuff. This sucks."

"See?" Trent said confidently, but that worry wrinkle above his eyes was still there. "It worked. Now we can let them go and be on our way with their employers still thinking we are here." He smiled, and I hated him. "They won't be expected to check in for twenty-four hours. We could be long gone by sunset."

Jenks's wings hummed, and Ivy's face lost its expression. "Sunset?" she said, and I grimaced. She wasn't going to like this, but it didn't matter. I *wasn't* helping Trent. Not after this. He had stood in my kitchen and performed two illegal charms, one of them black. Ceri was rubbing off on him and not in a good way.

"I'm not going anywhere with you, you little shoemaker," I said, trying to figure out what to do with these two. "Especially after that little stunt. Not in a plane, not in a car, not on a train . . . you've gone too far." I blinked. *What the hell?*

"Ah, Rachel?" Ivy touched me, and I jumped. "What's this about Trent needing your help. Help for what?"

Jenks hummed his wings for her attention, smirking at Trent as he said, "Trent wants Rachel's help. Quen won't do it. Trent says it's because Quen won't leave Ceri, but I think the little cookie maker plans to speak out against Rachel at the, uh, big meeting to get her under his thumb again, and Quen refuses to be a part of it. Trent won't have anything on her after she nullifies his familiar mark, so he has to move fast."

Jenks smiled at Trent, and Trent sighed. "It's not like that at all," he said, but his confidence was wearing thin.

Ivy glanced quickly at me before turning back to Jenks. "Not going to happen."

Shrugging, Jenks landed on the center counter where he could watch everyone. "Or Trent's telling the truth, and he's afraid of the weenie assassins here."

Jack scowled, and Jill made a little huff of sound, but I was glad Jenks hadn't dropped any names. They'd forgotten who had sent them and didn't need any reminders.

Trent frowned, one hand behind his back as he turned to me. Shoulders stiff, he asked, "Will you do it?"

I could not believe this, and I pointed at the two assassins sitting in front of my fridge. "No!" I said firmly. "I'm not helping you. Especially now."

Trent shifted, his confident poise lost when his hand slipped from behind his back. "They tried to kill me," he said, his brow furrowed as he glared at them. "You saw them!"

"Yeah?" I spouted off. "They weren't very good at it!"

Jenks was laughing, but I was mad and ready to throw Trent out. Throw them all out. Standing by the table, I dropped my forehead into my hands and rubbed at my temples. From the floor Jack sighed. "My old lady is going to be pissed. Her, I remember."

I pulled my head up. "Get out," I said bluntly. "Get up and get out. Both of you."

For a moment, Jack and Jill stared at me, but when Jenks clattered his wings threateningly, they slowly got to their feet. Okay, I knew who'd sent them, and it only solidified in my mind that I wasn't leaving Cincinnati on Trent's private jet. He was *still* lying to me. *Son of a bastard.*

"I don't feel so good," the woman said as she held her stomach and limped forward.

Jenks laughed bitterly. "That's because we beat you up. You cried like a baby."

The two people shuffled toward the door, feeling body parts as they began to complain. Jill looked at the weapons on the counter, but when I shook my head, they filed out under a pixy escort. Ivy seemed surprised that I was simply letting them go, but I had to be on a plane tomorrow at eight. I didn't have time for an extended smackdown.

"Jenks, you'd better tell your kids to leave them alone unless they come back," I murmured, and he flew up on a column of silver dust.

"Yeah-h-h-h-h," he drawled, his focus vacant as he imagined it. "I'll be right back."

He was gone in an instant, and from the front of the church, I could hear him shrill something, and then the door opening and closing. I turned to look at my kitchen, defiled by elven black magic. It wouldn't leave a visible mark, but it left me uneasy just the same. Al might be able to smell it.

"You, too, Trent," I said, listlessly picking up the roll of paper towels and trying to wipe the pixy footprints off the stainless steel. Trent's curse lay assembled on the counter, but he could just suck my toes and die for all I cared.

"I'm not leaving until you untwist the curse," he said stiffly. "It's all there. Do it now."

I hesitated in my motions to clean the counter. Ivy cleared her throat, and I felt more than saw her take up a stance. Still not looking up, I continued to clean the counter, picking up the scrying mirror and setting it down. Then the magnetic chalk, the five candles, the stick of redwood. He could go to hell. "Good-bye, Trent," I muttered, my head starting to hurt.

"Excuse me?"

His voice was harsh, and I balled up the paper towel, standing with my fists on the counter so I wouldn't jump over it and strangle him. "I don't trust you," I said softly, my knuckles going white from the pressure. "If I take that curse off now, you won't want me for anything and will speak out against me at the coven's meeting. You're going to have to wait. I'll do it after, not a moment sooner."

From the street came a faint "Is that our car?"

Trent grimaced when his car alarm began beeping, and he looked ready to murder someone as he fished a key fob out of his pocket and pointed it at the street. The alarm cut off, and he turned back to me. "That wasn't the deal," he said. "Take the mark off. Now."

"Neither was your coming over here trailing assassins," I said, letting go of the balled-up paper towel. Behind him, Ivy went to her stash of chocolate on the counter, opening a box and leaning against the counter. She was behind Trent, between him and the door, and he shifted to keep us both in his sight.

"Rachel," he warned, looking pissed.

"I'll do it," I said flippantly. "But you're going to wait until I'm safe. You don't like it?" I said, voice rising. "Then kill me. Right now. Go on!" I shouted. "Do it! Here I am!" I flung my arms wide to make a bigger target. "But if you do, you'll *never* get the mark off you! You slimy little thug!"

Jenks buzzed in with worried wing chatter, seeing me screaming at Trent and Trent looking like he'd swallowed a bug. The pixy exchanged a look with Ivy, who was now leaning idly against the counter, completely unworried as she ate a chocolate-covered orange slice. Her apparent indifference seemed to make Trent only more pissed.

Trent took a breath and held it. Saying nothing, he turned to the door, his stance stiff. Jenks snickered, and the man spun back around, even with Ivy there. His face was white with anger, and his eyes almost seemed to glow. "You are the most . . . unprofessional, irritating, frustrating person I have ever had to deal with," he said, and I shrugged. "I don't need your help. I'll get to California without you."

"Like I care," I said, and he turned on his heel and strode from the kitchen.

"Good riddance," I said, then, in a wash of self-preservation, I followed him to the hallway, leaning out into it as I shouted after him, "Go on! Leave! I'll get that mark of yours taken care of, but not until I get my freedom! You son-of-a-bitch elf!"

He never slowed, his dark silhouette flashing into a blinding whiteness when he found the sanctuary. More light poured in when he opened the church's door. It boomed shut behind him, and I pulled myself back into the kitchen.

Ivy was still slumped at the counter. Her eyes were hooded, and she looked . . . rather sexy from the anger Trent and I had been giving off. Grimacing, I stalked across the kitchen to the window, shoving it high to let in the breeze. Birdsong drifted in, and my hair tickled my neck. From the fridge, Bis sighed, his wings shifting as he settled back to sleep. I hadn't realized I'd woken him up. Peeved, I stared out at the bright afternoon, seeing the dark spot of the spell on a tree. I'd have to take care of that before the pixies got into it, even with Jenks's admonishment.

Beside me, Ivy casually took another piece of chocolate, succinctly biting through it with a snap of chocolate and sugar crystals. Jenks hummed closer, landing next to the brandy snifter on the windowsill. It was turned upside down to keep his cat, Rex, from eating the chrysalis Al had given me last New Year's Eve. Jenks's wings were unmoving and his expression worried as he looked at me, not the garden.

"What?" I said as I edged toward Ivy, leaning close to take a chocolate and then retreating. I looked down, seeing the dirt and grass clippings on my feet. My robe had come undone, and I tightened it back up. So much for getting a tan.

Ivy licked her lips and stood upright. "Do you think calling his bluff was the smartest thing to do?"

I exhaled, shaking as I leaned against the center counter. "No," I admitted sourly. "No, it wasn't, but I'm not going to give him what he wants until I know he's not going to give me to the coven." I bit into the chocolate, feeling the sudden give and the crunch of crystallized orange on my tongue. From the front of the church, Trent's car engine was racing harshly.

"It's the first smart thing she's done," Jenks said, making the short flight to the chocolate and using his sword to cut off a slice the size of his hand.

"Maybe, but something isn't right," Ivy said, clearly not convinced, and I followed her gaze as she took in the assembled ingredients for Trent's curse, next to the assassins' splat guns and knives and my broken sunglasses. An unsettled feeling tightened around my chest, and I fidgeted. I was glad I'd said what I had, and I wasn't going to "escort" Trent to the West Coast, but if truth be told, I agreed with Ivy. Something wasn't right, and I didn't think it was over yet.

Three

Hollows International wasn't a huge airport, but it was busy with early-morning flights, even at the ungodly hour of seven in the morning. It was way too early for me to be up, and I felt numb, the lukewarm cup of blah coffee almost slipping from my grip. Our flight was boarding in half an hour; we had lots of time. The air smelled like floor polish and plastic, and I sat in the fake leather chairs across from the check-in counter and people-watched as Ivy bought a ticket and checked our luggage. After the incident with Trent, she had gotten leave from her master vampire to come with Jenks and me.

Trent's prediction that I wouldn't be allowed on the plane had convinced me that the less I interacted with the gods and goddesses of air travel in their polyester blazers and winged lapel pins the better. So I sat waiting, our carry-ons strewn around me. Nervous, I pushed myself to the back of the chair and slouched. Jenks, though, wasn't fooled by my show of nonchalance.

"Trent's an ass, but he's right. We're not getting through security," he predicted, making his wings hum for some extra heat. It was chilly this morning, and all the warmth was escaping through the big plate-glass windows and the endless opening of the doors.

I didn't look at him, watching Ivy's slowly moving line. "Trent's just trying to scare me," I said, but when I realized I was spinning my wooden pinkie ring around and around on my finger, I stopped. I didn't need it to hide my freckles anymore, but if I didn't wear it, my brother, Robbie, would ask where my freckles had gone. What if we couldn't get on the plane? I had to be there in three days or my shunning would become permanent.

"Is it working?" Jenks landed on my knee where he could lecture me better. He was wearing his garden best, convinced that he wasn't even going to have to use the potion in my bag to go big to handle the air-pressure shifts. He hadn't even arranged for anyone to watch his kids, thinking we'd be back in an hour. His confidence in me was breathtaking.

I cocked my eyebrows, and he put his hands on his hips, finally starting to dust a little as he warmed up. "Rache, even if Trent is telling the truth and the Withons are gunning for him, that doesn't change that you being dead would make the coven's life a lot easier. You are *not* getting through security," he said, glancing nervously at a little girl in pink who had noticed him. "We should be thinking about how we're going to get you two thousand miles in three days, not chilling at the airport."

"I already have my ticket," I said sourly, noticing that Ivy had reached the front of the line. "How are they going to stop me?"

"Rache . . . ," he coaxed, and I shifted my shoulders, acknowledging that he had a point.

"Look," I said, slouching even lower. "If they don't let me on the plane, we'll take the train. Be there in no time."

His sigh was tiny, but I heard it despite the loudspeaker paging someone.

Silence grew between us, and I took in his pulled-back hair and his sharp black-and-green outfit with bluebells on the hem. It was the last outfit that Matalina had made for him, and I knew he wore it to feel close to her. It had been a very hard two months, even if he now knew for sure that his biological clock had been reset and he had another twenty years ahead of him. I, too, had my first twenty-six years back, and I figured this was why demons lived so long. By next spring, Jenks would be the world's oldest pixy. I didn't care that it had taken a curse to do it—as long as he was happy. He was happy, wasn't he?

Worry filled me as I watched him watch everyone else, his attention mainly on the cameras in the corners. "How you doing, Jenks?" I asked, the tone of my voice telling him I wasn't asking about the temperature. He turned, his sharply angular face showing a neutral nothing until I added, "Don't lie to me."

Jenks looked away as the sun started to stain the sky. "Fine," he said flatly.

Fine. I knew what fine was. I had been "fine" for the better part of a year after Kisten died. Since then I'd dated Marshal, had gotten shunned, and had sex with a nineteenth-century ghost named Gordian Pierce who'd been bricked into the ground alive in 1852 by the same group currently trying to give me a lobotomy and steal my ovaries.

Much as I hated to admit it, Pierce was everything I liked wrapped up in a package that might be able to stay alive through the crap my life dished out. He was Al's familiar, and I saw him every week when doing my stint as a demon student in the ever-after. We'd not had a moment alone together since he'd helped me get a temporary reprieve on my shunning, and it was aggravating, even if I didn't quite know what to think of Pierce anymore. He'd seen me through one of the most terrifying moments of my life, and we had opened up to each other in ways that left me wondering why I was still hesitant. He was a good man. But the same things that had once attracted me— power, tragic history, and a sexy body—now left me with a mild sense of unease. Ivy would say I was getting smarter, but I just felt . . . empty.

Twisting, I felt my back pocket for my phone, wondering what time it was.

"Seven thirty-two," Jenks said, knowing me better than I did myself.

"Thanks." Sighing, I tucked the phone away. Jenks didn't like Pierce, agreeing with Al that the charismatic witch would be the death of me, but Pierce wouldn't hurt me. He loved me.

The hard part was I thought I might love him, too, someday. I just didn't know, and Al wasn't letting me figure it out. It worried me that Pierce was a little too free with the black magic, even if it had been to help me. I was trying to prove that black magic didn't make you bad—but still I hesitated, whereas a year ago I'd have been head over heels and damn Al back to the Turn for getting in the way.

"Here she comes," Jenks said in warning, and I looked up. Sure enough, Ivy was making her way toward us, our two bags left behind on the conveyor belt and a blue-and-gold envelope in her hand. She was wearing an unfamiliar black business suit to make her look both sexy and capable, a mix of brains and body able to get *anything* done in the boardroom. I'd never be able to carry off that look, but for Ivy, it was easy.

"See?" I said as I sat up. "She got her ticket okay."

Jenks whistled softly as she maneuvered gracefully through the throng, ignoring the stares behind her. "The woman needs her own theme music," he said dryly.

I stood and he took to the air. "Cake. 'Short Skirt, Long Jacket.'"

"That'd do it," he said as Ivy picked up her briefcase with her laptop in it.

"So far, so good," she said, glancing at the nearby security line.

Jenks wasn't impressed. "Yeah, they just confiscated your luggage, Rache. Good job."

"Jenks . . . ," I complained, then turned to Ivy. "What gate? All my ticket has is the flight number."

"Doesn't matter," Jenks said bluntly. "We're not getting through security."

"A5," Ivy said, not looking at her ticket.

Ignoring Jenks humming a dirge, I grabbed my garment bag with my bridesmaid's dress in it. It had been easier than I had thought possible to coordinate Cindy's bridal shop with the one I'd worked with in downtown Cincinnati, making sure my hem length would match everyone else's. And for once, I liked this dress, steel blue-gray with no lace. I'd give Robbie's fiancée one thing—she had great taste.

"Next stop, Portland," I said as I threw away my coffee and fell into step beside Ivy. Boots clunking, we crossed the white tile.

Jenks was an irritating hum at my ear. "Woo-hoo! I haven't seen anyone strip searched all week!"

We got closer to the short line where the spell and metal detectors were, and Ivy began dropping back. "What?" I said, irate, and she shrugged.

"You first."

Exasperated, I got in line behind an old couple crabbing about the wait. "Why are you making so much out of this?" I asked. "If they were going to do something, they would have done it by now. They probably don't even know I'm here. Robbie bought the tickets, not me." But a sick feeling was slipping between my thought and reason as I noticed the two security cops eying me from the other side of the gate. Ahead of me, the old couple tottered through both the metal and the charm detection. The charm detection glowed a bright red, but the security people waved them on. In the distance, a plane roared into the air. I started to sweat.

Jenks's wings hummed, and I muttered, "This won't be a big deal. Let's just get through this as fast as possible, okay?"

His doubtful expression saying it all, Jenks darted through the detector and swung back around to land on it, waiting. With a feeling of foreboding, I dropped the garment bag on the belt and smiled at the severely emotionally deficient woman across from me. She was about twenty pounds too heavy for her uniform and didn't look happy.

"Any produce or high magic to proclaim?" she asked dully.

My heart started to pound. *Cool it, Rachel,* I thought, knowing they had charms to detect stress. "No fruit but for the pixy there," I quipped, pointing at Jenks only to have him flip me off, "but I do have a lethal-magic detection earth-magic amulet and a high-magic detection ley-line charm on my bag here."

If I didn't claim it, I'd get nailed for sure. They weren't illegal, just unusual. The curse in my bag to make Jenks big wouldn't even register, it being demon magic and all.

The woman looked up. "Pixy?"

Jenks clattered his wings for her attention. "Hey, hi," he said, trying to look innocent. "I'm not flying like this. I mean, I'm going on the plane. I've got a ticket."

The woman looked away. "We'll have to check your bag by hand" was all she said, and I gave Ivy a sarcastic smile. *See? No problem.*

"I guessed as much," I said cheerfully, handing it over. I couldn't move through the detector until she gave me the okay, but Ivy's briefcase slid past me, and the guard asked her to step through. Behind her, a young couple with a kid in a stroller were grumbling about the holdup. I was busy making bunny-eared kiss-kisses at the baby when the attendant cleared her throat, not sounding nice at all.

"Can I see your ticket, ma'am?"

I looked up, my expression going blank. *Crap, she called me ma'am.* "Um, it's in my handbag," I said, seeing it in front of her. "I'm going out for my brother's wedding."

She reached for my bag as she leaned to look at the screen. "Nice dress. Bridesmaid?"

I nodded, trying to stay calm. Her attitude had shifted from boredom to a sharp interest. On the other side of security, Ivy waited with her hip cocked.

"Can I reach into your bag for your ticket?" the woman asked, and I nodded again, hope sinking. "There's a problem here," she said, not even looking at the paper.

From behind me, the couple with the kid began complaining more loudly, a businessman and what looked like an entire high school cheerleading team behind them joining in.

"My brother gave it to me," I said, leaning closer, only to have her point at the floor and a yellow line I'd never even noticed before. "I checked it online," I babbled as I backed up. "It's still good. Look, my seat is verified and everything."

"Yes, ma'am," she said, my bag with all my identification in it in her grip. *Oh God, what if they slipped Brimstone in there or something?* "Could you step over there, please?" she asked tightly. "Just through here." She flipped the conveyor belt up and pointed to a laminated table and three chairs set to the side. Two guys and a woman in blue were waiting for me, hands placed behind their backs so their guns and wands showed. It was the wands I was worried about.

"Sure," I said, slumping, and Jenks darted to join Ivy. Taking a deep breath, I crossed the yellow line into enemy territory, the carpet changing from dirty and threadbare to only dirty.

"Rachel?" Ivy called out with Jenks on her shoulder. "What do you want me to do?"

I hesitated. "Wait for me on the other side?"

She smiled without mirth. "I was planning on doing that anyway."

I knew she was saying more than her words were, and I dropped my eyes. Twenty minutes. I had only twenty minutes to get to my gate. Damn it! I should have known better. I wasn't going to make it. I could either spend my time arguing with these guys or grab a shuttle back to the car. Screwing up my resolve, I eyed my shoulder bag on the table and my garment bag on the counter behind them.

"Look," I said as I stopped before the table, "I don't want to waste your time. If there's not a fairy's fart in a windstorm of a chance I'm going to make my flight, or any flight for that matter, will you just let me know now so we can all get on with our lives?"

One of the men inclined his head and gave me a cigarette-stained smile. "Not a chance."

"Okay." I nodded, trying to stay calm. Looking across the conveyors and archways, I found Ivy and Jenks and made a "kill" gesture.

"Well, duh," I heard Ivy say faintly, and I turned back to the security people.

"Can I have my bags back?" I asked. Apart from my car keys, the curse to make Jenks big, and my scrying mirror, I had all the materials to make Trent's curse in my shoulder bag.

The head security guy hesitated, and I stifled a surge of anger. What did Al do to scare the crap out of me? Oh yes. Get cold and pleasant.

"Don't mess with me, Johnny Boy Scout." Pleasant was too much to ask for, but I could manage cold. "I'm being really nice right now. Just give me my purse and my dress, and I'll be on my way and out of your hair. That is the first bridesmaid's dress I've *ever* liked, and I'm *not* leaving it here." I put my hands on the table, aware of but ignoring the fact that the two subordinates had dropped back and were touching their wands. "Do we understand each other?" I said softly. "Or do I need to stamp it on your foreheads with my foot?" I smiled. That would be the pleasant part.

I felt more than saw Ivy's sleek form slip back through the security exit. Jenks was a sparkle of dust on her shoulder. "Told you so!" she shouted, not slowing as she headed for the doors.

"Yeah, you did!" I exclaimed, not taking my eyes off the head guy.

As expected, my being left to my own devices made the security people more nervous, not less. I wasn't being abandoned; I was capable of handling this on my own.

"Well?" I said, again finding my pleasant inner demon. "You going to give me my dress and my car keys, or am I going to show you why I was shunned?" My smile grew even brighter, even as my mood became more pissed.

"Give it to her," the man said, his words clipped and precise.

"But they said to detain her!" the woman said, sounding disappointed.

Taking his eyes from mine, the head security man met his subordinate's eyes. "Give the woman her dress," he said, pushing my bag back to me across the table. "She's not the one they want."

"But . . ."

"Give the woman her God-blessed dress!" he shouted, and everyone looked at us, the noise of a plane taking off sounding all the louder in the sudden silence. His ears reddening, he hunched like a bear. "I have had an incident-free workplace for three years, and I'm not going to let you ruin that because you want a little gold star, Annie."

The woman huffed, but the man beside her had handed me my things.

Sliding the straps of my bag over my shoulder, I accepted the unwieldy garment bag. "Thanks," I said, surprised that calm and pleasant had gotten me further than hotheaded threats. Maybe there was something to a demon's methods. My bags had never been out of my sight, but I hesitated, finding and holding the man's attention. "Are they bugged?"

"No," he said, his eyes flicking from me to the distant doors behind me and back again. "But your checked luggage probably is. Good luck, Ms. Morgan. You helped my grandfather once. About three years ago, on a bus. I think you're getting a bum rap."

I hesitated, then smiled as I searched my memory for a familiar face and found a close match. "He was being harassed by Were pups? Winter, wasn't it?" I asked, getting a flustered nod in return. "It was my pleasure. You take care of yourself, okay? And thanks."

He smiled, totally ignoring the woman behind him having a hissy, and with my pride intact, I spun on a heel and strode for the big plate-glass doors.

The second I emerged from the low-ceilinged hallway, Jenks dropped down to me. "I told you so," he sang out, wings spilling a yellow dust over me like a sunbeam. Somehow, though, I didn't have it in me to be mad. It wasn't often that I ran into anyone who knew me, and even less frequent that they thanked me.

"Yes, you did," I said, disappointed. Six hours on a plane, and I'd have been there. Now I had three days to get to the

West Coast. Stiff, I pushed the automatic door aside when it didn't slide quickly enough. The fresh air hit me, and I hesitated, fumbling in my bag for a moment until I remembered that I'd sat on my sunglasses yesterday.

"What about your luggage?" Jenks asked, and I shook my head, squinting in the bright morning light and brisk wind, looking for Ivy.

"Forget it. It's bugged," I said. "I'd have to dip everything in salt water."

My new jeans, the silk sweater I was going to impress Robbie with, the swimsuit that took me three weekends to find . . . gone. *At least I still have my dress,* I thought, hiking it farther up on my shoulder. "Where's Ivy?"

Jenks's wings hit a higher pitch, and when he started swearing in one-syllable words, I followed his line of sight down to the end of the curb. Sighing, I pushed myself into motion and made my way past the chatting skycaps to the low black car. Ivy was there with her briefcase at her feet, the flat of her arms on the open front window as she talked to the driver. Her butt was giving the porters something to stare at, and not all the oglers were men. It had to be Trent. Whoopie friggin' surprise.

From somewhere above me, Jenks shrilled, "Listen to me! Listen this time, witch! This is Trent's doing! He wants to get you alone and brainwash you with a charm! Hit you with an enthrallment spell. What about yesterday, huh? You saw what he did! How stupid can you get?"

"Pretty stupid," I said, feeling my heels clunking all the way up my spine as I dodged oversize luggage and yet another cheerleading team. "Trent isn't going to charm me," I said, not so sure anymore. He had tried once before, the spell fizzling only because I'd been drenched in salt water at the time. I wanted to trust him but couldn't bring myself to do it, even if he'd shown me a part of himself that would be dangerous in the right hands. And what was with the elven magic? That stuff could kill you if you didn't do it right.

Jenks dropped down to my shoulder, reminding me of a

shoulder angel. "He's going to convince you to get in that car," he said. "And then you're going to believe everything he says."

I tried look at Jenks but failed. He was too close. "Probably. I want to talk to Quen."

Wings going full tilt, Jenks drifted backward off my shoulder, sputtering.

Ivy noticed my approach and pulled herself out of the window, a hint of relief in her dark eyes. They were dilated despite the early sun but not bad. Worry, not fear. Squinting from the morning light, I looked inside to find Quen behind the wheel. A real smile came over me, and I crouched to avoid looking bad next to Ivy's perfection. Despite, or maybe because of, having fought Trent's security officer in the past, I liked Quen, and by the honest smile on the older man's pebbly textured face, I knew he liked me, too.

"Hi, Quen," I said cheerfully. "How's Ceri?"

From the backseat, Trent cleared his throat, but I was mad at him and ignored him.

"Round, irritable, and as happy as if the world were hers," Quen said, the dark-complexioned man reaching across the seat to shake my hand. It felt small in mine but powerful, and it reminded me of Pierce's. His voice was as gravelly as his skin, both remnants of the Turn. It hit some species harder than most, but witches, vampires, pure elves, and Weres not at all. Quen had some human in him. Not that I thought any the less of him for it.

"It is," I said as I took my hand back. There was something wrong with me. I could free thousand-year-old slaves, outwit militant Weres, survive exploding boats and a vampire roommate once fixated on my blood and body both, but I couldn't find my own happiness. Yet seeing Ceri smile as she held her baby? That would be a good second place.

Quen was an honorable man. If Trent was up to something he didn't approve of, he'd tell me. Wouldn't he? Unsure, I angled my head to Quen. "If you were me, what would you do?"

"I'd get in the car." His eyes were focused out the front window, his jaw tight. He was Trent's security officer and abided by his wishes, but he'd also helped raise Trent and was probably the only one besides Ceri who could say no to him with impunity. And he wanted me to get in the car. A shiver ran through me. Something bad was coming. I could feel it.

"Good enough," I said, hearing Trent's exasperated sigh from the back.

My hand went to the handle, but Ivy's was already there.

"I am not sitting in the back with Trent," she said, eyes narrowing in warning. Behind her, Jenks pantomimed being hanged.

"Oh, for Tink's diaphragm!" the pixy said. "What is wrong with you women?"

The trunk popped open with a slow whine, and I went around back to stow the garment bag nice and flat. Quen met me back there, and I handed it to him. "Thanks," I said softly as Ivy and Jenks got in the front seat, arguing. The door slammed, and Quen gently put my dress into the trunk, already holding a bland but expensive-looking piece of luggage. We had only a moment. Time for only one question. Licking my lips, I blurted out, "Did Trent send those elves yesterday to persuade me to help him?"

Quen met my eyes, a lifetime of nobility in them. "No," he said simply. "I'd feel better if he had, though."

My shoulders slumped, and I didn't move as he eased the trunk closed and the power lock whined as it shut. Squinting, I looked up at a plane taking off, roaring overhead to who knew where. Portland, maybe. My gaze dropped to the bustle of people. Life was going on, and no one but a handful of people cared if I lived or died.

"Yeah. Me, too," I said with a sigh. Feeling trapped, I went to the door that Quen opened for me and slid into the leather-scented darkness.

Four

If looks could kill, my face would show the imprint of Jenks's thoughts. The irate pixy was sitting on the rearview mirror of Trent's big black car, heels thumping the glass and scowling at me as a green dust sifted from him, sparkling in the sun before it hit the dash to make an evil puddle, then spilling to the floor. Ivy was in the front passenger seat, talking softly to Quen about the success he'd had with Trent's highly experimental treatment to make vampire neurotoxins dormant. I could tell it bothered Trent that they were discussing the illegal, high-risk procedure, and the only reason it didn't bother me was because it wouldn't help Ivy in her quest to be free of her vampirism. She was a vampire, and making the neurotoxins dormant in her wouldn't save her soul when she died.

No, she expected me to do that.

Crossing my knees, I looked out the tinted window. We were passing through a weird mix of airport and industry on our way to long-term parking, and I felt cut off. The light making it through the tint was ugly, and it made me uneasy. No one was looking at us. We were just another black car. That made me uncomfortable, too.

From the far side of the backseat, Trent said, "Quen, could we have the roof open?"

Their conversation never hesitated as Quen touched a button and the small square of roof slid back to let the wind and sun roll in. I couldn't stop my sigh of relief, and I settled back into the comfortable leather. I hadn't meant to telegraph my unease, but I thought it telling that Trent was trying to make me more comfortable. Taking a deep breath, I tucked a stray curl behind my ear and looked at him. I'd called his bluff and was still alive. It must irritate him to no end.

He met my eyes and simpered, destroying any illusion I might have had about him being miffed with me. Damn it, he had warned me that I wouldn't be able to fly, and it rankled that I'd have to admit he was right. That jet of his was looking easy. Easy like a demon curse, and those always came back to smack you.

I smiled back, thinking of that curse I owed him. He wouldn't kill me for delaying it, but I was pushing him, and he would push back eventually. That he wasn't dressed for revenge, having gone extremely casual today, made me feel better, and whereas Quen was in his usual black outfit that looked somewhat like a uniform crossed with a martial artist's robe, Trent was wearing jeans and a lightweight short-sleeved shirt. Instead of his thousand-dollar boardroom shoes, he had on brown boots, scuffed from the stables and comfortable.

I was sure his appearance had been painstakingly contrived to remind me of the evening we had ridden over his fields. His number one man, Jonathan, had died under a pack of dogs that night for having attempted to kill me without Trent's permission. Killing an enemy's enemy was probably elven tradition for cementing a new relationship, but that Trent had run his own man down like some perverted version of the Hunt left me cold. Trent had insisted that it hadn't been Jonathan out there and stayed with me while the horns blew and the dogs bayed, but I hadn't seen Jonathan since.

Green was truly Trent's color, and I wondered if the buttons of his shirt were real silver. The wind shifted the collar to show a wisp of hair, and I looked away, my pulse quickening. The moon had been new that night, and it had been wonderful riding as Trent tried to show me what it was like to rule creation with dogs singing for the blood of the one who had hurt me. It had left me feeling curiously . . . lofty.

And then he goes and does black magic in my kitchen? My attention flicked back to Trent, his expression open and wondering, clearly curious as to where my thoughts had gone. Looking toward the front through the quietly moving car, I sighed and said loudly, "Okay. I can't fly. You told me so. I'm still not getting on your jet. And I'm still not going to remove your familiar mark until I'm free of the coven."

Jenks made a rude sound and a burst of dust came from his wings.

Trent shifted in his seat, inadvertently giving away his mood. "I never offered the use of my jet. There you are, jumping to conclusions again, Ms. Morgan."

My runner instincts kicked in, a soothing adrenaline starting to flow. Trent was trying to look relaxed when he was almost sweating. "Jumping to conclusions is my only option when every third word out of your mouth is a half-truth," I shot back. "The Withons trying to kill you for standing up their daughter is a good story, except I know she walked out on you, not the other way around. You're still lying to me. No."

Quen's eyes flicked to mine by way of the rearview mirror. His conversation with Ivy had cut off, and the tension in the car spiked. "You don't need to know why I need to get to the coast," Trent said softly, and Quen's grip tightened on the steering wheel. Crap on toast, whatever it was, it was bad. "All you need to do is get me there," Trent finished.

Jenks's wings were humming a warning, and even Ivy looked worried as she turned in the front seat so she could see me. Her window made a soft sound as she cracked it.

"You're the only one Quen . . . trusts," Trent added, his gaze on his fingers in the shaft of early sun, gray through the tinted windows.

There was that word again, and I grimaced as I looked to Quen and he inclined his head at me in unspoken encouragement. Damn it, I didn't want to be responsible for Trent. I didn't even *like* Trent. "Just get your little elf butt on your private jet and go," I muttered, jealous that his money made everything easy for him.

"I can't," Trent explained patiently. "I can't take the train, either. Tradition says I have to go by land, and I need to be there by Sunday night."

"Two days!" I yelped. "By car? Are you nuts? What do you need to do on the West Coast in two days that you can't do by phone?"

Jenks's wings hummed as if he was going to join us in the back, but a look from Ivy stopped him. The car turned a corner and the sun shifted, coming in to touch my knee without warmth. Trent leaned back into the shadows, reluctant to answer. "What's on the West Coast?" I asked again. "Trent, if you want my help, treat me like a professional. I need to know. Especially if lame-ass assassins are going to be dogging us."

Quen sighed heavily, and at the sound Trent seemed to get mad. "It's my personal business," Trent said, glancing at the back of Quen's head. "No one will be hurt by it, and it doesn't touch on your upcoming trial."

"It's not a trial, it's a pardon," I said quickly, but we all knew he was right.

Trent looked at me across the seat, his green eyes almost black in the shadows. "If you can get me there by Sunday, I should have time to speak for you at the meeting as well," he said, earning a bark of laughter from Jenks. "That is, if my familiar curse is gone by then."

Carrots. Sweeter than vinegar but still unpalatable, I thought, remembering the drug-laced carrots I'd eaten once while a mink trapped in his office. Son of a bitch, what was I doing?

"Get me there after Sunday, and I'll miss my window of opportunity," Trent added. "Three days, and there is no reason for me to go at all. If we leave immediately, we can make both of our deadlines."

My trial was Sunday night, and I met Jenks's and Ivy's eyes. This had all the earmarks of the tip of an iceberg. Trent was in trouble with the biggest elf family on the West Coast. And though he hadn't blamed me, I might have had some part in it. Guilt licked at my soul. I had a really bad feeling about this.

"Will you do it?" Trent asked. He sounded angry but not at me, and I could hear a whisper of past arguments with Quen in his tone. Though Trent was the boss, Quen ran Trent's life, had since Trent's father died. It had to rankle when the only way Quen would let him go would be with me.

"No," I said, sitting up straighter. "The last time I worked for you willingly, the boat blew up. That water was cold."

"Atta girl, Rache!" Jenks exclaimed, and Ivy leaned over to whisper a question to Quen.

Trent's expression was empty. "I kept you alive, didn't I?"

"Only so you could pound my head into a tombstone!"

"I was upset," he said, avoiding my glare as he gazed at the parking lot we'd turned into. The sun shifted to him, making his embarrassment easy to read.

"I had just saved your life!" I said. "And you try to kill me for something I hadn't done and wouldn't do. No, I don't think so. You're spouting pretty words like 'trust,' but you don't give it. I'm not going to help you get to the West Coast so you can run your *personal errand*. Especially if you are playing around with black magic."

Trent's eyes fixed on mine, his anger easy to read as he put one ankle on his knee, looking both cold and professional. "Ceri does black magic. You like her."

I squinted at him. "Ceri has morals," I said, and Quen winced. "I might not understand them half the time, but she's got them. You . . ." I almost poked Trent in the chest, turning the motion into a quick point. "I don't trust you."

"You need me," Trent said, playing it like it was his last card, desperate despite his attempts to hide his stress. "If I'm with you, the coven will be less inclined to take potshots at you. I'll admit that my dealings with you to date have been less than aboveboard." His jaw clenched. "I'm trying to change that. If not for me, you wouldn't even have this chance to clear your name. I swear, Rachel, that my business on the West Coast has nothing to do with you."

My foot braced against the carpet as the car gently halted. I looked up, seeing the back of my mom's car. *Finally.*

"Thanks. I have it from here," Ivy said with her usual calm control. Opening her door, she slipped out. Jenks followed her, shrilling something about his kids. Quen, too, got out, and the trunk whined as it opened. Ivy had a set of keys to my mom's Buick, and she opened the trunk, taking my garment bag as Quen handed it to her. Reaching for the door, I picked up my shoulder bag.

"You," I said to Trent, gripping my bag tightly, "are anything but aboveboard with me. You ask me to trust you, but even now you're not telling me everything. You must think I filled a prescription for stupid pills if you think I'm going to get you out to the West Coast in two days for 'personal business.' God, Trent, you told the coven I was a demon!" I could bear to say it now that Ivy, Jenks, and Quen weren't in the car, but my face still burned.

I pulled on the handle, but nothing happened. Damn it, the thing had child locks.

"I need your help," Trent said as I leaned over the front seat and unlocked the doors from the passenger panel. I flopped back in the seat and reached for my handle, shocked when Trent touched my arm. *"I need your help,"* he said again, letting go. *"Please."*

Oh crap. He'd said please. Gut clenching, I covered my arm where he'd touched me. His eyes were pinched, and I wondered if I was really seeing that whisper of desperate need in the back of his eyes, or if this was all a trick to get me to do what he wanted. "Why?" I asked, letting go of my arm. It felt like he was touching me still.

At the question, the tight press of his lips eased. Outside the car, Quen, Jenks, and Ivy were talking in a small huddle, but the drama was inside the car. Trent wasn't faking. He needed me—and he wouldn't tell me why.

Exhaling, I closed my eyes in a long blink. Crap, I was a sucker for helpless males, especially when they looked as good as Trent. A quiver rose through me, and I felt my resolve start to fall apart. He was powerful, he was suave, and he needed my help. He'd *asked* for it.

Damn it, damn it, damn it! I suddenly realized that no matter how much I complained and argued, I was going to do exactly what Trent wanted. Again. And it irritated me that he was right. If the coven *was* going to take a shot at me en route, they would think twice if Trent was with me. I didn't trust Trent, but I trusted the coven even less.

"I desperately need to get to the West Coast before Sunday night," he said, and my eyes opened. "It's a private matter. This is the most important thing in my life. *Please* help me."

The faint scent from his boots of stables was winding its way into me now that the car wasn't moving and the air was still. His clothes, the sun in his hair, everything combined to remind me of a summer afternoon when I was twelve and he had found me crying in the stables at summer camp, thinking I'd alienated my best friend. The thrill I'd felt, the power he'd given me when we took a fence together on his horse twined through me. Then a mere two months ago when we had pounded over his fields under the moonlight, believing the lie that the scream we had heard was a fox and not the man who had tried to kill me. Remembering it all, I quivered, feeling myself pulled to him. Shit. Maybe I was a demon.

I spoke to my knees. "If I get you to the West Coast by Sunday, you have to promise to help me at the coven meeting. I need them to reinstate my citizenship that you pushed them into revoking *and* guarantee that everyone stops gunning for me." Heart pounding, I looked up. "If I can't beat this, I'm permanently in the ever-after." I was going to regret this. I knew it.

"I didn't know that," he said, looking like he was realigning his thinking.

He went to say something more, but Jenks had dropped down through the open roof to hover between us. "You ready to go, Rache?" he asked, looking far too bright and eager.

"Yes," I said, tired as I gathered my bag to myself again. "We need to talk. I'm going to get Trent to the coast. I'm going to need your help, and don't try to stop me."

The pixy put his hands on his hips and grinned at me. "I know."

My lips parted, and I stared at him. *I know? He'd said, I know?* "Who are you, and how did you kill my partner?" I said, and Jenks spilled a silver dust.

"Cookie farts is right," he said. "Neither of you will make it out there without the other. And me, to help."

A huge sigh came from Trent instead of the expected bad temper at the slur. His eyes were closed, and when they opened, there was hope—it made him look more powerful yet. "We can leave within the hour," he said, opening the door. "They won't be expecting that."

I wondered if he meant they as in the Withons or they as in the coven.

Trent was gone, his door thumping shut. Jenks shot out of the roof. Scrambling, I worked the door and got out, blinking as I emerged in the sun. "They won't be expecting it because it's a stupid idea," I said, seeing Trent beside Ivy and Quen. "I need to go home and pack again," I said, striding to the trunk of my mom's car. "Jenks needs to find a babysitter."

Ivy shifted my garment bag to show two suitcases, my old blue one and the other I'd seen in the trunk of Trent's car. It had to be Trent's. *What was my old suitcase doing here? And Trent's? That was Trent's, wasn't it?*

"You've got your dress," Ivy said as I stared. "And everything you packed for the airplane is in your blue bag."

"Wha-what was in my checked luggage?" I stammered.

Ivy gave me one of her few full smiles. "Magazines," she said matter-of-factly. "They weren't going to let you get on that plane," she said coaxingly when my brow furrowed, "so sue me for thinking ahead. I just moved everything you packed to a different bag. I thought we'd hit the train station next, but this is better."

Not believing this was happening, I looked at everyone in turn, feeling like I'd been manipulated. "What about Jenks and his kids?" I asked.

"I called Jih," Jenks said as he landed on the raised trunk, his wings going red in the reflected heat. "Bis is going to watch them at night, and Jih is going to watch them during the day. Her husband wasn't going for it until I agreed that Jih could bring home whatever she wanted from the graveyard." His wings hummed and he took flight, warm again. "Ivy's going to bring me my good sword and some toothbrushes."

"You're coming?" I asked Ivy, not seeing her suitcase in the trunk.

She shrugged. "I'm going to close up the church and fly out to join you. You can get to St. Louis by nightfall. I already have my ticket."

Oh God. The one she'd bought today? Feeling used, I dropped back, eying them in disbelief. "This morning was all for show?" I said bitterly.

From beside me, Trent shifted his feet. "Is this why you suggested I dress casually?" he asked Quen. "You knew I wasn't coming back?"

Jenks hummed, close, darting off when I waved him away before he could land on my shoulder. "We had to be sure Ivy could fly," the pixy said. "Now we know she can. We're taking your mom's car."

The pixy looked too satisfied to live, but I wasn't happy.

"No, we're taking mine," Trent said suddenly, and I realized he hadn't known about this, either. It made me feel a little better. Especially when Quen cleared his throat and fell into a modified parade rest.

"No, Sa'han, you're taking Ms. Morgan's car."

I turned to Ivy and Jenks, both of them smiling in the sun as if it was all just a joke. Me and Trent in a car to St. Louis? The tabloids would love it. "You had this all worked out, huh?"

"Not all of it until just now," Ivy said. "But both Quen and I like to be prepared."

From my other side, Trent muttered, "Can I talk to you, Quen? Privately?"

"Yeah, yeah," Jenks said brightly when Quen inclined his head to excuse himself. "Go complain. It isn't going to change anything."

Gravel crunched under Trent's boots as the two elves went to have an argument that I was sure Trent was going to lose. Uneasy, I squinted in the sun as I faced Ivy. "You agree with this?"

Ivy nodded, and Jenks darted away to eavesdrop on Trent and Quen. "I think this is the safest way to get you there," Ivy said, and my focus sharpened on her. "The coven won't take a shot at you with Trent in the car, and the Withons' assassins aren't that much of a threat. It's the best of a bad situation. And if he is lying and he double-crosses you, I'll kill him for you."

From anyone else, it would have been an idle threat, and I smiled, feeling loved.

"Take this for me," Ivy said, handing me her laptop in the briefcase. "If for some reason I can't get on the plane, I'll bike out and join you. With luck, I'll see you in a few hours."

I took the briefcase as the heavy door of my mom's car slammed. Nervous, I gave her a hug. Jenks flew up, dusting us as he got included in there somewhere. "Be nice," Ivy whispered as she let go, and I shivered at the feeling of her words on my neck.

Flustered, I backed up, holding the briefcase before me like a fig leaf. Quen was coming toward us, and I shifted to make room for him. Trent was in the front seat, passenger side. Huh. He was in for a surprise if he thought he was going to ride the entire way.

Worry made the creases in the older man's face deeper.

Gripping my hand, Quen's expression smoothed out somewhat. "Thank you, Rachel," he said as he let go. "Don't let him do anything too stupid."

"If he does," Jenks said loudly, "we'll just leave him at a restaurant or something."

I didn't bother to hide my smile, but I shook my head to reassure Trent's security officer. I had more class than that. I think.

Quen hesitated as Ivy made motions to get back into Trent's car, then he said quickly, "Thank you from me. Ceri and me both . . ."

My smile grew wider, and for the first time, I started to feel good about this. "You're welcome," I said, knowing Quen couldn't leave Ceri. It was his child she was having, not Trent's. The woman could take on demons and win, but to have Quen beside her as she brought their child into the world would mean more to her than anything else.

"Bring him home safely so I don't have to mess you up," Quen added as he turned away, and my worry flowed back. I was responsible for Trent. I was responsible for keeping him alive on this magic carpet ride. *Remind me again of why I said yes.*

But Quen had gotten into the sleek black car with Ivy, and I did nothing as it looped forward and around, and left. The sound of the popping of gravel under tires gave way to crickets. A hot summer breeze rose, making my hair tickle my neck. My gaze went to the pale blue sky, then shifted to the cameras on the light poles.

I took a slow breath, and it was as if I could see the entire world spreading out unseen before me, making me small as I realized how far we had to go.

"How many miles is it?" I whispered to Jenks, and the sound of his wings melted into the morning, sounding right.

"One at a time, Rache."

Nodding, I dropped my eyes and scuffed my boots to the passenger side of the car. Yanking the door open, I met Trent's startled gaze. He was wearing a pair of classy, green-tinted sunglasses, and it made him look all the better. "You're driving," I said flatly.

Trent stared. "I beg your pardon?"

"I don't have a license," I said, waiting for him to get out. "The I.S. took it when I got summoned out on I-77 and plowed my car into a bridge railing. You're driving, bucko. At least until we get out of the city and no one will recognize me."

He blinked, then muttered, "For God's sake," as he undid his seat belt and slid over.

Jenks darted into the car as I got in, taking his usual seat on the rearview mirror. "You're not going to swear all the bloody Tink-blasted way there, are you?" he asked.

Feeling weird, I settled myself, my bag going on the back-seat. "I've got one more condition, or this stops right here," I said, and Trent sighed, his hands on the wheel, staring at the dusty trunk of the car in front of us. Overhead, a plane roared.

"What," he said flatly, more of a demand than a question.

My thoughts went back to the enthrallment curse and him wiping the memories of Jack and Jill, and I laboriously rolled my window down. My mom didn't trust electronics, and they were the old crank style. "You do nothing but drive," I said. "Got it? No wiping memories, no enthrallment, and no fighting if there's trouble. Nothing. You sit in a bubble and play tiddledywinks."

Jenks made a scoffing sound. "You're not good at this, greenie weenie, and you're going to slow us down if you try."

"You don't like my magic?" he said, a thread of pride in him.

"No," I shot back, stifling a shiver at the memory of his wild, elven magic. "I don't. Calling on the divine for strength is risky, and you never know what you're going to get. Keep it to yourself, or I'm going to zip-strip you."

His eyebrows rose mockingly. "Not a good feeling, is it? Knowing someone has the ability to do bad things and you just have to *trust* they won't."

"I only do black magic as a last resort," I said through clenched teeth. It was all I could do not to smack the smug, satisfied look off his face.

"Keys?" Trent said mockingly, and Jenks hummed his wings in anticipation.

Twisting, I reached over the seat for my bag, flushing when I got myself back where I belonged. Sheesh, my butt had been inches from Trent, and Jenks was laughing as I refastened my seat belt. Trent was still utterly emotionless, and I smacked the keys into his hand with enough force to bring his eyes to mine.

"She's all yours, Jeeves," I said, closing my eyes as I tried to gather my strength. This was going to be a long ride. They stayed shut for all of three seconds, flashing open when Trent revved the engine hard, jamming it into reverse and making me reach for the dash. "Take it easy!" I shouted, staring at Trent, his eyes on the rearview mirror.

"Watch where you're driving that piece of blue-haired crap!" someone yelled, and I turned to the businessman behind us, clearly hot and bad tempered as he looked for his car.

I went to shout something appropriately rude, but Trent had already yanked the wheel around and was accelerating, leaving him in a cloud of gravel dust. "When we get to St. Louis, we're renting a real car," Trent muttered.

"There is nothing wrong with my mom's car," I snapped.

Trent was silent, staring straight ahead, but I was fuming. There was nothing wrong with my mom's car. Nothing at all.

Five

A narrow slice of early-afternoon sun made it into the front seat to warm my arm, resting on the open window. I was driving—big surprise—and the wind had my hair in a tangle that would take half a bottle of cream rinse to fix. We'd stopped three hours out in the bottom part of Indiana for Jenks to find something to eat and somewhere to pee, and after that he told me he was going to nap. Elves had a similar sleep schedule, and though he hadn't said anything, it was obvious that Trent was getting sleepy, too, so I'd offered to drive.

Actually, I mused as I glanced at a somnolent Trent, the last four hours had been nice. Trent's face was pleasant when he wasn't scowling. His jeans and shirt made him look dramatically different—more attractive than his usual suit somehow. Accessible maybe. The wind shifted his baby-fine hair as he slumped against the door, as far from me as he could get.

I could reach right out and smack him if I wanted. I hadn't liked his quiet disdain of my mom's car. So it didn't have a six-speaker system or power doors or windows. It wasn't shiny, and the blue color didn't do anything for me, either. But I could do ten miles an hour more in my old-lady car than in my shiny red car and never get noticed. It had lots of cup holders, too.

Tucking a wayward curl behind an ear, I eyed his sunglasses in envy, just sitting on the dash while he slept. I bet they'd look better on me than on him. The sun was giving me a headache, and I almost reached for them—until I noticed that Trent's hands were clenched, even in sleep. Okay, maybe he wasn't as comfortable with this as he wanted me to believe. Still, it said something that he'd even fallen asleep.

Looking back to the flat landscape we'd been in for the last hour or so, I wondered if I'd be able to fall asleep with Trent driving. This was weird, and not just because a witch, an elf, and a pixy were on the Great American Road Trip. I still owed Trent that "freed familiar" curse, and guilt was tugging at me.

Bothered, I glanced at my shoulder bag where his curse was, then back to the road. A quick look at the rearview mirror assured me that Jenks was still sleeping, soaking in the sun like a tiny winged cat in the back window. Sighing, I returned my attention to the landscape. I'd never driven like this, and the open spaces were getting to me. The road had been built pre-Turn, and it was creepy driving past town after town that had been abandoned during the plague the Turn had been born of. The trees growing through the roofs of abandoned buildings and the tall yellow *M*'s and old gas station signs high above new forests made me positively uncomfortable.

The mix of vegetation covering the old destruction was reminiscent of the ever-after, and curious, I brought up my second sight. My scalp tingled, the sensation shifting over my skull to make me shiver as the red-tinted ever-after swam up, coating everything in a sheen of red. The sun seemed to cast two shadows, but apart from the road, which now looked broken and covered with weeds, everything looked pretty much the same. A sun-baked field of nothing but grass stretched from horizon to horizon. Demons congregated where the ley lines were, living under them in the ground where nothing changed much.

According to Al, the ever-after was a broken reality, unable to stand on its own, and was being dragged along behind ours, connected to and kept alive by the ley lines. Energy flowed like tides between them, preventing the ever-after from vanishing and giving the alternate reality a broken visage. It was a reflection of reality but shattered. So if Cincinnati put up a new building, a new one would show up in the ever-after, but would begin to fall apart even before it was completed. That's why demons lived underground. We didn't construct much below a certain level, so nothing changed there but what the demons fashioned for themselves. They used gargoyles like familiars, pulling ley-line energy deep into the earth to where they could use it.

But here, out in the spaces between big conglomerations of ley lines where the cities were, there was a whole lot of red-sheened nothing: trees, grass, bushes. You'd think that being an earth witch I'd like nature, but I didn't. Not like this anyway. It felt broken. It didn't help that the ever-after looked almost normal out here. Except for the black parts . . .

Squinting, I tried to figure out what they were. I'd never seen them in Cincinnati's version of the ever-after, and they glinted silver under the red-tinted sun, like a heat mirage or something, reflecting . . . nothing.

Still using my second sight, I looked over the trees to St. Louis, feeling better with the tall buildings, even if they looked broken with the overlay of my second sight. We were close, and I dropped my second sight and twisted in my seat to pull my phone out of my back pocket. I'd gotten a text from Ivy earlier when she'd boarded her plane, then again when she'd landed. We were going to meet at the arch. I should give her a call.

"What were you just doing?" Trent said suddenly, and I jerked, dropping my phone.

"Jeez, Trent!" I yelped. "How long have you been watching me?" I flushed, glancing in the back to see Jenks's wings shift and spill a silver dust as he slept on. "I'm calling Ivy."

Trent sat up, rubbing his right bicep where his familiar mark was, before he bent almost double to get my phone from under my feet. "You forgot I was here," he said as he handed it to me, smiling as if it pleased him. "What were you doing? Before, I mean. You were looking at something, and it wasn't the view. Your aura had a shadow on it. I've never seen that."

Great. He'd been watching me. Grimacing, I focused on the road. The traffic was starting to thicken as we approached the city. "Really?" I said shortly. Jenks had said the same thing to me once when I was doing some high magic. I didn't like that my "aura shadow" showed up when I was using my second sight. Smiling as if nothing was wrong, I tossed my phone to him, and he deftly caught it. "Will you call Ivy for me? Tell her where we are?"

He tossed it back, and it thumped onto my lap. "I'm not your secretary."

Dude, that was just rude, I thought, intentionally swerving from the right lane to the left as I flipped the phone open.

Trent clutched the door and the dash, and from the backseat Jenks shrilled, "Hey! Rache! What the Disney blasted hell are you doing?"

I was smiling my prettiest as Trent growled, "Give me the phone."

"Thank you," I all but sang, dropping it into his hand and rolling up the window so he could hear better. He seemed harmless in his jeans and shirt, and I wondered how much of his charisma came from his wardrobe. Jenks apparently appreciated the drop in wind, and he flew back to the front, looking rumpled and sleepy as he yawned and sat on the rearview mirror.

"Where are we?" he asked, rubbing a hand over his wings to check for tears.

"Still on I-70," I said as Trent scrolled through my call list, eyebrows going high when he found the mayor's number. Yeah, we had talked. Got that little misunderstanding about her son a few years ago taken care of. "We'll be crossing the Mississippi in a minute," I added.

Rubbing his arm again, Trent hit a button and put the phone to his ear. I wondered if he knew he was doing it, rubbing his familiar mark. "One of these days your smart-ass attitude is going to get you killed," he said softly.

"Not today," I said, then watched Jenks peer behind us.

"Huh," the pixy said, not sounding at all worried. "They're still there."

Nodding, I flicked my gaze to the mirror, seeing a gold Cadillac a way back. "Yup."

Phone to his ear, Trent turned to look. "We're being followed?"

"Relax, cookie maker," Jenks said as he continued to work over his wings. "They've been there since Terre Haute."

A knot of worry started to tighten. Was it me they were following or Trent?

There was a faint hail on the tiny speaker, and Trent continued to watch the car behind us through the side mirror. "Ms. Tamwood," he said, and I marveled at his voice. "Rachel would like to talk to you," he added as I held out my hand.

"Hey, hi," I said as I wrangled the phone to my ear. "We're almost across the Mississippi. How was your flight?"

"Lousy." Ivy sounded tired, but she'd been up longer than I had. "I'm at the arch," she continued. "Stay on I-70, then take the South Memorial Drive exit just after the bridge."

"Thanks, I already looked at the map," I said, mildly peeved. The woman had not only laminated the map, but she'd used a marker to star where we could stop for Jenks.

"Follow Memorial Drive all the way down to Washington," she continued, as if I'd said nothing. "There're signs everywhere to the parking structure."

"Okay, thanks," I said, exasperated, but Jenks was laughing as he landed on my shoulder.

"Rache, those guys are getting closer," he said, pitching his voice so Ivy could hear him.

"What guys?" Ivy asked, her concern clear through the tiny speaker.

I fluffed my hair to make Jenks take off. *Thanks a hell of a lot, Jenks.*

"Someone's tailing us," I said casually.

"For how long?" she said, loud enough for Trent to hear.

"Long enough," I said. "They aren't that close. Quarter mile."

"Two hundred feet, Ivy," Jenks said loudly, back on the rearview mirror and knowing her superior vamp hearing would pick it up. "Three guys unless someone's taking a nap."

The good news being that if they were that close, the car probably wasn't bugged.

"Maybe we should drive straight through. Where's the map?" Jenks said, taking off in a burst of sparkles and vanishing in the backseat.

Trent stiffened, his gaze sharp on mine. "We need to stop."

"I don't need a map, Jenks," I said, paying more attention to the road. We'd picked up a dump truck somewhere, and the road was getting crowded with semis and SUVs.

"If you're being followed, just keep going," Ivy said. "I've got a rental car, and I'll catch up, okay? Ram them or something."

"We are going to stop," Trent said again, looking militantly adamant. Maybe he needed to use the little boy's room after his nappies.

From the backseat, Jenks chimed, "I found it! Trent, be a pal and open it for me, huh?"

I jiggled the phone to my other ear, and the car swerved. Ram them? Was she serious?

"Rachel?" came Ivy's voice, and I put my attention back on the road.

"You're not going to ram them," I said, and Trent rubbed his forehead as if in pain. "And we aren't going to drive through. We are coming in. I'd rather meet up now than later, even if they are watching. They probably already know you're waiting for us."

Jenks darted up from the backseat, his hands on his hips. "Trent, I could use some help here. You just going to sit there like a pile of fairy crap the entire way?"

"We don't need the map," I said, starting to get mad. "And we are not driving through. We are stopping for Ivy!"

From my phone, Ivy was protesting, "There's a bunch of kids here. You really want to risk a fight with the coven?"

"The coven wouldn't dare," I said as I started to wonder. "Not with innocents around. We can have an ice cream or something. Make bunny-eared kisses at them from across the park."

"I suppose," she agreed, sounding doubtful. "Call me when you park, okay?"

Making a murmur of agreement, I closed the phone and dropped it onto my lap.

"Good plan," Trent said breathily, and a single warning flag went up, as smooth and sure as ice is cold. I don't know why, because he was agreeing with me, but his attitude—the overwhelming relief he was trying to hide—was at complete odds with what he should be feeling with someone tailing us. Frowning, I thought back to whose idea it was to stop in St. Louis in the first place. Ivy's, I think. She'd bought a flight going there.

The tires hummed as we found the bridge, and the world seemed to shift as we headed right for the city. The arch was huge. Word was that it pinned down one of the city's ley lines, which I thought suspect. Why would anyone do anything so stupid?

"You need the Memorial Drive exit," Trent said intently. "It goes right past the park."

"Thanks, Trent," I said, my eyes narrowed suspiciously.

"You're in the wrong lane," he added, and clenching my teeth, I wondered what he'd do if I just drove past the exit. Watching his body language, I shifted even farther to the left to get around a black car. Sure enough, he tensed.

Interesting, I mused, and then, checking the rearview to see that the gold car had done the same, I slid back to the right-hand lane, making the motion far too fast. Jenks yelped, taking to the air as the steering wheel spun. Trent clutched the dash, glaring at me as we rocked to a halt, but saying little else as his sunglasses slid off the dash and to my feet. Another warning flag went up. That should have gotten me more than a dirty look.

"You're going to have to do a lot more than that to lose them," Jenks said, misreading my motion, and I eyed the semi that roared up behind me, aggressively making his brakes flatulate in an effort to get me to move faster. Faster. That might be a good idea, seeing as that gold Cadillac was a car length away. Three guys. All blonds. Elves? Not the coven, then.

My phone hummed, and I ignored it. Trent jerked, his eyes showing a new alarm as he turned to me. "We need to get off this road. Now."

"Like how?" I snarled. "Our exit isn't for another two miles."

"Well, do something!" Trent exclaimed. "Someone is prepping a spell."

My eyes flicked behind us, seeing the three heads clustered together. The shoulder was on one side and that truck on the other as he tried to pass me. A little VW bug was ahead of me, full of people. "Are you nuts? No one would make a hit on the expressway. Too many people could get hurt. And besides, I don't feel—"

"Look out!" Jenks shrilled, and I gasped, jerking the wheel as a reddish-gold ball of something blossomed from the car behind us. Our tires hit the shoulder, gravel kicking up underneath as I struggled to maintain control at a suddenly too-fast sixty-five miles per hour.

The spell hit the VW bug ahead of us, and I watched in horror as it turned sideways and spun, right into the path of the truck barreling down on it. Sparks flew inside the small car, and the truck hit its brakes, the tires hopping on the pavement as three lanes of traffic became five, everyone trying to get out of the way. The little car spun into a roll, a protection bubble snapping into place, and I stiffened my arms, looking for an out. The truck was going to jackknife, and the rear of it was two feet away, coming closer, almost shoving us.

Behind us were the ugly sounds of screeching tires and plastic crunching. I didn't dare look as we sped ahead, the truck now taking up three lanes as it slowly began to topple over. The little VW had hit the wall, and I swerved into the path of the truck to avoid it. There was a huge crash, and the sound of scraping metal. I looked back to see the truck on its side, cars piling up behind it. Three cars had made it through: us, a station wagon with a white-faced woman driving it, and that gold Cadillac. *My God. What had they done?*

"Go, go, go!" Jenks shrilled, plastered to the back window. "They got through! Go!"

I floored it, weaving through the cars ahead of us, most of them just now noticing the truck sliding to a stop and taking up the entire road. Brake lights were going on, and my grip on the wheel became sweaty. *How had they gotten through?* I wondered, seeing that they had lost a fender but were still moving. The VW had become small in the rearview mirror, and feeling sick, I pulled my attention back to the road ahead of us. No one does a hit on a busy road. No one. Who the hell did these people think they were? Or perhaps my question should be, who the hell did these people think *we* were that they would do such a thing?

"We need to get off this road!" Trent exclaimed as I sped past a slow-moving Jag.

"Gee, you think?" I said, seeing the Cadillac clip another car as it tried to catch up.

"Where's the map," Trent muttered, leaning over the back-seat to find it.

Jenks looked scared, having moved to the front where he could stand on the rearview mirror and hold on to the stem for dear life. "Go right!" he shouted, and I jerked the wheel, looking back to see yet another ball of who-knew-what headed for us.

Trent yelped as the car swerved, his butt smacking into me

and a raised foot hitting the wheel. "Trent!" I shouted, shoving him off. "Sit down, will you? I'm trying not to get pasted here, and your ass in my face isn't helping!"

The orange blob hit the pavement behind us, the Jag I'd just gone around running right into it. The car flipped, and I started to get really scared. What the hell were they using to throw their magic? A grenade launcher? We were going over ninety!

Oblivious to it, Trent slid back into his seat with a huff, the map in his hand.

"Jenks, you got any ideas?" I asked as Trent buckled himself back in, and Jenks's wings stilled even as a green dust began spilling from him.

"Maybe Trent should have married the bitch," he warbled, and I shifted into the far-left lane to get around a bus. Sure enough, they stuck with me, and my heart pounded. I couldn't do magic and drive at the same time! Where the hell was Pierce when I needed him? No-o-o-o, the one time I have non-union assassins behind us, I have a *businessman* riding shotgun trying to find answers in a friggin' map!

"That's our exit," Trent said, trying to look cool, but his grip on the map was too tight. "We're sitting ducks on the expressway."

"Oh, thank you very much for that observation, Kalamack," I said sarcastically. "You think we should get off the road. And then what?"

"Just take South Memorial," he said, his eyes on the map as he swayed to my swerving through traffic, earning beeps and flashing lights. "We can lose them on the surface roads more easily than on the expressway. Do what I say, and we'll be fine." But he was sweating. I couldn't make a bubble—we'd drive right through it.

Jenks darted down to land on the map in Trent's hand as we flashed past the sign. "That's the one you want, Rachel. Right lane. Right lane!"

There was a big truck ahead of me in the far-right lane. If I slowed down to take the exit, the Cadillac would hit us. My fingers clenched and relaxed. Behind us, a new glow was starting in the car. I had to time this perfectly. " 'Do what I say, and we'll be fine,' " I muttered through clenched teeth. "Surface streets mean we put the entire city in danger. We're going to lose them right now."

"Rachel . . . ," Trent said, his voice tinged with anger and fear. "What are you doing?"

"Getting onto Memorial," I said, licking my lips. The engine roared as I pressed the accelerator, and my mom's car leapt ahead. My heart pounded, and I darted around a white car on the right, then a blue on the right. Crap, this was going to be close. There was a weird prickling through me, but I daren't look at Trent. It was wild magic, but I didn't think it was from him. It was like the tracers that the earth sends up to the cloud before the lightning follows it down. The next hit wouldn't miss. "Hold on!" I shouted, eyes wide.

"Rachel!" Trent shouted, the chicken strap in his hand.

"This is going to be close!" I yelled, and I jammed on the accelerator. The car bounced as we raced forward, and I yanked the wheel to the right at the last moment, skidding across all three lanes and onto the exit ramp. The semi blew its horn, but we were through and bouncing over the rough pavement, narrowly missing the cement wall.

"Ye-e-e-e-e-ha-a-a-a-a!" Jenks shrilled, and I hit the brakes hard so I wouldn't ram the car ahead of me. My heart was thudding, and we fishtailed. Scared, I looked to find Jenks in the back, face plastered to the window as he watched the traffic behind us. The awful prickling had stopped. *Thank you, God.* "They missed the exit!" he yelled. "They missed it! You lost them, Rache!"

I looked across the seat to Trent, white faced. From behind us came a crunch of metal, and someone's horn got stuck. My phone started to hum. *Ivy.* Where was my phone?

"We lost them." I breathed, then became worried. We had lost them, but what about everyone else? God, I hoped those people were okay. I was sure I'd seen a protection bubble on the bug, but at those speeds, it might not make a difference.

Ahead of us, cars were slowing for the traffic light. "It's red, Rachel," Jenks said, and I slammed on the brakes, adrenaline making the motion too fast. Jenks yelped, and Trent reached for the dash, glaring at me. I couldn't believe they'd tried to take us out on the interstate! I'd been under death threats before, but there were niceties to be observed, union rules. This wasn't them!

Silent, Trent folded up the map, tucking it away with precise motions. He looked calm, but I was starting to shake. "Nicely done," he said and I almost lost it, my hands clenching the wheel until my knuckles were white. *Nicely done?* There were people hurt back there, and I felt a sudden surge of panic as three ambulances went by, headed for the interstate. Everyone in that VW bug was probably dead. And the truck driver. And the four cars behind him. The guy in the Jag was probably okay. Probably.

My foot started to jiggle, and when the light turned green, I crept up on the car ahead of us, pushing it into moving. I wanted out of the car, like now.

Jenks flew to the rearview mirror when Trent rolled his window all the way down to get rid of the scent of cinnamon and wine, and something in me eased as I turned right onto Memorial. He was shaken and trying not to show it. More sirens wailed, and Jenks landed on the steering wheel, giving me a worried look as a fire truck went by, headed for the on-ramp. People were hurt. Because of me? Trent? Did it matter?

"We're going to stop, right?" Trent asked, his eyes on Riverside Park as we passed it.

"Why? Think you'll get a better view of the accidents from up on top of the arch?" I asked sarcastically. This was way more than I'd expected when I agreed to escort him to the coast, and I was long past wishing I'd told him to shove his little problem and taken my chances by myself. My foot was shaking as I stopped at another light. The church was right next to us, and in a split-second decision, I turned the blinker on.

"Okay," I said as I glanced behind us at the flashing lights on the interstate. "We're ditching the car. Get your stuff together."

"Ditching the car?" Trent stared at me like I'd said we were going to walk to the moon.

"Right now," I said as the light changed and I turned into the quiet parking lot, ignoring the DO NOT PARK sign. "You hear those sirens? We left the scene of an accident, one we helped make. There's no way we can go back there, which makes this a marked car, and not just by your friends from Seattle. Soon as we find Ivy, she'll carry your bag, Mr. Kalamack. Think you can handle it that long?"

"First smart thing you've done all day," Trent muttered, his fingers tapping.

Jenks exhaled loudly, his wings an excited red as I put the car in park and turned the engine off. I was moving almost before the car stopped, gathering my stuff and jamming everything but the bag of trash into my bag, Trent's sunglasses included.

Trent was already out of the car, and I popped the trunk. My fingers trembled as I worked the door handle, finally getting the stupid thing open. Cool air slipped in, and the sound of kids. Damn, that had been close. What the devil were they putting in their coffee in Seattle?

"Where's my phone?" I said, hearing it start to hum. "Jenks, have you seen my phone?"

Jenks darted to the floorboards. "It's under the seat!" he said, then added, "It's Ivy."

I stretched, reaching for it, exhaling loudly as my fingers found the smooth plastic. I wished my fingers would stop shaking. Jenks zipped out from under the seat, and flipping my phone open, I muttered, "I think we lost them. We're abandoning the car. Where are you?"

"From the sounds of the sirens, I'd say a couple of blocks away," she said. "What's going on?"

"I wish I knew." Getting out, I looped my bag over my

shoulder and grabbed my coat and Ivy's laptop. Jenks was a sparkle of dust as he searched the car, giving me a thumbs-up before he joined Trent. Trent already had our luggage out from the back, and he slammed the trunk shut hard, his hands going to his hips as he squinted at the busy road, the wind from the nearby Mississippi River shifting his shirt to show the familiar mark on his shoulder.

"We're at the church," I told Ivy. "I got your laptop, and we're going to walk in. Soon as we find you, we'll head to your car." Worry pinched my brow. "Ivy, they tried to kill us on the interstate. A semi tipped over, and I think they killed a carload of people. Someone will remember my mom's car."

"You're at the church?" she asked, not caring. "You can't park there."

"I'm not parking, I'm abandoning," I said, frustrated as I looked at the big, hand-painted sign. My mom would not be happy. She'd been royally pissed off when I'd left her car at a pull-off by the Ohio River last year. At least this time the car was in my name and she wouldn't be getting the impound notice.

"Ivy, I gotta go," I said, not able to handle everything I had and my suitcase, too.

"I'm on my way," she said, and I could hear the hoot of a steamship through the connection before it cut off.

I closed my phone and tucked it away, worry settling in deep as I looked from Trent, standing behind the car with our stuff, to the road. We'd find Ivy, and then we'd be out of here. "Can anything else go wrong today?" I whispered, thinking I could have been sitting on a dock somewhere drinking coffee by now if the coven had let me fly.

"Uh, you gotta stop saying stuff like that," Jenks said, darting up in a wash of dust. Alarmed, I followed his gaze across the busy street.

"Crap on toast," I said, the dappled sun going cold on me as I saw three blond men in slacks and polo shirts. They must have left their car on the interstate and walked. It wasn't that far, and a feeling of ice seemed to slip through me as I took them in.

One had really long hair; the other was short but perfectly proportioned; and the third, in the middle, reminded me of Quen, even though he looked nothing like him. It was his pace, both predatory and graceful. The other two carried themselves with a belligerent swagger, shoulders back, arms swinging, and hands well away from their sides. The Withons had gotten serious.

All three were watching us as they waited for four lanes of traffic to clear, but upon seeing me notice them, the one with the long hair simply stepped out into the street, his hand raised. Horns blew and cars screeched to a halt, the drivers yelling out their windows, ignored.

Trent turned to the noise, his lips parting as he took a deep, resolute breath. Funny, I'd have thought he'd look scared, not determined, and I stifled a surge of what might be a feeling of kinship.

"Well?" he asked me, looking surprisingly calm.

"Find Ivy," I said, digging through my shoulder bag for a stick of magnetic chalk and reaching out for the city's ley lines. I sucked my breath in as I found the one the arch was pinning down. Holy cow, it was big and way stronger than the one under Cincy's university. It felt slippery, being next to so much water, and had a metallic flavor, like fish.

I looked up with the chalk in my hands, surprised to find Trent still standing there with his suitcase, Jenks hovering between us. "Go!" I shouted, pushing the chalk into Trent's hand and giving him a shove. "Find Ivy. I'll take care of this and catch you up." Oh God. I could do this, right? Where was my black-arts bodyguard when I needed him?

"Rache . . . ," Jenks whined, but Trent looked at the chalk in his hand and nodded. Saying nothing more, he turned and walked quickly away, with his suitcase, headed for the arch.

"Stay with him, will you?" I asked Jenks, my attention on the three guys. They had gotten to the median and hadn't slowed down. "Maybe get him to run a little?" I added, trying to be funny as I glanced at the worried pixy. "I'll be right behind you. Piece of cake."

"I don't like this."

My eyes flicked back to him, seeing his worry in the slant of his brow. "Me neither, but who do you think needs you more right now? I'll catch you up. Go! It's just three guys. Once you get Trent to Ivy, you can come back and play."

He made a face, and with a harsh clatter, he bobbed up and down in agreement, then zipped after Trent, telling him to hurry up, that they had things to do today other than play tourist.

I felt better with Jenks watching Trent, but nervousness prickled through me as I turned back to the three blonds, now at the curb. The one with the long hair peeled off and started for Trent.

"Hey, Legolas!" I shouted, my boots grinding the gravel as I shifted. "You want him, you go through me."

Ignoring me, he continued on. That was just insulting, and gathering up a wad of fish-tasting ever-after, I threw it at him.

The guy with the long hair raised his hand, a protection bubble flashing into existence to deflect the ever-after. Standard move. I hadn't really expected my first shot to land, and I started backing up more, my feet finding grass as I moved under the huge trees. But the men stopped, and that was all I wanted for the moment.

Side by side, the three men looked at me, traffic passing behind them in an uncaring blur. The guy with the long hair seemed to be the leader, and he frowned at Trent, disappearing through the bushes, before turning back to me. "Whatever he's paying you, the Withons will double it if you turn your back for ten minutes," he said loudly, and my face burned.

Why was I not surprised? Elves were elves. "He's not paying me anything," I said, just now realizing it. I was either really smart or really stupid.

The short guy on the end snorted his disbelief. "You're kidding."

Embarrassed, I backed up until the roots of a thick tree stopped me. "And even if he was, I don't work like that," I said. "Obviously you do. Pathetic. I should have known you were amateurs when you tried to take us out on the expressway. You keep that up, and the union is going to come down hard on you. There are traditions for this kind of thing, procedures. Or haven't you been playing the game long enough to know?"

I was stalling, and the guy with the long hair knew it, taking a moment to tie his hair back and frown at the arch behind me. I glanced back, a knot of worry easing when I realized Trent was gone.

"Who wants the pleasure?" he asked, and the one in the middle, the one who reminded me of Quen, smiled.

"I'll do it," he said, and I tensed, shocked when a heavy lassitude filled me. My legs buckled, and that fast, I was on my knees, the tingle of wild magic coursing through me, robbing me of strength. There was music in my head, like green, growing things, and my hands hit the ground, bits of twigs biting into my palms, making them tingle. I gasped, my lungs reluctant to expand.

I fought it, finding strength from the ley line. I pulled it into me, feeling it burn. Teeth clenched, I looked up through the strands of my hair. The man in the middle widened his eyes as if in surprise. And then he started to sing.

My breath escaped me in a rush as his words washed over me, and my head bowed. My elbows trembled, and everything I had won back left me. "Stop . . . ," I whispered. I couldn't think, the thick, muzzy blanket swallowing me up as he sang, the lazy words unclear as they became my entire world. My pulse shifted, becoming slower, meeting his song beat for beat. It was too slow, and I fought for control, failing.

I felt myself start to fall, and a warm arm caught me, gently cradling me. I could smell cinnamon and wine, bitter and spoiled. I couldn't fight the music beating its way into my existence, making me live to a rhythm too slow, and my eyes shut as someone propped me up against the tree. I was losing my hold on the ley line, and in terror, I reached for it, trying to make a protection bubble in my mind to wall the music off. But it was already in my head, and I couldn't separate it from me. It was too beautiful. I couldn't help but listen.

"That was easy," I heard the long-haired elf say derisively, but I couldn't move. Couldn't fight the lassitude that had become my world, hated and familiar from my childhood.

"You have her then?" the voice asked, and finally the singing stopped. The fatigue lingered as the song echoed in my brain, circling over and over, going more slowly each time. It was killing me.

"Go," a breathy voice said, and my head landed on a shoulder. "I'll be done by the time you finish Kalamack."

Oh God. Trent. But the spark quickly died. My breathing had slowed to a shallow hint. I was faltering. I recognized it. I'd lived this before when I was younger. The grass sighed as two of them left, and it was only me and the elf singing me to death. So beautiful I couldn't let it go, couldn't forget it, mesmerized.

The air grew cold on my face, and I realized I was crying. I didn't want to die like this. Damn elf magic. Wild magic. Divine, slippery . . . alive, uncontrollable.

Uncontrollable, I thought, fastening on that idea. *Malleable.* I couldn't control wild magic, couldn't fight it. But maybe I could . . . change it.

My heart gave a thump, and refused to beat again as the man's voice faltered, leaving a single note in my mind to spiral down to a long, soft hum. Om, perhaps. The sound of peace, the sound of death.

Not yet, I thought, and then I added to it, giving my mind an ugly note to follow the one of pure beauty, and my heart gave a beat at the harshness of it, discordant and wrong. The arms holding me jumped in surprise, jarring me, and I added a new note to follow my first.

I could hear him singing again, the words unclear and so

exquisite it broke my heart. My jaw clenched, and I drowned the purity of his song with my own ugly music, harsh and savage—survival. It was never beautiful except for its pure honesty.

Again my heart beat, and I took a sip of air, breaking away from the elven spell, tingling with wild magic as control came flooding back, his hold on me broken. My eyes flashed open. I was sitting on the ground, my back to a tree, his arm around me like a lover, sleeping in the sun as he sang to me.

Son of a bitch.

I sat up out of his reach, turning to see the shock in his green eyes as his voice faltered. There was a hint of resemblance to Trent in them, and I felt a moment of doubt. *Could he do this, too?* "That was a mistake," I rasped, and then I plowed my fist right into his gut.

The man grunted, bending over and bringing his knees to his chest. I swung my legs around to kneel, reaching for his hair. It was soft, like silk, and I clenched my fingers in it, anger giving me strength. I slammed the back of his head against the tree, and as he groaned, I staggered to my feet, giving him a mean kick in the ribs, hard enough to at least crack one or two, if not break them. I was pissed.

"You son of a bitch!" I yelled, seeing the mothers nearby gathering their kids and moving them away. "Try to kill me with your magic? Have a taste of mine!" I shouted, shredding the last of the music in my mind, trying to get rid of it completely.

He looked up at me, the pain from his ribs making him squint. I put my hand on his face, and flooded him with everafter, burning the last of the wild magic from me with my own. He screamed and tried to pull away, but I followed him down, having to kneel when he fell over.

"You are slime, you hear me?" I shouted, wiping my eyes as I pulled away, my hand throbbing and me not caring. "Slime! And you know what? The Withons are slime, too, and Trent's going to make it to the West Coast if it kills me. And it won't!"

Heart pounding, I gave him another kick, thinking I should do a lot more. All those people dead on the expressway. Glancing at the empty park, I went and picked up my bag, searching until I found my lipstick. Throwing the cap away, I scrawled "I killed them" on his forehead.

Panting, I lurched to my feet and dropped the ruined lipstick on his chest. He whimpered, his synapses singed. He wouldn't be doing magic any time soon. Turning to the park, I pushed myself into a staggering, ugly run.

I did not like St. Louis.

Six

"Rache!" Jenks shrilled, scaring the crap out of me as he darted down from the tall trees.

"God, Jenks!" I yelped, heart racing as I paused, a hand on the tree beside me. "You scared me. Where's Trent?"

Dripping red dust, he hovered before me, taking in my haggard appearance and accepting it, knowing better than to ask what had happened. I was here, the assassin wasn't. It was enough for Jenks, and right now, it was enough for me. "In a hole in the ground," he said, and tension hit me. "Some kind of gardener's bunker. It was his idea. I told him to find Ivy, but he wouldn't listen. They're going to find him, Rache! It's not my fault! He wouldn't listen!"

I panted, turning to look back the way I'd come. "Show me," I said, and he darted away, dusting heavily so I could follow at my own limping pace. "If that man gets himself killed, I'm going to pound him!" I muttered, starting up the gentle incline.

The back of my mind registered how cool and restful it was here, the grass thick and well maintained. The trees were huge, rising high overhead like a distant ceiling. Seagulls called, swarming a crying kid with a box of animal crackers. Breathless, I caught sight of two men vanishing behind a row of tall shrubs.

Damn it, I don't want to do this again.

My shoulder bag held tight to me, I ran after them, seeing Jenks's faint trail leading down a damp sidewalk. Ahead of me, the two men stood at a bunkerlike door built right into a wall of earth. In the distance, one of the arch's huge legs rose up. Oblivious to me, the men slipped inside—and the door swung shut.

I slid to a panting halt before the brown-painted steel door, listening as I struggled to catch my breath and tried the handle. Locked—and not with a spell, which I could break, but probably with a mundane dead bolt from the inside. At least Jenks was in there.

"Damn it!" I hissed, dropping back and digging my phone out of my pocket. "Answer me, Ivy," I said as I hit the button and wrenched on the door at the same time.

"Right behind you," came her voice, and I spun.

"Where . . . ," I started, then shoved the thought out of my head. "The door," I babbled, dropping the phone into my bag. "Two of them. In there with Trent."

Ivy motioned for me to back up, and she gave the knob a side kick, yelling for strength. I heard metal snap, and I wasn't surprised when the knob came away in her grip as she gave it a tug and the door opened. God, I had good friends.

Shoulder to shoulder, we looked down a long, dimly lit room that narrowed into a black hallway. The electric lights were pale, and the sun streamed in for only a few feet. It was silent, and a cool breath of underground air, blowing out from the depths, moved my hair.

"Which way?" Ivy said, and I crept inside, feeling the chill take me. The faint glow of pixy dust showed when she pulled the door shut, and I pointed.

"There."

It smelled like oil and damp—of sweaty men, old machinery, and dusty paperwork that hadn't seen the light of the sun for twenty years. This was not on the regular tour, and I wondered where we were as we followed the corridor down and around, shunning doors and open archways when Jenks's dust pointed elsewhere.

"Where's the third one?" she whispered.

"Back at the car, out cold. Don't let them start to sing, okay?" I said breathlessly, and she nodded, taking that at face value.

We have to be almost under one of the feet, I thought, wondering how Quen kept Trent safe every day. I suppose watching Trent in an office was easier than trying to shake three guys in a Cadillac, but I was going to get the man a leash if we found him alive.

A soft crack of metal shocked through me, and then Jenks's yelp.

"Shit," Ivy swore, darting past me and running down a corridor.

Gasping, I bolted after her. Trent was shouting—it sounded like Latin—and, my boots skidding on the oil-slicked cement, I grabbed a rusty ceiling support and swung myself around a dusty machine and into a puddle of dirty light.

Squinting, I watched Jenks bust another bulb to make it darker yet. Two shadows were scurrying into the dark, Ivy's sleek form chasing them. The ceiling was low, and the space was crowded with abandoned machines. Trent had his back to me as he knelt next to his suitcase under a light, a protection bubble around him. Relief hit me, and I paused, torn between seeing if he was okay and following Ivy, busy thunking people into walls by the sound of it.

The circle was larger than I thought Trent could make, almost one of my size, and I was glad I'd given him the magnetic chalk. He had a ribbon draped over his shoulder, and a cloth hat on his head that I didn't recognize. I sniffed, wondering if that was an extinguished candle I smelled or just sulfur. He was kneeling and looked haggard as our eyes met, seeming almost scholarly with that hat and ribbon, but he seemed okay.

"Rachel! Some help here!" Ivy yelled, and I gave him a look telling him to stay put and ran. The glow of Jenks's dust lit a dark corner, and I winced at a loud clang. Crap, if that had been Ivy's head . . .

I barreled into another puddle of light, scrambling to catch the arm of the man she had flung. It was the short guy, and using his own momentum, I threw him into a rusty ceiling support. He hit with a thud, grasping weakly at it as he slid to the dirt-caked floor. With a dull crack, the beam he'd hit broke from the ceiling, falling right on him. A splattering of ceiling dust slipped over him, patterning him with rust. I wedged a toe under him and flipped him over to see his pained expression. "Surprise," I said, and his eyes widened.

"Duck!" Jenks yelled, and I dropped, feeling the rush of metal over my head.

"Son of a bastard!" I whispered as I rolled away, finding my feet when I hit a piece of machinery the size of my car. I scrambled up, the lethal-magic detection charm on the strap of my bag clinking. The guy with the long hair was in front of me with a metal rod the size of a baseball bat. *Damn it, is Ivy down?*

I couldn't see her, and I backed up as he came forward, swinging his pole in some lame-ass elf move as if it were a sword. My hands were empty. I had Jack's splat gun in my shoulder bag, but there were no charms in the hopper. Licking my lips, I tapped the ley line that St. Louis was built on. If he started singing, I was going to fry him, black charm or not.

Energy tasting of dead fish and electric lights slammed into me, and my eyes widened. It was as if it hit every square inch of my skin all at once, and I sucked in my breath, exhilarated. *Crap, I think we're right under the ley line!*

The guy I'd slammed into the pole was moving, and his buddy took a moment to help him up. "Ivy!" I called out, worried, and she coughed from the darkness.

"She's okay," Jenks said, darting in circles around my head.

The two men stood, a ribbon of blood seeping from a scalp wound the short one had. Grinning, ponytail guy pointed at me, then Ivy, and I cringed when someone pulled hard on the ley line humming somewhere above us. Their heads shot up as if surprised, and I dove for the shadows.

"Grab some air, Jenks!" I shouted, my heavy-magic detection amulet flashing red as I found Ivy, upright but holding her head. I never got a circle up as the tingle of wild magic hit me. *Too late,* I thought, doubled over in pain as a surge of energy swamped me. It was as if they had found a way to dump the entire line through me, forcing me to hold it. I screamed, trying to channel the entire ley line or spindle it—anything to get atop the massive force burning me.

Gasping, I managed to ride the wave of cresting energy, and with a triumphant cry, I shoved the spindled energy back out of me and into them, breaking my connection with the ley line entirely before they fried my synapses. It wasn't wild magic, and this I could handle. Son of a bitch . . . what demon had taught them that? And how much had it cost?

I looked up from my half kneel, not remembering having fallen. Ivy was standing beside me, and I peered through my watering eyes to see the two elves picking themselves up off the floor. I would have felt pretty good if my mind wasn't aching from the pain.

"You okay?" Ivy said, her grip on my arm hurting as she pulled me up. My skin felt as if someone had forced sand through my pores. She let go when I winced, but she didn't look much better than I felt, her cheek swelling and dirt caked on her entire right side.

"Great. How about you?" I snatched my bag up from the grimy floor and faced the two assassins.

"I'll live," she said darkly. "Which is more than I can say for them."

Yeah. I felt the same way, and I stifled a groan as I stepped forward with Ivy, ready to take them on if they wouldn't just go away. Somehow, looking at them, I didn't think they would. I took a breath to let them have it, hesitating when the faint sound of rumbling echoed up through our feet. A soft pattering of dust sifted down, and the two elves looked up. The one who'd hit the support looked terrified. Pointing up, he turned and ran the way we'd come in.

"Hey! Come back here!" I shouted as the other one bolted after him.

Jenks darted up, his face scared. "Out!" he shrilled, the sound of rumbling growing louder. "Run!"

"What?" was all I had time for, and then the earth moved. My balance left me, and I reached out for something, anything, to keep from falling. Chunks of concrete dropped where the elves had been. Ivy danced, somehow staying on her feet as I clung to another rusty ceiling pole.

"It's falling!" Jenks screamed, the only thing not moving in the suddenly choking air.

Wobbling, Ivy grabbed my arm, and we staggered to the door. The ground quit moving, and we broke into a run.

"Earthquake?" I guessed as we found Trent, dazed and numb in the middle of his fallen circle, that hat of his slipping off and my chalk loose in his grip.

"We're on a thousand-year-old swamp," Ivy said. "No fault lines here."

"Run!" Jenks shouted. "It's not over yet!"

I grabbed Trent's suitcase, and we all ran for the brown-painted door, getting three steps before a wave of dusty dirt rolled over us, clogging our lungs and making our eyes tear. The lights went out, and the earth shook again. Choking, I felt my way forward, squinting past Trent and following Ivy as she threw stuff out of our way.

"There!" she shouted, and the dim light of the sun spilled in.

The ground gave a hiccup, and noise crashed down, making me cower. Hand on Trent's arm, I yanked him forward as he hunched over and coughed. We spilled out of the earth in a cloud of dust, running several feet before stopping to turn and stare at the opening. Damn, maybe I shouldn't have swung that guy into the support pole.

"They're getting away," I said, hands on my knees as I

pointed to the dusty elves, a short distance up the walk. Seeing us, they turned and ran. Chicken.

"Let them go," Ivy said, and I turned to her, trying to ignore Trent throwing up in the nearby bushes.

"I owe them some hurt!" I said, tugging my shoulder bag back up where it belonged. "Damn it, Trent!" I shouted, pulling him up from where he was wiping his mouth with the red ribbon he'd pulled from his shoulders. "I told you to find Ivy, not go hide in a hole in the ground! I can't keep you alive if you don't listen to me!"

"Leave him alone," Ivy said, tugging my arm off Trent, her eyes on the sky and her lips parted.

I was bleeding, and I looked at my hand in horror, flexing my fingers until I realized that it wasn't my blood staining my fingers but Trent's. His right bicep was soaked where I had been yanking him forward. His ears, too, had blood leaking from them, and his hand was red when he wiped his mouth. It only made me angrier. Damn it, he was hurt.

"You are my *responsibility*!" I shouted, ticked. "If you *ever* do something like that again, I'll kill you myself. *Do you hear me!*"

Trent glared at me as he wiped his mouth with that ribbon, then let it fall. "You're not my keeper," he said, his green eyes vivid, reminding me of the elf who had almost killed me, lulled me to my death.

"Right now I am!" I shouted, getting in his face. "Deal with it!"

"Rachel, will you shut up!" Jenks exclaimed. "We have a bigger problem."

I suddenly realized Trent had gone white faced, and like both Jenks and Ivy, was now staring at the river. Turning, I felt my mouth drop open.

"Oh," I said, the sound of the approaching sirens taking on new meaning. I didn't think I needed to worry about having left the scene of an accident. The cops, both the I.S. and the FIB, had something bigger to worry about.

The arch was not there anymore. Sort of. The legs were mostly there, but the rest of it was in house-size chunks between the shattered posts.

My stomach clenched, and I looked at the bunker, realizing what had happened. "This wasn't my fault," I said softly, but my voice was quavering as if I didn't believe it.

"Maybe we should get out of here," Jenks suggested.

"Good idea," Ivy said. "Forget the rental. They have tracking charms built into the framework, and no one is going to be looking for you now."

Nodding, I grabbed Trent's sleeve and tugged him into motion. "They've probably got a tracking charm on my mom's by now, too."

"I can find any bug," Jenks said, then flew up when Trent shuffled to his wheeled suitcase and limped silently beside me. We came out from the sunken sidewalk together and joined the walking wounded, heading against the wash of help flowing into the park from the surrounding city. For once, our dusty and bloody appearance was unremarked upon. We were walking, and there were lots of people who weren't.

No way did a single support beam falling cause this. It had been the two elves and that magic that I'd pushed back into them. This was not my fault, and as I remembered the children playing on the grass, I vowed that the Withons were going to pay. *With interest.*

Seven

The faint smell of cinnamon, blood, and wine drifted forward from the backseat despite the fact that all the windows were down. My elbow was propped up on the sill, and my hair was a tangled mess. Jenks was on the rearview mirror, his wings flat against his back to keep them from being torn to tatters. Ivy was driving. We were an hour out of St. Louis, and no one was happy. I would have asked Ivy if she'd mind if I rolled mine up, but her grip on the wheel was tight and her eyes were halfway to black, slowly edging into hunger.

My chest hurt, and I wrapped my arm around my middle, staring out at the whole-lot-of-nothing we were passing through. The sun shifted as we took a slow turn. From the back where Trent sulked, a new burst of blood and cinnamon grew as the warmth found him. Ivy swallowed hard. That we hadn't stopped to give him a chance to change his clothes told me she was scared.

I exchanged a worried look with Jenks. Trent had tried to clean up, but there was only so much that bottled water and fast-food napkins could do. Dried blood cracked and flaked from the absorbent black cloth he'd tied around his bicep. It looked like a shoe-polishing rag, and I was sure he'd gotten it from his suitcase, thrown into the backseat before we tore out of St. Louis. At least his face was clean. Even his ears where the blood had dripped down. He had been bleeding from his ears! What had they tried to do to him?

I shifted, my foot scraping against the fast-food bag half full of candy wrappers, coffee cups, and water bottles. The scent of fries mixed with that of dried blood somehow reminding me of my prom. I'd be hungry, except my stomach was knotting over the news coming out of St. Louis.

"Experts claim that an adhesive that dissolves in salt water is to blame," the woman on the radio said, her voice a mix of urgent drama and calm journalism. "This salt-water-dissolving adhesive is routinely used in major road construction in no-frost zones outside the coastlines, and it's thought that the salt used to de-ice the nearby sidewalks soaked into the soil, eating away at the foundation over the years until today's disastrous toll."

Salt-dissolving adhesive, I thought darkly. That was Inderland speak for a magic misfire. No need to scare the humans. Despite all the integration we'd achieved, the equality that we managed, there were still secrets, still hidden ugliness.

Jenks's wings hummed from the rearview mirror. "Anyone mind if I change the station?" he asked. "They're just repeating themselves now."

His tone was heavy, and I looked at Ivy. She was the one who'd turned it on. From the back, Trent sighed, finishing off a bottle of flavored water enhanced with B vitamins and complex amino acids or something, capping it and tossing it to the front for me to jam in with the rest of the trash. Ivy clicked off the radio, her motions just shy of vampiric speed.

I squinted out the window in the new silence as I shoved the bottle in the trash, not really seeing the gently rolling grasslands. They looked hot under the lengthening afternoon sun, and I wished I had my sunglasses to cut the glare. I'd put on Trent's, but he'd probably want them back, and I didn't know what to think of him anymore. The third assassin hadn't been at the car when we'd stumbled back to it. Neither Trent, Ivy, or Jenks had asked what happened, and I wasn't about to admit, especially to Trent, that I'd almost died. I hadn't known elven magic could be so insidiously deadly, and a new wariness, or respect maybe, had me quietly thinking.

Depressed, I hoisted my shoulder bag with its early-warning amulet higher onto my lap, the ley-line amulet glowing briefly when it fell into my aura's influence. Thanks to them, Jenks had looked for and found the explosive charm stuck to the car before it blew, and then the bug they'd put on it in case we found the bomb. Ivy had been ticked. Trent, impressed. It was the bug that had prompted Ivy to take 44 southwest instead of jumping on 70, ticking off Trent, whose ultimate destination was Seattle. I wasn't going to Seattle. I was going to San Francisco. The deal was the West Coast in two days, not Seattle.

I turned to look at the man, wondering if he could sing. "How's your shoulder?" I asked. He'd missed a smear of blood just under his hairline, and I forced my attention from it. I could see it in peekaboo snatches when the wind hit him just right.

Trent's sour expression shifted to one of irritation. "Better," he said, the word clipped. "I don't think I'm *bleeding through my pores* anymore."

From the corner of my eye, I saw Ivy tighten her grip on the wheel, her French-manicured nails catching the light. Jenks hummed his wings in worry, and I took an uneasy breath. "Sorry," I said shortly, wondering if I should ask Ivy to stop.

"You care?" Trent muttered.

"No," I said, resettling myself to look out the front. "But I told Quen I'd keep you alive. Even when you do stupid stuff like hide in a hole instead of finding Ivy like I told you to."

"I wasn't aware that keeping your word was important to you," he mocked.

My eyes narrowed. Jenks shook his head, warning me not to rise to the bait, but I couldn't help it. "It is," I said, eying my nails. There was blood under my cuticles. *Trent's?*

"And that's why you refuse to take my familiar mark off?" Trent asked.

Ivy exhaled loudly, and I looked sideways at him. "I don't trust you," I said. "Duh."

Seeing my irritation, Trent put his leg across his knee and lounged in the backseat like it was a limo, the sun in his hair and eyes as he looked out at the hot, flat view. How could someone with a bloody rag around their arm look that confident? *Because he could sing someone to death?* "That's patently obvious," he said softly, almost like a rebuke. "But you *did* agree."

I huffed and turned back around. "Like you hold to all your agreements."

"I do," he said quickly. "Agreements . . . and threats."

Jenks's expression had gone dark. Ivy, too, was clenching her jaw. The scent of cinnamon and wine grew stronger. Trent might look calm, but he was losing it on the inside. I might not have noticed it last year, but after spending almost a day with him, I could now.

"Then why haven't you killed me? Huh?" I said, turning and holding myself back from the seat so I could look at him square on. "Go for it, you little spot of sunshine! I just beat off three assassins, one by myself. I'm stronger than you, and you know it." I smiled insincerely. "It bothers you, doesn't it? You rely on Quen far too much."

His eyes flicked to mine, then away. "That's not it at all," he said mildly, the wind playing in his hair, showing that smear of blood again.

"Is so," I said, and Jenks cleared his throat. "You're lucky I pushed that magic back into those idiots and got them to back off. There was enough there to kill both of us."

Irritation crossed his face, so quick I wasn't sure it even existed. "That's not what I meant," he said, dabbing a bloody cloth against an ear. "Obviously you're more capable than I in magic. It's why I wanted to *hire* you in the first place," he said, making it sound like an insult. "The deal was that I give you until the witches' conference to resolve this issue." I made a "well?" face at him, and he snarkily added, "We aren't there yet. You've got a day or two before I start trying to kill you again."

My mouth dropped open. From behind me, Jenks coughed, covering up a laugh. "I just saved your life!" I said loudly, anger spilling into my voice. "Again!"

"Will you two stop bickering?" Ivy suddenly said, and I flicked a look at her, seeing her about ready to lose it. The blood, the anger, it was adding up. Trent had pissed me off, and I was filling the car with it. I wasn't done, but for Ivy, I'd shut my mouth.

"Screw you, Trent," I said as I flopped back into my seat. In hindsight, it might not have been the best thing to do since Ivy took a deep breath and shuddered.

"I'm just saying—" Trent started, his voice cutting off as Ivy put on the blinker. We hadn't seen a car in miles, but she flicked it on and took the exit ramp, right before the interstate rose to go over a grass-covered road running north and south.

"Uh, Ivy?" I asked. Trent, too, had put both feet on the floor and sat up straight. I'd almost say he was worried.

"I'm good, Ivy," Jenks chimed in. The guy had a bladder the size of a pinhead.

"I'm not." Ivy looked at Trent through the rearview mirror. "You stink."

I looked over the seat, wincing at the sight of his blood-soaked shirtsleeve and the wad of red tissue he had pressed against his ear again. "Sorry," he said sourly. "Didn't mean to offend."

"You're not offensive," she said shortly. "You're turning me on. Get out. Clean up."

I turned back around, mouth shut. Tires popping on pebbles, Ivy pulled onto a seldom-used road bracketed by two deserted gas stations and a derelict fast-food joint. Slowing, she made a beeline across the grassy pavement to the station with the least weeds. She brought the car to a halt, sideways to the faded parking lines, and put it in park. Sighing, she turned the engine off.

Silence and crickets took over. It was four according to my cell phone, but it felt like five. Somewhere we'd crossed a time line. "Where are we?"

Jenks looked up through the strip of blue-tinted glass at a faded sign. "Saint Clair?"

The sound of Trent's door opening was loud, and above us, a car drove by on the interstate. "Good," he said as he got out, with a wince, to peer at it. "That's 47 going under the expressway. If we take that, we can hit I-70 in an hour and cut twenty hours out of the drive."

Ivy leaned back and closed her eyes. "I'm not driving on a two-lane road. Not out here in the abandoned stretches. And not after dark."

"You're afraid?" Trent mocked.

Jenks rose up and down in nervousness, but Ivy just settled deeper into the sun. "Absolutely," she said softly, and I bobbed my head, totally agreeing with her. I didn't want to get off the interstate, either. There were bad things in the empty stretches, especially out west, where there'd been less of a population to begin with.

"Release the trunk, will you?" Trent said, clearly not going to push the issue.

While Trent shuffled to the back of the car, I began gathering the trash. *I don't remember anyone buying Milk Duds . . .*

"Be quick about it!" Ivy said loudly as she reached for a lever and popped the trunk. "And don't go in the building for water. I've got wet wipes in the outside pocket of my bag."

"I know better than to knock on doors," Trent said, feeling his jaw as he pulled his suitcase out and moved to the back of the car.

I watched him in the side-view mirror until the lid of the trunk lifted, blocking my view. Fidgeting, I finished shoving trash into one bag. I didn't believe his crack about trying to kill me, but I was going to have to make good on our deal at some point. Here in the middle of nowhere might be better than in the middle of San Francisco with witches breathing down my neck. I didn't trust him, but now was better than later. It might get him to shut up, too.

"Ivy," I said as I grabbed my shoulder bag. "Do we have twenty minutes?"

"You gotta pee, too?" Jenks guessed, darting outside the window to warm himself in the sun. "Tink's panties, I don't know why it takes you women so long," he said from outside.

"Maybe because we don't have to do it every twenty minutes," I suggested.

"Hey!" he said indignantly, but Ivy had opened her eyes, waiting for an explanation.

"I want to take care of his familiar mark," I said, almost angry.

"Feeling guilty?" she said, eyes closing.

"No," I said quickly. "And I'm not afraid of him killing me, but it will give him one less thing to bitch about."

Ivy's lips quirked, and the sun hit her fully. "If it will shut him up, take an hour."

"All I need is twenty minutes." Sublimely aware of Trent rustling in the back, I got out with my bag in one hand, the trash in the other, using my foot to shut the door. Jenks lifted high to do a perimeter, and looking at the abandoned gas station, I sighed. Yellowed weeds grew in the cracks, but there was a nice bit of concrete under the gas station overhang. That was likely the best spot to make a circle, and I did want this done in a circle.

"Rachel?" Ivy called, and I turned to see her leaning across the front seat, to my window. "Find out why the Withons are trying to kill him, will you?" she whispered, her brown eyes going darker. "We're going to hit desert soon. That's a lot of space for bad things to happen in."

Squinting from the sun, I followed her gaze to the lifted trunk lid and settled my bag on my shoulder. The memory of the attack outside St. Louis sifted through me, and then my nearly succumbing to wild magic. And then the arch falling on us? It was a far cry from the "assassins" in my kitchen, and I wanted to know myself. It was times like this when I missed Pierce. He'd probably threaten Trent with a curse and be done with it, which wasn't much better than Trent, but I did appreciate his results. I had to be more circumspect for my answers.

Nodding, I started for the back of the car. Jenks was sitting on the rim of the upraised trunk talking to Trent, and upon seeing the man, I stopped, blinking in appreciation.

Trent had his shirt off, wadded up and in a pile at his feet. His suitcase was open, but he quickly shut it when my shadow touched him. A wad of wet towelettes was in his hand, and his skin was glistening in the sun where he'd wiped himself down. Damn, he looked good. Lots of definition and not a single tan line. Not to mention the six-pack abs disappearing into a pair of faded jeans. *Murdering drug lord. Bio-drug dealer. Pretty like a toxin.*

His expression cross, Trent dropped the used wipes on his bloodstained shirt and snatched up the one draped over my garment bag. "What?" he said shortly, and I flushed.

Sitting on the highest part of the hood, his feet dangling down, Jenks sighed.

"I need something from my bag," I said as I dropped the trash into the nearby fifty-five-gallon drum and edged closer. Shoving Trent down with my mere presence, I pulled my scrying mirror from the side pocket of my carry-on. The rest of the curse—five candles, magnetic chalk, finger stick, transfer media, and stick of redwood—was in my bag. It was a simple curse, really.

"I'm tired of you bitching at me," I said, jamming my carry-on bag back where it had been. "I'm going to take care of your familiar mark. Right now."

"Here?" Trent said, the sun making his surprise easy to see.

"That's generally what 'right now' means, yes, unless you want to do it in a car going ninety miles an hour down the interstate."

His motion to wrangle a black T-shirt on across his shoulders was fast. "Now is fine," he said as it settled over him, not too tight, not too loose. Oh. My. God. He looked good, unaware that I was watching. His hair was mussed where he'd tried to slick it back after wiping off the blood, and it was all I could do not to reach out and smooth it. My hand gripped the scrying mirror tighter as he tucked the black cotton shirt behind his waistband in a move that was both casual and intimate.

Upon noticing my eyes on him, he stopped, a mistrustful wariness coming over him. Motions sharp, he zipped his suitcase closed and slammed the trunk shut. "What can I do to help?" he asked.

"You help?" Jenks said, flying since Trent had shut the trunk out from under him. "You're the reason we're in this trouble. The day we need your help—"

"Relax, Jenks," I interrupted. Sure, Trent had sicced the coven on me, but he wasn't the one getting filmed being dragged down the street by a demon. Jenks made a hum of discontent, and I gripped my scrying mirror tighter, it feeling slippery in the sun. "There've got to be pixies here," I said, leaning to look at the gas station overhang. "Can you talk to them? Find out where the local big bad uglies are so I don't do my magic on their doorstep?"

Face screwing up, Jenks shifted his wings in sullen affirmation. His hand rose to slap his bicep to make sure he had on his red bandanna, then dropped to rest on the butt of his sword, again on his hip thanks to Ivy. "Sure," he said, buzzing off with a noisy wing clatter. "Tink's a Disney whore, Rache. Why don't you start thinking with something other than your hormones?"

"Hey!" I shouted after him, stiffening when he was suddenly surrounded by pixies in brown shirts and pants. They had spears pointed at him, but they soon dropped them and he went with them willingly. Slowly I exhaled. Trent scuffed his boots, and I looked over the abandoned gas station. A car went by, looking a thousand miles away on the overpass.

Hiking my shoulder bag up, I headed for the man-made

shade of the overhang. Trent moved to stay with me, dropping his bloody shirt and wet wipes into the trash can along the way. "Ah, I should apologize for not doing this sooner," I said, feeling a pang of guilt.

"You were scared," Trent said, his lofty attitude making my eyes narrow.

"I'm not talking about yesterday," I said tartly, guilt vanishing. "I mean the last two months. Al wouldn't tell me the curse, and it took me a while to find it."

Trent glanced at me, his pace going stiff. "It's a new curse," he stated flatly. "I thought you would simply untwist the one you put on me."

"I didn't curse you," I said sharply. "I took ownership of the one Minias claimed you with. But don't worry. This one won't hurt. I'll take the smut." *Crap, I'm taking his smut.*

"Ah . . . ," he started, and I scuffed to a halt, my toes edging shadow as I squinted at him in the sun. Damn, he looked good in that T-shirt, and looked even better out of it. *Stop it, Rachel.*

"I'm not going to ask you to pay for it," I said, tired. "I'm so covered with smut that this little bit won't show. On you, though . . ." I slipped under the gas station's overhang, appreciating the cooler temp. "We don't want to jeopardize your bid for mayor, do we?" Okay, that might have been catty, but everything about this bothered me. Pulling my magnetic chalk out, I dropped my shoulder bag. "How's that going anyway?" I asked as I set my scrying mirror beside it. "The Weres have had the mayoral seat for over fifteen years."

Trent edged under the overhang, his eyes on the holes in the roof. "Not as well as I'd like," he said, a practiced polish coming across with his words, as if he had been saying it a lot lately. "I'm writing off the Were demographic. There's been a marked increase in registered Were voters in the last two months, which will make things difficult. If I knew it was an intentional block by you, I'd be irritated."

He went silent, spinning to keep me in his sight as I walked around him, bent almost double to trace a circle on the dirty concrete. Straightening, I kicked out an old pop can, and sank to the ground. His eyebrows rose, and I shrugged. "Have a seat," I said, indicating a spot about four feet in front of me.

Still silent, he bent his knees and found his way to the ground in a graceful move that was as far away from the boardroom as his present clothes were. He had an almost animal-like grace now that he wasn't in a suit, and something twisted in me. *Stop it, Rachel.* Jenks was right. I thought way too much with my hormones. But seeing Trent sitting cross-legged in jeans, that thin black T-shirt, and blood-splattered boots, I was struck by how quickly the businessman was slipping away. It kind of worried me—even as I liked it.

Trent's gaze dropped from the broken roof to me, and I warily shuffled my things around, trying to figure out what was going through his mind. He'd known Ceri for almost a year now, and her old-school, black-magic-using elf mentality had been rubbing off on him. She'd believed demon magic was a tool. A dangerous tool, but a tool. Trent had been taught to fear it, much like the coven had. But clearly that was changing. I didn't know what he could do anymore, and it moved him from a familiar threat to something I had to be wary of.

Looking across the two-lane road, I whistled for Jenks, getting a burst of green dust signifying that we were good. On the horizon, the waxing moon rose in the bright light of afternoon. At the car, Ivy was busy cleaning the backseat with her special orange wipes. Nervous, I wiped my palms on my thighs. The wind moved my hair, and I tucked the strands, still caked with the dust of the arch, behind an ear. Ivy wanted to drive all night, but I wanted to rent a room to shower, if nothing else. I felt icky.

"I meant it when I said I didn't mean to drag this out to the last few days," I said as I pawed through my bag. "Al wouldn't tell me how to do the curse, just gave me a book. Demon texts don't have indexes, so I had to look page by page. It wasn't in there. But it does have a page or two with info like substitutions, sun and moon tables, conversions . . ."

I found the index card with the Latin Trent was going to have to say, and I handed it to him. He automatically took it, his expression one of surprise. "The curse to free a familiar was—"

"At the back with the metric to English conversions, yes," I said sourly. "I guess they don't do this often." I set five candles on the cement. They were from my last birthday cake. How sad was that? The finger stick and shaft of redwood were next. I had a moment of panic until I found the vial of transfer media. I could buy it, sure, but not anywhere near here.

I twisted where I sat to reach my scrying mirror, setting it between us as the platform on which to do the curse. Trent looked at the dark wine-colored hues that it reflected the world in. His boots shifted. He was nervous. He should be.

"You need the mirror for this?" he asked, though it was obvious.

"Yes," I said, thinking the plate-size piece of etched glass was beautiful for all its dark purpose. Etched with a stick of yew, the pentagram and associated glyphs were how I accessed the demon database in the ever-after. It also let me chat with my demon teacher, Algaliarept. I guess you could say it was an interdimensional cell phone that ran on black magic, and since this curse needed to be registered, I'd have to use it. Suddenly suspicious, I asked, "Why?"

Trent's eyes fixed on mine, too innocent. "I was remembering having used it to talk to Minias. It wasn't hard."

I flicked the top off the finger stick with my thumb and jabbed myself. The brief pain was familiar, and I massaged three drops of blood into the transfer media. "Demon magic never is," I said softly as they went plinking in and the expected redwood scent was quickly overshadowed by a whiff of burnt amber. I glanced at Trent, hoping he hadn't noticed. "That's why you pay for it the hard way. He's dead, by the way. Minias. Newt killed him."

Suddenly tired, I slumped. "I can't get the familiar bond annulled," I admitted, knowing he wasn't going to be happy.

"The best I can do is file an emancipation curse. That's why I need the mirror."

Sure enough, Trent clenched his jaw. "I'd still be counted a slave?"

"Deal with it!" I exclaimed angrily, eyes flicking up when I heard a pixy whisper from the roof and realized we were being watched. "You were caught, Trent. You were on a demon's auction block. You had a little red bow around your neck, and you were a commodity. I'm sorry, but you were!"

Scowling, Trent looked past me to the yellow grass.

"If it helps," I said softly, "the only reason I was able to get the familiar bond between Al and me annulled was because it couldn't be enforced. And before you ask, if you want to go that route, I'd have to complete the familiar bond, use it, and you'd have to successfully beat me down. After that little stunt at the arch, I think we can agree that *that* is not going to happen," I added, not sure if I had the right to be so confident anymore.

Looking as if he were swallowing slugs, Trent gazed past me. "I will be a freed slave."

I winced in sympathy as I rubbed at one of the candles to get the dried frosting off. "The upside is that no demon can ever claim you. Even Al. At least as long as I'm alive," I added, watching him as he took it in and his frown eased into a thoughtful expression. It was a serendipitous bit of CYA, but it was true, and it felt good knowing that he wouldn't be trying to kill me again. Ever. Na-na. Na-na. Na-a-a-a. Na.

His response was a quiet "mmmm," and I wondered if he thought I was making it up.

Leaning forward, I wiped the glass clean and pressed the candle at the tip of the pentagram to Trent's right, wiggling it a bit to get the wax to melt a little and stick. "So-o-o-o," I drawled, not looking up. "You want to tell me why the Withons want you dead so badly that they'd drop the St. Louis arch on us?" I said, and his knees shifted.

"I'd sooner tell you what I wanted to be when I grew up,"

Trent said sarcastically, then frowned when our eyes met. "It could have been the coven."

My hair was getting in my way, and I pushed the nasty curls behind my ear to make them less obvious. "Come on, Trent," I said. "We all know the Withons were after you. They said as much after you left."

Trent looked at the holes in the ceiling, silent. I pressed the second candle into the mirror on the point counterclockwise from the first, surreptitiously eying him from under my tangled hair as I took in his tells. He was nervous. That's all I could determine. *I'm doing demon magic at an abandoned gas station within sight of I-44. God! No wonder they shunned me.*

I moved to the third candle, rolling it between my fingers before I wiggled it into place. "Quen was so scared that he picked me up from the airport, ready to send us out right from there in the hope of shaking the Withons' assassins," I said, and Trent cleared his throat. "They attacked us on the interstate, risking dozens of lives, and then again under the arch. And you knew they would," I said, suddenly realizing it, "or you wouldn't have gone to that bunker, looking for that ley line when I told you to find Ivy."

His head came up, and he glared at me, still refusing to say anything.

"That's why you were so adamant that we stop there, wasn't it," I said, leaning forward. "And why you went to ground. You knew they were after you and you didn't trust Ivy and me to hold them off. You had your magic all prepped, with your little hat and ribbon," I accused, and he held his gaze, angry. "And after you did your magic, the arch fell down." *It fell on us, and children, and dogs playing in the park.*

Trent's eye twitched. "I didn't make it collapse," he said, his beautiful voice strained.

Feeling used, I set the fourth candle, my hair falling onto the mirror to meet its reflection. "I never said you did," I said. "But they want you dead, and they want you dead now. What are you trying to do that the Withons will sacrifice a park full of people to prevent?" I looked at him, thinking he appeared sharp and cold in the shadow with me. "People got *hurt* because of us. Killed. Kids, Trent. If I hadn't gone to St. Louis, the arch would still be standing and those kids . . . those *kids* would still be okay. I deserve to know why!" I said, not wanting to get back in the car without an answer.

Trent, his expression a blank nothing, looked into the field where the pixies were showing off for Jenks. "It's something between Ellasbeth and myself," he finally said reluctantly.

The fourth candle fell over when I let go of it, and it rolled almost off the mirror before I caught it. "You going to kill her?" I asked outright, my heart pounding.

"No!" I felt better at the horror in his voice, and he said it again, as if I might not believe him. "No. Never."

The wind shifted his hair, and I couldn't help but think he looked better now than in a thousand-dollar suit. Silent, I waited. Finally he grimaced and looked at his feet. "Ellasbeth has something that belongs to me," he said. "I'm going to get it. She wants to keep it, is all."

"We caused a pileup on the interstate and hurt a bunch of kids over a family heirloom ring?" I guessed, disgusted. "A stupid hunk of rock?"

"It's not a hunk of rock." Trent's green eyes lowered as he looked at his hands in his lap, fixing on me fervently when he looked up. "It's the direction the next generation of elves is going to take. What happens in the following days will shape the next two hundred years."

Oh, really? Thinking that over, I tried to get the candle to stick, holding my breath as I let it go, watching it carefully. I didn't know why I was helping him. I really didn't.

"You don't believe me," Trent said, his anger showing at last. "You asked why they want me dead. I told you the truth, and you haven't said anything."

My gaze coming up from the mirror, I looked at him from under my straggly hair. I was so friggin' tired it hurt. "The

Withons are trying to stop you from getting this thing so they can shape the next two hundred years of elfdom, not you, eh?"

"That's it." Trent's shoulders eased at my sarcasm. "Our marriage was supposed to be a way to avoid this. If I can claim it by sunrise Monday, then it's mine forever. If not, then I lose everything." His expression was empty of emotion. "Everything, Rachel."

I stifled a shiver, trying to disguise it by wiggling the last candle into place. "So this is kind of like an ancient elven spirit quest, rite of passage, and closed election all in one?"

Trent's lips parted. "Uh, ye-yes," he stammered, looking embarrassed. "Actually, that's not a bad comparison. It's also why Quen couldn't help and why air travel was out. I'm allowed a horse, and the car is the modern equivalent."

I nodded, jumping when the fifth candle fell over. "And me? What am I?"

"You're my mirror, my sword, and my shield," Trent said dryly.

I looked askance at him to see if he was serious. *Mirror?* "Times change, eh?" I said, not sure what to think. The candle wasn't sticking, and I was getting frustrated.

"I have to be in Seattle by Sunday or it means nothing. Rachel, this is the most important thing in my life."

The candle went rolling, and Trent jerked his hand out, catching it. I froze in my reach, eyes narrowing as Trent breathed on the end and quickly stuck it to the mirror. My gaze went to the moon, pale in the sunlight. Maybe that was his deadline. Elves loved marking things by the moon. "I don't have to help you steal it, do I?" I asked, and he shook his head, unable to hide his relief that I believed him. And I did believe him.

"If I can't claim it on my own, then I don't deserve it."

Back to the coming-of-age elf-quest thing. "I want a say," I said, and Trent blinked.

"Excuse me?"

I lifted a shoulder and let it fall, carefully spilling a bit of primed transfer media onto the mirror. "If I'm your mirror, sword, and shield, then I want a say as to how it's used. I've seen you work, and I don't like your way of getting things done. Maybe Ellasbeth's family would be better at directing the elven race than you."

Trent's eyes were wide. "You don't believe that."

"I don't know what I believe, but I want a say." *Especially if it bothers you so much.*

Mouth moving, Trent finally managed, "You have no idea what you're asking."

"I know," I said flippantly. "But here we are. Yes or no?"

Trent looked like he was going to say no, but then his posture slipped and he smiled. "I agree," he said lightly, extending his hand over the scrying mirror. "You have a say."

His eyes were glinting like Al's, but my hand went out, and we shook over the prepared curse. His fingers were warm in mine, pleasant, and I pulled away fast. "Why do I feel like I've made a mistake," I muttered, and Trent's smile widened, worrying me more.

"Rachel, I've been trying to get you involved for two years. If this is how I'm going to get my foot in the door, then so be it." His eyes went down to the curse. "Is it ready?"

Crap, had I just gone into a partnership with him?

Feeling ill, I nodded, taking up the stick of redwood and dipping it in the primed transfer media. I made a quick counterclockwise movement before touching the tip of it to the back of Trent's hand, then mine, making a symbolic connection between us.

Trent frowned at the damp spot on his hand as if wanting to wipe it off, and I set the stick down beside my bag with a snap. "Don't wipe that off," I said sharply, still uneasy because of his last comment. "And put your hand on the mirror, please—without touching any of the glyphs or knocking over the candles."

He hesitated, and I set my hand down first, making sure my thumb and pinky were on the center glyphs for connection. The cool stillness of the glass seemed to seep up into me—until Trent's fingers touched the etched mirror. Jerking, I met his startled gaze, sure he'd felt the zing of energy leaving him. "You're connected to a ley line?" I asked, not needing to see his nod. "Um, let go of it," I said, and the faint seepage of power ceased. "Thank you."

Satisfied everything was set, I reached behind me with my free hand to touch the ring of chalk. *"Rhombus,"* I said, wincing as my awareness found the nearest ley line. It was all the way back in St. Louis, thin and weak from the distance, but it would be enough.

Warmth textured with silver poured into me, and Trent sucked in his breath in surprise, connected to the line by way of the mirror. A molecule-thin sheet of ever-after rose up, arching both overhead and underneath, within the earth, forming a sphere of protection. Nothing stronger than air could pass through except energy itself. The sheet was colored with the gold of my original aura, but the demon smut I'd accumulated over the last couple of years crawled over it like arcs of unbalanced power, looking for a way in. At night, it wasn't so noticeable, but out here in the sun, it was ugly. Looking up, Trent grimaced.

Nothing you've not seen before, Mr. Clean. Looking up at a car on the interstate, I took a deep breath. There was no better time to do this, but I wasn't comfortable. Trent, too, looked uneasily at the forces balancing between us, and I dampened the flow until his shoulders relaxed. My thoughts went to the energy I'd shoved into the assassins under the arch. There was no way all of that had come from Trent, but I didn't think it had come from the assassins, either. What had he been doing with that little cap and ribbon?

"Okay," I said, starting to fidget. "What's going to happen is that I'm going to light four of the candles. Then you say your words. I'll register the curse, and we're done."

Trent's gaze flicked from the index card to me. "That's it?" I nodded, and his attention went to the candles. "There are five candles. Do I light that one?"

"No, it will light on its own if we do it right." The wind brought the sound of pixy laughter to me, recognizable but faster and higher than Jenks's kids, and I inhaled slowly. A quiver went through me. I'd never shown anyone outside my friends that I could do demon magic. But Trent was looking at his card, squinting as if he didn't care.

"What does it say?" he finally asked.

A flush warmed me. "Um, *bella* usually means beautiful, doesn't it?"

Trent scrunched his face up, clearly not knowing, either, but I bet he'd find out thirty seconds after he got to his phone. "You want to wait until I find out?" I asked, already knowing the answer, and sure enough, he shook his head.

"It doesn't matter. I want the mark off. Now."

Yeah, me, too. Jittery, I looked at the candles, hoping they'd stayed put. The curse didn't physically change anything or break the laws of physics, so the smut would be minimal; Nature didn't care about the laws of demons or men, only her own. Break them, and you pay.

"Ex cathedra," I said, carefully scraping a bit of wax off the first candle at Trent's right and holding it under my nail. I didn't need a focusing object most days, but I wanted no mistakes in front of Trent. Thinking *consimilis calefacio* to light the candle, I pinched the wick and slowly opened my fingers to leave a new flame. *Ex cathedra,* "from the office of authority"; I hoped my pronunciation was right. It wouldn't mess up the curse if I was off, but this curse would be registered in the demon database, and word would get around.

Lighting the candle had taken an almost minuscule drop of ley-line force, and I met Trent's startled gaze. "Ceri knows how to light candles like that, too," he said.

"She's the one who taught me," I admitted, and Trent's frown deepened. Guess she hadn't taught him. *"Rogo,"* I said, lighting the second candle on my left. *I am asking,* I thought, watching until I was sure the flame wasn't going to go out.

Trent cleared his throat at the rising power, and the hair on my arms pricked. *"Mutatis mutandis,"* I said, lighting the candle to my right, continuing my counterclockwise motion. Counterclockwise. This was really wrong, but it was for a good reason. *Things to be changed.*

"Libertus," I said as I lit the candle to Trent's left, almost completing the circle. Just one right in front of him to go, and if it didn't light on its own, then I was in trouble.

"Read your card," I said as I stared at the unlit candle. "And for God's little green apples, don't blow anything out in the process."

Much to his credit, Trent didn't lick his lips or give any indication that he was nervous, and with a smooth, enviable accent, said, *"Si qua bella inciderint, vobis ausilum feram."*

I felt a sinking of self, and my hand pressed firmly into the glass. It was as if the world had dropped out from under me and I was suddenly not just under an abandoned building's overhang in the middle of nowhere, but also in the theoretical black database in the ever-after. I could hear whispers of demons talking through their own scrying mirrors, sense the bright flash of a curse being registered. The double sensations were confusing, and my eyes had closed, but they opened when Trent roughly said, "Nothing happened."

Dizzy, I tried to focus on him and the fear behind his anger. Clearly he wasn't feeling the same thing I was. "It's not done yet. I have to register it." Heart pounding, I closed my eyes, praying this wasn't going to swing around to bite me on the ass. *"Evulgo."*

I stiffened as a flare of ever-after shot through me, and my eyes opened at Trent's hiss. "Keep your hand on the glass!" I warned him.

The four candles went out, the thin trails of smoke and the scent of sulfur rising like curls of thought to heaven. My gaze went to the as-yet-unlit candle. *Please, please, please . . .*

Relief pulled the corners of my mouth up as the last candle burst into flame, covering the scent of honest sulfur with the acidic, biting scent of burnt amber. "I pay the cost," I whispered as I glanced at Trent, even before the smut could rise.

Trent grunted, his free hand clutching his shoulder where the familiar mark was. A wave of unseen force pulsed out from me, breaking my circle as it passed through, pressing the pixies into the air, and heading out in an ever-widening circle. From inside the abandoned building, something crashed to the floor. Still holding his arm, Trent looked to the gaping windows.

I let go of the ley line and took my hand from the scrying mirror. It was done, for better or worse, and I lifted my head and took a deep breath. I didn't know what Trent would do, and it was scary. From the car, Ivy called out, "You good?"

Trent's face was empty of emotion as he turned where he sat and pulled his sleeve up, twisting to see on his arm where the mark was—had been—I hoped.

"Good," I called out to Ivy, my voice cracking. "I'm good!" I said louder, and she slumped back into the seat. She'd felt it. That was curious.

Trent made a small noise, his expression ugly. "What is *that*!" he exclaimed, his face becoming red as he twisted to show me his arm, and my lips parted. The demon mark was gone, but in its place was a dark discoloration of skin that looked like a birthmark. A birthmark in the shape of a smiley face. All it needed was the phrase "Have a nice day!" tattooed under it.

A mild panic hit me. This was so not fair. I had done the charm—curse—whatever—right, and I still ended up looking like a fool.

"What is that!" he demanded, the flush rising to his ears. From the open field, the pixies rose high then back down.

"Uh, it looks like a birthmark," I said. "Really, it's not that bad."

"Is this your idea of a joke?" he exclaimed.

"I didn't know it was going to do that!" I admitted, voice rising as I shifted to a kneel. My foot hit the mirror, and the candles all fell over, the one going out in a puff of smoke.

"Maybe it's so the demons know to keep their mitts off you!" Oh my God, it looked like a smiley face.

He sniffed at it. "It stinks!" he said. "It smells like a dandelion!"

I closed my eyes in a long blink, but he was still there when I opened them. "Trent, I'm sorry," I apologized, hoping he believed me. "I didn't know. Maybe you can add a tattoo to it. Make it something more butch."

Trent wouldn't look at me as he got to his feet, his boots scraping on the cement. "This is clearly the best you can do," he said shortly. "We have to get going."

"You're welcome," I said, peeved that that was all I was going to get out of him. His becoming my familiar had only been to save his little elf ass. For my trouble I'd gotten my head bashed into a tombstone. And now that I'd gone and added more smut to my soul to break said familiar bond, incidentally giving more ammunition to the coven of moral and ethical standards to use to prove that I was a black witch, all I got was "We have to get going"?

"Have a nice day," I called snidely after him as I shoved everything into my shoulder bag. Standing, I started to follow. The sun hit me like a heavy wind, and I bowed my head, wishing I had another pair of sunglasses. They might have a pair in the gas station, but I wasn't going in to look. And I wasn't going to give Trent his back, either.

Trent's pace was stiff as he walked to the car. I turned to the nearby field, squinting for Jenks. Not a wing caught the light or broke the stillness, and a sliver of worry colored my anger. "Do I smell better?" I heard Trent ask Ivy sarcastically as he got in the back of the car.

"I liked the way you smelled before, Trent. That was the problem."

I dumped the candles, transfer media, and finger stick into the barrel with Trent's bloody shirt and our trash. Tapping a line, I made the appropriate ley-line gesture, and with the final words, *leno cinis,* I threw a ball of unfocused energy in on top to get the entire thing burning. Flame whooshed up, fueled by my anger as well as the demon curse. Ivy looked at me through the open window, her eyebrows high as I destroyed any evidence of us and the curse.

Without a word, she started the car. Hands on my hips, I looked to the field for Jenks. A sneeze tickled my nose, and I let it come, hearing it echo against the broken buildings. My eyes narrowed, and sure enough, I sneezed again. There was only one reason I sneezed more than twice in a row, and I held my breath until the third one ripped through me.

Damn. It was Al. Maybe he'd felt the familiar emancipation curse being registered.

"Ivy, we got a minute?" I asked as I tossed my bag in through the open door, then sat down sideways with my feet still on the cracked cement.

She knew what my sneezing meant, too. "A minute." Still reclining, she honked the horn. "Jenks! Let's go!"

The tightening in my gut eased as Jenks flew up, a veritable cloud of pretty dresses and flashing wings left hovering forlornly over the meadow. "Crap on toast!" the pixy said, his long hair loose and looking disheveled as he straightened his clothes. "I think I almost got married."

There was a flash of red on his feet, and as I placed the scrying mirror on my knees, I blinked in surprise. "Where did you get the boots, Jenks?"

"You like them?" he said as he landed on the glass to show them off. "Me, too. I told them about you, and they gave them to me. They think I'm some kind of wandering storyteller, and it was either take these or the nasty honey made from sedge flowers." He made a face, his angular features twisting up dramatically. "What does Al want?"

I sneezed in the middle of saying, "Three guesses," and he took off, flying to the back to show his boots to Trent. "I'm coming!" I shouted at Al as I placed my hand on the center glyph and tapped into the ley line. Feet in the sun, I set my thoughts on Algaliarept, his ruddy complexion, his overdone

British accent, his cruelty, his crushed green velvet coat, his cruelty, his voice, and his cruelty. He was nice to me, but he really was a depraved, sadistic . . . demon.

"Can't you do this while we're on the road?" Trent asked from the backseat.

"Al!" I said aloud when I felt the connection form to the demon collective, and my thought winged away to be immediately answered. A second consciousness expanded mine, and I heard Jenks clatter his wings.

"You ever see anything freakier than that?" he said to Trent.

"Yes, about three minutes ago," Trent answered back.

What in the arcane are you doing? came Al's unusually angry thought within mine, and shoved away the whisper imagery of him either cleaning his spelling kitchen or tearing it apart.

"Filing an emancipation curse," I said aloud so Ivy and Jenks could hear half the conversation. "And before you start, what I do with my familiars is my business."

Do you have any idea what you've done? Al shouted, and I winced. *Please tell me you didn't teach him anything.* Al hesitated. *Did you?*

I shook my head even though Al couldn't see it. "I didn't teach Trent anything. Not even respect," I said, and I felt Al sigh in relief.

Itchy witch, Al thought, his dark musings seeming to insert themselves into my head. *There's a reason we kill familiars when we're done with them. He's got a new mark, doesn't he?*

"His familiar mark turned into a smiley face," I said, feeling myself warm.

From the backseat, Jenks exclaimed, "No way! Let me see!" and Trent's negative growl.

Damn my dame, Al thought, seeming to fall back into Ceri's comfortable chair by the small hearth in his kitchen if I was interpreting his emotions right. *You did it correctly. Nice going, Rachel.*

"Hey, you're the one who gave me the recipe," I shot back,

thinking the modern phrase sounded funny coming from the old-world-charm demon.

I gave that one to you because it's bloody impossible and I thought you wouldn't be able to do it! he exclaimed, loud enough to give me a headache. *You just made Trent able to call any demon without fear of being snatched. Nice going.*

Fingers pressed to the glass to maintain our link, I looked back at Trent. *So? You can still smack him around, can't you?* I said, and the demon chuckled, making me shiver.

Technically, no, but that's a matter of interpretation.

I pushed my fingers into my forehead, tired of it all. Demons. Their society's rules were not worth the blood they were written with unless you had the personal power to force everyone to abide by them. But the snatching thing? That was probably ironclad.

"What did you say?" Jenks asked belligerently. "Hey! You're talking and not telling us. That's rude, Rache."

"Tell you later," I said, turning to look at Ivy, her hands on the wheel as she waited. She looked worried. Hell, I knew I was.

"Look, I wasn't going to use him as a familiar," I said to Al. "And now he's going to help get my shunning removed." The part about the West Coast elves trying to cack him, I'd keep to myself, not because it made this look more dangerous, but because Al wouldn't care. He'd just as soon see me fail. If I lost our bet, I'd be living with him in the ever-after—hence the reason he wouldn't just pop me over there.

Trenton Aloysius Kalamack? Al thought, a tweak of magic running through me when he lit a candle. *Why? You going to be his little demon in return for his vouching for your sterling character, dove?*

"Absolutely not," I said with a huff. "Trent's on some elf quest. I promised I'd see him to the West Coast is all. I'm his mirror, sword, and shield all in one. It was a *deal,* Al. Just because I can break them with impunity doesn't mean I will."

"You're on an elf quest?" Jenks said loudly, and Trent sighed. "You shitting me?"

You make the most interesting mistakes, my itchy witch, Al thought, and I didn't care if he could sense me slump in relief. If he was back to calling me itchy witch, we were okay. *Don't teach him anything,* he finished. *Nothing.*

"Not a problem," I said and lifted my hand, breaking the connection before Algaliarept caught my first whisper of unease.

Don't teach him anything, Al had said. Like how to free a familiar, maybe? *Too late.*

Eight

The hum of the engine shifted, becoming deeper. It stirred my unconsciousness, waking me more than the bright sun determined to wedge itself under my eyelids. Beyond the cover of my coat draped over me, it was cold, so I didn't move. Somewhere between Ohio and Texas, the cinnamon and wine smell of elf had joined the familiar scent of vampire and witch, mixing with the leather of my coat. Under that was the faint hint of lilac perfume, evidence of my mom lingering yet in the cushions of the backseat of her car. It was relaxing, and I lingered, dozing and slumped against the door. If I woke up, I'd have to move, and I was stiff from riding in the car for the last twenty-four hours.

A sigh that wasn't mine moved me, and I jerked awake. Crap, I wasn't slumped against the door. I was leaning against Ivy!

Great, I thought, carefully sitting up and trying not to wake her. I wasn't being phobic, but I didn't want a misunderstanding.

Her eyes opened as I pulled away, and I met her sleepy expression with my own, taking my coat and covering her up where my warmth had been against her. Ivy's smile turned sly even as her eyes closed again, and I shivered at the slip of teeth. The clock on the dash said it was about nine. Way too early for me to be up. Jenks must have changed it to Central time.

Scooting to my side of the backseat, I flicked my attention to Jenks sitting on the rearview mirror. He had on a new red coat I didn't recognize, matching his boots. Seeing me look at them, Jenks shrugged and continued his conversation with Trent about financial trends and how they parallel the size of successful pixy broods. I vaguely remembered hearing them talking in my dreams, and I sat there, ignored, as I tried to figure out what was going on.

The last thing I remembered was Ivy stopping for gas and Trent waking up from his midnight nap to take over the driving. We'd been in Oklahoma, and it had been dark, flat, and starless. Now, as I sat slumped in the back and blinked at the bright sun, I wondered where we were. The terrain had changed again. Gone was the sedge that had dotted the dry, rolling plains and turned everything in the distance into a pale green carpet. It was true desert now, the vegetation dry and sparse. Under the glaring sun and cloudless sky, the colors were thin and washed out: tans, whites, with a hint of mauve and silver. I'd never seen such a lack of anything before, but instead of making me uneasy, it was restful.

My mouth tasted ugly, and I checked my phone, my brain still fuzzy as it tried to work without caffeine. I'd missed another call from Bis, and I frowned, concerned. He'd be asleep now, but if it was anything important, the pixies would call Jenks. Bis was probably just checking on me again, still worried about me having pulled on St. Louis's line so heavily. He'd called yesterday shortly before sundown, throwing me until I realized it was dark where he was. But what bothered me now was that he'd felt me pull on a line when he'd been asleep.

Trent's voice was pleasant as he talked to Jenks, and I tucked my phone away, wondering what it might feel like to have that voice directed at me. I was not crushing on him, but it was hard not to appreciate a man who was rich, sexy, and powerful. Trent was all of that and scum, too, but the respect in his tone as he talked to Jenks was surprising. Respect, or perhaps camaraderie.

But Trent and Jenks were a lot alike in many ways, stuff that went beyond their similar sleep schedules. Jenks had the same frontier-justice mentality that irritated me when I saw it in Trent. I knew Jenks killed fairies to protect his family, and I didn't think any the less of him. Ivy, too, had killed people to survive until she had managed to escape Piscary. I was sure Pierce had, though he hadn't told me of any except the four hundred innocents in Eleison, dead because of his previous lack of skill. Everyone made sacrifices of some kind to save what was important to them. Maybe Trent had a lot more things that were important to him than most people.

"Where are we?" I said softly as I pulled on my boots, not liking where my thoughts had taken me. I felt fuzzy, like I'd been asleep a long time.

Jenks shifted to face me, his wings catching the light and sending snatches of it about the car. "About an hour outside Albuquerque."

Albuquerque? As in New Mexico? "You're kidding," I said, scooting forward to drape my arms over the passenger seat into the front. There was a fast-food bag on the floor. No, it was a take-out bag from a chain of high-priced gourmet eateries. "What time is it?" I asked, looking at the clock on the dash. "And where did you get the red coat, Jenks?"

"Nice, isn't it?" he said, rising up to show it off. "I got it when Trent picked up some breakfast around sunup. All I had to do was tell a story, and the pixy girls gave it to me. I don't know what time it is anymore. My internal clock is all screwed up."

Trent glanced at me, his eyes showing the strain of too much driving. "We crossed into another time zone. The clock is right, but I feel like it's eleven. I'm tired."

I did the math, and I looked at the speedometer, seeing it was a mere sixty-eight miles per hour. "Holy crap!" I exclaimed, then lowered my voice when Ivy moved. "How fast have you been driving?"

Jenks's wings hummed as he returned to the rearview mirror. "Ninety mostly."

Silent, I turned to Trent, seeing a smile lifting his lips. "I have to make up the time somewhere," he said. "You sleep a lot, and the roads were empty."

I tried to stretch by pressing my palms into the roof of the car, but that wasn't doing it. "I don't sleep any more than you do," I said as I collapsed back over the seat. "I just don't have to do it every twelve hours." Trent raised an eyebrow, and I added, "You want to stop for some breakfast? Maybe rent a room for a shower or something?"

"Lunch," Jenks said brightly. "*We* ate at sunup."

I stifled a smile at Jenks's satisfaction.

From the backseat came Ivy's low, gravelly "I'm hungry," and Trent smoothly took the next exit, the off-ramp clean of debris, indicating that it was well used and likely had civilization at the end of it. Though the space between the cities was mostly abandoned, there were clusters of oddballs for gas and food holding back the emptiness.

"Breakfast for the witch and the vamp it is," Trent said, sounding like he was in a good mood. Relaxed almost. I ran my eyes over his clothes, seeing that he'd changed into a pair of dark slacks at some point. Not jeans but still casual. His boots were gone, and soft-soled shoes had taken their place. I'd be willing to bet they were still pricey, but the shine was gone. The businessman was vanishing, being replaced by . . . something else. *Quen,* I thought as I slumped back into my seat, *might not be pleased.*

"Good," Jenks said as Ivy pulled herself together. "I gotta pee. Maybe get me a red hat or something. I gotta call my kids, too."

"Taking up a new profession, Jenks?" I asked, and he slipped a silver dust.

"I like the color," he said, flushing. "And where else am I going to get new clothes?"

My gaze went to the weird landscape as I thought of Matalina. Most pixies died of heartache when their spouses passed, but Jenks had lived, partly due to a demon curse that had accidentally given him a new lease on life, and partly due to his desire to see beyond what was real and into what might be. He had spent half his life breaking pixy traditions, learning about both the grief and the reward that came from taking chances. Matalina had told him to live, and somewhere he'd found the courage to do it. It was the smaller things, like who was going to make his clothes or cut his curly hair, that tripped him up. The obvious choice would be one of his daughters, but the thought had probably never occurred to him.

I slumped as Trent pulled into the single cluster of buildings on the right, sporting a tidy-looking gas station, a small motel, and an eatery. The southwestern flavor made everything look alien. Tires popping on gravel, Trent parked in front of the long, low restaurant. Behind us, a green two-door Pinto slowly turned into the lot and parked at the outskirts.

"Hey, look who caught up," Jenks said, wheezing slightly as he landed on my shoulder.

Alarmed, I turned to look closer, relaxing when I recognized the woman. It was Vivian, the youngest member of the coven of moral and ethical standards. Of the five remaining members, I liked Vivian the best, and might even count her as a friend if circumstances were different. She'd given me a bit of blackmail to use against Oliver, and had enough guts to think on her own. *She drove a Pinto? I'd put her down as a BMW kind of girl.*

"I saw her at the airport, too," Ivy said sleepily. "I'm surprised she found us at all."

"Hey, I got all the bugs off," Jenks said in a huff. "Don't look at me."

I eagerly opened my door, and the new air coming into the car smelled of dry grass. My faint headache seemed to ease. Vivian was a concern, but if she'd wanted me dead, she would have done something by now. The woman was lethal despite her diminutive looks and childlike voice. "Think we should go talk to her?" I said, and Trent stared at me like I had lobsters crawling out of my ears.

"You think you can knock her out? Buy some time to slip away from her?" Trent asked, totally misreading my words.

I snorted, and even Jenks laughed. "Vivian is *not* the one trying to kill us," I said as I gathered up the trash. "And the last thing I want to do is lose her. They might give the job of tailing us to someone else, someone more likely to throw spells and ask questions later." No, Vivian and I understood each other, and that was more conducive to a good night's sleep than a cauldron of sleep charms. Even so, I was glad she hadn't been around when I'd done the demon curse to free Trent. That would have been hard to explain.

Trent opened his door, and the breeze went right through the car. "You do make the oddest friends, Rachel."

"You want me to buzz her anyway?" Jenks asked. "Pix her, maybe?"

I shoved another empty box of Milk Duds in the garbage. *Who is eating the Milk Duds?* I glanced at Trent and Ivy, and seeing that they were leaving it to me, I shook my head.

"Good," Jenks said from my shoulder. "The elevation is kicking my ass. I can't fly worth a Tinker's damn."

I carefully got out, catching my hair before it could hit Jenks. Vivian had her head against the steering wheel as if exhausted, her straight blond hair falling to hide her face. She was alone, and therefore likely hopped up on a charm or a spell. She'd pay for it later. Big-time.

"Trent, will you pop the trunk?" Ivy said, standing beside it. "I'm going to shower."

I plucked my chemise away from my skin, thinking a shower sounded fantastic. Breathing deeply, I took in the air, tasting the differences. My body felt like it was almost noon, but the sun wasn't that far above the horizon. Nine o'clock and the sun was already warm as it hit my shoulders. It felt good to be warm, and I squinted at the distant horizon, missing my sunglasses. The hard-packed earth had a pink tint to it. Rusty, almost. It was as if I could sense the salt beneath the earth, just under the surface. The wind moving my limp curls had the feeling of distance.

While Ivy stretched in what I recognized as her martial-arts warm-up, I reached out a finger of awareness and looked for the nearest ley line. My lips curled up in a smile. There was so little water in the ground here that it seemed as if I could feel the earth forever. The mental landscape of ley lines stretched as far and as clear as the flat horizon. There was space here, both visually and in the more nebulous regions of the mind. Lots of space, and nothing to stop any of the senses until the very earth curved from you. It was odd, and I took a moment to just taste it.

Breaking my line of sight, Ivy grabbed her overnight bag from the trunk. "I'll see if they'll rent us a room for an hour," she said, flicking her gaze at Trent, daring him to protest. "You want to shower, Rachel?"

"Absolutely," I said. "After I eat. Want me to order you something?"

Ivy shook her head, her gaze on the interstate. It was almost empty at this hour. "No. I'll get something to go while you're cleaning up."

Moving with an uncharacteristic stiffness, Trent started for the cloudy pair of restaurant doors. Jenks took to the air as if unsure of who to follow. His new boots and jacket caught the light, shining brilliantly.

"Trent, you going to want a shower?" Ivy called.

"Yes," he said, not turning. "Then I'm taking a nap."

Jenks's wings clattered in relief. "We'll get a table," he said quickly, then hummed heavily after Trent.

Ivy's smile was faint but sincere. "Someone found a new friend," she said dryly.

I chuckled, thinking Trent looked dead tired. It was weird seeing him like that, so far from the usual polished, put-together face he showed the world. "Can you believe where we are? It's not fair. If I drove ten miles over the limit, I'd get pulled over."

She made a sound of agreement, then glanced at Vivian, sleeping with her head propped up on the steering wheel. "You sure you don't want to shower first?" she asked.

Grabbing my bag from the backseat, I flicked my lethal-magic detector. "Nah. I'm hungry. I'll babysit Trent until you're done. I don't mind going last. Save me some water."

Nodding, Ivy turned on her heel and headed for the faded OFFICE sign and the wilted flowers in the huge earthen pots decorated with Aztec-looking figures that reminded me of ley-line glyphs.

I pulled my suitcase to the front of the trunk to grab a new shirt, bra, panties, and socks. My jeans were okay for another day. I shoved everything in my shoulder bag, and slammed the trunk shut. Across the parking lot, Vivian jumped awake. Waving at her, I went in. Poor girl. You'd think they'd give her some help in spying on us. Maybe it was a punishment of some sort.

The windows fronting the road had been tinted, and only the barest glimmer of light and warmth made it inside. As soon as the milky glass doors shut behind me, I felt cold, as if I had stepped into a cave. My attention went to the cash register, hoping for a stand of sunglasses, but there was nothing. Maybe the next stop.

The few people were clustered in such a way that it was obvious they didn't know one another. A pinball machine flashed silently, trying to attract a quarter, and the carpet was almost threadbare. It smelled like Were more than vampire in here, but they had an MPL posted on the door, so I knew it was a mixed-population restaurant. Not that humans ever drove much through the between places anymore. Entire human populations had died in small towns during the Turn, and the fear lingered. It was only in the cities that there had been enough of a support structure to keep them alive in any numbers.

No one looked up as I entered except the waitress, and after I pointed at Trent, she turned away. True to his nature, Trent had taken a table in the center of the place, not in the sun but close. Oddly enough, even though he didn't fit in with the rough Weres and brooding witches smoking I-don't-want-to-know-what, he didn't look out of place. It might have been Jenks on the napkin dispenser.

"We can't take all day with this," Trent said as I pulled out the seat across from him, sitting down with a tired thump.

"We can skip your shower if you want," I said, arranging my bag so I could see the lethal-amulet detector hanging off it.

Green eyes looking black in the dim light, he frowned. "I didn't drive ninety miles an hour all night so you two could waste it under a showerhead."

"I still have the dust from the arch in my hair," I said, turning my mug over to hopefully get something in it soon. "I know we're in a hurry. I want to get there as much as you do."

Trent was silent, and Jenks looked between us, an unhappy expression on his face.

"You look tired," I finally said when Jenks made a motion for me to say something.

Trent's pinched brow eased. "I am," he admitted, and Jenks perked up.

"Me, too," he offered.

"I don't mind driving for a while," I said, trying to catch the waitress's eye.

"That'd be nice, Rache," Jenks said snidely, hands on his hips and slipping a silver dust. "Since you've only driven about two hundred miles so far."

"No," Trent offered. "You need to stay hands free in case the coven . . ." He hesitated, lifting a shoulder and letting it fall. "In case the Withons send someone else," he finished.

"Yeah, okay," Jenks said, but I was surprised he'd taken Trent's side in the first place.

The waitress finally came forward, two pots in her hands. She looked about sixty and smelled of both Were and witch, so

I couldn't easily tell what she was. She had cowboy boots on and an apron, wearing both like they were comfortable slippers. "Morning, folks," she said, her sharp-evaluation look clearly trying to peg us as well. "Regular or decaf?"

"Um, regular," I said, and Trent put a hand over his mug.

"Decaf," he said, and the smell of the coffee rolled over the table as she poured first mine, then Trent's. Jenks flew to my cup and dipped a pixy-size portion out, the waitress watching the entire time. She looked suspicious, not charmed, and I guessed that she had had dealings with pixies before.

"What can I get you?" she said as Jenks lifted from the rim of my cup and I took a sip.

"Oh God, this is good," I said, and the woman beamed, her wrinkles folding in on themselves to make her look windbeaten beautiful.

"Thank you, hon. We've got some batter in the back. Want me to have Len make up some pancakes for you?"

I nodded, willing to put myself at the woman's mercy if she gave me coffee like this.

"I'll have the tomato soup," Trent said as he slid his menu to her, and the woman made a small sound. Jenks, too, turned to Trent. Ordering tomatoes wasn't unusual, especially out in the wild where there weren't many humans, but for Trent it was. He'd been masquerading as a human his entire life. Getting out of Cincy must be a new experience for him. Freeing, perhaps. "That is, if Len makes a good soup," he added, smiling up at her.

"The best this side of the Mississippi," she said, tucking the menus under her arm. "You want the spicy or mild?"

"Mild."

Leaving both carafes, she wandered back to the kitchen. For a moment, silence but for the pinball machine and the comfortable kitchen noises swirled around us as we all lost ourselves in the pleasure of sitting somewhere other than in the car, drinking something that wasn't coming out of a can or a bottle.

"The best coffee I ever had in a restaurant was in this little place in downtown Cincinnati," Trent said suddenly, looking like a different person as he set his chipped mug down. The memory of the smile he'd given the woman, genuine and sincere, wouldn't leave me. "It had pictures on the walls of babies—"

"Dressed like flowers?" I blurted out, and Jenks let a flash of gold dust slip from him.

"You know it?" Trent asked, eyes wide.

"Know it? She's been banned from it," Jenks said, laughing.

"Junior's," I said over the rim of my coffee, then set the mug down. I could smell pancakes, and my mouth began to water. "Mike's," I said, correcting myself. "He banned me when I got shunned. That was the night I tried to arrest the banshee that had been terrorizing the city last New Year's. Remember the fires at Aston's roller rink and Fountain Square?"

Depressed, I looked into the depths of my coffee. I'd never gotten any public credit for that one, either.

"His name is Mike?" Trent asked, and my attention came back up at the amazement in his voice, and when I nodded, Trent shook his head. "You know a lot of people."

I lifted one shoulder and let it fall. "So do you."

This was kind of freaky. I was sitting with Trent, and neither one of us was baiting the other. Maybe my mom was right. Whenever Robbie and I got on each other's nerves, she would make us clean the garage or something. My mom had had a very clean garage.

"Food's here," Trent said, sounding relieved as he pushed back from the table to make room for his bowl.

"One stack of hotcakes," the woman said, setting a plate of three very brown pancakes before me. "And a bowl of tomato soup."

Trent was already reaching for the bowl. "Thank you, ma'am," he said with such eagerness that she smiled.

"Can I get you anything else?" she asked, setting the bill between us, facedown.

Jenks clattered his wings for attention but didn't take flight. "Would you mind if I browsed in your flowerpots? I'm just about dead on refined sugar and processed peanut butter."

The woman's brow pinched. "You're welcome to what you can find, but it will be a mite thin. There's been some singing in the rills lately. We've got a rove clan about somewheres. Not that they bother us big folk, but they might not take kindly to you."

Jenks beamed. "I'll be fine. Thanks," he said, taking a slurp of his coffee to make his wings hum faster. "One more cup of coffee, and I could take on an entire fairy clan."

"You just be careful," she said as she went back to the kitchen.

The smell of my pancakes was heavenly, and shunning a knife and fork, I rolled the top one up in a tube and took a bite. Trent sighed heavily, carefully polishing his soup spoon with a paper napkin before taking a cautious taste.

His eyes blinked and started to water. "It's hot. She gave me the spicy. This is good." Still gasping, Trent started eating in earnest, wiping his eyes and blowing his nose on his napkin.

I doubted she gave him the hot. It was more likely that the mild was hotter than most volcanoes. The light shifted as the door opened, and I turned to see Vivian standing alone and small in the narrowing band of sun arching to nothing. Giving us a halfhearted wave, she shuffled to the bar and ordered something, putting her head down on her crossed arms when the waitress yelled back to the cook to make up a milk shake.

I chewed, looking at her slumped petite form at the bar, remembering her honesty at Loveland Castle, and then her phone call that had given me leverage with Oliver, the coven's leader. When I'd first met her, she'd been polished and refined, wearing a cashmere coat and having a trendy bag. By the end of the week, she was begrimed, sore, and full of the knowledge that everything she'd been told had been a lie. Right now, she was somewhere in between, wearing jeans and a sweater that looked too hot. Everything was designer label, though, and her makeup, though thin, had been expertly applied.

"You mind if I ask her to join us?" I asked Trent, and he looked up, green eyes watering.

For an instant he was silent, and then his spoon clattered against the white porcelain. "Why not?" he said as he stood. "Since you're so sure she's not going to kill you. I've not yet made her acquaintance."

"I was going to do it," I said, but he'd already crossed the room.

"Why not?" Jenks mocked, his wings a bright red from the caffeine. "Get him away from Quen and he thinks he's cock of the world."

"You noticed that, too?" I said softly. "I like his new shoes."

"Thief shoes," Jenks said around a belch. "I wonder what he's stealing."

"Not our problem." *I hope.* Taking another bite, I watched Vivian sit up, startled when Trent came up beside her, and then her quick glance at me. "Are you doing okay?" I asked Jenks, seeing his flushed face and slowly moving wings.

"I'll be fine." Jenks tugged his new red jacket straight and rinsed his cup out in my glass of water, leaving a thin ribbon of coffee trailing down. "I want to see if she put a bomb under our car. You going to be okay alone with them?" Thinking of Ivy in the shower, I nodded, and he rose up to leave a fading glow of yellow sunbeam on the table. "I'll be in back in five."

"Be careful," I said as he flew off, and he gave me a flash of red dust, the pixy equivalent of rolling his eyes.

At the bar, Vivian was sliding off her stool, one hand holding a tall glass of milk shake and a dangling napkin. Behind her, Trent followed, smiling as if he were crossing a ballroom floor, not a bar/restaurant surrounded by nothing in the middle of New Mexico.

"Ah, I don't know what to say," the small woman said as she approached, and I pushed out a chair for her.

"Sit," I said, smiling. "Trent won't bite. It's Ivy you have to worry about, and she's in the shower."

Her milk shake hit the table, and she sat. The heavy-magic detection amulet on my bag started to glow, but the lethal one remained dark. It didn't go unnoticed by Vivian, and she took a sip of her drink while Trent resettled himself. I couldn't help but be reminded of the last time I'd sat with her and had coffee. It had been in Mike's, actually, and she'd been prepared to shoot me if I hadn't gone with her. But that had been before she'd watched me stand next to a demon and try to save her mentor, Brooke.

"Ivy said you were at the airport," I said, taking a sip of coffee and probably getting Jenks's glitter on my lips. "You're not going to kill me, are you?" I asked, and Trent choked on his tomato soup.

Eying Trent, she shook her head, her eyes red rimmed and tired looking. "They're hoping you do something demonic on the way, and if so, I'm to report it," she said, nervous until Trent stopped coughing. "Not that everyone isn't pretty much set on how they are going to vote already. Except for whoever they elect to take Brooke's spot. Oh, anything you say to me is going to be used against you in the vote."

Vote? I thought, my gaze going to Trent as I realized he'd been right. They were going to try to put me away despite what Oliver had promised. "This was a done deal!" I said, then lowered my voice. "Oliver said if I dropped my claim that the council is corrupt, you'd pardon me!" I almost hissed.

Vivian shrugged as she sucked on her straw, and Trent wiped his mouth, red faced but finally under control. "Ms. Morgan is somewhat naive when it comes to world powers," he said.

"Why? Because I expect them to keep their word?" I said darkly.

Looking innocent drinking her milk shake, Vivian sat back, her blue eyes downcast. The diamonds on her watch glittered, and the time was off. "It would help a lot if you brought back Brooke. She'd vote for you then."

I couldn't stop my rueful laugh. "No, she wouldn't."

Trent had gone back to his soup, watching us both. It made me feel like I was on trial not once, but twice.

"And we're not corrupt," Vivian said, almost as an after-thought.

Why is she saying this crap? I thought, rolling up a second pancake and taking a bite. It was like she was reading a script. Maybe she was afraid of what Trent thought? Maybe she was bugged and this entire conversation was going to end up in someone else's ears?

Regardless, I couldn't let that one go without a rebuttal, so, taking a huge bite of pancake, I mumbled, "Right. Okay. Let's just say the coven is lily-white, but Brooke *was* dabbling in demonology." Swallowing, I added, "She summoned Big Al all on her own, knowing that's who she was going to get, not me. She didn't pay or threaten anyone into doing it, she did it herself. I warned her not to. I went out of my way to try to stop her. Burned my synapses and fried my brain trying to jump a line to get to her in time. If I'm to be shunned, then she should be, too."

Sure enough, Vivian didn't look appalled or insulted. Though we were alone, we were not unheard. "Can you . . ." She looked at Trent, hesitating.

"No," I said, knowing where her thoughts were. "I can't rescue her. Brooke *summoned* Al. He broke her circle because she didn't know what she was doing. I'm sorry. I know you think I control him, but I don't. I'm just trying to stay alive here."

Vivian bent her head back over her milk shake. "I had to ask," she said, her thin fingers looking cold on the glass.

The table grew quiet. I kept shoveling pancake in my mouth, not knowing what to say now that I knew we were being eavesdropped upon.

"Vivian," Trent said, his attention lifting from my unused syrup as he broke the awkward silence. "What role do you have in the coven? You seem to be involved in everything."

"I'm the plumber," she said with pride. "It's traditional for the junior ley-line magic user."

Plumber was a nice way of saying that she plugged information leaks and kept the crap moving. And I almost laughed at the junior tag. Junior or not, she could smear my face in the playground dirt with her white magic.

"I fix things," Vivian added to make sure Trent understood. "Make things run smoothly. That's why I . . ." Her words faltered, and she looked embarrassed as she took another pull on her straw.

"Got this gem of an assignment," I said, and she nodded. "Sorry about that."

"It's what I like," she said, shrugging. "Usually."

The last was said rather dryly, and I wondered if it was for our listener's benefit.

"Just be careful," I said, not entirely in jest. "That's what Pierce was before they cemented him into the ground."

Trent was still eying my syrup, even as he scraped his spoon to get the last dregs of the soup, and I pushed the little container to him.

Vivian's face showed her disgust. Pierce had beaten her up last spring, and that was not easy for the self-assured woman. "Pierce," she said, mouthing his name like it tasted bad. "He was dead. You brought him back."

I could almost hear her think *black witch,* and my jaw clenched. Why was everyone so fixated on labels? Across the table, Trent dunked his clean fork in the syrup, pushing the little container back after he'd tasted it. If he didn't like it, then Jenks wouldn't, either, and I left it as I put my napkin over my last pancake. I was done.

"I didn't bring Pierce back to life," I said, not seeing what difference it made, but wanting to clear it up. "He was in purgatory, and I accidentally woke him while using a white spell to talk to my deceased father for some parental advice. Did it on a dare. I got Pierce instead. Al was the one who made him alive again so he could use him as a familiar. Dead witches can't tap lines, and they make lousy familiars."

I sipped my coffee, trying not to think about it. Pierce was living out the rest of his life in another's—a dead man's—body. It gave me the willies, and I only hoped I'd never find myself facing such a decision. It was hard to blame the guy. I just wished he had given me a chance to find a better way before he'd given himself to Al until death do them part.

"But you woke him first?" Vivian said intently, her eyes red rimmed from lack of sleep.

"It's a white spell," I said, glancing at Trent. He had known for a while that I could do this. "And it doesn't work on the dead, only on those in purgatory."

Vivian moved her straw around to remix her milk shake. "I know it's white," she said. "I've tried it. You got it to work when you were how old?"

Oh. That. Uncomfortable, I looked out the window at my mom's car. "I don't remember," I lied. I'd been eighteen and stupid, but clearly there was someone under the grass Vivian wanted to talk to. "Pierce started haunting me last year. He was buried in my churchyard." I started to warm, getting angry. "It was your precious coven that killed him."

"I know," Vivian said, as eager as if she was talking about someone from a history book, not a real person I once had breakfast with, hid in a little hole with, owed my life to. "I read up on him after he . . . after we met," she said slowly. "He was a coven member gone bad. They had no choice but to kill him."

Trent was silent, drawing back as I pointed a finger at her. "He wasn't just killed. He was buried alive."

"Because of Eleison—" Vivian said, eyes alight as if discussing a long-argued point.

"Eleison was a mistake," I interrupted. "It wouldn't have happened if he had known even the basic defensive arts for demonology. Your coven turned on one of their own. Gave him to an ugly rabble instead of trying to understand what he was warning them about." Frustrated, I leaned forward. "Vivian, this lily-white crap the coven sticks to can't protect you anymore. It took five of you to subdue me, and I didn't use a black curse. A real demon would have. You saw how easily Al took Brooke."

"Rachel—" Trent said, and I cut him off.

"Knowing how to twist curses doesn't mean that you're evil," I said, hoping I believed it myself. "Using demon magic doesn't necessarily mean you're bad. It just means you created a whole lot of imbalance."

"You," Vivian said hotly, "are rationalizing. White is white. Black is black."

Trent picked up both bills, pulling a wallet from his back pocket and dropping enough cash on the table to cover them both. "Madam Coven Member disagrees with you," he warned me, and I frowned, my gut tensing.

"Look," I said, aware that I was probably sealing my fate, but this might be my only chance to actually say anything in my defense. "Knowing demon magic has saved my life. I never use curses that require body parts or ones that kill . . ." *Shit,* I thought, hesitating. "I've never killed . . ." Sighing, I paused once more. "I've never used it to kill anyone who wasn't trying to kill me first."

Vivian's lips parted, and her fingers slipped from the condensation-wet glass. "You admit you killed someone? With black magic?"

Trent's expression was questioning as he sat back down. My shoulders slumped, and I grimaced. "The fairies your precious coven sent to kill me," I admitted.

"No," Vivian said, shaking her head. "I mean people."

"Fairies *are* people," I said hotly. "I saved the ones I could, but—" Frowning, I shut up, glad Jenks hadn't heard.

Vivian was silent, her milk shake gone and her fingers damp as she dried them on a white paper napkin. "Well, I have to use the little girls' room," she said, looking uneasy. "Don't leave until I get out, okay?" she said hopefully. God, she didn't even know why I was insulted.

"No promises," Trent said as I continued to steam. "The road calls."

Vivian stood, her chair bumping on the floor. "I'm going to pay for this little chat when this is over," she said as she flicked the amulets around her neck. "See you at the finish line."

"It was a pleasure meeting you, Vivian," Trent said, standing as well, his hand extended, and I huffed when they shook. Vivian, though, was charmed, beaming at him.

She turned away, and I cleared my throat. "You going to vote for or against me?" I asked bluntly, and the woman's eyes pinched.

"I don't know," she said softly. "Thanks for breakfast."

"Our pleasure," Trent said as he sat back down.

Vivian paused, looking like she wanted to say more, but then turned for the short corridor with RESTROOMS over it. She turned a corner and vanished with a squeak of a hinge.

Trent wrapped his hands around his mug and took a sip. "I don't understand you," he said. "I truly don't. You know they were listening, right? Editing it and putting it on the closed-circuit TV at the convention hotel?"

"I know," I said, depressed. "The sad thing is that she's probably the only coven member who might side with me, and I think I just alienated her." Disgusted, I pushed my plate away, trying to shove my dark thoughts along with it. Looking up, I caught the waitress's eye and pointed to my coffee cup, signaling another one for the road in a to-go cup. "You want another coffee?" I asked.

"No. Mind if I shower next?" he asked, and I gestured for him to have at it.

"Be my guest," I said, hoping he left me more than a hand towel.

Trent tapped the table once with his knuckles, hesitated,

then left. The Weres at the end of the bar watched him as he walked to the door. There was a flash of light and a jingle as he opened it, and then the restaurant returned to a dim coolness.

The waitress sashayed to my table, a jumbo disposable cup in her hands. It was Were size, and if I drank it all, I'd be stopping to pee more than Jenks. "Thanks. That will wake me up," I said, reaching for my bag and wallet as she set the cup down.

"We're good," she said as she picked up the bills Trent had left behind and smiled.

Standing, I slung my bag over my shoulder and lifted the huge cup of coffee. It took two hands. This thing was not going to fit in my mom's cup holders, and I walked carefully to the door, opening it by leaning against it and walking backward.

The heat and light hit me, and I carefully let the door slide off me and close. This time-zone jumping got to a person. Two hours in one day was hard. Squinting, I shuffled to the car, now parked under the gas station overhang with a hose stuck into it. Trent wasn't anywhere, but Ivy was standing halfway across the lot, confronting a heavy, grungy trucker who looked not scared but concerned.

Her long hair, wet from her shower, glinted, and I paused at the car to set my coffee down and sigh at how much it took to fill the tank. Ivy had changed her clothes, her long legs managing to make the retro bell-bottoms look work. Her white shirt set off her figure nicely, and the short sleeves were going to make her day a lot cooler. She looked upset, and a faint feeling of unease tightened in me.

"Ivy?" I called, and she spun, the fear on her face striking me cold. She was moving fast—vampire fast—and her eyes were fully dilated in the bright sun.

"He's gone," Ivy shouted across the lot, and the fear dropped and twisted.

"Who?" I said, already knowing.

"Jenks," she said, eyes wide.

Coffee forgotten, I ran across the lot, squinting when the sun hit me. "Gone! Where?"

The trucker looked forlorn in a bearish sort of way, clearly wanting to help us but not understanding why we were upset. "I'm sorry, ma'am," he said, holding his hands like a fig leaf. "I don't pay much attention to the little winged critters unless they hit my windshield. They're a bitch to get off."

God help me, I thought, panicking.

"I don't know if it was pixies or fairies," the man said, "but a whole mess of noise of 'em just rose up, taking a little fella in red with them. He didn't look like he was hurt any."

My heart was thudding, and I backed up, sharing a terrified look with Ivy. Oh God, we were in the desert. There was nothing between me and the horizon but wind, sand, and scrub. Pixies could fly faster than I could run and in every direction.

We'd never find him.

Nine

"Trent!" I shouted, hammering on the bathroom door. It was thin and hollow, and I could hear the water running in the shower. He had to have heard me, but he didn't answer.

Fidgeting, I hammered on it again. "Trent! We have to go!"

"I've been in here two minutes!" he shouted back.

My breath came fast, and I looked out the open door to the parking lot. Ivy was still talking to the trucker, explaining the difference between pixies and fairies to hopefully narrow down who had taken him. We'd never find him if fairies had taken him. Not in time.

I should have insisted that he use that curse to make him big, I thought. *I should have made him safe.* "Get out!" I shouted, my voice muffled by the low ceiling and faded curtains. "We have to go." *Go? Go where? I had no idea, not even in which direction.*

"I just got in here," Trent muttered.

My eyes narrowed to slits. I looked at the door, took a deep breath, grabbed the chintzy fake-brass handle, and twisted. It wasn't locked, and the door cracked open. A moist, foggy warmth spilled out over my feet and then my face. I peered into the tiny room, grimacing. It was clean but old. An ugly toilet was right before me. A simple pedestal sink on two spindly, rusted legs was beside that. There was a small, tidy bathroom kit open on it with clean stuff laid out. The tiny window had peeling self-stick privacy film. The tub/shower combo was to my right, with a masculine shadow moving behind the thin curtain.

"Trent," I said, and the shadow jumped with a half-heard oath.

"What are you doing in here?"

My heart pounded. "They took him," I said, reaching through the curtain to turn the water off. Trent protested, but he moved to the back of the tub. "They took him, and we have to get moving," I said, handing in a large towel.

The curtain shifted open, and I jerked my attention up to Trent's face. He was rubbing it dry with the towel. *Don't look down. Don't look down,* I thought, though I don't know why. He'd seen me naked in Fountain Square.

Hair still dripping, he draped the towel around his hips and tucked the end in the folds to hold it there, looking more appealing than if he'd been stark naked. "Took who?" he said calmly.

Flustered, I stared at his face, avoiding his damp, taut skin sliding easily over his muscles. His hair still looked pale, plastered to his face. The tub gurgled as the last of the water drained away, and still I stood there.

"Who did they take, Rachel?" he asked again, and I shook myself.

"Jenks." My eyes suddenly started to swim, and I looked away. "You have two minutes to get dressed and get in the car, or we leave without you. They took Jenks." My throat closed, and I choked out, "The longer I'm standing here, talking to you, the farther away they're getting." Damn it, I was almost crying. "It's a desert out there!" I shouted, pointing. "He can't fly at this altitude. I have to find him!"

Trent's head dropped. "Okay . . . ," he said tiredly, and I just about lost it.

"It's not okay!" I yelled. "Get moving!"

Trent stepped from the shower, and I flung myself back, jumping when his shower-wet hand gripped my arm and propelled me toward the door. "Okay. Get out so I can get dressed."

"Oh." Heart pounding, I blinked. "Okay." Only now did I look at his feet. *Nice feet.*

Trent cleared his throat, and I backed out of the bathroom. "Two minutes," I affirmed.

"Two minutes," Trent said, and the door shut between us.

I backed up until my calves found the bed. Not looking, I sat on it. The air was cool and dry out here, and I nervously smoothed the coverlet, my fingers catching where the stitching had pulled. It smelled, and I stood, arm around my middle as I looked out the door to Ivy and the trucker. I could hear Trent moving around, and I wiped my eye. Damn it, I was crying. I had to find Jenks. He had saved my life so many times. I couldn't imagine a day without him.

"Rachel, are you still in here?"

I spun, finding the door cracked, a slip of fog drifting out like Trent's irritation given substance. "Yes."

"Hand me my clothes, will you? Or leave. One or the other."

I scanned the room, finding a pile of dark clothing on the chair beside the window. Moving fast, I strode to it, hardly feeling the softness of the fabric as I tried not to mess up the folds of his shirt and pants. "Here," I said awkwardly. The door creaked open a little more, and the flush of warmth and steam rolled out.

"Thank you," he said, and the door shut, leaving the clean scent of his deodorant.

"I'll wait outside," I said, glancing at the door.

"Thank you."

It was short and clipped, and even through the door I could hear his irritation.

"Sorry," I said as I moved away. He hadn't been flustered at all by my bursting in on him. But then again, he didn't have anything to be ashamed of. The man was built like one of his horses. Not an ounce of flab on him.

What is wrong with me? I thought as I snatched my bag up

from the bed and went out, slamming the door hard enough to shake the windows and let Trent know I'd left. Jenks had been kidnapped, and I was thinking about Trent naked in the shower?

Ivy was walking toward me, the trucker revving up his diesel engine behind her, and she turned and waved when he yanked the horn cord to send an echo of it across the flat desert. I had to content myself with trying to guess her news by her posture as she made her slow way to me, arms wrapped around her middle and her head down. My head started hurting.

"It's pixies," she said when she got close enough, and my breath slid from me in relief.

"Are you sure?" I asked, hand on her arm.

She nodded. "He said they all had silver wings that made a lot of noise. The only noise fairies make is when they clank their swords against each other."

I looked back at the motel, wishing Trent would hurry. "He's probably alive then," I said, my worry coming right back. Pixies wouldn't kill an intruder wearing red, and Jenks had on enough to blind a horse. But why kidnap him at all?

The jingle of the restaurant door caught our attention, and we turned to see Vivian coming out, her head down as she looked at one of her amulets.

"Maybe she arranged it," Ivy said, her dark eyes getting darker. "To slow us down. If you don't make it in time, your shunning is permanent."

Squinting at the slight but powerful coven member, I shook my head. "Not her style."

Vivian looked up, blinking as she saw us standing in the parking lot. Turning, she looked to the west, then down at her amulet, then up again, clearly confused. Steps slowing, she halted on the covered wooden walkway that connected the motel to the restaurant.

My pulse hammered, and sweet, beautiful adrenaline poured into me. "She's got a tracking amulet," I whispered, knowing now how she'd been following us through the night.

"What?" Ivy said, but I was already moving to Vivian, arms swinging loose and free, my every motion full of intent. Vivian saw me, and her foot scraped as she took a step back.

"She's got a tracking amulet tuned to Jenks!" I exclaimed without looking over my shoulder. "Like I made for Mia. That's how she's been following us!"

Vivian took another step back, her gaze darting from me to her Pinto.

"Rachel!" Ivy exclaimed. "Rushing a coven member might not be the best thing!"

I smiled at Vivian. That tracking amulet was mine.

Vivian's eyes were wide. She swore, then turned and ran, her boots thumping on the walk running alongside the motel. She was headed for her car.

Instinct kicked in, and I bolted after her. Arms pumping, I gave chase, my boots hitting the dirt as I tried to head her off.

"Look out!" Ivy shouted, and my gaze shot to Trent, head down as he came out of the motel room. My pace faltered, and glancing at me, Vivian put on a burst of speed, turning her head just in time to smack right into Trent's door.

The *thunk* of her head on the thick wooden door was loud, and I winced, slowing to a jog.

Trent scrambled, dropping his toiletry bag as he narrowly caught her. Her hand opened and the amulet dropped, going dark as it rolled off the raised wooden walkway and to my feet, falling on its side in a tiny puff of dust.

I snatched it up and looked at Trent, now holding Vivian as her head lolled and her feet splayed askew. "That wasn't quite what I'd planned," I said, then turned to the waitress leaning half out of the restaurant and waved, shouting, "Can we have a bag of ice? I think she's okay."

The woman ducked back inside, and I shifted to make room for Ivy.

"I missed the meeting, didn't I?" Trent said, and I helped him ease her to the walk. She was breathing okay, and when

Ivy lifted her lids, her pupils contracted equally. Given a little time, she'd likely be fine.

"Thanks, Trent," I said as I hefted the amulet, glowing again now that I was holding it. "You're being useful today. I think you just saved me from beating up a coven member."

Ivy looked from Vivian's Pinto to my mom's car. "Now what?"

I looked at the amulet, my heart pounding as I saw how far apart the two little red dots were. I wondered if Oliver had made it. Looping the cord around my neck, I crouched beside Vivian. "You take her feet, I'll take her hands."

Immediately Ivy shifted, and together we lifted her, me straining far more than Ivy.

Trent backed up a step, confused. "What are you going to do with her?"

"Put her in the car," I puffed, moving awkwardly to my mom's car.

Trent scooped up his toiletry bag. "You're joking, right? Rachel, she's coven. We can't take her with us."

"I'm not going to leave her here," I said, and Ivy's eyes flicked to him as the unconscious woman seemed to gain fifty pounds with every step. "Will you get the ice?"

Frowning, he turned away, but I couldn't help but be impressed as he gave the waitress a story about us traveling together and knowing her and her friends, and that we'd make sure she got home okay. Pace fast, he caught back up with us in time to open the back door.

"You can't be serious," he started in again, his eyes pinched as he held the door open. "They want to kill you!"

"Maybe I'm trying sugar instead of vinegar," I grunted as I scooted backward into my mom's car, hitting my elbow as I pulled Vivian in after me. Ivy wrestled with her feet as Trent stood behind her and watched, his toiletry bag in one hand, the ice in the other. He looked totally different in his black clothes, his hair slicked back, his expression worried.

"You should be tucking her away in that hotel room you rented," he said, "and throwing her keys into the desert. She'd never find us then."

"Maybe. Or maybe it would just tick her off," I said as I tossed my bag to the front seat and tugged Vivian farther in. My back hit the far door, and puffing, I opened it and backed out. Exhaling, I looked at him across the roof, tired. "I'm not leaving her unconscious in a hotel room a hundred miles from civilization to maybe wake up as someone's desert-bunker wife. You put a zip strip on her, and she goes from coven to incapable. But frankly, the real reason she's coming with us is that I'd rather have her tell the coven all our secrets than have a twenty-four-hour gap that they can use to invent stuff." Seeing Vivian laid out on the seat, I carefully shut the door and looked out over the desert. "I'm driving. Who has the keys?"

Ivy opened the driver's-side door. "I'll drive, you work the amulet," she said, and I just looked at her, my heart pounding and adrenaline surging through me like a sugar high.

Her eyes dilated at the fear I was giving off, and smiling wryly, she tugged the keys out of her pocket and dangled them for me. "Okay, you drive," she said. "I'll sit with my head hanging out the window like a golden retriever."

"Thanks," I said, shaky as I came around to her side, got in, and adjusted everything. Ivy slipped into the front passenger seat as I cranked the engine over, tossing her overnight bag with her dirty clothes in it over the seat at Trent. He barely got his hands up in time, having been trying to arrange Vivian in a somewhat upright position.

"You want to wait a minute so I can move some of this to the trunk?" he said, dropping the ice bag on the bump just now starting to rise on Vivian's forehead.

"No." Everyone's arms and legs were inside the vehicle, and I put the car in reverse, hitting the gas hard.

Ivy already had her hand on the dash, but Trent went flying as the car jerked backward. Teeth clenched, I hit the brakes hard, and he was flung into the backseat where he belonged.

His door, which had been open, bounced shut from the quick stop, and I jammed the gearshift into drive while ignoring Trent yelling at me.

"You think you like speed?" Ivy said as I spun the tires and we left a cloud of dust, bouncing wildly until we found the road. "You've never seen Rachel drive with purpose."

Yeah, purpose. If purpose meant scared to death and to hell with everyone else, then I'd be driving with purpose.

The ride smoothed out, and my eyes flicked to the rearview mirror, not to see the restaurant grow smaller in the distance, but to see Jenks's absence.

I had a chance to find him. A chance. And if he wasn't okay, I was going to do some serious damage to my already wafer-thin credibility as a good witch, even if I was a black one.

Ten

My grip on the wheel tightened until my knuckles hurt. I was trying to keep my worry from turning into anger, but it was hard. Especially now that Trent was awake. "I don't care how far we've *not* gotten," I said tightly, glaring at Trent by way of the rearview mirror. "If we only make three hundred miles today, then we'll deal with it. They have to stop sometime."

"I understand you're concerned about your partner," he said in that same persuasive voice that was starting to sound patronizing, "but I doubt they're planning on sacrificing him to their local god. You have a locator amulet. You'll find him. Slow down. Let them land. They're running because they know you're chasing them."

It was a nice thought, but they weren't running because of us. They were running to somewhere, their path arrow straight and their pace unflagging. I wasn't about to slow down, and Ivy didn't look up from her map, a long white finger touching where our paths might cross again.

Vivian kicked the back of my seat as she tried to find a more comfortable spot. On the other side of the backseat, Trent frowned out the window. Okay, so maybe I was going a little fast, but I'd been driving a huge, frustrating zigzag for the last four hours. I had raced down I-40, then gone south on 602 to get in front of them, as Ivy had suggested. We had, only to see them rise up right over the car and swear at us. We spent another hour on 61, watching them go a rather speedy forty miles an hour, paralleling us until we roared ahead to where 191 crossed their theoretical path. They simply flew higher, shooting arrows at us when I demanded they stop.

From there, we'd taken 191 north in an effort to get back to the interstate. We didn't know the next time we'd find gas, and Ms. Worries-a-lot in the front seat next to me was getting fidgety. By now, Ivy had enough data points to predict where they'd cross the road next. I was hoping that if we could get far enough ahead of them in time, I could hide behind a rock and simply catch them in a big bubble. Every time they saw the car, they raced out of my reach.

Right now, they were somewhere behind us, me going about eighty and the pixies hitting a steady forty miles an hour. It was their top speed—which meant Trent was wrong and that this was a planned snag-and-drag; pixies couldn't go that fast for that long. They were switching off and carrying Jenks. Carrying Jenks who knew where.

It was about two in the afternoon and hot. I was frazzled and ready to snap. Ivy wasn't much better, leaning over the seat to shake Vivian awake every half hour in case she had a concussion—which was totally pissing off the coven woman. Trent had been up for only a few minutes, but he already looked bored, staring out the window and clearly irate that the time he'd made was *being wasted*. It was all I could do not to reach over the seat and slap him.

As I fidgeted, Ivy rolled her window down to let in a warm blast of air, overpowering the hefty air-conditioning my mom's car had. Her eyes had gotten dark and her posture was tense. She wasn't hot, she was randy, and I rolled my window down a bit as well.

"I think they stopped," she said, eying the amulet. "Somewhere by 180. See?"

She held out the map with her notations and calculations. I

didn't look, teeth clenched as I blew past a van with a wizard painted on the side.

"Rachel?"

"Just tell me what road to take," I muttered.

She pulled a strand of her blowing hair out of her mouth. "The next exit," she said, putting on a pair of dark glasses to hide her eyes. "You're going to have to go north for a few miles before it loops around and goes under the interstate."

"More backtracking?" Trent said, hardly audible.

"Shut up! Just shut up!" I yelled, then exhaled, trying to relax. "I mean, I understand your concern," I said softly. "I'll get you to the West Coast in time if I have to buy a trip for you from Newt." *If only Al would've jumped me there, but he wanted me to fail.* "But if you don't shut up, I'm going to pull this car over and shove you in the trunk!"

Trent sighed and shifted his knees, and Ivy looked up from the map, eyebrows raised.

"I'm trying," I said softly to her. "He's got about as much empathy as a demon. It's always me, me, me. What if it had been Quen who was kidnapped? I bet he'd be all over that like pixies on elf trash."

Trent cleared his throat, and I huffed. Point made.

"You want me to drive for a while?" Ivy said. "You need a break."

"No, I've got this," I said quickly, then added, "If I don't do something, I'll snap."

I waited for Jenks's comment that I had already snapped, but of course it never came. Checking the speedometer, I pressed the accelerator. We had to stay in front of them, and there was a whole lot of distance left.

"We'll find him," Ivy said, the amulet getting dark as she set it aside to fold up the map.

Silent, I scanned the distant horizon for cops, my senses stretching as I took in every nuance of light and shadow. Jenks was out there somewhere. My stomach clenched. This shouldn't have happened. He didn't need me to watch him, but this altitude thing had caught us all by surprise. I should have made him take that curse.

Ivy shook the map out with a rattle. "Trent, jiggle Vivian. Ask her what her name is."

"My name is Vivian," the irate witch grumbled, clearly awake. "And if you touch me, Kalamack, I'll turn your hair pink. I do *not* have a concussion! *Leave me alone and let me sleep!*" In a huff, she repositioned herself in the corner, her feet kicking the back of my seat as she shook out my mom's shabby car blanket and rearranged it over her head.

"I think she's fine," Trent said sourly as he looked out at the changing nothing.

The car was full of unhappy people heading west. It was the Great American Family Road Trip, all right. Whaaa-hoo!

I sniffed, my stomach hurting from too much stress and not enough food. I was upset, but it was hard not to see the scenery and call it beautiful. It was nothing but dirt and rock, but it looked clean, pure, the angles and gullies standing out in the strong sun. I could tell that Trent was hot with the window open and the air-conditioning going full bore, but I was comfortable. He'd have to suck it up.

"That's our exit," Ivy said suddenly, and I slowed, not wanting to take it at ninety miles an hour. Trent sighed again, and I tapped the brake to shake him up.

"It's a state park," I said, seeing the faded PETRIFIED FOREST sign. "Maybe this is where they're heading."

"The Petrified Forest?" Trent said, sounding interested. "I read about this place."

Ivy leaned forward. "Everyone who's been to school has read about this place."

"I've never been here," Trent said, his words clipped as he tried to hide his interest. "It's not the kind of thing that—"

"They let you do, huh?" I finished for him, pissed for some reason. *I'm chasing down my partner from kidnappers, and Trent's more interested in chunks of rock?*

Ivy handed the map to him over the seat. "Now's your

chance, Johnny Boy Scout," she said, apparently not needing it anymore. "We're going right through it."

My heart gave a thump before settling into a faster pace. There was a park-ranger hut straddling the road. *Crap.* "Vivian? Are you going to give us any trouble? Tell me now."

"Just let me sleep," she grumbled. "Let me sleep, and I'll sign a paper that you're a fucking angel."

"I didn't know they let coven members talk like that," Trent said dryly, probably trying to cover his curiosity, but he was leaning forward, wanting to see more.

"Fuck you, Kalamack," the usually posh woman shot back.

Oh yeah. We were *all* having fun now.

Ivy shrugged, so I pulled up and rolled my window completely down.

"Hi. Can we have a day pass?" I asked after reading the rates painted on the brown sign.

"That will be five fifty," the weathered woman said, and Trent shoved some money at me over the seat.

"Let me get you a receipt," she said, ducking inside her window to hit a few buttons. "Are you camping?" she said as she leaned back out and handed me a receipt stapled to a brochure. "We don't suggest it this time of year. And you'll need to take a class before you can get your camp permit. If you're not prepared, the desert can be deadly. The class just takes twenty minutes."

Twenty minutes to preserve your life? I thought. *Is that all?* "We've got lots of water."

Seeing Trent's eager hand on the seat, at my shoulder, I handed him the brochure, and he settled back like a kid with a new toy.

"It's not just the water, it's the heat and elevation," the ranger said, her gaze on Vivian. "Is she okay?"

The bar ahead of us was still down, and I took a deep breath.

"Too much partying," Trent said over the crackle of new paper, surprising me. "She's not even going to get out of the car."

The ranger smiled, and the bar rose. "The gift shop is up on the right. If you change your mind about the class, they start every half hour."

"Thanks," I said, wanting to floor it, but she hadn't given me our sticker yet.

"Well, enjoy the park. There's a large group of Weres out at the hotel for a company retreat, but other than that, all the exhibits are open."

Finally the little yellow sticker was stuck to the inside of my window, and I exhaled, turning it into something I could blame on the heat instead of relief. "Thanks! Bye now!"

Waving, the woman went back into her air-conditioned hut, and I crept forward at the posted forty miles an hour. After blowing down the interstate at ninety, it felt like I was crawling. I started to fidget.

"It says here the average person needs a gallon of water per day," Trent said, reading from the brochure. "How much do we have?"

"None." I eyed the empty water bottles in the cup holders. "It's twenty miles to any road. I think we'll be okay."

"All I'm saying is if we have to walk, we don't have any water."

Ivy glanced at him. "You're not walking anywhere. You're staying in the car."

From the lump of blanket came an irate, "I'm *trying* to *sleep*! Will you *shut up*!"

Ivy settled back, and I said nothing, dividing my attention between the unmoving dot of Jenks on the amulet, the winding road, and the shocking views of sharp-angled ravines and colors that were like nothing I'd ever seen before. We passed pull-off after pull-off, Trent rolling his window down, sucking the cooler air out of the car, the flat of his arms on the frame to get a look at the admittedly spectacular views. It wasn't until we found flat desert again that he sank back into his seat. As expected, we crossed under the overpass and headed south.

"Think we'll get to the place in time?" I asked, my mood

vacillating wildly between relief and impatience as I hit the gas.

"Lots of time," Ivy said, fingering the amulet. "They aren't moving anymore."

"He can't fly. Not at this altitude." Damn it, I was babbling.

"He's wearing his red," Ivy said, pointing out the sign for the auto tour. It went into the desert, and Trent perked up, his gaze going up and down as he traced our path on his brochure. "They might have taken him because he collapsed. Maybe they were trying to help."

"Yeah, and that's why they were swearing at us when we caught up with them," I said. Double damn, what if I found him, only to find that the size difference prevented me from doing anything? The curse in my bag was for making little things big, not the other way around.

Driving with one hand, I looked at my bag, where my phone was. If worse came to worst, I could call Ceri for the curse to make myself smaller. I'd do it in front of Vivian if I needed to.

Again Trent put his window down, and the dry smell of the desert lifted through my hair as we drove a level course on the top of the world, the canyons dipping an impossible distance down, colored with purples, grays, and blues—like mountains in reverse. It was a weird way to see things. We'd met no one since entering the park, just seen a few ravens and buzzards. Silence, still and uncomfortable, and the sun hammering at everything without mercy.

"Slow it down," Ivy said, eying the amulet.

"Are we there yet?" Trent said sarcastically, and Vivian groaned, pulling the blanket over her head despite the heat.

I drove past a sign about an ancient ruin, and Ivy stiffened. "Back up, Rachel! We're close. I think they're at the ruins!"

My heart pounded as I jerked the car to a halt so fast that Vivian hit the back of my seat, and even Trent had to catch himself. Ignoring Vivian's snarl, I flung my arm over the back of the seat and put the car in reverse. Trent's eyes widened as I whipped the car around, landing it between two white lines and jamming it into park. Intent, I turned the engine off and bolted out of the car, my boots scraping on the pavement as it threw up a wave of heat.

The silence hit me, and I hesitated, shocked almost.

There was nothing out here, impinging upon me the impression of magnitude. The hot wind shifting my hair had been in motion for hundreds of miles without impediment, giving it a slippery feel as it molded around me and continued on, elastic and not even recognizing me. I couldn't see far enough, my eyes failing due to their own limitations for the first time in my existence. It was . . . immense. *Jenks* . . .

The sun beat down, making even the shadows hot. I sent my senses out as I stood on the road to the ruins, looking out over the purples and mauves, searching for anything, every part of me taking in the feel of the air, listening for the hum of a wing and hearing only an aching emptiness. I looked for a ley line, finding a crisscrossing of faded nothing, like hints of what had once been but was now gone. Empty. Everything was empty.

My head ached from the echo, and I took in every nuance as I looked for a sign, a breath, a wing chirp. Every chip of rock, every shadow stood out in sharp relief as I searched for him, the image of the desert almost scratched on the inside of my mind and built around the faded images of ley lines that no longer existed. They whispered, hinting at a time when there was grass and trees here, and huge animals roaming, living, dying . . . until they vanished along with the ley lines. I wondered which had disappeared first.

Al had once told me that demons made the ley lines in their efforts to escape the ever-after, but magic was older than that. Was what I was seeing now the faded remnants of lines gone dead? Had the demons destroyed the original source of magic in their attempt to banish the elves? I squinted, closing my eyes and reaching for a breath of understanding, wrapping my awareness around an empty shell of a scratch between the present and the past, finding no energy but only the lingering idea that power had once run here, now gone, leaving only the skeleton, dry and dusty, to hint at what had been. It made me feel so damned alone.

A door slammed shut, and I turned, my last thought heavy in my heart. "Get back in the car," I said to Trent, and Ivy slowly got out, her head bent over the amulet in her hand.

Trent looked me up and down, his expression closed. "It's an oven in there," he said, turning to the map on the brochure. "And besides, it's a bunch of pixies. How bad can it be? Just go and get him. You're a thousand times their size." Irate, he leaned against the car and squinted at me in the sun. The wind playing with his wispy hair, and the heat, made him look tired. "I'll stay here unless you scream for me. Promise," he said sourly.

Yeah, like that will happen. Jittery, I looked at the map sketched on the big brown sign beside a trail, seeing that there was a quarter-mile footpath that circled around a ruin. According to it, about four hundred people had once lived here, almost a thousand years ago.

Ivy shut her door with a backward kick, the *thump* not going on for long before the silence soaked it up. "You should listen to Quen more," she said, looking up from the amulet to frown at the slight rise of land before us. "Pixies are deadly."

Trent frowned at the sky, and I ran a finger between my ankle and the heel of my boot. "A clan of wild pixies kidnapped an experienced runner," I said. "They live in the desert. What does that tell you?"

"They aren't smart enough to move?" Trent said, and I made a noise of disgust. Ivy headed for the narrow footpath of paved asphalt, and I turned to follow. According to the plaque, archaeologists had begun to reconstruct the village site, but there were no walls higher than my knees.

Reaching my awareness out past the faint scratchings of what might once have been ley lines, I tapped the nearest real one. My eyes closed as I found hundreds of them, some as far away as the next state. The lack of water had extended my reach, much like the lack of trees expanded my sight. Having so much visual mindscape to play in was almost nauseating, and I quickly spindled a wad of ever-after energy in my head. I remained holding on to the line, knowing this was not going to be easy. I didn't want to resort to magic. If I couldn't convince them to let Jenks go, I wasn't sure if I could force them to without hurting them.

The click of Vivian's door opening was loud as I started out after Ivy, but she was only propping it open to get a cross breeze.

Yeah, there was the Vivian angle to consider, too. Anything I did was going to land in the coven's ears. Frowning, I picked up the pace until I caught up with Ivy, my heart pounding as we went up the slight rise. The altitude was getting to me. I tried to walk softly to listen for the clatter of pixy wings, but there was only the wind.

How anything could survive out here was beyond me, much less flower-loving pixies. The only plant life I'd seen was tough and herbaceous, something that I'd never give a second glance at if I was home, but here, the tiny flowers stood out. "Trent is dumb enough to make me want to cover him in honey and toss him into the middle of them," I said tightly as we passed down a narrow alley, slumps of rocks to either side.

Ivy didn't look up from the amulet, too worried to notice the stark beauty around her. It felt good to be moving, even though the idea that I was a ghost walking down an abandoned alley lost to history was creepy. I didn't like the fatigue creeping up my legs. We'd walked only twenty yards, but it felt like a mile in the heat and elevation. No wonder Jenks couldn't fly.

The path turned, and we halted at the end of the village, looking over what was once probably the refuse dump. Below us at the bottom of a steep drop-off were figures etched into the rock, the dark surface chipped off to show the white stone underneath. Most of the glyphs were indecipherable circles and spirals, but the one with the bird holding a man in his beak was clear enough. It looked kind of Egyptian, and I wondered if demons had been here.

"Look at those cave drawings," I said, pointing out the one with the storklike bird.

"They're called petroglyphs." Ivy didn't even look at them, focused on the amulet.

"Okay, but that huge bird is eating that man," I said, and she glanced up.

"I think it says 'stay close to the village, or the boogie man will get you.'"

I lifted my eyes to the open spaces over the glyph, feeling like we were being watched.

"Right," I said, not convinced. "And those little tally marks under it are what?"

She shrugged, and I hugged myself, wanting to scream for Jenks. "Where is he?" I said, stifling my urge to take the amulet from her, knowing better. Ivy felt helpless, too.

"I can't tell." Ivy turned in a slow circle, her expression one of the lost. "I know they're watching us." Pursing her lips, she whistled.

Below us in the parking lot, Trent pushed from the car. I waved him to stay, and he kicked a stone as he crossed the parking lot to crouch and feel the dirt between his fingers.

Ivy and I strained to hear something, but not even an insect broke the sound of wind on stone. I didn't like this. If they took Jenks to ground, we'd never find them. "Jenks!" I shouted, then spun at a tiny rock falling.

"Careful . . . ," Ivy said, her hand on my arm, and we went forward together, following the path over a small ridge and out of sight of the parking lot.

I crept along, uncomfortable under the sun as the heat evaporated the sweat before it dampened my skin. Twenty feet ahead of us was another part of the village, the corner wall rebuilt almost to waist height. A small motion caught my attention, and I stumbled to a halt.

There atop the wall, hogtied and with his own bandanna shoved into his mouth, was Jenks. I couldn't see his face, but his quick motions told me he was ticked, squirming with his words muffled by distance and his bandanna. His wings weren't moving, either. A black dust sifted from him. He looked like a sacrifice, and Ivy's words about the local gods echoed in my thoughts along with the image of that bird with a man in his beak. Maybe it was a pixy.

"Son of a bitch!" Jenks shouted, finally getting the bandanna off his mouth. "You cowardly sons of bitches!" he said again, then accidentally rolled off the wall to vanish behind it with a yelp.

"Jenks!" Ivy shouted, lunging forward.

"No, wait!" I shouted, reaching after her and feeling like the earth was going to drop out from under us. A piercing whistle echoed. My adrenaline pulsed.

"Rhombus!" I shouted, cowering as my molecule-thin layer of ever-after rose up around us. The protection circle snapped into place with a mind-jolting echo, and I looked up as tiny arrows plunked into it. The sun seemed darker, scaring me. *Have I put that much smut on myself already?*

"Stop!" a shrill pixy voice cried out ahead of me. "Or we kill the black-haired woman!"

"Rachel, stop!" Jenks shouted, and I looked up. And blanched. Thirty. No, fifty, maybe more, pixies surrounded Ivy, all with a bow or a sword or both. She wasn't in my circle. Her vampiric speed had moved her too far.

"Ivy!" I called out, and she slowly licked her lips, fingers spread as she put her arms up in capitulation. Her face was deathly pale, and she barely breathed as the pixies, in shades of brown and violet, hovered over her, their dust coating her in a sheet of red, savage as they hooted and brandished their weapons. I had the ugly realization that this was how they survived out here—bringing down animals to supplement the traditional pixy diet of pollen and nectar. *Shit, we were in trouble.*

"Ah, sorry about this," Ivy said, freezing when the pixies above her told her to be still.

"If you hurt her," I threatened, and my gaze darted to the

ridge. Trent was there, tense and looking like he was ready to do something. Damn it, I couldn't protect both of them. What was he doing? If they saw him, they'd attack, and I tried to tell him with my eyes to get the hell out of here.

The bright flash of yellow drew my attention back, and I frowned at the colorful pixy dressed in a flaming yellow, billowing outfit as he hovered before me. He looked like an ill eighteen-year-old who'd been into the Brimstone too much, his dark skin wrinkled by the sun and too little rest. His grip on his six-inch toad sticker of a spear was firm enough, though, and his green eyes were as sharp as any I'd ever seen.

"Why are you following us, witch?" he demanded, hovering inches from my barrier. His words were so fast, I almost couldn't understand him. My eyes flicked back to Trent, and I shifted my shoulders as I realized he was gone. *Just start the car and wait,* I thought, knowing that was too much to ask. He was going to do something, and it probably was going to make things worse. *Stupid elf.*

From behind the wall, I heard Jenks shout, "What the Turn is wrong with you? They're my friends!"

The pixy confronting me darted to the wall. "Liar!" he exclaimed, gesturing for two pixies to get him. "They're lunkers!"

"They're my friends." Two pixies dropped down, depositing Jenks back on the wall right where he'd started from. Looking pissed, Jenks stood, wobbling as he tried to find his balance. It looked like they'd weighted the tip of one wing to keep him from flying.

"I'm not making this up," Jenks said in disgust. "I'm Jenks! Of Cincinnati. I'm traveling to the West Coast on a job, and I can't stay here. And I'm not going to marry any of your women! I have a wife!"

I exchanged a shocked look with Ivy, and she rocked back, centering herself. *They had kidnapped him as stud material?*

"Liar!" the head pixy shouted, his wings moving fast in the heat. "You said she died!"

I opened my mouth, but Jenks beat me to it, shouting, "I

don't want a new wife! I love my old one. Do you have troll turds in your ears? Get this thing off me!" Jenks shook his wings, dusting heavily as the clip weighed him down.

Two more pixies, both in matching shades of sage green, had risen to flank the head pixy. "He did complain the entire way," the one with the length of steel said.

"Lifted his ass 150 miles, him bitching nonstop," the other with the bow said. This was weird. I'd swear they were the same age, but they didn't look like they were from the same clan. Pixies didn't cooperate like this. At least, pixies east of the Mississippi didn't. Maybe they had to band together in the desert to survive. That might explain why they thought Jenks should take a new wife, too.

"He can't even fly," the second one said, pointing at Jenks with his bow. "Even without the shackles. I say let him go. They want him, and for all his finery and height, he can't fly."

"He's from the east," the pixy in yellow said. "He'll adapt. He's not used to the air. Look at how water fat his flesh is. And his sword," he said, hoisting the one in his hand, and my eyes narrowed. It was Jenks's. "This is pixy steel. Pixy steel! Fifty-four kids he says he has. All living."

At that, the surrounding pixies rose up, gossiping in words too fast for me to understand.

"He lies!" a pixy said. "You can't keep that many children alive."

"Jenks can," I said.

"You're not helping," Ivy called out, and I winced.

"I bet he can!" The head pixy in yellow waved Jenks's sword around. "Look at him!"

Jenks stood with his hands tied before him and his gossamer wings dripping a black dust. Even I had to admit he looked good, especially compared to the gaunt, smaller pixies surrounding him. In another world, in another time, in another size . . . but he was Jenks, my friend, and my anger grew. I daren't move, though. Not with Ivy having a dozen poisoned arrows pointed at her.

Around us, the pixy women tittered, and I burned when one said loudly, "I don't care if he can fly or not. I'd just unwrap him and wear him like a fur."

"We stole you," the head pixy said to Jenks, gesturing for them to back off. "You belong to us."

"Jenks doesn't belong to anyone!" I shouted, but Ivy was silent. She was a vampire, and vampires were born to be treated like objects, given to others as favors for a day or a lifetime.

At my exclamation, the pixy flew to the bubble and poked at it with Jenks's sword. "You're not big enough to stop us. Get in your car and leave, or we'll kill the vampire."

I swallowed, feeling cold. "Please. I know this is weird, but Jenks has been working with us for over two years. He owns the church we live in. I pay him rent. You can't keep him. He has responsibilities. A job. A mortgage. He's got to get back to his kids because I'm not going to watch them!"

"He owns property?"

It had been the one with the bow, and I nodded as the pixies buzzed over that.

"His garden has so many flowers you can't step without crushing one," I said. "The grass grows so fast, I have to cut it every week. His children are so clever, they stay awake all winter. They play in snow."

"It sounds like paradise," a pixy wearing a flowing brown tunic said with a sigh.

"You aren't helping . . . ," Ivy said softly, her voice rising and falling like music.

The pixy with the bow frowned, taking a higher position than the other two. "I told you we should have asked. They do things differently across the Mississippi."

"We caught him!" the leader insisted, but hope rose in me as I saw a crack in their resolve. "Dragged his sorry ass across six clans, and you want to give him up? His wife is dead, and he's on a quest to spread his seed to the wind. Why else would he be wearing all that red?"

Excuse me?

Ivy made a small sound of disbelief, and I turned to Jenks. He looked as mystified as me.

"Uh, that's what we do where I come from to get safe passage through another pixy's territory," Jenks said.

"You don't just let them cross?" a pixy woman asked, her brown silk furling as she darted up. "How do you find enough food to survive?"

A cultural difference? I thought. The entire mess was the result of a misunderstanding over the color red? "I'm sorry for the mistake," I said, for the first time thinking we might get out of here without a fight. "Can we have him back? He won't wear red anymore. We didn't know."

The pixies were flitting in the sun, the shadows of their wings flashing over Ivy as they argued in small knots. Slowly I began to relax.

"He's a proven provider!" the head pixy said. "We need new breath in our children!" But the bows had been eased and the sword tips had fallen.

"Look," I said, taking a half step forward and halting when the pixies bristled anew at me. "He didn't know wearing red meant that he was trying to spread his, uh, seed."

"Yeah, I didn't know!" Jenks said, flushing. "I can't stay. I gotta get back to my kids!"

"I'm sure we can work out an exchange for your efforts in kidnapping him and bringing him here," I added. "Honey or something. What do you want?"

I held my breath as the three leaders looked at one another and then at their surrounding people as if considering it. I'd buy them an entire tanker of honey if that's what it took.

"Can you get us . . . maple syrup?" the pixy in yellow said. "A gallon, maybe? The real stuff, not that lizard shit with the corn syrup in it."

I exhaled, my breath shaking in my lungs. "Yes," I said, seeing the lines in Ivy's face ease.

The head pixy's wings became a neutral silver, and he

turned to the other two leaders. "For each of us," he added, wanting more after I'd given in so quickly, and I nodded, smiling.

"Three gallons. But Jenks gets his sword back."

"Done!" the three pixies said simultaneously, raising their weapons in salute, and the pixy standing beside Jenks cut his bonds. Jenks gave the buck a nasty look, letting the cut rope fall to his feet. His wings still flat to his back, he raised his hand to catch his thrown sword. Clearly not happy, Jenks jammed his sword away.

It was over, and the pixies by the far rock slide rose up in a whirlwind of sound and color, shouting, "Ku'Sox! The Ku'Sox Sha-Ku'Ru!"

A party? I thought as the air around Jenks and Ivy was suddenly empty of pixy wings. *In celebration of a peaceful resolution and three gallons of maple syrup?* Smiling, I strode to Jenks, still perched atop the wall. "Are you okay?" I asked, falling to kneel before him, hands curling around him but unable to touch. Never able to touch.

"I'm fine," he muttered, looking embarrassed as he wedged that clip off his wing and wobbled three inches into the air and back down. "Bought for the price of a gallon of syrup."

Ivy's shadow covered us, and I looked up at her as she chuckled. "It was three," she said. "And better that than my life."

Jenks nodded ruefully. "I'm never going to wear red again. Can we just write them a voucher and go?"

I stood, pushing my nasty hair from my shoulder in invitation. "One of us will run into town for it, and then we'll get out of here. Trent will just have to suck it up."

Jenks rose unsteadily and laboriously flew to my shoulder, and my earring pulled as he fell against it. I looked up the path to the unseen car, taking Ivy's arm to be sure she was okay, too.

"You didn't get hit by anything, did you?" I demanded, but she wasn't listening, her eyes riveted to the outcrop of stone behind me. The pixies were shrilling at the piercing croak of a bird, and I turned.

A bird? I thought, and then everything shifted. The Ku'Sox Sha-Ku'Ru wasn't a party; it was a bird. A big-ass bird, like a stork. And it was . . . "It's eating them," I whispered, horror filling me. "Oh my God, that bird is eating them!"

I stood frozen in disbelief, not comprehending it. The second and third leaders were shouting directions, so fast and high-pitched that I couldn't understand them, but it was clear enough as the arrows and spears once pointed at us now fell on the bird. It cawed, the harsh sound crawling through my mind and making me shudder as it echoed off the stone.

"Oh my God," Ivy gasped.

I spun, blinking when a new shadow fell over us. "You!" I exclaimed stupidly as Trent half-slid to a halt beside us, breathing hard and looking tired. "I told you to wait in the car! We've got this!"

"I can see that." His words clipped, Trent eyed the battle, his lips pressed tight. "Shouldn't we be going?"

Pixies were screaming, the sound becoming panicked. "What, now?" I exclaimed. "We have to help them!"

"The pixies who kidnapped your partner?" Trent said, frowning. "Why?"

"Why?" I echoed him. "Because it was a misunderstanding! We got it worked out. I just need three gallons of maple syrup!"

Trent's face became white. "Oh." He licked his lips and shifted from foot to foot. "Um, maybe we should leave anyway," he said, taking my arm and pulling me a step up the path.

"Rache?" Jenks warbled. "I can't fly."

"Do you not see what's going on here?" I said as I yanked out of Trent's grip and pointed, my finger dropping when a pixy screamed, trying to free itself from the bird's long beak, even as it vanished in a toss and a sharp snap. The pixy's clansmen and women were stabbing at the gray, storklike bird, firing arrows and throwing spears, but it simply jerked its head to catch another warrior who got too close, wings flapping as it hopped to a rock where its footing was better. Feathers gave it protection, and it seemed immune to the poison.

"There is a *bird*," I said, "eating *pixies*. Do you have any idea how wrong that is?"

"We need to get out of here," he insisted, and my attention snapped back to him. He tossed the hair from his eyes, and my heart seemed to stop. His ears were bleeding. Again.

"What did you do . . . ," I whispered, scared. Trent began walking away, and I glanced at Ivy, seeing her closed expression. Pushing into motion, I followed him, my heart pounding. He stank like cinnamon and spoiled wine. "What did you do?" I demanded, and he ignored me, not slowing down.

"I thought you needed help," he said, and I yanked at his arm, pulling him to a stop at the top of the hill. Frightened, I grabbed his chin and shifted his head. He let me do it. There was a handprint on his neck, but it was the blood dripping from his ears and nose that struck fear in me. The arch. He had bled at the arch, too, and he smelled like elven magic. *Thought we needed help?*

"Tell me what you did!" I said as I looked down the hill to the car. The trunk was open, and my scrying mirror was out, glinting in the sun. Vivian was slumbering in the back as if immune to the noise. Sleeping or out cold? "Oh my God!" I exclaimed as I pieced it together. "Did you use my mirror to make a deal with a demon?"

The bird cawed. Ivy stood next to me, and Jenks started swearing. Trent's jaw clenched, jerking as a horrible croaking came from over the hill. "Yes," he said.

The single word hit me like a slap. "That was you under the arch?" I stammered, being drawn forward as Trent doggedly paced downhill to the car. "You put yourself in a ley line and called on a demon under the arch!" I accused. "That force I shoved into those assassins wasn't from you, and it wasn't from the assassins. It was from a demon! And when I pushed the energy back into him, he tried to bury us all under the arch. You asked a demon for help and it almost killed you. And now you go and ask for his help again? Are you insane?"

Jenks had taken to the air, hovering backward and watching our backs as well as our faces. He looked as scared as I felt.

"It can't kill me now," Trent said, his jaw clenched. "You'll be fine. Trust me."

"Trust you!" I shouted, and Ivy grabbed my arm as I went to shove him. Feeling it, Trent stopped, looking angry and unrepentant as he turned to me.

"It can't snatch you because of me!" I exclaimed, shaking off Ivy's hold and pushing him in the chest. Trent stumbled back, but I was moving forward, getting in his face. "You used me! I freed you as a familiar, and you used me!"

Trent became more grim looking, his gaze darting behind me as the sound of fighting pixies grew loud and the harsh cawing of the stork echoed. Ivy was at my shoulder, a hand on her hip. "The coven might be interested in that. Trent Kalamack dabbling in demonology."

"If you tell her, then Rachel doesn't have a chance," he said, and I realized it was true.

"Uh, Rache?" Jenks said nervously, perched on Ivy's shoulder. "They're coming this way."

"You are an idiot," I said softly, shaking inside. "You have no idea what you've done."

Trent tugged his clothes straight as if he were wearing a three-piece suit and not a black T-shirt and a pair of jeans. "I suggest we leave before it finishes eating them."

I dropped back a step, almost laughing, as disgusted as I was. Ivy was staring at him in disbelief. "I'm not going to walk away from this. It's *eating* them!"

"Rachel, no!" Trent shouted, but I was beyond listening, and I leaned back as he came forward, bringing my foot up just in time for him to run right into it. He hit with a jarring that shifted me, and he fell backward holding his middle, taking Ivy with him. They sprawled on the paved footpath, and as Jenks darted to my shoulder, I turned to the bird.

"Celero inanio!" I shouted, throwing a ball of glowing ever-after at the harshly croaking stork, its ugly neck skin flapping. Yes, it was a black curse, but it was a bird eating pixies—pixies I had found a way to deal with peacefully. I was already mumbling, "I take the smut," as the curse to boil the blood in a living creature sped across the short distance, slamming into the bird to destroy it in a ball of curse-ridden magic.

Except it didn't.

My ball of death exploded inches from the bird, breaking against a flash of black that had enveloped the large bird, protecting it. Sparkles lit the afternoon, falling like a cascade over the protection bubble. The pixies darted back with frightened cries, gathering in a hazing cloud as the bird shook itself and the protection circle vanished.

Cawing, the ugly black stork turned a red eye to me. My gut clenched as I noticed it was slitted like a goat's.

"You stupid fool," Trent gasped from the ground, his eyes tearing as he tried to catch his breath. "It's not a bird. It's a demon."

Eleven

"Um, Jenks?" I said, taking a stumbling step back into a cloud of pixies now seeking shelter with me. "Tell me the sun is up."

"The sun is up," he said, hearing the panic in my voice and knowing what that black bubble had been about as much as I did. "Damn, Rache. You telling me that's not a bird?"

Ivy shoved Trent off her and got to her feet. Trent was next, and we walked backward to the car, the pixies retreating with us as they continued to shout insults at the bird. The sun was up. It couldn't be a demon. But it wasn't a bird, either, and I didn't know if that scared me or simply made me angrier. An ignorant bird eating people might be forgiven, but not if it was another intelligent being, demon or not. My instincts screamed demon, but the sun was up. *This isn't possible. Maybe it's a really bad witch Trent thinks is a demon.*

The cloud of pixies behind me started talking, too fast for me to follow, shrilling about Ku'Sox and fables and the past coming to life. "Kill it!" the head pixy shouted, and the snick of Jenks pulling his sword rang in my ear.

"No!" he yelled, and they halted, hovering behind me. "It's not a bird! You can't fight it as if it is!"

My mouth went dry as the stork croaked, eying me as it jumped from rock to rock, coming closer. Crap, it was getting bigger, too. My thoughts went to the petroglyph of the bird with a figure in its beak, and I paled as the memory of a pixy scream echoed in my mind, the bird gulping it down. "Uh, guys . . . ," I stammered as I turned, seeing Trent and Ivy still standing there, scared pixies wreathing them. "We'd better get to the car."

We ran. Arms pumping, I followed Trent and Ivy down the hill to the car, hitting the rocks and jumping over low walls to make a beeline for it rather than the safer, serpentine route. I could make only one circle. We all had to be in it, Vivian included. Behind me, the bird squawked, and the pixies scattered with shrill sounds of panic as heavy wings beat the air.

"Make a circle!" I shouted as I saw Vivian, awake and standing next to the open trunk, my scrying mirror in her hand, her mouth hanging open as she gaped behind us.

"Make a friggin' circle!" I shouted as the path became level and I ran on pavement instead of asphalt. The heat ballooned up, almost a wall. Ivy and Trent reached the car first, landing against it to turn and stare. I didn't look as I skidded to a halt beside them, searching my pockets for chalk that I didn't have. I had been hunting pixies, not a friggin' day-walking demon!

It couldn't be. But I'd seen its eyes. It had made a circle.

Behind me, the bird croaked out a weird call. It echoed in the heat-beaten stillness as if coming from time itself. Leaning into the car, I found my bag, and digging through it for my chalk, I thought about my scrying mirror in Vivian's hands. *Did Trent swipe my chalk, too?*

"A circle won't hold him," Trent said grimly, and I pulled myself out of the car, chalk in hand. Vivian was beside Ivy, and pixies circled, darting about in an eye-hurting mass.

"It's the Ku'Sox Sha-Ku'Ru," one shouted. "You brought the left hand of the sun upon us!"

"Chalk," I said triumphantly, holding it up and turning. "Oh, crap," I whispered. It was flying. And it had gotten even bigger—the size of a small plane, maybe.

"Rachel, duck!" Jenks shrilled as it angled for me, but I was already dropping.

I screamed as I felt talons rake my hair, and I dropped to the pavement, rolling under the car. My cheek burned from the pavement, and I held my breath as the wind shifted my hair. Then it was gone, and I looked up to see it swooping around. Holy crap, I had to do something.

"Is it a demon?" Jenks shrilled, inches from my face as I rolled out from under the car and got to my feet, squinting in the sun as I wiped the grit from my palms. Trent looked shaken as he crouched beside the car, and Ivy was helping Vivian off the ground. Pixies were a cloud over them, drawn to the very person who had caused their kinsmen's deaths. "Well, is it?" Jenks asked again.

"I don't know." Dazed, I looked at the frightened pixies seeking shelter with us. A day-walking demon? It couldn't be. But as I looked at Trent, I had a bad feeling that it was. *Just trying to help, eh? Thanks a hell of a lot.*

"What is that thing?" Vivian asked.

"I think it's a demon," Trent said, trying to wave the pixies away.

"You *think*!" I exclaimed, but the hard look he gave me stopped my next words cold. Ivy looked up from wiping her palms, and even Jenks turned, hovering in the hot air over the car. And as Trent slid his gaze to Vivian, then back to me, my jaw clenched, and I remained silent. I could say nothing. If the coven knew he'd summoned a demon, even to help us, his words in my defense would mean nothing. *Damn it!* Damn it all to the Turn and back!

"It can't be," Vivian scoffed, missing the hatred I directed at Trent. "It's daylight!"

"It's coming back!" the pixy leader exclaimed. "Scatter!"

"No, come closer!" I called out. "Jenks, get them closer!" Then immediately wished I hadn't as he laboriously flew from the car to try to corral them.

So Trent had summoned a demon to help us. God save me from businessmen with too much money and not enough to do, I thought as I leaned against the car and tried to imagine a circle big enough to hold us all. It would be large for most witches, but I could do it. It wouldn't hold long, either, but if I did it right, it would give me time to make a real one.

The pixies vacillated between following their leader, now flying away, and Jenks, almost browbeating them to get them to the car. Croaking three times, the huge bird came at us, talons outstretched. I quivered, remembering the time I'd been a mouse.

"An undrawn circle won't hold," Trent said softly, his eyes wide as he stood beside me, two of the pixy leaders at his shoulder. Stupid-ass elf might get hurt, but the demon couldn't snatch him, and he knew it.

"You need to shut up," I snarled, starting to shake. "I think you've helped out enough for one day, okay?"

He dropped his head and rocked back, looking not nearly chagrined enough. Turning to the approaching bird, I touched the line, pulling it into me and imagining the strongest, bird-hating circle I could think of. Oh God. The yellow claws looked as big as tree roots, and they were getting bigger.

"Now!" Jenks shouted.

"*Rhombus!*" I screamed, flinging my hand out to give my spell more strength.

I went down on one knee as I pushed the energy out of me instead of letting it flow naturally. With a clap of sound that reverberated like thunder, my bubble flashed into existence. Screeching, the bird tried to back-wing, head flung high and claws yanked tight to its body.

"Hold," I whispered, hands in fists as it hit. "Oh God. Please hold."

The bird hit, and I shook, bowing my head as the impact reverberated through me. And then my circle fell. Panting, I looked up. The bird had glanced off the top of the bubble, pulling up enough to avoid a full, neck-snapping strike. Tumbling, it hit the ground, getting smaller as it rolled across the parking lot and smacked into a rock.

"Did you kill it?" Trent said. "Rachel, did you kill it!"

He sounded frightened, and I gave him an ugly look. For all the smooth callousness he showed the world, perhaps he wasn't as immune to death as he wanted everyone to think.

"We should be so lucky," I said sourly, crab-walking a quick circle around the car with the chalk to make a more secure barrier. Ivy looked frustrated, pixies perched around her for security since Trent had driven them from himself. Vivian was pale. Scared. The lump of feathers now lying at the base of the rock wasn't moving, but I invoked the circle, shaking in the hot sun, waiting.

"Are you going to go look at it?" Vivian asked and Jenks landed on my shoulder.

"Yeah. Right," Jenks said, dusting heavily in exhaustion. "You don't poke the monster when it's down. You run away."

"I'm not getting out of this circle," I said. "Give it an hour or two, and if he still doesn't move, we can throw rocks at him." Demon. I was starting to believe that it was one.

Trent edged closer, stopping when I gave him a withering look. But whether we should poke the downed bird or simply drive away became moot when the lump of black shifted and stirred. Fear tightened my shoulders as a man rose, shedding feathers, the foot-long shafts of obsidian gray falling from him to reveal the simply cut gray pants and shirt underneath and the soft gray slippers. His slate gray hair was silver where the light hit it, and when he turned, he smiled as if pleased that I'd hurt him. He was taller than me. Pale. Silver. Shiny. *Demon.*

I glanced at Trent, thinking I'd rather have him as an enemy than a friend if this was his idea of helping. Trent's head was down, and it ticked me off that I was the reason he was safe and the rest of us weren't. God! I was a fool. Al had been right.

Vivian was staring, slack-jawed, at the approaching form, and Jenks hovered at the edge of the bubble, hands on his hips as he assessed the new threat. Ivy was scared but trying not to show it as the demon came to a halt before us, looking stronger and more certain of himself. He looked young, even with the silver hair, and I squirmed when his goat-slitted eyes moved from Vivian to me.

"But it's daylight!" Vivian whispered, and Ku'Sox smiled in delight, his attention leaving me to touch upon Trent and slide away. *Can't touch this.* His look at me had been one of casual disinterest. Bet it wouldn't stay that way.

"It's the Ku'Sox!" the pixies shouted from the car, and Ivy waved at them to go away as they swarmed her. "The Ku'Sox Sha-Ku'Ru!"

"I'm the eater," the narrow-faced man said, and I breathed. Crap, his voice was as gray as he was. Silver and gray, with a weird accent I'd heard only once. It was Newt's.

Ku'Sox squinted at my bubble, making me even more nervous as he leaned one way, then the next, evaluating its size and the black haze of demon smut crawling over it. I blanched when I realized the smut crawling over my bubble was being attracted to him, congregating where he was, looking like it was trying to get to him. "Guys," I said, wishing I could back up even more. "I don't think I can hold a drawn circle this size against him."

"No, you can't," Ku'Sox said, his eyes landing on me. "Aren't you an odd sort of witch." He breathed deep, surprise cascading through his expression. "Wearing a man's clothes," he added, his bloodred eyes shifting to a pale blue. "How curious. You're female."

"Look out!" Jenks shrilled, but I was suddenly gagging, my hands digging at Ku'Sox's fingers gripping my throat. He had me, his hands lightly around my neck as my feet dangled. Somehow he had yanked me out of my circle, broken it without a thought. It was too large for me to hold against him, and he'd taken it.

From Ivy's and Jenks's shouts of protest, I guessed that Vivian had reset the circle. She wouldn't have a chance of holding it, either, except Ku'Sox didn't seem to care about them anymore. No, I was freaking demon candy. It must be the red hair.

"Wait!" I choked out, still able to breathe and feeling his

fingers firm around my neck. He didn't stink like a demon. And his eyes, though still slitted like a goat's, had become a pale blue with a thin rim of slate gray on the edges. His lips were thin, and his chin was narrow. Al had once said he could change his eyes if he made the effort. Had Ku'Sox made the effort, or were his eyes naturally blue?

Fear was a cascade of sparkles through me, and I shuddered as my toes touched the earth. "Uh, can we talk?" I managed, and the man smiled wider. His teeth were flat and blocky, like Al's, and very white.

"Can we talk?" he echoed softly, looking at me in a not-so-nice way. "Perhaps. Hel-l-lo-o-o," he drawled. "Nice to meet you, little red-haired witch."

"Let me out, Vivian!" Jenks shrilled, and I tried to see them.

"Don't you dare . . . ," I managed, then looked back to Ku'Sox as the grip around my throat shifted to my shoulders and my heels touched the pavement. I could breathe freely again, and my gaze was fixed on the man . . . demon . . . Ku'Sox. Washed-out, pale blue eyes flicked behind me, then back.

"I don't know who you are," I said boldly, his long, narrow fingers pinching my shoulder, "but you need to leave."

"Brave," he said, and I punched him in the gut when he tried to tuck me under his arm.

I didn't know what my fist connected with, but he dropped me. I got a gasp of breath in, and then the pavement hit me hard. The chalk was still in my hand, and I refused to open it. Ku'Sox's slippers were inches from my eyes, and my knuckles were bleeding, scraped open when I fell. I still had my chalk. Damn it, I still had my chalk.

I could hear Ivy yelling at Vivian, and I prayed she'd keep her circle closed. "Let me handle this!" I warned everyone, pulling my head up to see Ivy ready to throw Vivian into her own circle and risk all their lives. "Please," I begged Ivy, and with a pained expression, she let Vivian go. The coven witch hit the car and slid to the pavement, shaken. Trent was a silent observer, and Jenks . . .

I looked away. Jenks was beside himself.

Ku'Sox only laughed, but he looked cross as he felt his ribs. "You'll be my first in a long time," he said, bending down to look at me with his hands on his knees. "Do you have anything in particular you're not fond of?"

"Shove it up your ass," I panted.

Ku'Sox straightened. "Lady's choice," he said, then reached for my shoulder.

"Owwww!" I howled as he flooded me with energy. Pissed, I rose up under his hand, shocking the hell out of him as I spindled the force and flung it right back at him. "Knock it off!" I shouted as he staggered back, his silver clothes seeming to shift to black in the sun.

Ku'Sox caught his balance eight feet away and blinked, amazement on his thin face. "Who the hell are you, witch who dresses like a man?"

I took a breath to tell him to screw himself, my words going unsaid as my head seemed to explode. Gasping, I fell to my knees. He was in my head. *Oh, God, he was in my head!* I was seeing snatches of my life with him standing in the shadows: an orderly at the hospital when I was thirteen, his blue eyes mocking my pain as my dad lay dying; then he was at camp on the horse behind mine; then he was at the park, walking the dog I'd seen when I'd made the deal with Al. He hadn't been at any of those places in reality, but now, as I lived it again, he was there, learning everything, missing nothing.

"Get out!" I shouted, hands on my head as I tried not to hammer my forehead into the pavement.

"Rachel Mariana Morgan," Ku'Sox said, flinging a hand out; I heard Ivy fall back with a grunt. The circle was down. *No. Please no.*

"Who has been teaching you such dangerous tricks?" Ku'Sox said, and there was a touch on my shoulder, soft and hesitant.

"Go to . . . hell," I panted. *No, not that memory,* I thought in anguish as I saw his reflection in the mirror while I held Kisten as he died.

"Algaliarept?" The stitching in Ku'Sox's sleeves glinted in the sun as he threw magic at Jenks, and I felt tears form, falling hot on my knees. They were trying to fight him as I sat crumpled on the hot pavement, living my life for the demon. "Why is the dullard letting you wander about here in the sun, little familiar?"

"Get out of my head . . ." I breathed as I tried not to remember that I wasn't a familiar but almost an equal. "Get out!"

"Oh!" he exclaimed suddenly as a memory of Trent grew strong. Jonathan was there, his face having Ku'Sox's eyes. And then I was gasping, my fisted hand scraping the pavement as I tried to get up, alone again in my thoughts. Panting, I bowed my head as the heat soaked into me. Oh God, it had been awful. *My life. He'd seen my entire life.*

"You can invoke demon magic?" Ku'Sox said softly, bending over me with the faintest hint of burnt amber between us. But if it was from him or me, I didn't know.

My breath came in fast as I felt arms go around me. Head lolling, I tried to focus, failing. He was holding me, and I was too tired to even protest. I'd lived my entire life in eight heartbeats, and the heat washed out of me as I fell into shock.

"S-stop," I managed, jerking when Ku'Sox murmured a word of Latin, and Vivian cried out in pain. The only reason they were still alive was because he was interested in me.

My hand was in a fist, and he brought my bleeding knuckles up to his mouth, licking my blood. Working at it, I managed to focus on him. He had a scar on his eyelid, like Lee. He'd be minus an eye if I could move my other arm.

"You're a link," he said, grinning at me like he'd won a doll at the fair. "And you have red hair and wear pants. I *adore* red hair. I once gave an entire generation of witches that color. That was before they locked me in the ground."

"Put me down," I demanded, and he did, holding me until I

got my balance, but when I tried to escape, his grip tightened about my waist.

"Seems as if I got out just in time," he murmured, looking me over again. "Why are you dallying with Algaliarept? He's a hack. But then, he's probably the best they have now. Unless Newt is still alive. I've been gone for . . ." Squinting, he looked up at the sun in evaluation. "Somewhere in the vicinity of two thousand years?" Frowning, his gaze dropped to me. "Two thousand years and you have red hair. How's that for a legacy!"

He seemed happy about it, but I was still trying to stand on my own feet. I didn't like what I was hearing, and I was sure Vivian was even more pleased than she had been. Ku'Sox was indeed a demon. In. The. Sun. I needed answers, but I wanted them from Al, not . . . Cute Socks here.

Vivian was ashen faced, standing in front of the car with a bit of chalk in her hand. There was an uninvoked circle around Ku'Sox and me, and her intent was clear. Ivy was next to her, and Jenks. The wild pixies still with us were under the car. I met Jenks's eyes, and he shrugged, pantomiming slugging him. *Might work,* I thought. I'd have a better chance of holding him in a smaller circle than keeping him out of one as large as a car. My heart pounded, and I pulled my foot back and slammed it into Ku'Sox's shin.

The demon howled, his grip easing just enough.

"Roll!" Jenks shouted, and I dove for the pavement, feeling Vivian's circle lick my heels as I made it through. A grunt slipped from me as I hit the parking lot again, finding my feet a little more slowly. Hand still clenched around my chalk, I turned, panting. The demon was in a circle—a coven-made circle—and it wasn't going to hold.

Sure enough, Ku'Sox was pushing at it with a determined expression, smoke rising from where his fingers touched. The familiar scent of burnt amber grew obvious, and I scrambled into motion. Hunched, I crab-walked around Vivian's circle, praying that the magnetic chalk wouldn't skip, wouldn't leave a gap. It had to be perfect. And it still might not hold.

"*Rhombus.*" I inhaled as I finished, sitting back on the hot asphalt as the circle formed.

"Son of a Were whore!" Ku'Sox shouted as his smoldering fist broke through Vivian's barrier only to smack into mine. Yanking his hand back, he shook it as if stung. His washed-out eyes dropped to mine, and I scooted back. It was perfect. It would hold. It had to.

"I couldn't hold him," Vivian panted, and I looked to her, haggard and slumped against the car.

I jumped at Ivy's touch, then relaxed as she helped me up. "You okay?" she asked, and I nodded. Slowly her touch slipped away, and I took a deep breath as if trying to find myself. Trent was leaning against the car, avoiding everyone's eyes. *Bastard.*

I exhaled, scooting back a little more before I got up and wiped the grit from my palms. "Thank you," I said to Vivian as I tucked the chalk in my waistband, then glanced at Trent, wondering what the hell his game was. Idiot summoned a demon he couldn't control. What did he expect to happen?

"I couldn't hold him!" Vivian said again, and I shuffled to her, tired. The upside? At least now the coven had proof that demons could be in reality while the sun was up. Al had done it once while in Lee's body. But I didn't think Ku'Sox was possessing anyone. This was something different. *Swell.*

"I couldn't hold him!" Vivian said a third time, and I frowned.

Pierce might have been able to make a circle to hold him. But he wasn't here. "He's a big guy," I finally said, glancing at Ku'Sox and away. "Everyone okay?"

Much to my relief, Ku'Sox didn't start spouting threats or monologing, and the chorus of pixy shouts brought back memories of Jenks's kids, memories that Ku'Sox had now. I didn't like that. If he knew my history, then he knew what I was going to do to him.

"It wasn't even a very big circle." Clearly shaken, Vivian sat sideways in the open front seat, dejected and weary.

I looked back at Ku'Sox patiently waiting, and Vivian's useless scratchings on the pavement. "It's a tough world." Limping to Ivy, I leaned back against the warm car. "I don't know this one," I said, talking to Vivian but accusing Trent. "He's nasty."

"Nasty?" Ku'Sox said, and my eyes jerked to his at the hidden threat his words held.

"If you *ever* touch me again," I said softly, "I will explode your 'nads. Got it?"

Trent had his head down in thought, worrying me. If I wasn't so darn tired, I would have barked at him, too. "Demon," I started, and Ku'Sox grinned in anticipation, making me shiver. He wanted to be released.

"Wait!" Trent said, his hand outstretched.

"You will leave this place and return to the ever-after, not to bother us again," I finished.

Trent slid to a stop, turning away to hide his disgust, but I'd seen it.

"For now," Ku'Sox said, his eyes going from Trent to me. They vanished first, then his body, until finally all that was left was a black obsidian feather, making me shudder when it finally melted in the sun.

My eyes shut, and I heard Ivy sigh. "I really hate demons," she said. I agreed.

"Okay, everyone smaller than a teapot, get out of the car!" I said loudly. "Jenks, you stay. And I swear, if you feral pixies give me any trouble, I'm going to jam you all in a box! I'll send you your syrup by mail, and you'll be happy with it. Clear?"

Without a protest, the pixies began to leave in threes and fives, their excited chatter making my already pounding headache hurt all the more. The head pixy wasn't around, and I didn't care. Like he'd ever say thank-you. My headache throbbed when Trent walked stiffly past me, sweat matting his pale, baby-fine hair.

"Letting him go like that was a mistake," he said in passing, and I lashed out, spinning him around to a shocked, angry halt against the car.

"You think we could have used him?" I shouted, and Ivy, putting my scrying mirror away in the trunk, hesitated. "Maybe traded a jump to Seattle for his freedom? Stick to helping with your checkbook. We'll all live longer."

Jaw clenched, Trent held his ground as Jenks joined me. "I'm just saying—"

"Nothing!" Okay, I was shouting, but I had a lot of adrenaline to burn before I got back in that car and drove out of here as if nothing had happened. "That was a demon! One in the sun. You think you're smarter than him? You're not! You mess with demons, and you *die*!"

His gaze flicked to Vivian. "You work with them," he said. "Think you're special?"

That had been barbed and pointed, and it made me angrier still. "I wish I wasn't, Trent," I said, managing not to shove him. "I'm so special it's going to kill me. That one . . ." I pointed to my empty circle. "That one is bad. Banishing him might cause a problem tomorrow, but nothing like keeping him around and trying to harness him would, and the sooner you get that through your thick skull, the longer we *all* will live. It was my decision to banish him, and you will sit down, shut up—"

"And enjoy the ride," he finished, the last of his suave businessman exterior vanishing as he bent at the waist and smoothly slipped into the car. He slid to the opposite side and slammed the door shut, waiting.

Ivy gave me an unreadable look, scratching her neck as she got in the backseat beside him and rolled the window down. I was hot and sticky, and Vivian slid across the bench seat to put herself behind the wheel, freeing me to weave my way through a passel of pixies and ride shotgun.

I got in, feeling Trent's glare on the back of my neck, the heat of the sun on the fake leather seats warm under me. My neck itched, and I realized that we'd been pixed somewhere along the way. Damn it, this was not my day. "I thought you were tired," I said as I looked across the seat at Vivian, and she frowned.

"I'm awake now." Saying nothing more, she cranked the engine over, and I fiddled with the vents, aiming them at me. I felt awful, not having showered two mornings in a row.

The pixies were gone, and I whistled for Jenks. He zipped into the car without his usual flair, almost falling as he latched on to the stem of the rearview mirror. His long curly hair swung as he dusted heavily, and I wondered where during the last 150 miles he'd lost his hair band.

"Thanks for driving, Vivian," I said, and she carefully pulled out onto the road, actually using her turn signal.

The young woman was silent, pensive as she rolled her window up while the air-conditioning took over. "He pushed through my circle like it was nothing," she said, gaze flicking to me and back to the road, looking embarrassed. "And what was he doing in the sun?" She looked at me, scared. "Did you call it?"

I rubbed the blood off my knuckles, stiffening as I forced myself not to turn and glare at Trent. My blood looked like anyone else's, but everyone who had blood like mine died unless they'd had three years of illegal genetic tinkering disguised as summer camp.

"Did you?" she asked again, frightened, and I shook my head, staying silent. Jenks's wings clattered, and I couldn't meet his eyes. Trent's voice might be all that stood between me and an Alcatraz jail cell, and I wasn't going to get him labeled as a demon summoner—yet. Jenks would be quiet, too. And Ivy.

"Demons are coming, Vivian," I said as I rolled my window up and angled the vents to me. "They're finding ways around the rules. The genetic checks and balances have been broken, and the demon genome is going to repair itself. We're going to become who we were. Maybe not this generation, maybe not the next, but when it happens, the witches can either be ready, or they can be pixies being eaten by giant birds."

Vivian stared at the road, her thoughts on my words. "I have to get to San Francisco. I have to talk to the coven."

"Me, too."

Leaning back, I turned my face to be in the light, seeing the bloodred spots of sun even behind my eyelids. I didn't want to be labeled a black witch and imprisoned, but I was giving the coven a very clear picture of what might happen if they let me live.

And I couldn't stop myself.

Twelve

The warmth of the sun on my face turned into an irritating come and go of shadow and light, and I stretched. The crackle of a fast-food bag reminded me of why my back ached and why I was sleeping sitting up. Feeling fuzzy, I opened my eyes, glancing at Vivian, currently alternating her attention between the busy urban street and the clock she was trying to change. It must have been the beeps that woke me up. Apparently we'd crossed into another time zone. Six-eighteen. But I felt like it was nine. Somewhere, I'd missed another meal.

Vivian gave me a quick, neutral smile, and turned away. I looked up at the washed-out buildings on either side, wishing I had my sunglasses. We were off the interstate, and there were palm trees, but it didn't look like L.A. The timing wasn't right, either.

The street was busy, clogged with traffic and people. Pedestrians were everywhere, and my eyes widened at the three guys dressed in velvet capes. Vampires in the sun? Living, to be sure, but they were Gothed to the max. "Where are we?" I asked.

"Las Vegas," Trent said from the back, his voice sour.

"Vegas?" Lips parting, I sat up and looked a little closer. Oh yeah. Where else would you get a pyramid and the Eiffel Tower on the same street? Leaning over, I found the map at my feet. "Why are we in Vegas? I thought we were headed for L.A." *Which probably had vampires roaming the streets in capes as well, come to think of it.*

Vivian tightened her grip on the wheel as if I'd brought up a sore subject. Her professionalism was running thin, and the petite woman frowned. "I'm not driving 40 to Bakersfield," she said through clenched teeth. "We're going the long way."

My gaze went to Ivy in a question, and she shrugged. "What's wrong with Bakersfield?" I finally asked, feeling the tension between Vivian and Trent.

"Nothing." Vivian frowned, but she still looked cute. Tired, but cute. "It's 40 I'm worried about. There are no gas stations after Kingman, and we would have run out."

"Someone's bad planning," Trent said softly. "The right person could make a killing."

Vivian made a huff of noise. "Someone's good planning, and make a killing is right. The people there don't want anyone driving through. Going to Vegas doesn't add much time. Stop complaining. We all want to get to the West Coast as soon as possible."

I hid a smile. Apparently Vivian and Trent hadn't been getting along, either. Settling myself, I ogled the people and buildings, acting like the Midwestern goober I was. I'd never seen so many flamboyant people flaunting their differences. It was easy to pick out the tourists with their pale faces and cameras. I'd never thought of myself as a conservative person, but this was like Halloween and Mardi Gras lumped together, a true Inderland playground.

"As long as we don't stop," I said, thinking it would be easy to lose a day here.

"We're stopping," Ivy said, voice low and confident.

From behind me, Trent muttered, "She speaks, so we must obey."

"*You* showered this morning," Ivy said, more loudly than she needed to. "I showered this morning. Vivian and Rachel didn't, and Rachel fought off a demon in hundred-degree heat.

We can stop for an hour." There was a hesitation, followed by a soft "Besides, I'm hungry."

"Fine," Trent said, sounding like a passive-aggressive teen-age girl. "But when we get back in the car, I'm driving."

A shower sounded more than good, and worried about the backseat dynamics, I stretched again. "Could you pick me up a burger or something?" I said around a yawn, eying a tall, blond vamp pacing down the sidewalk in six-inch heels, her clothes hardly covering her important bits. "The faster we get out of here, the better."

"Burgers?" Trent's voice dripped disdain, and my tension spiked. "We are in Vegas. This is the first time we might find something that passes for food, and you want burgers?"

I turned in my seat, surprised by how tired he looked, washed out and worried. Trent was never worried. Not enough to let it show, anyway. "Dude, why don't you stop and think about what your mouth is saying?" I said tightly.

"Children," Vivian said, not entirely joking, "if you don't stop arguing, I'm driving right through."

I turned back around, and Trent muttered, "I get to pick the restaurant."

Ivy sighed.

"And the hotel," he added, and she growled in annoyance.

I suddenly felt a whole lot ickier. And hungry. Leaning forward, I began tidying the front seat, tucking the map away and picking up trash. *More Milk Duds boxes?* "Jenks, you okay?" I asked, still not having seen him. It wasn't like him to miss a chance to join in with picking on Trent, and he wasn't on his usual seat on the rearview mirror.

"Peachy," came his voice from under the napkin draped over the open dash ashtray.

"He's altitude sick," Ivy said.

I resisted lifting the napkin, but just. "Are you okay?" I asked again, eying the white square. "You don't sound good."

"Leave me alone," he said, a green dust spilling over the rim of the ashtray, then sifting to the floor of the car. "I'll be fine."

"You want some pop or anything?"

It wasn't the right thing to say. In a flurry of motion, Jenks flung the napkin off, flying to an empty cup and throwing up in it, his wings flat against his back as he retched.

"Oh God!" Trent exclaimed. "He's doing it again."

"Jenks!" I exclaimed, almost frantic. I mean, when someone throws up, you're supposed to hold their hair back or make sure nothing hits their shoes, and I was way too big to do either.

"He's fine," Trent said so callously that I glared at him. "There's some honey on the dash. It helps."

I was ready to smack him, but Vivian handed me the packet, saying, "Flagstaff was really hard. He'll be okay."

"I don't feel so good," Jenks said, flying wobbly as he got back to his nest.

I shoved the cup in the bag with the rest of the trash, really worried. I knew Jenks tried to hide it, but if he didn't eat every couple of hours, he suffered. Throwing up could be a big problem. "Are you sure you're okay?" I asked as I tore open the packet and set it next to him.

Looking pale, he pulled a pair of chopsticks from his back pocket, nodding. "My head hurts." Eating a bit, he sighed, slumping to fall back when Vivian stopped at a light. We were right on the Strip, but worried about Jenks, I couldn't look up to see the sights.

"Better," he said with a sigh, then gave me a look of clarity before the honey kicked in. "I'll be okay. Just keep the honey coming."

I exhaled, relieved. He'd tell me if there was a real problem, wouldn't he? "Just what we need," I said, finding a smile. "A drunk pixy in Vegas. We'll fit right in."

"Not if I eat it slow enough," he said, easing back, looking relaxed but worn out. "Crap, now I have to pee."

My smile turned real, and I looked out the window at the people. I wished I had my camera, but then I'd stick out. Well, stick out more than two witches, a vamp, an elf, and a pixy in a powder blue Buick with Ohio plates already did. But then I saw the pack of Weres trotting down the sidewalk, and I decided we didn't stick out at all.

"I said, I have to pee," Jenks said again, louder this time, and I appreciated that he wasn't going to go in a cup.

Vivian leaned forward as she made a turn. "Hold on. I know a quiet hotel off the Strip."

"Off the Strip?" Trent complained, and I realized just how this trip was wearing on all of us. "We are *not* stopping at some Were-bitten hole in the wall when we can stay at a decent establishment."

Vivian said nothing as she pulled my mom's car into a low-budget chain with very little neon on the sign. "We're not staying," she said when Trent voiced his disgust. "We're taking a break, and we're stopping here because you won't get past the front desk of one of the big hotels without being recognized." She turned to him, her childlike face smiling cattily. "You want to be recognized?"

Trent said nothing, and satisfied, she put the car in park at the front office. "You've been nothing but a pain in the ass," she said as she grabbed her purse, just about the only thing she had since we'd kidnapped her. "No wonder Rachel doesn't like you. I don't like you, and I like everyone."

His hand went to his chin, and Trent silently looked out the window, clearly peeved but seeing her logic. Ivy, though, was stirring, putting her boots back on and grabbing her purse.

"Is that Elvis?" I had to ask, seeing a Were in a white leisure suit and gold boots coming out of the office door. The stitching was glowing in the shadows. The man was wearing neon, and he had a Chihuahua in his arms. The dog's collar was neon, too.

Vivian reached for the door handle, barely glancing at him. "That's Bob and Chico," she said shortly. "I lived here before I moved to the coast. Well, not here, exactly, but just outside town. The ley lines are spectacular."

Really? I thought as she opened her door and got out. I'd

heard they were numerous, but I had always thought it was part of the sell line.

"Everyone stays here, okay?" she said from outside, looking harassed, a hand on her hip and her clothes rumpled. She hadn't put on any makeup, and her once-slick hair was more like straw now. It made her trendy purse look like a cheap knockoff. "I'll get a room and then you can all go get something to eat," she said, eyes narrowed in annoyance. "I don't need a bunch of you in the office with me. I can handle this."

Ivy, of course, was getting out, and Vivian gave her a tired look. "I don't trust you," Ivy said with absolutely no remorse or guilt. "No hard feelings."

"None taken," the small woman said with the same detachment. "The rest of you stay."

Jenks's wings hummed, but he didn't move from the tissue-lined ashtray. "I gotta pee," he grumbled, but Vivian had shut the door, and the two walked in together, Vivian looking small next to Ivy's bruised and battered height.

"I really have to pee," he said again, this time his eyes beseechingly on mine.

I cranked the window all the way down, and he rose unsteadily into the air. "When did Vivian become everyone's mother?" I said, and he flew in a wobbling path outside. "Stay close, okay?" I said, noticing that he didn't have a scrap of red on him.

"Yeah, whatever," he said, then flew giggling to the sheared rosemary lining the path to the door.

I watched him, unable to stop my sigh. Silence descended, and as the insects buzzed, I became keenly aware of Trent, in the back. He had summoned a demon, not once, but twice. A day-walking demon. He said he'd done it to help. I wanted to believe him, but this had to stop. He wasn't proficient with magic, and he was doing more harm than good.

Twisting to see Trent, I said, "We need to talk."

His eye twitched. Without a word, he unlocked his door and pushed it open, his foot catching the heavy door as it bounced back into him. Getting out, he shut the door and leaned against it, his back to me as he looked toward the Strip, a few blocks away.

Peeved, my eyes narrowed. I was too tired right now to push the issue. After I had a burger, I'd pin him to the wall and demand some answers.

Even though we were off the Strip, there was a definite flow of people headed for it, passing us with either a fast pace with loud chatter or silent with a dull drudgery. The high-magic amulet detector on my bag was glaring red, but the lethal-magic one was quiet. Remembering what Vivian had said, I reached for a ley line to see how some little city in the desert stacked up to my Cincinnati.

"Oh my God," I breathed as the reason for my slight headache became apparent. The ley lines were everywhere, thick, thin, long, and short, crisscrossing in a chaotic mess in every compass direction. It looked like someone had dropped a handful of pickup sticks. Las Vegas was on a damn rift or something, time fractured and barely holding together. Awed, I shook myself from the mental sight of so much power hovering over the desert sand, then promptly sneezed, my hair flying in my face at the quick jerk.

Oh, great, I thought as I wiped my nose, but the sun was still up, so there was no reason not to answer Al, if Al it was. Leaning over to the driver's seat, I popped the trunk and got out.

"What are you doing?" Trent asked belligerently as I shuffled through the trunk for my scrying mirror, giving him an insincere smile as I pulled it out.

"You ever use my mirror without my knowledge again, and I'm going to bust it over your head," I said. "And we are going to talk. We could all have gotten killed back there, or worse. Leave the magic to the professionals. Businessman."

He frowned as he took in my threat, and he looked like a spoiled brat standing there with his arms over his middle, wearing black from head to toe, a slight flush to his cheeks.

Damn, he looked good, though, and I sneezed again as I sat down, leaving my door open for the cross breeze.

Trent turned to watch me set the mirror on my lap, and I shivered as the cold glass seemed to adhere to me, going right through my jeans. The silver-and-wine color threw back the haze of the setting sun, looking more beautiful yet. Another sneeze shook me, and I frowned. Yup, it was Al.

Ignoring Trent as he moved around the car to better spy on me, I put my hand on the scrying mirror in the cave of the pentagram. I connected to one of the smaller lines, and the rest was easy. *Rachel calling Al, come in Al . . . ,* I thought dryly.

The link formed in an instant, with a fury that left me blinking. *Son of a bitch!* echoed in my thoughts, foreign adrenaline slamming into me. Al was in pain. He wasn't talking to me; he was in excruciating, mind-numbing pain.

Al? I thought, confused as flashes of power and half-understood spells roared through my consciousness, too fast to be realized. My lips parted, and I pressed my hand more firmly into the glass. Furious Latin uncoiled from his mind as he twisted communal stored spells. They rose from the depths of two thousand years, created during a time of war, and all the uglier for having been roused and thrust into existence with no warning. Black and sickly, I felt them pass through my mind, coating me in Al's memory of what it was like to be in pain and how to crush another with one's thoughts.

Al! I screamed into our shared thoughts, scared that the magic might turn on me. He was pulling on a line through me, and damn it if it didn't feel good even as I tried to cut him off.

Get over here, Rachel. I need your—ow! Al thought as he finally heard me, but then his splinter of awareness jerked away, and his howl at a burst of energy created to liquidize fat burned itself into my brain. He nullified it in an instant, leaving me dizzy and panting but knowing how to do it.

Al! I thought, but I must have said it aloud because Trent's shadow covered me.

"What's going on?" Trent asked, more irritation than concern in his tone.

Heat exploded in my chest, and Al and I both reacted—him with a furious shout and a thrown counterspell, me slamming my rising palm back to the mirror before my fingertips could leave the glass.

Line. Give me a line! Al thought, and I did, loosening my grip and letting the energy flow through my hand and into his mind.

The pain cut off, and I groaned in relief. My hand was trembling, and I pressed it more firmly into the scrying mirror. I looked up, feeling unreal. Past the car windows, the sky had gone hazy with red, and the gritty wind was blowing. Somehow I was using my second sight, seeing Las Vegas as if it was on fire. It looked like hell, the casinos and buildings burning, crumbling, and re-forming to crumble again. It had to be from the ley lines. There were so many that nothing was stable. I stared, transfixed, as, in the back of my mind, Al moved, dodged, and fought someone using spells so complex they looked like another language.

"Rachel, what's going on?" Trent asked again, his voice a faint buzzing as I struggled to hold my connection to Al. He'd all but forgotten me as he fought. Al was fighting hand-to-hand, teeth clenched as he struggled to keep something from his eye.

"Al!" I shouted, shoving the line into him. It burned through his mind, and he groaned, directing it into his attacker's face. Outside the car, an explosion in the ever-after ripped off the corner of a building. I watched in awe as it fell in slow motion, a red dust rising from the impact. In Al's kitchen, I felt him shove someone away, and Al rolled to his knees, his savagery making my lips pull back in a snarl.

I blinked, and I was suddenly seeing reality—the demolished building became whole and serene, its elevator rising up, the windows glittering with neon.

Trent touched my shoulder, and I jumped as our auras connected.

From Al's kitchen, a savage explosion shook me. The curse falling from Al's lips was like tinfoil between my teeth, serrating into my spine and brain, and Trent felt it, too. I gasped as Al pulled on not only me, but Trent, and with a bellow of rage, Al flung the ball of death he'd pulled from us across his kitchen, exploding it against a quick black figure with silver hair. The attacker hit the wall, the tapestry that I hated going up in green flames. The fabric screamed, and with a clap of rushing air, the figure attacking Al vanished. On the floor, the tapestry shrieked and writhed as if in pain.

Trent's yelp of shock echoed in me as he pulled away. Stunned, I sat alone with my hand on the mirror. A slithering blackness had risen, and I felt it settle over Al as he huddled on his cold black floor, whispering, *I take this, I take this,* before the smut could hurt him. I shivered as the smut lapped about my consciousness, touching me and recoiling like a living thing before it slid back to Al.

Sweet everlasting shit. We're in trouble, I felt in our joined thoughts.

The attacker was gone, and I cut off the energy flowing between us. *Al?* I cautiously offered, and I felt his consciousness gather, trying to pretend that he hadn't almost just died.

Rachel . . . , he started, and then we both clenched in pain. A new rush of adrenaline poured into me, and I heard in our joined thoughts, *You little runt!*

There was another grunt of pain, and I doubled over. With a pop, I felt Al's thoughts leave mine. It wasn't the snap of disconnection because I could still feel what he was feeling. It was something else. Something was wrong, and this time, Al was in trouble. His mind wasn't working. At all.

"Al!" I shouted, forcing my thoughts into his and finding a glimmer. "Bring me across!"

I gasped as my body dissolved in a flash of thought. There was the burst of an expanded awareness, and then the awful division of self when I was again alone in the universe. A ping of fear lit through me. With a speed that left me reeling, I was yanked through the nearest ley line, stumbling as I suddenly found myself holding my scrying mirror and standing in Al's acrid-smelling kitchen. A thick haze of dust in the air, stinking of burnt amber, choked me, and the only light was coming from a book burning in the corner.

Chunks of rock had been gouged out of the raised circular fire pit where Al twisted his larger curses. More chunks of rock from the ceiling littered the floor. If it was wood, it was charred. If it was glass, it was broken. The tapestry was silent, a liquid black dripping from it like blood as it hung askew, half on the floor.

Before the smaller hearth, on his back, was Al, out cold and bleeding from several gashes as he lay before the black fireplace. And over him was Pierce, a black ball of death in his hand.

"Pierce!" I shouted, and he turned, shocked.

"What are you doing here?" he exclaimed, the blackness in his hands flickering.

Al groaned. Pierce spun to him, Latin coming from him fast as Al's eyes opened in fear.

I didn't think, just moved. Slipping on the chalky stone dust, I lunged at Pierce, knocking him from Al and landing front first across the demon. Frantic, I scrambled up, hearing Al grunt in pain as my elbow dug into his gut. Almost in the fireplace, Pierce had gotten to his feet as well, the invoked curse still in his grasp.

For an instant, our eyes locked, and then, after shaking his head, he threw the spell at Al.

What is he doing?

"*Rhombus!*" I shouted, and Pierce's curse hit, pinging through my awareness as I slapped his magic aside. It went spinning into the broken remains of Al's kitchen, and my anger peaked.

"Are you addled?" Pierce yelled, his blue eyes showing his anger as he stood, his hands bereft of magic. "What the blazes are you doing?"

At my feet, Al groaned, and I felt a twinge on my awareness as a red-sheened sheet of ever-after coated him, dropping away to leave him looking half dead but no longer bleeding.

"I had him!" Pierce shouted, arms waving. "I bloody had him, and you knock me away? Deflect my curse? What's wrong with you, woman! I could have been free!"

My mouth dropped open, and I glanced down at Al gazing up at me. *Holy crap, had I just saved Al's life?* "Uh," I stammered as Al levered himself up onto one elbow, his head drooping to the floor and his dark hair covering his eyes.

"I had one chance!" Pierce shouted, shaking as he stood by the fireplace. "And—"

"Septiens," Al wheezed, and Pierce collapsed, seizing as if having hit an electrical field.

"Al! Wait!" I shouted, seeing Pierce writhe.

"And you blew it," the demon said, ignoring me as he staggered to his feet before the small hearth. His red, goat-slitted eyes fixed on Pierce. "Killing me when I'm down . . . not very sporting."

My heart pounded, and I remembered the ugliness leaking out of Pierce's hand. Pierce was a demon killer, and I was basically a demon. Would he try to kill me next? I had to believe no, but I hadn't thought he'd try to kill Al, either. I hadn't thought at all, apparently.

"Let him go," I pleaded as Pierce shook, his neck muscles straining as he tried to breathe. "Al!" I shouted, smacking the demon's shoulder. It wasn't hard, just enough to get his attention.

For a long second, Al looked at me, his goat-slitted eyes searching mine. Then Pierce's breath rasped in, and his entire body went flaccid. Panting, he lay on the floor and didn't move.

"Perhaps you're right," Al said, looking disheveled as he leaned against the fireplace and eyed his kitchen. Half-burned wood was scattered on the floor, and the book in the corner was going out. Seeing it, Al snarled and muttered a word at

Pierce. Pierce screamed, shocked into pain again as his back arched. "Selling him might pay for this mess," Al finished, his expression ugly.

I reached out to protest, then hesitated. Pierce had saved my life, but he had tried to kill Al. "Stop," I finally whispered, touching Al's sleeve, but what I was thinking was, *Why did I help you?* If I'd let Pierce kill him, all my troubles would have been over. Except they wouldn't have been. Al was my protection in a world that I was probably going to be trapped in very soon.

Al frowned, and he looked at me as if only now seeing the dirt, grime, and bruises. He twitched, and I heard Pierce collapse behind me. My gut unclenched as it grew quiet, Pierce's breath sobbing in and out in relief. Part of me was angry, part of me wanted to lift Pierce up and wash off his face. I didn't know which part was stronger.

Moving slowly, Al staggered to the stone bench circling the center fire pit, coughing on the dust as he began arranging sticks for a fast fire. His fingers were shaking. It was dark, and I looked for a candle to light. All I found were puddles of wax, spattered like blood. At a loss as to what to do, I looked at the devastation, then went to help Pierce.

"You did this?" I asked as I pulled him upright against the broken remains of a bookcase, and Pierce winced, his eyes still closed. The shelves were leaning askew, and a thick tome fell, glancing against his shoulder. Still, he didn't open his eyes, but pushed me away, grimacing. I'd seen them fight before. Almost a year ago, Pierce had gone into this familiar partnership with the intent to kill Al. I hadn't thought he might actually do it.

"He wishes." Al's tone was flat, and I turned to see his thick fingers nursing an infant fire in the circular fire pit. "He's a cowardly runt."

The new flame flickered, lighting Al's features into an ugly mask, and from Pierce came a ragged "I utilized my resources to the fullest, demon spawn."

"You're a bloody coward!" Al shouted, then coughed. "Trying to kill me when I was down."

I stood between them, not knowing who to help. *He had tried to kill Al.* "What happened?" I asked, remembering the deadly, world-killing curses that Al had drawn through me. My God, the power they could use and didn't . . . I was like a child playing, and I suddenly felt both scared and stupid.

Al looked up, his wavering gaze landing immediately on Pierce. "You. Go," he said, pointing, and before Pierce could do more than widen his eyes, he vanished.

"Hey!" I exclaimed, and Al pushed himself up. He looked beaten, and his clothes were dusty, showing blood and rips, though the skin under them was unmarked.

"He's alive," the demon muttered, dropping a chunk of what had once been his chair on the flames. "I simply shoved him in a box for when I decide what to do with him. He tried to kill me. Please tell me you aren't still clinging to the idea that he lo-o-o-oves you?" he mocked. "That witch is a demon killer. You're simply lower on his list than I am. Grow up and accept it."

I didn't want to believe it, and I searched the floor, hoping I hadn't cracked my scrying mirror. Pierce had said he loved me, and I truly believed he hadn't been lying. But the memory of him standing over Al, hurt and unconscious, with a black curse flickering over his aura, ready to kill him . . . Could I afford that kind of blind trust?

Depressed, I picked my way through the devastation to get my scrying mirror, breathing shallowly to avoid the dust. Feeling awkward, I sat beside Al, the slight curve of the bench between us. "You don't look good," I said, my thoughts on Vivian. Trent would tell them what had happened. Jenks would be angry that he hadn't been there. Ivy would be ticked because Trent hadn't done anything, and Vivian would have another chapter in her "Let's Shun Rachel" book. Even better, I was going to stink like burnt amber when I got back. If I got back.

"I don't look good?" Al wiggled his fingers at his own scrying mirror, just out of reach, and I leaned over to get it, feeling a dizzying amount of other selves trying to get through to him as I handed it over. He wasn't wearing his usual gloves, and it made him look vulnerable.

Exhaling heavily, Al put his thick-fingered, shaking hand on the mirror and it fogged up. "You say I don't look good, but you're the one in trouble."

My gaze went from his foggy mirror to my crystalline one. "But I stopped him!"

"Not that," Al said, and he let his mirror slide to the bench. Sighing, he rubbed his forehead, leaving a smear of black ash. "I've temporally blocked the collective because I can't answer that many calls at once, but pretty soon, I'm going to be entertaining. Lots and lots of irate, angry demons in my tiny little living room. It will be embarrassing. My reputation will be utterly ruined. I don't have enough chairs," he finished lightly, turning his lip in and chewing on it.

"You mean Trent?" I said, standing up and distancing myself with the excuse of gathering bits of broken furniture. "I told you already, I didn't teach him anything." But a sliver of worry had started to wiggle in me. Trent had summoned a demon. I hadn't taught him that, but they wouldn't believe me.

Al chuckled, low and long, and I stifled a shiver. "If only it was that," he said wryly. "I know you're driving to your little witches' meeting. Tell me you weren't in St. Louis yesterday."

Oh God. I'm in trouble. "The arch falling was not my fault," I babbled, the broken chair leg in my hand clattering to the floor. "It was Trent! He did it, not me!"

"Damn my dame. It was you," Al said, grimacing as if he'd eaten something sour.

"It was Trent," I said, wondering how he knew the arch had fallen, but my voice lacked conviction, and I became more worried yet when Al wouldn't look at me. Nervous, I tucked my rank hair behind an ear and fidgeted.

"I don't know what kind of spin I can put on this," Al finally said, his eyes on his dirty fingers and his shoulders slumped.

"Al?" I said, really concerned. He looked up, and I blanched at his empty expression.

"And then this afternoon," he said, reaching out to rub my hair between his fingers. I didn't pull away, and he leaned forward to sniff it. "You were in the badlands of Arizona. Yes?" he asked, looking up at me from around his sweat-soaked bangs.

I didn't feel so good, and I sat down, a hand to my middle. "This is about Ku'Sox, isn't it," I said, more of a statement than a question.

He made a sighing groan, and I knew it was. "Then you've met," he said, his thoughts clearly on the day-walking demon. "Funny, you don't look dead." His hand touched my chin, shifting it so he could see where I'd been pixed, the blisters itchy and red. "I'm surprised you survived the little designer dump. I nearly didn't. At least he doesn't know who you are yet."

I winced, and Al's hand fell away. "He knows, doesn't he," Al said flatly, and I nodded, making the connection now between Ku'Sox and the shadowy figure I'd seen fighting Al before I'd come over and found Pierce ready to finish him off. Maybe I shouldn't have banished Ku'Sox to the ever-after.

"He lived my entire life in eight heartbeats," I admitted. I tried not to whine, but I knew by Al's "So what?" rise to his eyebrows that it was there.

"Bet that was fun," he said, and I wondered if Al could do the same and hadn't, knowing it for the gross violation of self that it was. Not rape, but worse almost. "That adds something a little unexpected to the mix," he said as an afterthought.

"Sorry," I said, and Al slumped, rubbing his forehead with his stubby fingers. From behind us, the tapestry finally became quiet, and the silence was almost creepier than the weird burbling sound it had been making. Licking my lips, I stood. "What is he?" I asked. A shiver went through me, and I wondered if it was the need to feel like I wasn't alone, that I wasn't a freak. "Is he like me?" I asked, lips barely moving.

Al's eyes were glowing in the light of the fire when I turned to him, the demon seeming to be gaining strength as the flames warmed him. Still he said nothing, and after dropping the broken seat of an upholstered chair on the fire, I stood next to the weary demon, seeing him slowly regain his strength and knowing that we were really, really in trouble. "Al?" I asked again.

"He's you."

Twin feelings of fear and excitement lit through me, but the fear won. If he was me and he was bad, then everyone would think I was bad by association.

"A link between demons and witches," Al continued, nodding to acknowledge that I realized what this meant. "But not made by Trent's father. Ku'Sox Sha-Ku'Ru was our attempt to bridge the gap when we found out what the elves had done. It didn't work," he said sourly, "and we decided not to do that . . . anymore. He's missing something."

"Yeah, he looks a little crazy," I said dryly.

"Crazy? Perhaps. He's missing something from his soul," Al said, and my lips parted.

"That might explain him eating pixies," I said, and Al cocked his head at me, the glimmer of his usual bluster returning.

"Ku'Sox was eating pixies?"

Cold, I wrapped my arms around myself and sat down while Al built the fire higher, his chairs burning with the smell of varnish and burnt amber. I shrugged, then scratched at a little welt under my shirt. "Trent thought we were in danger." My fingers slowed, and I tucked a foot under my leg as I gazed into the fire. "The idiot called Ku'Sox to get rid of the pixies. He showed up as a bird, and when Ku'Sox started eating them"— I looked up at Al—"I hit him with a curse. It sort of got his attention."

"You're a bright girl for someone so stupid," Al said, and I frowned, affronted, as he got to his feet and unsteadily went to his bookshelf, nudging the books scattered on the floor until finding the one he wanted and retrieving it. "I told you to take that elf firmly in hand, my itchy witch." Al sighed as he sat back down, closer to the fire than before. Square reading glasses had appeared on Al's nose, and he squinted through them as he turned the pages of the book on his lap. "That new mark of his makes him immune to everything." His eyes met mine, making me shiver despite my anger. "*Everything,* Rachel. He's probably the only person on the planet who could free Ku'Sox Sha-Ku'Ru without getting killed in the process."

"Free him?" I asked. Al made a questioning face at me, and I figured it out. The arch falling, the power I'd shoved back into someone. Ku'Sox saying he'd been gone for two thousand years, locked in the ground. "You mean Ku'Sox was imprisoned under the arch? Trent didn't summon him, he freed him?" I said, aghast.

Al had gone back to his book. "I told you . . ."

"To take him firmly in hand, yeah," I said, seething. Stupid on top of stupid. God! I was ready to smack Trent into next week. "But he loosed Ku'Sox before I gave him his freedom," I said, remembering the blood coming from Trent's ears and nose. Maybe Trent was stronger than I gave him credit for.

Al made an uninterested sound and turned a page. "And of course the first thing Ku'Sox did was find me."

"Because you're my teacher," I said, and Al laughed, the sound ending in a short cough.

"No," he said, clearing his throat and waving his hand. I shivered as the dust in the air fell like rain, and I brushed it off. "Not everything is about you, itchy witch. Ku'Sox and I go back a long way. The son of a bitch completely yanked Asia out of my grip just when things were becoming interesting. I couldn't get a familiar there for nearly a hundred years until Newt finally trapped him and tucked him safely away in reality. The demon is a genius."

Ku'Sox was Al's rival? Great. "And he can be under the sun," I prompted, wondering if he had meant Ku'Sox was a genius, or Newt.

Al blew the dust off a page and turned it. "That was the entire point of creating him," he said distantly, as if it bothered him and there was nothing he could do about it.

I wanted to go, but I thought he was working on something for me. The drip, drip, drip of the blood falling from the silent tapestry was loud, and sullenly I said, "I'm sorry."

A short guffaw broke from Al, and he looked at me. "That makes me feel so-o-o much better. I'll be sure to tell everyone that. My student freed her familiar, who let loose a demon we didn't want to kill and just barely managed to imprison? Newt will be most vexed. Honestly, you told me you were going to be smarter. This isn't it."

"It's not like you ever tell me anything," I said sourly. "If you'd said, 'Don't go to St. Louis and free the crazy demon under the arch,' I wouldn't have." Nervousness pulled me to my feet, and I went to the bookcase, shelving the scattered books one by one in no particular order—which might be a problem since none of them had names. "And I didn't free Ku'Sox. Trent did. What Trent does is not my responsibility."

A hint of deviltry was in Al's voice when he asked me, "You severed all responsibility?"

"Yes," I said as I shelved another book. "One hundred percent."

"You didn't even keep a call-back clause?" Al asked, then waved his hand and answered his own question. "Of course not. You've had the worst upbringing of any demon I've seen."

I turned, the book I held pulling the heat from me through the binding. "I'm not a demon," I said, and Al stood to bring me the book he was looking at, splayed open on his palm.

"Which emancipation clause did you use? This one, right?"

I leaned over to look at the curse he was pointing to, and though it was in a different book, I could tell it was the same. "That looks like it."

Al smiled, and seeing it, a knot of worry eased. For the first time, that awful smile of his made me feel . . . good. "Trent is bound to come to your aid when you ask. Did you know that?"

Al snapped the book shut and shelved it beside the one I'd just placed there. "I think that puts him in a slightly higher standing, thus freeing you from responsibility for his actions."

"Really?" I said, willing to give Trent the high ground if he'd get in trouble, not me.

His pace a jaunty limp, Al crossed his kitchen, kicking bits of rock and wood out of his way. "I do believe your do-gooder tendencies have finally come home to save you," he said as he pulled a chest from the wreckage, opened it, and fingered through whatever was inside. "Trent's in trouble, not you. Go back to your little scavenger hunt."

"It's not a scavenger hunt," I said indignantly. "I'm trying to clear my name."

"Whatever." Al dramatically waved a silver amulet. "You're taking the runt with you."

"Pierce?" I came up from the floor with another book in my hand, the image of him standing over Al, ready to kill him, sifting through my mind. "He just tried to kill you!"

"Yes, but for all his anger, he still thinks he loves you." Al squinted at the black jewel centered in the amulet, muttering a word of Latin to make the stone glow a brilliant silver, and then darken. "You're going to need protection if Ku'Sox is free to come and go. A demon killer is just the thing to keep you safe. I'd do it myself, but I don't want any taint of interference to mar our agreement that if you can't get your shunning removed, you abandon reality."

"Al," I protested, thinking my strolling into the coven meeting with a witch they'd buried alive for black magic wasn't going to look good. "He's going to get me labeled a black witch."

Al looked at me over his glasses, almost pouting. "You're going to be labeled a black witch anyway, love." He smiled, snapping the chest closed and dropping it down the stairway to his herb cellar, to shatter by the sound of it.

Remembering the look of fury on Pierce's face, directed at me, I shook my head, reaching for books as fast as I could place them, as if helping Al clean up might win me some favor. "I do *not* want Pierce tagging along on this magic carpet ride." But just yesterday, I had.

"Which is why this is so perfect." Smug, Al dramatically snapped his fingers, cocky again. In a soft pop of displaced air, Pierce flashed into existence, his clothes disheveled and his hair everywhere. Immediately his confused look turned to one of anger—deepening when his gaze landed on me.

"You're a mess," Al said, almost his old self as he smacked the man so hard he stumbled.

The smack had been a curse of some sort, because Pierce stiffened, shuddering as a sheet of red ever-after coated him, changing his outdated clothes into something more modern. He was still wearing creased black pants and a long-sleeved shirt, but now there was a colorful patterned vest and a sharp-looking, trendy hat in his hand. He looked good, even with his hair disheveled, and I squashed the thought.

"You're going on a field trip, runt," Al said as he looped the amulet he'd taken from the chest over Pierce's head. "You will keep my student alive or die trying."

"Hands off," Pierce all but growled, and Al smacked his face, taking the hat out of Pierce's hand and smashing it smartly on the witch's head. I tensed, but clearly Pierce was used to the manhandling, and he only frowned more deeply.

"You will make sure that nasty demon Ku'Sox doesn't kill her," Al said conversationally. "Understand? You're angry, but you still like her, yes? Want to have wild demon sex with her even if she ruined your attempt to kill me? Keep her alive, and you might get some. Eh? Eh? You'd like that, mmmm?"

"Al . . . ," I protested, and Pierce looked at me like I was trash.

"I'd sooner lie with a whore," Pierce said, and I gasped, affronted.

I half-expected Al to smack him again, but all the demon

did was brush off the amulet and say, "Well, she's been called that, so where's the problem?"

"Al!" I exclaimed, but no one cared.

"Better," Al said, nodding once sharply as he took a step back and looked Pierce over. "All nice and pretty for itchy witch."

Pierce took his new hat off and dropped it to the dusty floor, even though I saw that he liked it. "You're doing this because I can kill you. I could kill you right this moment."

I gasped as Al reached out and slapped him, the sound of hand meeting flesh giving the fast movement away. Pierce reeled, catching himself against the broken chair that had once belonged to Ceri. "I'm getting rid of you," Al said calmly, "because you're a clever witch who won't stay in his box."

Glaring, Pierce straightened from his half fall, looking at me as if I was the source of his woes. *Hey, dude, I wasn't the one trying to kill Al.*

"Al. No. This is not a good idea," I said, seeing Pierce's anger as I backed up a step.

"It's a capital idea!" Al took three steps to close the distance between him and Pierce. The shorter man tensed, but Al only put an arm over his shoulder. He looked like a dad threatening a date, and I half-expected him to tell Pierce to have me home by ten, but what he said was "Keep her alive. Keep her alive, or I will know about it."

Pierce looked at me, and I remembered his hand, painful against my mouth, forcing me to be quiet as inches overhead Trent's horses and dogs searched the woods for my blood. He loved me. I was sure of it. But he had tried to kill Al with black magic—and as the memory of him leaning over Al with power leaking from his fingers replayed itself in my mind, I began to question my judgment of him.

My face became cold as I abruptly realized that for all Pierce's claims of compassion, for his clever mind and quick loyalty, for all his justifications of black magic as acceptable if the cause was good, Pierce truly was a black witch. He had tried to kill with magic. It didn't matter if the charm was white, black, or polka dotted with silver sparkles. The coven of moral and ethical standards had been right about him. *They were right.*

And if they were right about him, maybe they were right about me.

"I don't care if she dies," he said, and I looked away, remembering: *And I will cry when I go, because I could love you forever.*

Son of a bitch. I'd done it again.

Al smacked Pierce's face a little too hard. "Then let's just say you keep her alive, or I will give you to Ku'Sox like a free toaster for opening an account in the bank of degradation."

Pierce shoved Al's arm off him with an indignant look. "You'll be dead first."

Al shook his head. "I thought you might say that. You will excuse me and itchy witch for a moment."

Pierce opened his mouth to say something, and Al punched him. Hard.

I blinked, shocked, as Pierce dropped and the demon swore and wrung his hand. "Damn, I forgot how much that hurt!" he said, then reached down and hauled the unconscious would-be demon killer up by his vest front. It was silk and linen. Enough to put even Trent's wardrobe to shame. I stood there feeling like I should protest at the brutality, but I didn't know what to think anymore. Pierce was black. *Was I?*

"Rachel," Al said as he held Pierce like a drowned kitten. "I'm hanging by a thread, both my life and my reputation. Take Pierce and keep him away from me. Ku'Sox is not crazy. He is smart, clever, and has had two thousand years for his hatred of everyone on this side of the ley lines to fester into his chaotic nightmares. He knows everything I do, everything that Newt has forgotten. He can't be reasoned with or pacified. We're in trouble, and I can't have a familiar who is ready to take advantage of a moment's lapse. Pierce knows more than you, and you'll need him. Turn your feminine charms on and seduce him if you need to in order to have him save your scrawny witch ass."

God help me, I thought. No wonder the coven wanted to kill me. Pierce was a black witch, and I had been defending him.

Unaware of the confusion swirling through me, Al's attention lingered on Pierce. "I don't think he'll ever forgive you for saving my life. Pride. He's full of pride." I shivered as his eyes came to me, that same look of evaluation in them—but this time, it was tempered with gratitude. "Thank you," he said as he shoved Pierce at me. "For . . . helping me."

At a loss, I took Pierce's weight, staggering until I found a new balance. "No good deed and all," I said, not knowing how to say, "You're welcome." I was glad I'd done it, but did accepting his thanks mean that I was aligning myself with demons all the more? Did it even matter anymore?

Unaware of my thoughts, Al nodded, looking tired. "Don't forget your mirror," he said as he handed it to me, and I struggled to hold it and Pierce both. "And don't let your freed familiar use it again."

Better and better, I thought as I felt Pierce's weight vanish, and then me, too, dissolve into nothing for the trip back to reality. I hardly had time to form a protective bubble around myself and Pierce before we misted back into reality. My boot heels scraped as I got my balance. I was standing in the sun-drenched parking lot where the car had been. The shadows had shifted, and I let Pierce slide to the pavement, not caring how he hit the hot ground as long as my mirror didn't break. From a second-story walkway, Ivy, Vivian, and Jenks were collectively yelling at Trent as they looked for their room number.

The soft *oof* of Pierce hitting the pavement caught Jenks's attention, and his long whistle pulled everyone to a stop. Ivy's eyes found me next, and she was smiling as she looked down, leaning against a support pole. Trent was silent, plucking the key from Ivy and vanishing with a bang behind a red-painted door. Vivian stood in openmouthed awe, her small figure looking small next to Ivy.

"You're back!" she said, eyes wide as she recognized Pierce, just now starting to stir. "Is that . . . Gordian Pierce?"

I bent to help Pierce rise, and he pulled from me, holding his jaw and not meeting my eyes. "Yup," I said, feeling hurt somehow. We were back. But for how long, I didn't know.

Thirteen

If it wasn't for the lack of an ocean, I would have believed I was in Florida, sitting at a tourist-trap, beach-themed restaurant whose target audience was college kids on spring break. The floor was of gray dock planks. The stairs had stiff rope railings. Fishing nets that had never seen the water were strung under the high ceiling. It was busy, and Trent's hundred bucks had bought us a booth in front of the stage, bypassing the forty-minute wait. Maybe money couldn't buy happiness, but it could get you a table that looked like the back end of a deep-sea fishing vessel.

Tired and disillusioned, I looked over the booth. It even had fake fishing poles out the back between us and the stage where a scruffy Were was singing about a last shaker of salt. No, his *lost* shaker of salt, according to the paper place mat. It must bother Jimmy Buffett that no one could understand his slurred lyrics even if he had them painted on the thick support beams, too. Yep, we were in Margaritaville, and it was steaming Trent's shrimp that we were still in Vegas.

Uptight, I ate my last piece of shrimp cocktail and took a sip of soda, eying the beautiful servers moving around the tables. Every last one of them was a living vampire, and I thought it odd that vampires and the beach seemed to mix so well.

Still hungry, I ran my finger through the shrimp sauce and licked it off. I was on the outside of the semicircle with my back to the kitchen. Ye olde demon killer was to my left, then Trent, Vivian, and Ivy on the other end. Jenks was on the candle centerpiece, almost asleep despite the noise. My phone said it was seven thirty, but it felt like ten thirty, naptime for pixies and elves on East Coast time. Jenks looked better now that we'd quit moving. I was feeling better now that I'd had a shower and was in a fresh pair of jeans and a black camisole. I hadn't yet talked to Trent about his new friend, Ku'Sox; I was still trying to wrap my mind around Pierce. He was a black witch. There was no denying it. Maybe instead of trying to figure out if it was wrong to like him or not, I should do the smart thing and . . . forget about him.

Grimacing, I turned my phone to vibrate and tucked it in a back pocket. Jenks had talked to his kids earlier, and I'd fielded another chat with Bis. Apparently he'd woken up this afternoon for a few minutes and wanted to talk to his folks about having seen the sun. They were at the basilica, a good five minutes' flight away, and he didn't want to leave the pixies alone unless we knew about it. He was a good kid. I was surprised, though. Most gargoyles couldn't stay awake during the day until they were much older.

"Hey, Ivy," I said, leaning across the table. "How come everyone working in here is a vampire? Some kind of union thing?"

Vivian looked up from her corn chips, clearly eager to answer, but Ivy was quicker. I'd seen her watching some of the prettier ones with more than a passing interest. "They're working off their debts," she said as she sipped her soda, looking as sexy as a vodka commercial.

I glanced at our server flirting with a table of four businessmen, then the vampire stud Ivy had been eying since we walked in. "Really?"

"Really," Vivian said when Ivy air-kissed her chosen one. "The head vampire in Vegas has a policy of free movement on his turf. Otherwise there might be a drop in revenue from the gambling. No one leaves with an outstanding debt. Dead or alive."

Trent was nodding as if he'd known, but I'd never heard of an undead vampire having control of another vampire's family member, even temporarily. I turned to Ivy to see her blushing a faint, eager red. "That's why we're stopping in Vegas," I guessed, and she nodded, eyes on the table as Jenks snorted himself awake with a burst of yellow dust.

"Fewer issues to deal with when I—" She stopped, eyes on the vampire she'd culled from the herd. He was pretty enough, I guess. "You think a human is bad at not knowing when to quit at the gambling table?" she said, chewing the toothpick the cherry had come on. "Try being a vampire, bored and seeing an eternity to find the money you might lose tonight." She licked her lips for someone else's benefit, and I stifled a shiver. My eyes flicked to Trent and Pierce. Okay, they were watching her flirt, too, both of them weirdly intent and detached.

Pierce was not happy to be here, which I thought rude since his other option was Al's box in the ever-after. He'd showered as well, so he smelled like hotel shampoo instead of burnt amber. Frowning, he watched everyone from under his funny hat—it had shown up during his shower—gulping his bubbly soda and wiping his eyes when he drank it too fast. Tumbling his clothes in the hotel drier had taken care of most of the stink on them, and he was back in his tidy slacks, casual shirt, and a vest that was probably from his 1800s closet but looked new. He was still wearing that silver amulet. I had no idea what it was, but I thought it telling that Pierce hadn't taken it off, even when he'd been in the shower.

Trent wasn't good company, either, seeing that our planned pit stop had turned into a four-hour break at a restaurant he hadn't picked out. We *all* had to get out of the car for a while, and I still wanted to talk to Trent about Ku'Sox—to find out if he knew how bad Ku'Sox was before he let him out or after.

Ivy shifted, her motions screaming sex as she smiled up at our waitress when she came back with another soda for Pierce.

"Do you know what you want?" she said as she set it down, voice raised over the music.

"I'll have the pasta," I said, pointing to it on the menu.

"Same," Pierce said, and I wondered if he could read anything other than Latin. He'd been born in the early 1800s, and it was possible he couldn't.

"Clam chowder," Trent said as he handed his menu over.

"I'll have the tilapia," Vivian said brightly, a vestige of her usual polished self showing as she settled into a familiar haunt. "With asparagus."

"Oh God, save us," Jenks said, dramatically holding his nose. "We do have over a thousand miles left to go in that tiny car."

"My mom's car isn't tiny," I said, and Trent frowned.

"It is with five people in it," he muttered.

Ivy was handing her menu to the woman. "I want the steak sandwich," she said. "In a to-go bag."

I gazed at her in question, but the woman was nodding. "I'll put these in," she said, making a last note on our bill. "Anyone else need anything?"

By the look of it, and the slight nudge Vivian was making at Trent to get him to slide over, Ivy needed someone's neck. I shook my head, but Trent spoke up, handing the waitress a folded bill. "I want another beer," he said. "And if you can get everyone's meal out here in five minutes, there's another one of those in it for you."

The woman looked at Ben Franklin's face and tucked it away. "I'll see what I can do, honey," she said, smiling at Ivy before she sashayed away.

"Beer and soup?" Jenks said as he dusted a thin sliver of silver, his own light hardly making a dent in the dusky shadows in here. "That's going to mix well."

"You'd be surprised by how a good beer mixes with clams," Trent said, his attention on the male waiter Ivy was blinking at slowly. God, this was getting uncomfortable, and I put a hand over my neck as it started to tingle.

"He's uptight about his timetable," Ivy said, almost sighing the words.

"And you're not?"

Trent's expression froze when she turned to him, smiling to show her little fangs. "Excuse me," she said as she got to her feet in one languorous move that made Pierce shiver. 'Course it could be the cold pop he'd just slammed down.

No one said a word as Ivy sat on the back edge of the fake boat and swung her feet over. Moving with liquid grace, she made a beeline for the vampire she'd had her eye on. People were getting out of her way, and the vamp in question was smiling, waiting for her.

"What is she doing?" Trent asked, but Vivian knew, her eyes cast down as she shifted on the bench to make more room for the rest of us. Hell, even our waitress knew what Ivy was doing.

I took a sip of my soda, watching Ivy drape her arms around the man and whisper something in his ear. "Keeping the rest of us safe," I said, trying not to worry about her. She'd be okay. And if Vegas had a freethinking master vampire, then this was probably the only spot between home and the coast that she'd be able to take the edge off.

Jenks frowned, clearly not happy, but as willing as I was to let her take care of her own needs. I didn't know if I should feel upset or not. I wasn't her keeper—but I *was* her friend.

Pierce was ignoring everyone, and Trent didn't seem to care apart from Ivy's tryst possibly slowing us down. Vivian, though, pushed her glass around, clearly screwing up her courage, and I wasn't surprised when she asked, "She and you—"

"No," I said before Jenks could offer his opinion. "We're not sharing blood." I felt Trent's eyes on me, but Pierce didn't look up from his drink. "We tried," I said, talking to the entire table though my gaze was on Vivian. "Well, we tried it enough to know that for it to happen, one of us would have to change too much. If I bend, she'd lose what she loved in me, and if she bends, I lose what I love about her." I shrugged, flaming red in embarrassment, but that was my problem.

Jenks clattered his wings, rising up and down as if testing

his strength. "I'll keep an eye on her," he said, then frowned when Pierce made a rude noise. "To be sure she stays safe!" he added sharply. "I'm not going to watch. Tink's a Disney whore, I'm not a Peeping Tom."

Jenks gave me a meaningful head toss to Trent and flew away, taking a high path between the ceiling and the fake fishing nets.

"We don't have time for this," Trent said suddenly, and I wondered if Ivy's and my relationship bothered him. *Curious.*

"You're the one who wanted to eat," I said.

"I meant the rest of us could grab a decent meal while you showered, not a five-hour sightseeing excursion ending up in a sideshow restaurant."

That was just rude, not to mention an insult to Jimmy Buffett fans everywhere. "We've been trapped in that car for two days," I said. "We need a break." *And I need to talk to you, stupid elf.*

Trent ran a hand over his hair, leaving it attractively mussed. His eyes showed his mood, dark and irate, as he looked over the vacationing people who had nowhere to go for the rest of the night. His frustration peaked. "I need to be—"

"In Seattle by Sunday," I said, interrupting him. "Yeah, I got that part." I took a sip of my drink, which infuriated him for some reason. "Will you relax? Have a margarita or something. I told you I'd get you there, and I will. Trust me." That last jab had been sarcastically bitter, but I was ticked. I mean, why ask me to protect him on his way out to the West Coast, then free a demon to do it?

Vivian was watching me, her intelligent eyes squinting in question. She knew something was up, just not what.

"Trust you." Trent shifted in disapproval. "Seattle is fifteen thousand miles from here. Just getting to San Francisco will take us eight hours, even if we take 95."

"Whoa, whoa, whoa," Vivian said loudly, and the couple in the next boat over looked at us. "Are you crazy? No one takes 95!"

"Which means we can go as fast as we want," Trent said, his eyebrows bunching.

"We are not taking 95," Vivian said fervently, and I tuned them out, watching Ivy and her blood buddy slip out the back. Jenks gave me a color flash of green, and I turned back to the table. "If you get on 95, you don't stop!" Vivian finished intently.

Trent took a swig of his beer, looking normal. "I don't plan on stopping."

Vivian tossed a hand up in the air and pushed herself back into the cushions. "I'm coven, not one of God's angels. It's too dangerous."

Maybe he's relying on his demon *friend,* I thought bitterly. I didn't think any big, bad uglies on 95 would be a problem, even if we had to stop. Hell, we'd already evaded elven assassins and one severely disturbed demon. A soul eater. Crap on toast, I had to talk to Trent. He'd better not have any idea of what he had unleashed, because if he did, and he'd done it intentionally, I might be pissed enough to just walk away from this completely.

Trent leaned toward Vivian. "I don't see any other way of getting to Seattle in time other than taking 95," he said softly, his anger just in check.

"I said I'd get you there," I said, watching Pierce eye two women in shorts, his ears turning red. "Have some faith in the people you ask to protect you."

Feeling a hint from my last words, Trent leaned back, giving Pierce a good view of the female vamps making out in the corner.

His back against the cushions, Trent unrolled his silverware and arranged it perfectly with stiff motions. "I've seen how you protect people. Telling me to have faith isn't inspiring."

Oh, but summoning day-walking, soul-eating demons is?

Pierce pulled his eyes from the vamps long enough to snort his agreement, and my face flamed. "Have I ever not come through?"

Trent fingered his knife. "No, but your collateral damage is generally more than I want to pay—Morgan."

This from the man I had to save by going into a partnership with a demon? I frowned; Pierce looked happy for the first time since he'd gotten here. "And what's on your mind, demon bait?" I snapped at him. "Enjoying the show?"

Immediately Pierce's smile shifted to a frown. "I could have killed Al if not for you," he said, and Vivian started.

"You almost killed a demon?" she asked, eyebrows going high in interest. Her attention flicked from the two women to me and back to him. "Her demon?"

"Aye," he said, glancing at me darkly. "She stopped me."

"Who's going to protect me in the ever-after if not Al!" I said, fumbling my words as suddenly everyone at the table was looking at me like I'd killed Bambi's mother. "Al is the only thing between me and Newt, or worse! You look at me and think I've got this all under control, and I don't!"

Trent smiled as he moved his nearly empty glass of beer just so. "That's not what I see when I look at you."

"Me neither," Pierce said under his breath, and may God strike me dead if the two men didn't start to bond.

"What I meant," I said patiently, feeling like the butt of a joke, "is you think that I'm safe with them, but I'm not. If Al dies, I'm up crap creek."

Pierce spooned a piece of ice out of his drink. "Not my problem," he said, teeth clattering against it.

My jaw dropped. "Hey! *You* were the one who went to him with some stupid idea to be his familiar just so you could kill him."

"It's a capital fine idea," Pierce said indignantly, glaring at me from under his hat. "And it would have worked if not for you."

Vivian leaned closer. "You tried to kill a demon?"

"I almost made a fist of it, yes," Pierce said, his features still holding his anger at me. "It was the only reason I did tuck with them, and I opine that if the truth were known, then the coven might have to apologize for burying me alive, and they wouldn't want to do that, would they?"

Expression becoming pinched, Vivian sank back into the seat. I said nothing. As far as I was concerned, he *was* a black witch. And it bothered me, probably because I thought I might be one, too. Maybe I was being too harsh. *Maybe.*

Pierce gave me an angry look. "I'd be free tonight if not for your misguided, ignorant stupidity."

"Yeah, yeah, yeah," I said, unable to look up at him. "It's all my fault. And if you killed Al, where would I be? *You* can't protect me from Newt. Like it or not, I need Al. Go kill someone else's demon to make yourself a man, Mr. Black Magic User."

Pierce became silent as the Were in one flip-flop finished his set and got down amid a too-enthusiastic round of cheers.

"To freedom," Trent said, startling me. His glass was raised and, fingers fumbling, Pierce picked up his mostly empty glass and the two clinked.

Men. "Well, excuse me for trying to stay alive," I said, elbows on the table. I didn't like being here without Ivy or Jenks. "And I thought you didn't like Trent."

Pierce had taken a gulp, his eyes watering at the bubbles popping. "I can drink with a man and not like him," he said, and Trent smiled that infuriating men's-club smile.

"I bet you can," I said, but I was busy looking over the moving heads for Ivy. Shouldn't she be back by now? How long did it take to bite someone, anyway? Or was it the cleanup that took so long? I'd never been bitten where I wasn't fighting for my life three seconds later. Must be I was doing it wrong.

"Excuse me," Trent said suddenly, and my attention jerked to him as he rose and nearly pushed Vivian out of the booth.

"Where are you going?" I asked suspiciously.

Trent hesitated next to the table, and Vivian slipped back in. "The washroom." His eyes went to his empty beer glass, then back to me. Slipping into the narrow path, he wove his way to the back of the restaurant, past the kitchens and the big sign proclaiming BUOYS and GULLS. *Catchy.*

My head started to hurt. This might be my only chance to talk to Trent alone. Sighing, I stood, saying, "Vivian, you got Pierce, okay?"

Vivian looked at me in bewilderment, letting go of the straw she was downing her soda with. "He needs watching? What's he going to do?"

"I don't need watching," Pierce said indignantly, and I swung my legs over the edge of the boat the way Ivy had. She'd probably looked better doing it, though. Not answering Vivian, I pushed into motion to follow Trent, noticing that he was getting some appreciative glances from the surrounding patrons. He didn't give any indication that he knew I was behind him as the noise of the restaurant was replaced by the clatter and steam of the kitchen, and then the muted noise of the back hallway.

"Trent," I said as he reached the door to the restroom. Arm stiff, he pushed the door open and went in, not acknowledging that I was behind him.

I didn't slow down, following him in with my breath held and my shoulders tight.

Trent was at the mirror, head down as he held the sides of the white sink with a resigned air about him. Glancing up, his eyes twitched when they found me in the mirror's reflection. "Get out."

Arms swinging, I let my held breath out and decided it didn't stink too much in here. Ugly things, urinals. Going past him, I looked under the single stall, then kicked it open to make sure no one was standing on the toilet. *Trust me,* he'd said, but he had summoned Ku'Sox, and I needed to know why.

"You hired me for protection," I said stiffly. "That's what I'm doing."

Trent turned to lean against the sink. "It's a bathroom. Wait outside."

I stood with my hand on my hip, angry. "Seems like I remember that the elves who attacked you under the St. Louis arch had the same bits that you do," I said, and he frowned. Sauntering forward, I all but pinned him against the sink. "Remember St. Louis? The arch fell down? Why the hell did you free a day-walking demon? Didn't trust me to get you there, huh?"

Turning his back on me, he pumped the soap dispenser, having to go to the next one before anything came out. The rims of his ears were red, and my anger grew. "I know you girls go to the bathroom in packs, but I'd appreciate some privacy," he said, his jaw tight and the skin around his eyes pinched. "No self-respecting assassin takes their mark in the john."

"And no self-respecting assassin makes a hit on an interstate, either." I moved closer, well within his discomfort zone. "You want to tell me what in the *hell* you thought you were doing freeing a day-walking demon from under the St. Louis arch?"

Trent didn't pause, his smooth motion never bobbling as he turned off the water, shook his hands, and reached for a paper towel. Silent, he turned, his expression closed.

A quiver rose through me and tightened my gut. I wanted to shove him, but I managed to keep my hands where they were. Through the cement walls, I could hear cheers as the next band took the stage. "Ku'Sox was halfway to killing you until I shoved that energy back into him. He knocked down the arch, trying to kill both of us," I said, pushing forward until we were only inches apart. "And then I freed you from your familiar bond and made you immune to him. What I want to know is whether you've been planning this from day one, or if you're making this up as you go along."

He turned his back on me, not looking at my reflection as he arranged his hair. "I've known about Ku'Sox since last year," he said, and I dropped back, not knowing if I believed him or not. His eyes flicked to mine in the mirror. "You think Ivy is a planner? She has nothing on a motivated elf with too much money." He looked away, shifting one thin lock of hair over his ear. "I've got this under control."

I blinked, trying not to lose it, but my hands shook. I could almost hear him add, "Don't worry your pretty little head about it." "Yeah?" I barked, glad I'd waited until we were alone to bring this up—this way, there'd be no witnesses when I killed him. "Do you have any idea how much trouble you're in? The demons are pissed. They can't control this guy, can't kill him! That's why he was imprisoned!"

Trent slowly turned, gesturing as if waiting for me to leave.

"Trying to catch him the first time was a friggin' war," I said, remembering Al's spells slithering through our connected brains. "Ku'Sox isn't confined to the ever-after during daylight, and he eats people to absorb their souls! He *eats* people, Trent."

A flicker of emotion crossed the back of Trent's eyes. A soft twitch at his lips. I pounced on it, seeing a sliver of humanity.

"You *saw* him eating those pixies!" I said, hammering the guilt home. "That's what he does. He *eats* people because his soul doesn't work right. Ku'Sox is a magically engineered disaster the demons created while trying to break the curse your people put on them in your *stupid* war! What they got was something so horrendous and disturbed that they buried it in the *next world over*. And you go and *free him*?"

Trent's green eyes hardened. "I *have* this *under control*."

I snorted. "Like you got him to stop eating pixies? Just because he can't kill you doesn't mean you control him! The demons aren't blaming me for this, they're blaming *you*! This emancipated-familiar thing makes you liable. You're going to have demons with little red robes coming at you for breaking the law of uncommon stupidity if you're not careful."

His gaze on mine narrowed, and he turned away. "I have this under control. He's sworn to protect me."

Did he not get it? "Protect you?" I yelped. "He *ate* pixies—alive—to distract them so we could escape with Jenks."

"You're welcome for that," Trent interrupted, and my head pounded.

"If you didn't think I could protect you, then why am I here?

Huh?" I asked, hands on my hips as I stood between the door and him.

A small, infuriating smile showed on his face, shocking me. "Because Quen wouldn't let me out of Cincinnati without you."

My teeth ground together, and I forced them apart. I didn't think Quen knew about Ku'Sox, and I sure as hell believed that Ceri didn't. "You are an idiot," I managed, hands in fists.

Trent turned back to the mirror and brushed nonexistent dust off himself. The motion lost something with his being in a casual shirt instead of a thousand-dollar suit. "Right back at you, babe."

Babe? Did he just call me babe? Shaking, I turned on my heel. This guy was a piece of work. "I'll wait outside for you," I said, not trusting myself with him right now.

"If you feel you have to."

Pissed, I stiff-armed my way out of the bathroom. *You can die here for all I care,* I thought, the warmth and noise growing as I stalked down the empty hall. Trent was a jerk. A jerk and an ass. The demons might not blame me, but the coven would. And then I'd have to take care of Ku'Sox myself. What in hell was I? Trent's maid?

Not looking at the man I pushed past, I peered out over the kitchen archway to the restaurant—then paused. Cinnamon. Cinnamon and wine.

My anger vanished, and I turned to the man now heading for the men's room. Nice slacks, nondescript windbreaker, soft shoes, dark hair, well built. Smelled like a snickerdoodle dunked in wine.

Shit, the guy was an elf.

Fourteen

Heart pounding, I ran back down the corridor. I hit the men's room door with a bang that reverberated from my arm to my toes. Breath held, I slid to a stop as the unknown elf turned.

Trent still stood beside the row of sinks, hunched under a claustrophobically small circle. Something close to panic was in his eyes, quickly turning to his familiar cool dispassion, but I'd seen it, and I knew he was glad to see me. The air smelled like ozone, and the last of the attacking elf's green aura trying to break through Trent's circle flickered and went out.

I put a hand on my hip, and gestured with the other at the man in his trendy windbreaker and utterly blank expression. *Trying to kill Trent on my watch? I don't think so.* "If I can't kill him, then neither can you," I said, and the assassin's lips twitched.

I moved, tapping one of Las Vegas's lines even before he threw a ball of magic at me. Striding forward, I flashed a circle into existence for the bare second I needed to deflect the green-hazed ever-after into the corner. It hit the tiled wall and spread out, a gelatinous ooze smelling of bone dust emanating from it.

"Nice," I said, thinking it must be a charm to break someone in half. "You want to leave before I hurt you?"

Hunched, the elf backed up, trying to keep enough distance

between us so that he could throw something at me and not have it bounce back at him. I kept going forward, trying to get under the guns, so to speak. Grasping him by the front of his windbreaker, I shoved him into the wall, slapping aside his attempt to flood me with ever-after.

"I said, you need to leave," I said, unimpressed, but I hesitated when I felt the prick of wild magic brush across my aura like sandpaper. Eyes wild and frightened, the man smiled at me, and a quiver rose in my chi as I thought of black snakes unwinding from Al's head to kill Ku'Sox. The man made a gesture, lips moving and fingers twisting into an awkward figure. He gasped as his hand contorted and I heard knuckles pop, and hazy black enveloped his fist.

Alarmed, I dropped him before his magic could flood into me.

"Demon whore!" he shouted, clearly in pain as he threw whatever it was at me. I flung myself back to dodge his spell, hitting the stall door and falling backward into the toilet even as my protection circle sprang up. Arms and legs flailing, I caught myself with the oh-so-helpful railing they put in there. Sprawled across the seat with my arms straining, I stared at the horrifying green aura only a handsbreadth from me, slithering over my bubble as if looking for a way in. It was wild magic. It had hurt the assassin to cast it. It might make it through. I didn't think it was going to be sunshine and lollipops if it broke my bubble.

In the corner, the assassin was getting to his feet, shaking the pain from his hand. I wasn't keen on the gleam of anticipation he still wore. Licking my lips, I glanced at the charm burning its way to me, then back to him. *"Stricto vive gladio . . . ,"* I started, and the man's eyes widened in fear as he recognized the "bounce back" charm. He scrambled to his feet, almost flinging himself at the door in his effort to flee.

"Gladio morere transfixus," I finished, and the green haze coating my bubble vanished.

The fleeing elf skidded to a halt between Trent and me, his

back arching as all his muscles seized. Mouth open in a silent scream, he reached behind him as if trying to touch something. Gurgling wetly, he collapsed, his back scraping on the sticky floor.

Horrified, I broke my bubble and pulled myself out of the stall, looking at the man contorting under the charm meant for me. His lips moved as foam bubbled at the corners while he tried to speak the countercharm. "Sorry," I said, wincing. "Maybe you should have tried to kill me with something that didn't hurt so much." A soft pop sounded, and Trent's face turned ashen. I think the guy had just dislocated something.

Groaning, the man collapsed, but it had been the curse breaking, not the man's spine, and he lay on the floor, gasping for breath.

"Maybe you should leave now," I suggested, and he rolled to his hands and knees. Reaching for the sink, he pulled himself up. Grime from the bottoms of a thousand shoes coated his back, and sweat glistened on his neck. Panting, he looked to the door as it creaked open, becoming even more frightened.

I looked as well, and a heavy spike of fear slid through my ribs and into my lungs. *Ku'Sox.* "Damn it, Trent," I said as I edged over to stand by him. "I told you I have this. I do *not* need any help!"

Ku'Sox stood before the closed door in a blue-gray, trendy suit, his pale eyes gleaming as he adjusted his silver tie. He had upgraded, it seemed—eaten an executive on Hollywood Boulevard, maybe. With one hand, he opened the door. Music drifted in, along with muffled conversation and kitchen clatter. The assassin didn't need to be asked twice. Soft shoes squeaking, he fled.

"You'll never make it in time," he said to Trent as he slipped past Ku'Sox.

"Oh yeah?" I shouted as the door started to close. "You don't know nothing!"

Silence fell as the door clicked shut. Crap.

"As compared with you, who thinks she knows everything?" Ku'Sox said, smiling.

My thoughts flashed to him as an ugly stork, in his beak a pixy fighting for life even as the demented demon tossed his head to shift him headfirst down his throat. Stifling a shudder, I nudged Trent's bubble to get him to take it down, but he didn't, his face set in grim determination. No fear, though. Stupid man.

"Hey, hi, Ku'Sox," I said, mouth dry. "Uh, no hard feelings, okay? Al had you beat before I got there."

Instead of the expected threats, the demon nodded as if I'd answered a question. "I thought it was you Al had slipped into," he said, blue eyes slitted. "If it had been Newt, I might have been hurt. You are full of unexpected talents . . . Rachel. I can call you Rachel, can I not?"

He came in another step, and I backed up, hitting Trent's bubble and slipping backward when Trent took it down. There was a new caution in Ku'Sox, and that gave me hope, even as my palms started to sweat. *Damn it, Jenks, where are you?*

"I should have guessed," Ku'Sox said, sniffing as he took in his image in the mirror and his nose grew a shade narrower and his tan deepened. "Even Al knows better than to let Newt hold his energy field. She might have snuffed him for the fun of it." Blue eyes meeting mine, he frowned. "This alliance with Al doesn't bode well for your future. I will take drastic measures if you persist in it. It's all in the early training. I should know, having been . . . trained. Get us young enough, and we can do anything. Wait too long, and we never break our bad habits."

I took another step backward, teeth clenched. I was going the wrong way, but this guy scared the peas out of me. "I'm not being trained, and Trent's not in any danger," I said, proud of the way my voice didn't crack. "You can go now. He's safe."

I had held Al's energy field? I thought even as I looked for a way out of this. I'd assumed it had been the other way around, but maybe not.

"Go?" Ku'Sox shifted his shoulders, watching his reflection as his suit broadened and he became wider across the shoulders. The scent of carrion seemed to tickle my nose. "Going is an excellent idea. We shall start your rehabilitation right away."

"No, wait!" I said, my hands raised to fend him off, but it was too late and he wrapped an arm around my waist and tucked me under his arm. "Watch it!" I cried out when my head almost hit a urinal as he spun. I was still connected to a line, and I smacked him with it.

Ku'Sox trembled, shuddering in what could have been pain but what I was betting was pleasure. Maybe it was both. "More than adequate to get started," he said as he headed for the door. Trent stood at the sink, helpless as Ku'Sox picked me up like a kitten and walked away. Maybe he'd get it now. It only looked like I was safe around demons.

Fingers scrabbling for the edge of the stall, I managed to stop us for a half second. "Still think you can find a way to control this? Then tell him to stop," I said to Trent, then yelped when my fingers burned as Ku'Sox yanked me off the stall. My butt hit the door, and the music got loud as we left the men's room. Three steps later, Ku'Sox swung me up, putting me over his shoulder. I was helpless. If I threw anything at him, I'd get it back in spades.

"I won't let you jump me," I said, his shoulder cutting into my lungs and making it hard to breathe.

He slowed as we entered the restaurant, seeming to enjoy the music and high spirits. "To the ever-after? Why would I want to go there when we have the sun here?" he said, adjusting my weight to make my breath huff out. "There must be a boat somewhere in a sea of salt. I'm going to pick you apart, find out how much of a pain in the ass a natural-spawned demon is going to be to raise properly, or if I'd be better off destroying you all in the womb, so to speak."

Oh, that didn't sound good. "I'm not a demon," I said, jamming my elbow into his back, wondering if I grabbed a knife off a passing tray and hit his kidney hard enough, he might drop me. The blood was pooling in my head, hurting.

"I've tasted you," Ku'Sox said softly. "You're like me, only natural born. With a mother and a father."

Even over the noise, I could detect his jealousy. And why was no one saying anything? Maybe men toting women out of the back were normal here. I hit his back harder, and he tightened his grip.

"You might be strong enough to give me pain," he said, heading for the door. "You might not be. I want to know before more of you show up."

"Let me go, you freak!" I shouted, feet kicking as we started to pass tables, but everyone thought it was part of the show and only clapped. *Where is Trent? Washing his hands?*

"I'm not a freak," he hissed, pinching my middle until I gasped in pain.

Extending my arms to his back, I pushed myself up, looking wildly for Ivy. Jenks. Hell, even Vivian would be a help. Orienting myself, I sent my gaze to our table. "Pierce!" I shouted, and the man turned from where he'd been watching the two vamps in the corner. Beside him, Vivian's eyes widened. "A little help here, maybe?" Jeez, did I have to sing it for them?

Pierce stood, his face ashen. "Rachel!" he called, cutting through the music and catching everyone's attention. Without missing a beat, the band shifted to "Love Lifts Us Up Where We Belong" and the crowd exploded into cheers. I could understand their confusion. Ku'Sox looked like an especially attractive billionaire, rescuing his woman of the week from a lifetime of minimum wage.

Tight over my head came a clatter of pixy wings, and I looked up to get a face full of pixy dust. "Jenks, get Ivy!" I shouted between coughs, the image of a pixy and a bird flashing through my mind—terrifying me more than Ku'Sox carrying me away. My head dropped as I wiped my eyes, and I glimpsed Trent at the top of the kitchen corridor. Focus blurry, I felt more than saw Ivy at the front of the restaurant in a puddle of light by the register, hands on her hips and looking svelte and refreshed.

Finally I could see again, and I let out a little shriek, ducking when a black ball of ever-after arched toward us. Pierce. He'd thrown something.

It struck Ku'Sox right in the head, little pinpricks of his aura hitting me like sleet. Ku'Sox stumbled as if shocked, and I scrabbled for a grip as he began to fall. The curse flashed through Ku'Sox, jerking his muscles stiff, but then it was me screaming when the son of a bitch shoved Pierce's curse into me instead.

I howled as the arc of electricity jumped from neuron to neuron, burning. I caught a glimpse of Pierce, horrified, and then the pain was gone and I was panting, trying to breathe as I hung limp over Ku'Sox's shoulder.

"What are you doing?" Vivian shouted from a thousand years away.

"You think your white charms are going to do anything against that?" Pierce yelled back, and the band started to falter—except for the drummer, lost in the throes of his passion.

"Please don't do that again," I slurred, head hanging. Conversation hummed in my stunned ears, and I caught a few uneasy whispers. We passed another table, and I started to rally. It was up to Ivy. Magic wouldn't do it—it had to be physical.

"Thank you, God," I said as I heard her scream at him. The world spun, and I hit the floor, sprawling and hip bruised. I looked up to see Ivy and Ku'Sox in a tangle on a table. Shouts of protest rose high as glasses and plates hit the floor. My phone was humming, the buzz in my back pocket almost lost in the vertigo that was hitting me. Dizzy, I rolled to get out of the way. People were starting to scatter. We had to do this fast, or the freak would start eating people.

"Jenks!" I shouted, ducking under the table when a chair Ivy had thrown shattered near my elbow. "Get Trent out of here!" I shouted again, thinking that maybe if Trent was gone, the demon might be constrained to follow.

Jenks hesitated in midair, hovering between Ivy and me, clearly torn.

"Tell him to get the car!" I yelled, a little *ding* from my back pocket telling me whoever it was had left a voice message. "Bring it here!" The demon would follow him or not. Either way, we'd have a quick way out of here when the shit quit hitting the fan.

Leaving a burst of frustrated dust, Jenks darted from Ivy to me, his long hair swinging. His sharply angled face twisted up in indecision, but before he could say anything, Ivy yelled in pain. We both looked to see her slide across the floor on her back until slamming into the bottom of the stage. Blinking, she shook her head, trying to focus. The drummer finally stopped, and in the sudden hush, she slurred, "I'm okay. Get the freak of a demon."

That did it, and even as Ku'Sox dramatically turned, people surged to the doors in a panic. In seconds, the emergency door began screaming, and the people trying to get out of the jam-packed front surged to the rear. Ku'Sox seemed to be enjoying the chaos, raising his arms in benediction and soaking it all in as the fear rose and the noise grew louder.

I jumped when Jenks landed on my shoulder. Beside me was Trent, and I grabbed his arm and started dragging him to the kitchen. There had to be a back door. Vivian and Pierce could take care of themselves. My phone was ringing again, and I ignored it.

"Nice going, Trent," I said as I yanked us to a halt to avoid a panicked waitress, her eyes black in fear. "I had this under control until you called in Ku'Sox."

"Yeah, you stupid cookie maker," Jenks snarled, resting on my shoulder. "Quit trying to help, okay?"

"I didn't call him. He just showed up," Trent said indignantly, and I would have laughed but it sounded too familiar. "Why don't you just hit him with some magic?" he said, and I stopped in the hallway, just outside the kitchen doors. People were screaming, trying to get out, but no one was coming this way.

"What, and end up dead?" I said, not having a problem admitting that there were people stronger than me. "Ku'Sox almost killed Al," I said, my pointing arm dropping when I realized Ku'Sox was eying the frantic people as if mentally culling the herd. "I can't beat that! You freed a serial killer!"

Trent flinched, but I think it was from the explosion behind me more than from what I'd said. I spun to the wave of heat at my back, and by the familiar green tint to the fading aura, I'd guess that Ku'Sox had deflected one of Pierce's curses. A table was burning with a green flame, and the fire licking the nets was beginning to crawl along the ceiling. A drop of it fell to the floor, and I felt myself pale when someone collapsed with an ugly scream, writhing in pain and clutching his leg. In three seconds, the man was engulfed, creating a second panic as people trampled one another to get away.

Okay. Safety note. Don't step in the green fire.

"Pierce!" I shouted. The choking air smelling like burned limes. "You're hurting people!"

His long coat furling, he spun to me. My face went cold. There was no remorse in him, no softness. Only the demands of the fight. "He needs to die in flame!" Pierce shouted angrily. "Demons die in flame!"

True, but so do people.

I strengthened my hold on the ley line when Ku'Sox started for Ivy, but the shrill sound of the man burning pulled Ku'Sox's attention like a siren's song. He shifted his focus and started for the screaming man instead, flinging people aside if they didn't move fast enough. Standing before the writhing man, Ku'Sox hesitated for a blissful second, soaking in the sound of the alarm and the fleeing people as the man gurgled his last. The demon's eyes widened in anticipation, and he flushed before plunging his hands into the slumped, still-burning form. Ku'Sox shuddered in pleasure, his expression one of gleeful enthusiasm. Pulling back, his two-handed grip was holding something hazed with a soft glow. Holding it over his head, Ku'Sox squeezed his hands and a black, viscous substance oozed from his fingers to fall into his mouth. His soul? Was it the man's soul, burnt and burning?

"Holy crap," I whispered, scared to death. I looked across the restaurant to Pierce, seeing that he was as horrified as I was. Beside him, Vivian shook, utterly terrified—she had nothing to stop a soul-eating demon. I hadn't even known you could pull someone's soul out like that.

Both Vivian and I jumped when a rifle shot exploded through the sound of alarms and terrified people.

Only the ringing door alarm broke the sudden silence as everyone turned to the front where a huge bear of a man, a Were by the look of it, stood in a sifting of ceiling dust. There was a rifle as big as he was in his thick hands. "All right!" he said, and I nudged Trent to get the hell out of here. "The cops are coming. You just clear out, and we'll have no more trouble!"

It was a nice thought, but he clearly didn't know this wasn't your average brawl, supernatural or not. "Get the car!" I all but hissed at Trent, and finally the man started to drift back toward the kitchen. Under the ringing alarm, I could hear a woman crying. Ivy stood slowly, able to focus again apparently. She had a hand to the back of her head, and I hoped she was okay. I didn't dare move yet. Ku'Sox seemed to have forgotten me, and I was too chicken to remind him; maybe we could all just slink out of here real quiet like . . .

"Stay with Trent, Jenks," I said, unable to look away from Ku'Sox, and the pixy dropped to hover in front of me.

"Don't make me leave," he said, his fear obvious.

"What is that marvelous creation!" Ku'Sox exclaimed, looking across the restaurant at the rifle, and when he moved, people started for the door again. At least the alarm to the back door had gone quiet, and it was only people screaming this time.

My gaze flicked to Jenks, and I felt a stab of shared fear. "I don't trust Trent. We need the car. Do this for me." My palms were sweaty, and I wiped them on my jeans. "You've got my back, Jenks," I said as he hesitated in frustration. "Make sure Trent brings the car. I'm counting on you."

"Damn it back to the Turn," Jenks swore, looking both pissed and scared as he darted through the swinging kitchen doors to follow Trent. A silver sparkle dripped from his path, and I prayed Trent wouldn't cross us. Jenks would kill him.

Shaking, I turned back to the restaurant. Maybe I could salvage something.

"I don't want no trouble," the Were manager said as he cocked the rifle again.

Maybe not.

My shoulders slumped and I held my middle as I exchanged a look with Ivy across the tables, knowing what was going to happen next. We could do nothing but watch as Ku'Sox strode forward, his hand outstretched. The Were shook his head in warning, grimaced, lowered the weapon, pointed, and pulled the trigger. I jerked as the bullet exploded the wall behind the demon, people screaming as the splinters of wood and plaster went everywhere.

The manager's mouth opened, and Ku'Sox yanked the gun from him, not angry at all, but curious. "Please make it fast, God," I whispered. I couldn't stop this. *I couldn't stop it!*

"It works like this?" Ku'Sox said, turning the gun around and blowing a hole in the man's chest.

I couldn't tell if the noise or the color came first: the blood and tiny bits of bone coating the register in a speckled red wash of thunderous noise. People screamed, and the Were looked down at the hole in his chest in shock. Red bubbles frothed from his lips as he tried to speak. Then he dropped to his knees and fell forward into a puddle of his own broken insides.

It was ugly, and I leaned against the wall as the rising fear hit me along with the stench of gunpowder and hot metal. I wished this had never happened, that I'd never agreed to help Trent, that I'd never, *ever* gone to the library two years ago looking for a way to do whatever it was I'd been hoping to do.

I didn't even remember anymore. Whatever it was, it had been a mistake.

Shutting my eyes wasn't making it go away, though, and I opened them to find Pierce standing resolutely on a table, his moving fingers wreathed in blackness as his whispered Latin buzzed through my brain, an echo of his rising curse. I turned to the exits, seeing that everyone had gotten out but the few collapsed in fear. "Vivian!" I shouted, seeing her not panicking, but not knowing what to do, either. "Get them out of here!"

Thank God Jenks is gone. I don't want him to see what I do next.

"What a waste," Ku'Sox said as he looked at the rifle in his hands, then tossed it from him to clatter across a table. "It killed you far too quickly." Scanning the nearby tables, he found a woman in white, sobbing, curled into a ball and spending her five minutes in hell.

"You're still alive, though," he said, and the woman shrieked as he plucked her from under the table. "I'll eat you instead," he said, and the woman came to life as he held her up, ignoring her clawing hands as he pulled her closer, his jaw opening to fix on her throat.

It was like a demented kiss, and the woman had one breath to scream—a terrifying shriek of pain and fear—of shock at what was happening. And then he pulled her from him with a sudden jerk, his face bloody and a two-pound gap of flesh in the woman's neck. She still struggled though her head flopped at an impossible angle, bits of bloody froth spraying from her torn throat as she tried to scream, her lungs still working though her voice box was now inside Ku'Sox.

I wanted to turn away, but I couldn't. I wanted to run, to leave it for someone else to deal with, but I couldn't. It was me or no one.

"Oh my God," Vivian said, and I jumped when I realized she was next to me, clutching my arm. I swallowed my bile down before I emptied my stomach. "This is why I know how to do black magic," I whispered.

Vivian looked at me as Ku'Sox finally ate enough of the woman to kill her. Vivian's eyes were wide, her mind not yet having found a way to believe what her eyes were telling her.

"Even dead vamps remember pity," Ivy said, coming up on my other side.

"He-he . . . ," Vivian stammered, white faced and unable to say it.

"You think I know black magic for kicks?" I said harshly. "I'm trying to survive." I shoved the sight of a demon in a silver suit biting a woman's throat out to the back of my brain to wake me in a cold sweat later. *What can I do?* I thought as I found Pierce throwing up behind a table. Burn him? Like the curse I almost did in the garden? Could Pierce, Vivian, and I kill a demon together? My heart pounded, and I took a step forward, feeling Ivy's hand take my bicep. I doubted we could kill him, but it was all I had. Killing Ku'Sox wasn't murder, it was survival. And if it made me a black witch, then so be it.

My memory flicked back to Pierce crouched over Al and ready to end the demon's life for his freedom. Maybe there was no difference between us after all, and the reason I was mad at Pierce was because I was seeing reflections of myself in him, and I didn't like it.

Ku'Sox looked to the ceiling as a cascade of red-tinted everafter washed over him, rebounding at the outermost point of his aura and soaking back into him. Tucking the dead woman under his arm, he headed for the door. I could hear sirens out there, and my heart hammered. Black craft or not, I couldn't let him leave.

"Are we letting him go?" Pierce shouted, angry as he wiped his mouth and came out from behind the table.

I glanced at Ivy to tell her we weren't, then Vivian, who still didn't understand the reality of demons. "Yep," I lied, leaning back and crossing my arms over my chest and rocking back on one foot. "This is not my problem."

"What?" Vivian said, and I lifted a shoulder and let it fall. "You can't let him walk out of here! He just killed two people!"

she raged, her anger at her own naivete, her fear, and her disbelief finding an easy scapegoat in me.

I should have told her that this was all Trent's fault, but I held my tongue as Ivy slinked away to take up a defensive position. "What do you want me to do, Ms. Coven Member? You're telling me to do black magic? Huh? 'Cause that's the only thing that he's going to notice!"

She licked her lips, clearly at war with herself. Ku'Sox, though, was almost to the door.

"He'll notice this," Pierce said, and then, pulling on the line so heavily even Ku'Sox felt it, he threw a spell. Vivian gasped as it flew the distance, burning the very air as it passed. Ku'Sox spun, bouncing it back at us with a quickly instigated bubble.

"Down!" I shouted, and I dropped to the floor. The curse hit the stage, and the amp exploded, sending sparkles of ozone over us. "Damn it, Pierce! Watch what you're doing!"

"Mmmm," Ku'Sox said as he started back in our direction. "Curious accent to your spell work. Not at all like hers. Who taught you?"

"We can't stop him!" Vivian exclaimed.

"Duh," I said, trying to decide if Vivian was scared enough yet. If I could convince her that someone needed to know black magic, they might let me keep my mind when they shoved me back in Alcatraz. Sort of a plan B in case demons came visiting again.

Pierce jumped onto a table, shouting Latin, and seeing that he had Ku'Sox's attention, I pulled Ivy and Vivian to me. "I have an idea," I said, silently thanking God that Pierce was here—even if he was a black witch. I needed him. Al was right.

Vivian hesitated, but it was Ivy who said, "Like the fairies?"

I nodded, even as my heart seemed to clench. I was going to burn Ku'Sox—and I wasn't going to stop the curse. "Vivian, we need your help." Her face became more frightened, and I looked at Pierce, winding up and throwing another curse at

Ku'Sox. Okay, the man not only knew what he was doing, but he looked good doing it.

Pierce followed the first charm with a second, scoring on the demon when Ku'Sox didn't see the one hidden behind it. A black sticky something coated Ku'Sox, and the demon dropped the dead woman to claw his way out of the green aura covering him.

"A casting," I said, watching Pierce flick his hair back as he caught his breath. "We have to do a casting. I doubt it will kill him, but he might go somewhere else to lick his wounds. Pierce?"

His gaze never leaving the demon, Pierce raised his hand in acknowledgment.

My heart gave a hard pound. Ivy. She'd be safe, but she'd have to stay with me.

"That's—" Vivian began to say, starting to look aghast again, and I wondered what it was going to take to convince her.

"Casting isn't illegal," I interrupted her. "Just the curse. And I'll twist it, not you."

"Down!" Pierce yelled, and I dropped, yanking Vivian with me and snapping a protection circle over us. A red-tinted ball of death exploded behind us, and the smoke alarm started going off. Outside, I could hear sirens.

"We need a decision here!" Ivy said, looking shaken.

"I can't do a black curse!" Vivian babbled, the last of the professional young woman dropping away as she pushed her hair out of her eyes. "I'm coven!"

"Bloody hell paste!" Ku'Sox was shouting, still not altogether out of Pierce's last spell.

"All you need to do is hold the inner protection circle against all creation," Pierce said, his blue eyes sharp with an old anger at the reluctance of uptight women. "You don't need to sully yourself—we'll do that."

I dropped my bubble so Pierce could join us, and he took a symbolic step forward. He knew the spell I wanted to use. "My outer circle won't hold him long. Pierce, you'll have to be quick in the casting. If he breaks it, the curse will incinerate half of Vegas."

Ivy looked scared. "Get it right, witches."

"'Scuse me," Pierce said with a grunt, throwing another ball of goo at Ku'Sox.

This time, Ku'Sox absorbed it, the black mass dissolving in a cascade of sparkles. He had mastered the countercurse. We had to work fast. "I'm of a mind to see if you're as grand as you think you are," Pierce said to me, and I smirked back.

"Same here," I said, exhilarated even as I was scared to death. "Okay! Let's do this!"

"Look out!" Vivian shouted, and I jerked as Ku'Sox backhanded Pierce into Ivy. They slid across the floor in a tangle of arms and legs, the spell that Pierce had begun fizzling in a sparkle of green and red. Crap! When had he gotten that close?

"Hey!" I shouted as Ku'Sox wrapped an arm around my neck and started dragging me away. I struggled, trying to break his hold as he headed for the door. Shit, shit, shit! I could still make the outer protection circle, but I wasn't ready to sacrifice myself to get rid of Ku'Sox. But then I remembered him tearing that woman's throat out and her silent screams as she tried to breathe. Burning would be better than that. I think.

"You have the nicest hair," Ku'Sox said as he yanked me up and I felt him touch behind my ear. I stiffened when he ran his nose down my neck, and my breath sucked in as he found the vamp toxins sunk deep in my tissues. "Ohhh, you're flawed," he murmured. "How delightful."

"Oh shit," I whispered, scrambling for anything to slow us down.

"Shit," Ku'Sox said speculatively, and he loosened his grip until my heels dragged on the floor again. "I've heard that several times now. Is that the word of choice? I do so like all-encompassing words. Verb, adjective, noun. Yes, you are shitted."

My heels thumped as he dragged me backward. "You'd better let me go!" I cried, reaching out to grab a post. Ku'Sox yanked me off it, pulling me another foot until I snagged a table. I wouldn't let go, and the added weight slowed him down even more. We were almost to the door, and I could hear radio chatter and yelling people in the street.

"You know why my brethren didn't kill me?" Ku'Sox said as the table I was dragging hit a post and we stopped. "They couldn't. Even Newt, and she tried. They made me special, the wonder child of the future, now our ignoble past, designed to bridge the gap between demons and witches and bring us back into the sun, able to walk in reality and the ever-after both, and all of us capable of holding as much energy as a female." He hesitated, yanking me until my grip slipped and we moved forward again. "You can understand why male demons might want to fix that unfair quirk of nature. I think I turned out quite nicely, don't you?"

"You don't look special to me," I panted, seeing Pierce horrified and afraid to do anything. He was next to Vivian, and Ivy was at their feet. *I have to get back to them.*

"But I am," Ku'Sox snarled, sounding almost unhappy. "You know why Newt killed her sisters? I told her to. Newt I could control, but the others? They were a danger and had to be killed. Females can hold more energy than males. They have to in order to hold a second independent field of energy inside them without absorbing it."

That was interesting, and my thoughts went back to what Ku'Sox had said earlier about my holding Al's energy, supplementing it. Had I been able to do it because I was female?

"Two souls in one body," Ku'Sox said, shifting his hold on me and smacking my hand until it went numb. My grip slipped away, and he started forward again. "Two energy fields bound by one aura without the smaller being crushed or absorbed. That's where babies come from, Rachel, not cabbage leaves. And once I got Newt to kill all her sisters, there was no one left to tell me no, especially when all I needed to do was slide into reality to escape. And then I find you. Natural born. Unknown possibilities. Stronger? Weaker? Let's find out."

Crap, we were almost to the door. "I'm all for finding out who's stronger," I said, and then I reached for the line I'd never fully released, demanding all that Vegas could give me.

Energy raced in, hot and electric, tasting of dust, sand, and lightning that beat on the desert floor, the power of the sun kept clean and unblemished, the sands storing it like a battery.

I pushed it out through my pores, teeth gritted. It didn't hurt, but it burned like fire.

Howling, Ku'Sox flung me from him.

I arched through the air, grunting when I hit a table. I slid to the floor, hurting. Damn, it felt like my back was broken. "You're right," I slurred as I felt Ivy's hands reach under my armpits and drag me back to Vivian and Pierce. "I can hold more than you."

When I could focus again, I looked up to see Vivian, fear on her face for what she was about to do. Pierce took my hand, and I dampened the energy flowing through me so I wouldn't fry them. Vivian took my other, and when Pierce grasped her free fingers, completing our circle, I took a deep breath, feeling the alien-ness of them with me.

"Fire in the hold," I whispered, opening my mind and gathering both Pierce and Vivian into my thoughts, now realizing that I could, like a mother with twins. It was akin to sharing a spell, as we had done in my garden, but there would be no will but my own here. For an instant, their souls were mine—my strength was lent to them, and they didn't know the difference, didn't know that I directed them. Mine.

Vivian's bubble snapped up around us, coated with my smut. I felt Pierce's aura shift, melting with Vivian's so his magic could pass through her bubble. My outer circle was next, encompassing most of the restaurant's front room and a slice of the unseen back alley.

Ku'Sox ran for us, his clawed hand looking like a bird's foot as he screamed and tried to break it, but Vivian's will was supplemented by mine, and he couldn't.

"Celero inanio!" The words ripped from Pierce's throat, pushed by my will and his fear. I could feel Vivian's despair and shame, but fear for her life burned in her. I felt Pierce's pride, then wallowed in his shock when he realized I was holding him, holding them both.

In slow motion, I felt the lava ribbons of the curse snake out from Vivian's bubble, moving like lightning as the energy darted to the edges of my containment bubble, snaking up the sides and running to the peak above us. As one, the six ribbons struck the apex. A flash of energy exploded from it, crisping everything in a burst of heat.

"I pay the price," I whispered, gathering the rising smut to me as if it were a blanket. The black curse was mine. I deserved the price.

Pierce's head was down, and Vivian was staring upward in amazement as more power than she knew existed spun through her. It wasn't that the dark side was stronger, but that *everything* was the dark side. All magic was inherently wrong, and it was only us fooling ourselves that some of it was good, some of it was bad. Magic . . . just was.

And so it was only I who saw Ku'Sox's face go white in the realization that I might be as strong as Newt, but not insane and therefore not easily twisted. The cloud of burning molecules drifted to him in slow motion, sparking from one to the next as fast as an electron can spin—and in a bare second before the air in his lungs turned to flame, he vanished, snarling in anger.

He was gone, and the air burned—empty of his flesh.

I closed my eyes, and the sound of glass breaking sliced through my disappointment. We had missed. Damn it, we had missed.

"God forgive us," Vivian whispered.

The curse felt me weaken, and it broke upon itself, flashing upward and turning into real flame. With a snap, both my and Vivian's bubbles collapsed. Hands pulled from mine in haste, and I dropped to my knees. Ivy caught me—her hands gentle with compassion, tender with hesitation.

I opened my eyes to find that the sound of breaking glass had been the lights. We were in the dark, lit only by real, honest fire, dancing at the ceiling. It grew even as I watched, the light becoming brighter, more dangerous. "The ceiling is on fire," I whispered. "We should go."

Disappointment made me slow, and Ivy helped me to my feet as the smoke detectors continued to scream and the water system clicked on. Ivy and I searched each other's expression in the dim glow of the flames, the water mixing with her tears, shining in the come-and-go light from the fire. She knew by my expression that he'd gotten away, and yet she thought nothing less of me, either, for failing to kill him or because I'd tried in the first place. *Evil witch, black demon.*

"Let me help you," she said, and I nodded, thinking she was beautiful inside.

"We-we . . . ," Vivian stammered, clearly in shock as the water misted down.

Pierce started for the kitchen, turning when he realized no one was following him. "Time to pull foot," he said, yanking Vivian, not me.

"We . . . ," she tried again, slipping, but at least we were moving. The floor was charred, slick under my steps, unseen in the dark. The air was heavy, a weird mix of heat and moisture. I glanced toward the front, glad I couldn't see the smoldering bodies of the people dead and left behind. I could smell them, though, and see the little puddles of wax burning on the tables still left standing.

"Kitchen," I said, leaning heavily on Ivy, weary. Cops and firemen weren't coming in, which meant they were going to count the building as a loss. As soon as the right people arrived, they were going to circle the place and let it burn. We should probably get out before then.

We hit the kitchen at a staggering run, Ivy grabbing a take-out bag in passing once we got past the arc of my circle that had contained the curse. I wasn't sure if she was supporting me or if I was supporting her when we hit the kitchen's service doors and a slice of harsh mercury lamplight from outside spilled in. My head came up as the air changed. It was still hot but now it had the stink of garbage. Ivy was first out, looking at Trent, waiting beside my mother's car, before taking the three-foot jump to the lower pavement and looking up at me.

Vivian sat down to slide off, leaving a long, wet mark glistening in the streetlight. Pierce hesitated only briefly before he jumped, hitting the ground in a soggy splat. Ivy's hand was extended for me, and I took it, still shaky. Ku'Sox had left, sure, but now he knew I was a threat.

"We got the devil," Pierce said, clearly in a good mood as we all limped for the car, just twenty feet ahead. It was running. Maybe Trent had learned something after all.

"You think Ku'Sox is dead?" I said as I stumbled beside Pierce. "I didn't see a body in there. Did you see a body? Anyone see a body? I sure as hell didn't!"

Pierce jerked to a stop, and Ivy left me with one hand on the car for support as she got in and slid to the driver's seat, water dripping from her. Vivian dived into the back, yelling at us to get in.

"No one could survive that!" Pierce said, water flinging from him as he pointed at the burning building. I jumped when the city's fire codes clicked into play, and the building-wide circle snapped into place to contain the fire. Thank God we were out of it. We had only moments before someone would come back here and find us. They might have been waiting for us to get out. *Maybe.*

"If killing that *freak* was that easy, don't you think that the demons would have done it?" I said, feeling Ivy's eyes on me. "He's still alive," I said as I slowly got in the car, numb.

He was alive, but I might know how to kill him now, and I dropped my eyes, ashamed to even be thinking it. It was said that Newt had killed her lovers by running a line through them. Obviously I could do the same. Otherwise why had Ku'Sox convinced Newt to kill the female demons that the elves had missed?

I looked at my hands, trying to see them shaking in the dim light. I had to talk to Newt. Great. Just friggin' great. Maybe she'd think I was a demon and decide to kill me, too.

"Pierce, get in the car!" Ivy shouted from behind the wheel, and he shoved me to the middle as he got in, the car shaking as he slammed the door.

A cop car's light played over our car, and swearing, Trent ducked. Ivy gunned it, bouncing my mom's car's fender off the bubble containing the fire as she spun in a tight circle. Pierce gaped behind us as Ivy drove like the devil himself was after us, jumping curbs and driving over the bare ground. Vivian and Trent cried out in protest from the back. There was a final, jolting thump, then the road smoothed as Ivy found the way to the interstate. No one followed.

I closed my eyes, enjoying the smell of excited vampire on my left and the rich tang of witch on my right. The lights of oncoming traffic glowed through my eyelids, and I opened them when my phone started to hum. Jenks's wings were a beautiful web of silk and diamonds as he held on to the rearview mirror's stem, watching our back. Always watching our back.

"Everyone here?" I needlessly asked, my fingers shaking as I flipped open my phone to see that it was Bis. The last two calls were from him as well. He had to be feeling me pull heavily on the lines. He was waking up in the day, too. Maybe he *was* older than I thought.

Jenks's wings hummed to life, turning as gray as my soul as they deflected the light, their beauty lost. "Yeah, everyone's here," he said, clearly not believing they were just going to let us drive away.

I hesitated briefly before letting Bis's call go to voice mail and tucking the phone away. I couldn't talk to him right now.

Vivian was sobbing in the back, trying not to be obvious about it. I thought it callous of Trent not to give her any comfort, but if she was anything like me, his show of compassion would only get his face bitten off and he probably knew it.

The hum of the engine grew steady, never varying as we sped north on 95. I flexed my hand, trying to see it in the faint green glow from the dash. The memory of how much energy I'd channeled into Ku'Sox had left my body unmarked, but it had shaken me. It had been enough to fry anyone else to a cinder.

My fist closed, and I saw Ivy look from it back to the road. Her eyes were worried. Taking a breath, she pushed her wet hair back, steadying herself for whatever I might do next. She looked too young, too beautiful, too perfect to put up with my crap, and when I touched her hand, she jumped.

We'd gotten away, but my heart was like ash, as black as the coating on my soul. Vivian had seen the depth of it, taken part in it. Maybe she'd leave this part of the trip out of her report.

"Hey," Jenks said, his thoughts clearly on the same path as mine, "is it true what they say about Vegas?"

"No," Vivian said, and I caught sight of her red-rimmed eyes in the rearview mirror when the lights of a passing car lit up her misery. "I'm telling them. I'm telling them everything."

Trent shifted uncomfortably, and Jenks took a breath, a darkly glowing dust spilling from him. I calmed him with a soft nod. I wanted them to know. It might be the only thing that was going to keep my body and soul on this side of the lines. That and maybe Trent's testimony that I was a good person. I was in trouble if they ever found out Ku'Sox was his demon.

"Double jeopardy," Trent whispered. "It's double jeopardy." His eyes met mine when I turned to him. "It always has been."

Fifteen

It was the changing sound of the engine that woke me, but the car's motion never shifted, so I snuggled deeper under my coat and leaned more heavily against the door. A bleary glance at the clock told me we'd been on 80 only for about an hour, and therefore were probably coming into Reno. Four hours of driving a hundred plus in the dark had been more than a little unsettling, but we'd made great time.

Trent was driving again, had been since getting off 95. He could keep the job for all I cared—even if he bitched incessantly until we cut our bathroom and coffee breaks down to almost nothing. The road between Las Vegas and 80 had been nerve-racking, even though we hadn't seen anyone. There'd been lights. In the air. Lots of them. And they'd kept pace with us no matter how fast Ivy had gone. Trent and Jenks had slept through it all.

Three eighteen, I mused as the clock changed, and I resettled myself against the door, still achy from hitting the floor, wall, table, and whatever else Ku'Sox had thrown me into. The mercury light of a truck stop flashed over me, then another. I slowed my breathing, trying to seduce sleep back to me. If this was almost Reno, then San Francisco was only about 240 miles away. A spike of adrenaline lit and died. Tomorrow. It would all start tomorrow.

"She'll get you there in time," Jenks said, his soft voice

paced a shade slower than usual, and carrying a hint of both irritation and the altitude sickness he was dealing with. I'd offered him the charm to make him big, and he'd refused, saying the car was crowded enough.

"You keep saying that," Trent said just as softly. I'd never have heard them if I hadn't been in the front seat.

"Well, you keep pushing the pedal to the floor," Jenks shot back, his voice putting him in the ashtray, not the rearview mirror. "You should trust her. She had every right to dump you on the side of the road for freeing Ku'Sox, and she didn't. That must have been some conversation you had in the john, because if it had been me, your ass would be under the grass right now."

Sleep vanished, but I didn't move. Jenks would know I was awake because of my "aura brightening" or some such crap, but Trent wouldn't, and I worked to maintain my slow, sedate breathing. Vivian, too, must be asleep or Jenks would never have brought up the demon.

"You don't know when you got it good, elf boy."

It had been a soft mutter, but I knew Trent heard, as there was a creak of plastic and the vent started blowing cold air. "I have my reasons," Trent said.

"You have trust issues is what you have," Jenks said. "And turn the air off. What are you, a friggin' penguin?"

"You don't know half of what's going on."

You got that right, I thought as the air turned warm again. My nose was tickling from a thread on my coat, but I didn't move, hoping Trent would say more. He might. Jenks and Trent had been spending a lot of time together while the rest of us slept, and Jenks liked to talk. Especially when he was cranky. Anything over 2,500 feet above sea level and he had a hard time flying. Hit 3,000 feet and he was down.

"Well?" Jenks said sarcastically, almost daring him.

A small sound of mistrust slipped from Trent. "You'd tell her."

"So?"

"So I don't want her sympathy."

Sympathy? I cracked my eyes open enough to see a faint haze of pixy dust in the ashtray, glowing in the predawn gloom. "Come on, Trent," Jenks wheedled as he shoved the doughnut napkin off himself and sat up. "What is so damn important in Seattle? Maybe I can help."

Again came Trent's huff of disbelief. "You talk too much."

Indignant, Jenks flashed his wings. Making a wobbling flight to the dash, he stood with his hands on his knees, bent over and wheezing. "I helped Quen lift your paperwork from the FIB," he said between breaths. "I never said anything. I can help. It's allowed. I checked. If you're really on an elf quest, you're allowed a pixy. Pixies helped elves on quests all the time."

Elf quest, I thought. It sounded so . . . undignified, like an overdone renaissance fair show, and I stifled a smile imagining Trent in costume riding through his woods to rescue the imprisoned princess. *Crap, is he going to come back to Cincy with Ellasbeth?*

"I'm breaking into a high-security location, not riding across the countryside on some fairy-tale adventure," Trent said tightly, his thoughts clearly akin to my own.

"So you're in a borrowed Buick instead of on a mighty steed, and your pixy sidekick can short out security systems instead of spot orcs. It's the times, Trent. Roll with it."

Jenks was laughing at him, and though I couldn't see Trent, I could imagine his tight mouth and red ears when he grumped, "It's not like that."

"It looks like it to me," Jenks said. "Even got your band of ragtag misfits."

In the seat behind me, Ivy shifted. For a moment, neither one said anything.

"What are you doing?" Jenks whispered. "Scrambling the Withons' tax returns?"

I let out my held breath, almost missing Trent's soft, "I'm claiming something. Ellasbeth has it. It's mine."

He wasn't after Ellasbeth then. Thank God. And why did Trent have to prove himself? Old traditions? Apart from going into the ever-after for that elf DNA sample, he'd been coasting on his father's legacy. Was this some way to prove to the remaining elves that he could lead them? As if the cure for the demon curse wasn't enough?

"I can help," Jenks said. "Tell me what you're doing."

The car drifted to the right, avoiding traffic by the sound of it. Reno must be close. "Why do you want to help me?" Trent asked as he settled into a new lane. "You don't owe me anything. I've given Rachel nothing but trouble."

"True," Jenks admitted. "But working with Quen got me a church and security for my family," he added, and I slitted my eyes to see him sitting on the dash in front of the wheel, his wings almost blue with cold and altitude. "But mostly it's because if you get caught, Rachel won't have you to speak for her at the coven meeting."

There was that . . .

"That's not enough to risk your life for me. I want to know why," Trent insisted.

Jenks's wings hummed, and I lifted an eyelid a bit. Through the windshield, gray buildings passed in the gloom. "Where are you going?" Jenks asked, his tone one of mistrust as the turn signal clicked on again. We were changing lanes, the buildings seeming to tilt as the car moved.

"Seattle."

I bolted upright, stiff muscles complaining. "Hey! We're going to San Francisco!"

Trent jumped, clearly shocked. But the car was in an exit-only lane. "H-how long . . . ," he stammered, but I was more concerned about the SEATTLE-395 THIS EXIT sign that flashed past.

"We are *going* to *San Francisco*!" I hissed, not caring if I woke everyone up. "Get the car back on the interstate!"

Trent stared. "How long have you been listening to us?"

My teeth clenched seeing the broken white line turn solid. "So help me, Trent, if you don't get back on the interstate, I'm going to, to . . . hate you forever!"

Jenks's wings hummed as he laughed. "I'd get your ass back on the interstate, cookie maker. You wouldn't like it if Rachel hated you forever."

"I don't have time to stop in San Francisco," he said stiffly. "Two hundred miles might be the difference between my making my appointment or not."

My side hurt, and holding it, I stared at him. "I'll get you there."

"I don't see how!"

"I'll get you there!" I exclaimed. Oh God, the triangle of gravelly pavement was getting bigger. "Trent, trust me. Just trust me. You *asked* me to trust you!"

I could see the frustration in the set of his jaw. On the dash, Jenks waited, tense and not a slip of dust escaping from him. *Trust me. If he didn't, then why should I trust him?*

In a moment, there would be a metal barrier between 395 and 80—and an even larger one between Trent and me.

Trent's face became ugly, and with a growled curse, he yanked the wheel to the left.

"Hey!" Ivy exclaimed from the backseat as the car swerved violently.

My heart was beating fast, and I pulled my hand from the dash. Jenks had made it to the rearview mirror, and he was grinning.

"Are we there yet?" came Vivian's sleepy voice, and I glanced back to see her with a really bad case of pillow hair.

"No, go back to sleep," I said, noticing that Pierce had never even woken up, pressed into the corner behind Trent and huddled under his long coat.

I settled back, pulling my own coat up in the chill Trent kept the car in. His face was set in a determined, angry expression. We were back on 80 and headed to the coven meeting, but he wasn't happy. He'd said he trusted me, but his body language said otherwise.

"I'm not going to make it," he said, and I smiled when the

SAN FRANCISCO—217 MILES sign flashed over us. He was going to make it. And even better, I was, too.

"Thank you, Trent," I said, my headache easing a little.

"I'm not going to make it," he said again, sounding more lost now than angry.

It wasn't like I could pretend to be asleep anymore, so I reached for the bag of sugar and carbs we'd gotten in another state and rummaged around until I found a squished brownie. *Who in the Turn is buying the Milk Duds?*

"You'll make it," I said as I tore the cellophane open and the scent of enriched flour and chocolate hit me. I took a bite: the chocolate had too much wax and the peanut chunks tasted stale, but it was sugar. Leaning forward, I handed Jenks a chunk as big as his head. "Soon as I check in with the coven, I'll have Al pop you up there," I said around my full mouth. "QED."

The noise that came out of Trent was sort of a strangled cough of outrage caught in a steel trap of fury. I turned from Jenks, who was saluting me with his brownie, to Trent, now staring at me. "Want any of this?" I asked, holding my brownie higher in explanation.

"You could have jumped me there at any time?" Trent said hotly.

"Yeah," Jenks said, voice muffled from the brownie. "You just click your heels and think there's no place like being pwned."

Trent clenched his jaw and corrected for the truck we were barreling toward. "Rachel," he said, that one word holding an entire argument. He was pissed, his grip tight on the wheel. Our speed, too, had gone up by about fifteen miles per hour.

"No, I can't do it at any time I want," I said with a huge grin, lips closed so I didn't look like a goober with brownie in my teeth. "The magic doesn't work until you learn a life lesson," I teased. "Wasn't it fun, though? Only two hundred miles left. We can do that on our heads! Unless it violates your elf quest?

I mean, if I'm your sword, your shield, and your mirror, then it's fair if I'm the one who gets you there, right?"

There was a snuffle from the back. Clearly Ivy was still awake, but I think that had slipped Trent's notice. "Two thousand miles, Rachel," he said tightly, and I guessed that no, it didn't violate the rules of whatever he was doing out here, because he sure wasn't out here keeping the coven from attacking me. "I have eaten nothing but slop for two days and used facilities I wouldn't let my dogs urinate in. And what about that couple in the RV outside Texas? I'll never get that memory out of my head."

I nodded, working the brownie out of my teeth. "I could've done without that visual myself."

"I could have done without the entire trip," Trent grumbled, but his anger was slowing as he realized he was going to be in Seattle in a matter of hours.

I tucked my foot under me and turned to him. "You want me to work with you, right?" I said as I crumpled up the cellophane and tossed it into the bag. "Consider the trip your interview."

Jenks choked on his brownie, looking at me as if I'd lost my mind, red faced as he alternated his attention between me and someone in the back, probably Ivy. I shifted my lips in a soft grimace at the pixy. What was I going to do here, realistically? Either I cozied up really close to Trent to get him to say the right things at the meeting in two days, or I wound up first in Alcatraz, then the ever-after when I admitted I'd lost my bet with Al and fled to his protection. Some choice, but really, Trent was the better of the two. Even if he had let Ku'Sox out of his box. Stupid elf.

Trent made a huff of noise. "You were interviewing me. *You*. Interviewing *me*?"

I stifled a shiver. "Maybe." I could feel Ivy staring at the back of my head. It almost hurt.

His lips turning up, Trent smiled at the road, his expression becoming one of confidence and satisfaction. Not surprised, I collapsed in on myself and rolled my eyes. He was going to milk this forever. "So you're saying you might work with me?" he asked, apparently needing to hear it. The tone of the engine dropped, and for the first time since leaving Las Vegas, the speedometer dropped into double digits. "How did I do?" Trent asked, a smile in his voice. "On my *interview*?"

Damn it, he was laughing at me, but a knot had loosened in my gut. I might work with him. I'd said it—admitted it to myself. I wasn't going to sign his paper—become his witch—but a job . . . I might do a job. I was going to need something while I earned the trust of Cincinnati back and the work trickled in. "You're not much of a team player," I said as I scraped the last of the sticky cake off my fingertips with a napkin so stiff it was nearly useless. "Inclined to take on too much and not let other team members know what you're doing, which causes problems that could easily have been avoided."

Trent's entire demeanor had changed. Relaxed, he let one hand fall to his lap and drove with the other. It just about pegged my attraction meter, but I frowned when he said, "Sounds like you."

"But on the whole, a good risk," I added sourly. "If the benefits were there. And I felt like it." *And I can't make rent.*

Jenks dropped down to his ashtray, burying himself under a tissue and a doughnut napkin. "All this good feeling is making me sick," he said, hidden away. We had the mountains to get through. It was going to be a rough couple of hours.

"I can't believe you let me sweat over this. Rachel, I ate fast food," Trent complained.

"And tomatoes in public," I said, remembering the soup. "It felt good, didn't it? Not hiding what you are?"

A slow smile came over him, hard to see in the dim light. "It did," he said so softly I might have missed it if I hadn't known it was coming.

"And you got to see the Petrified Forest," I added.

From the ashtray came Jenks's voice saying, "And pixies being eaten alive."

"Totally his fault," I said, and Jenks poked his head out, not looking that good. "And you got a vacation," I offered, my own mood brightening. It had been a long, tiring run out here, and I'd be glad to see it done.

Jenks laughed, sounding like wind chimes in the snow. "Vacation. The Tink-blasted arch fell on him."

"Again, his own fault," I said, blinking innocently at Trent. "Gee, Trent. Maybe we should have left you at home after all."

Trent said nothing, his gaze fixed on the road stretching out before us, and I fiddled with the heat until it blasted out to warm Jenks. "I think you enjoyed this," I said, and Trent looked askance at me, appearing charmingly irate. "You had the chance to see what it was like to be in a family," I added, and his eye stopped twitching.

"And to answer your question, yes, it was exactly like being in a family," I said as I leaned to dig out one of Ivy's bottled waters from the bag at my feet. I'd rather have had a coffee, but I knew he wouldn't stop. "And really, I couldn't just pop you there whenever I felt like it," I said as I opened it. "Al owes me big. He wouldn't have done it before."

Silent, Trent shifted in his seat as he angled the vents away from himself. Sighing, I looked in the back at Vivian, slumped between my vampire roommate and my black-magic-using, shunned, demon-familiar beau whom I didn't trust.

All the black magic that I'd done in front of Vivian—asked her to help with; maybe now that she'd seen what they faced if they ignored the coming problem with the demons, they might think more kindly of me. Maybe having Ku'Sox attack us would help my case. Would they really try to kill me if there were worse uglies out there, uglies they couldn't handle? People had died in the last few days, but not because of my magic, and more would have died if I had feigned ignorance and let Ku'Sox do whatever the hell he wanted.

"You sure you know what you're doing, Trent?" I whispered, hoping he knew I was talking about Ku'Sox, and his fingers stiffened slightly. "I won't say it's not like you, because using dangerous things like they're flash paper has you written all over it, but do you have any idea what you've done?"

Jenks was basking in the new warmth, but his eyes flicked from mine to Trent.

"Is it Ceri?" I guessed. "Are you trying to impress her? Be the elf she thinks you should be?"

Lips twitching, Trent ran a hand over his head to get his vent-blown hair to lay flat. It was one of his tells, and he caught himself, lowering his hand to grip the wheel. "I have my reasons," he said simply.

"Yeah, because you don't trust me to keep you alive." I set the bottle in the cup holder and put my boots on the dash, knees bent as I tried to find a comfortable position.

"Trust has nothing to do with it," Trent said as he glanced at my boots, and Jenks made a rude noise. "I trust you, Rachel. I never would have left Cincinnati if I didn't. I trust you, though you're quick tempered and jump to conclusions too fast. God knows why."

My brow smoothed out, and I took my feet down. "Really?"

He gave me a sidelong glance. "It's important to you, isn't it?"

I looked out at the world starting to go from black to gray. "Yes, it is. No one likes to be given a compliment, then find out it's fake."

A small noise came from Trent, and he frowned. "I never thought of it like that. Sorry."

"Tink's a Disney whore," Jenks swore from the ashtray. "Did he just say he was sorry?"

Trent glanced at him in irritation, but I was grinning. "Shhhh, don't ruin the moment, Jenks," I said. "It might never come again."

Trent chuckled, his good mood returning. I could fix that, though, and after a moment, I asked again, very softly, "So why did you do it?" *You little goober,* I added in my head.

Eyes on the mountains, he was silent. "I didn't do it because I didn't trust you. I did it because he's part of my . . . quest," he finally said, clearly embarrassed.

"Oh my God!" Jenks exclaimed. "Take me with you, Trent. I've never been on an elf quest before! Ple-e-e-e-ase?"

"Quiet, Jenks," I murmured, not wanting Trent to stop talking, then turned to Trent. "So you've got a way to take care of what you, um, started, right? When it's over?"

"I won't know until I finish it," Trent said. Looking at me in snatches, he shrugged. "I never intended all this to happen."

I turned away, having a hard time getting mad at him. I was too tired. "Welcome to my world," I said, thinking I'd done some pretty stupid things in my day, too.

"I've got a way to take care of things," Trent insisted, but I doubted it. And his usual tells weren't telling me anything. My gaze dropped to Jenks, and he shrugged, at a loss as well. Jenks's going with him was looking better to me. I wanted to know what Trent was doing that was so risky he needed a demon to help him. God, what was wrong with us?

Still . . .

I looked inquiringly at Jenks, twitching my fingers in the pixy signal that meant scout, and he nodded. Maybe that had been Jenks's intention all along. Sitting up, I looked over the seat at Ivy, lurking under a blanket. She was awake, her eyes black in the dim light. She grimaced, rolling her eyes at Trent and nodding as well. It was unanimous, then.

"I think you should take Jenks with you," I said as I turned back around.

His grip tightened on the wheel. "No."

"No-o-o-o?" Jenks whined. "Hey, if it's about the altitude sickness, Seattle is lower than Cincy. I'll be fine."

I exhaled loudly, gathering my strength. "Jenks is right. If you're allowed a pixy on an elf quest, you should take one."

"I'm *not* having this conversation," Trent said, and Jenks's wings hummed.

My eyes narrowed, and I turned the heat up even more. "Trent, you are a stiff-necked, overbearing, cold—"

"I'm not cold."

"—impersonal son of a bitch. Try making a decision by

looking at something other than logic. You might have more friends that way."

Jenks's mouth shut, and he looked surprised. Trent, too, seemed taken aback. "Just because I don't wear my heart on my sleeve—"

"You don't even wear your heart in your chest," I interrupted. "But one thing you aren't is stupid." I flung a hand in the air, exasperated with him and not even knowing why I was trying to help. He'd given me nothing but grief. And a chance to save myself.

"I don't know what you're doing," I said. "Frankly, I don't care as long as you don't land your butt in jail when I need you standing up for me at the coven meeting. So just consider this me being selfish, asking you to let Jenks help you. Do me a favor, huh?"

Jenks's wings shifted, and Trent stared out at nothing as we drove into the dark.

"Or are you so proud that you can't accept a sidekick?"

Trent looked at Jenks. "He's not a sidekick," he said, and I blinked. *A compliment?*

"Awww, I think I'm going to fart fairy dust," Jenks said, clearly pleased as he managed to make the flight to the rearview mirror now that he was warm again.

From the back, Ivy piped up, "Take him. It will save me from pounding you when you don't show up by midnight tomorrow."

Trent jerked his head to glance at her. "You're awake, too?"

Vivian stretched, yawning. "I think you should take him," the coven member said. "You can't be expected to work alone. No one but a fool works alone."

Trent cleared his throat dryly, and I exchanged a worried look with him, hoping she hadn't pieced together that the "thing" we'd been talking about was Ku'Sox. "How about you, Pierce?" I said, trying to distract her. "You want to weigh in on this decision?"

"Aye," he said, the lump he made not moving. "I'm of a mind you should do it alone."

Surprised, I turned to look at Pierce as he sat up, his mood surly.

"But only so that devil of a demon doesn't eat Jenks," he added. "I wouldn't give a horse apple for the son of a Kalamack, but Jenks is a fine warrior, and I'd be sad to see him make a die of it for whatever foolish quest you're on."

Oooooh, strike one.

Not a twitch, not a single movement gave away Trent's thoughts. He wasn't going to go for it, and whatever idiotic thing he was about to do in Seattle was going to bitch-slap me with no advance warning, probably at the least opportune time. I glanced at Jenks.

Jenks shrugged, the slight rise of his shoulders almost unnoticed with the thin glow of pixy dust sifting from him. "Face it, you little cookie maker," Jenks said, almost sounding fond, "in the last couple of days, you've seen what it's like to be in a family, with all the touchy tempers and irritation that goes on. Now you get to see the other side, where we do stupid stuff for each other just because we like you. Rache is the little sister. Ivy's the big sister. I'm the uncle from out of state, and you're the rich nephew no one likes but we put up with you anyway because we feel sorry for you. Just let me help, huh? It won't kill you."

I'm the little sister? I thought, looking back at Ivy for her opinion, finding her smiling a soft, closed-lips smile.

Silent—thinking, I hope—Trent drove, not really seeing the road as we barreled into the mountains. "Fine," he eventually said, to make Jenks explode with a burst of pixy dust. "But I'm not telling you what I'm doing until we get there."

"Okay. Okay," Jenks said, making a swooping flight to his shoulder. Both Trent and I stiffened, but Jenks was oblivious. "Tell me when we get there. I can adapt. Damn! Rache, this is going to be fun!"

"Yeah, fun," I said, giving Trent a sharp look. If Jenks didn't come back, I would be all over Trent like a pissed . . . demon. "No airplanes on the way home," I added, and Trent nodded carefully, so as not to unbalance Jenks.

"No airplanes," Trent said.

"And keep him warm. He likes it warm."

"God, Rache. Shut up!" Jenks said, sitting down, looking right on Trent's shoulder. "I'll be fine. We're probably just going to steal his grandmother's ring back."

Somehow, as I settled back into the leather, I doubted that, and I couldn't help but wonder if I'd just saved or damned my ass.

Sixteen

The sun was almost up, and I stretched beside the car in the brightening, predawn damp, feeling all the bruises that I'd gotten in Margaritaville. There weren't many people around this time of day, either Inderlanders or humans, and a quiet hush held our voices down. It was either that or we were all too numb to say anything. Here among the buildings, the fog had retreated, but the glimpse I got of the bay on the way in said that it would be a while before it lifted and I'd get a glimpse of Alcatraz.

Squinting up at the brightening sky, I breathed deep to bring in the scent of salt, old garbage, exhaust, and the sticky smell of the petunias in the huge planters outside the hotel. The air felt slippery from the salt, and I shifted my shoulders as if trying to fit in a new skin. The hotel stretching above us looked nice, I guess. Ivy had made the reservations, so it would have to be. Trent had a room here, too, which was convenient. He was currently with Vivian and the doorman. I lifted my bag out of the trunk, then Trent's. Ivy already had her bag, and was heading in, the small carry-on rolling quietly behind her. I hurt all over, and I set the bags down with a click of plastic.

"Jenks, stay close," I said when I caught sight of the pixies tending the huge flowerpots. They looked almost militant. A traveling pixy was almost as rare as a sole traveling vampire.

Jenks darted from me to prove he wasn't scared, the overhead light glinting on his sword. "God, it feels good to be at sea level," he said, facing the unseen bay. "Smell that?"

I winced, my thoughts drifting to Alcatraz. It seemed a whole lot more real that I might end up there now. "Sure. Nice." But it did feel good to get out of the car. "You want to go in and check the lobby for lethal charms?" It might be overkill, but we did have reservations, and I wouldn't put it past the coven to hit me here—seeing that Vivian had ridden almost the entire way with us and they probably didn't want a credible witness to my death.

Giving me a thumbs-up, he followed Trent inside when the doorman returned to his station to call a cab for Vivian. She was staying down on the bay with the rest of the coven in someone's house. Glancing at Pierce, who was standing alone and looking like a doorman himself with his vest and hat, she came up to me, smiling.

"I don't know if I should thank you or not," she said, her purse over her shoulder. Her hair was mussed and her clothes were wrinkled. She was far away and distant from the trendy, polished coven member I remembered from the grocery store this last spring. The confidence was still there, though.

She stuck out her hand, and I took it, feeling an odd sense of peace when her small fingers met mine. "I'll say it, then," I said. "Thank you. For helping." Hesitating, I pulled my attention from Pierce trying to talk to the hotel pixies. "I'm glad you saw everything."

Vivian squinted as she ran a hand over her tangled, car-trip hair. "I have to tell them."

I nodded, thinking she looked positively bedraggled. "Good. Maybe they'll begin to understand the inherent problems in shunning black magic to the point of ignorance."

My gaze went to Pierce. I didn't know what to think anymore. My world had gone from black and white to shades of gray a long time ago, and there were no answers, easy or otherwise. I couldn't condemn Pierce for trying to kill Al by using magic unless I condemned myself for having tried to kill Ku'Sox with the same. Sure, Ku'Sox was bad, but so was Al. That Al was important to me wasn't a good enough reason. Everyone was important to someone.

A deep breath went in and out of Vivian, and she couldn't meet my eyes. "They're afraid. Hell, Rachel, I'm afraid. We're at such a disadvantage. They're going to want to bury everything and hope we don't have to deal with it for another generation."

My gaze flicked back to Pierce. *It worked last time. Why try anything new?*

Clearly having heard her, Pierce turned, a mix of determination and irritation on his face. "That's what I've abided by all along, and look where it got me."

Hands in her pockets, Vivian shrugged. She was one of six and the youngest.

I carefully lifted my bridesmaid's dress out and shut the trunk with a thump, hearing the solid sound echo. It was as if the world was still asleep, here on the verge of a new day. "They should be afraid," I said as I draped the dress over my arm. "It's not going to go away. They have to do something." I hesitated, hoisting my duffel bag in my free hand. "Besides giving me a lobotomy, that is."

Vivian rocked back as her cab pulled up and the doorman opened the door for her. "Well, thank you," she said, chuckling ruefully. "It's been an education." Her gaze went to Pierce, now standing beside me and trying to take my suitcase. "If I don't get the chance to see you alone again, good luck."

Good luck. I'd need it. "Oh! Wait!" I said as she started to turn away, and I let Pierce take my bag, then made him hold my dress, too. "I've got something for you," I said, head down as I rummaged in my shoulder bag.

Vivian paused, and I held my breath in annoyance until my searching fingers found the little Möbius-strip pin. "This is yours," I said as I handed it over, feeling flustered for some reason. "I didn't magic it or anything. I thought you might want it back. Seeing as you don't have one . . . any-more."

A huge smile spread across her face as she took it, pleasure and real gratitude in her expression. "Thanks," she said softly, her smooth fingers curving over the pin possessively. "I'll probably have to give it up because you touched it, but thank you. Brooke—" Her words broke off and her gaze dropped. "Brooke gave me hell for losing it."

There were new wrinkles at the corners of her eyes when she looked up, and a deep sadness. Leaning forward, she gave me a hug, her fist holding her pin, pressing hard into my back. She wasn't very tall, and I was again struck by how someone so slight could be so powerful.

"Thanks," she whispered as she stepped back, her eyes flicking to mine as if embarrassed. She had smelled like red-wood, and I wondered if she had sensed the stink of burnt amber on me when she turned and headed for her cab, her eyes unable to meet mine.

The door thumped shut behind her, and she waved, looking worried as the car pulled away. The sound of the engine was muffled in the rising fog, and it was just Pierce and me stand-ing outside a squat hotel in the middle of San Francisco, the doorman waiting for the keys so he could park my mom's car.

Pierce had my stuff, so I handed the attendant my keys along with a couple of bills, and the guy thanked me, his sus-picions easing. Pierce's eyes widened at the amount, but he was probably still running on eighteenth-century gratuities, and I don't think a nickel would have done it. The car vanished in the same way as the first, and I looked at the hotel, almost losing my balance as I ran my eyes up to the brightening sky. The thought of earthquakes slipped through me, and I took my garment bag back from Pierce. It would be just like the coven to destroy an entire building to get to me.

My lethal-amulet detector hung conspicuously from the side of my bag as I headed to the double doors with my dress over my arm. It felt like I was entering a war zone.

A minor shiver lifted through my aura as I passed over the threshold, and my shoulders dropped. Pierce grunted as he felt it, too, and I was guessing it was a rather expensive calming charm, temporary, to be sure, but effective.

"This looks nice," I said as I looked over the deep reception/living room designed in solid blocks of color that were rich and sophisticated. The ceilings weren't that high, but they were decorated to hide the retrofitted earthquake support. To my right was the reception desk where the night clerk was talking to Ivy. Trent was standing before it chatting amicably to the manager. He must have been dropping hundred-dollar bills again because the man in the suit was almost bowing and scraping. Ivy, though, was having trouble, clearly not happy with the woman behind the desk. Jenks was snarling something at her, a red dust pooling on her keyboard.

"Trouble," Pierce muttered as he set my bag down and put his hands behind his back, feet spread wide as he scanned the place.

"Of course there's trouble," I said as Ivy stepped from the desk. Her eyes were black, and her motions were edging into that eerie vampiric quickness. Jenks's wings were clattering in anger, and I sighed, knowing what was coming.

"They lost our reservation!" Jenks shrilled. "The Tink-blasted hotel didn't hold the room. 'So sorry,'" he said in a high falsetto. "'Nothing we can do.' We drove two thousand miles, and we don't have a room! No one in the city does because of the convention!"

Ivy's lips were pressed tight, her anger in check. Las Vegas must have helped. "I made that reservation through Rynn Cormel's secretary," she complained.

"It was a good thought," I said as I tried to think, but I was too numb. "We'll find something." A park bench. Maybe the parking lot of the local Wally World. Yeah, that'd be safe. I could wear my bridesmaid's dress and fit right in with the kooks.

Trent ambled our way, a hotel envelope in his hand. He

looked too satisfied to live. The manager with him scooped up my bag, and I felt a surge of adrenaline when he dropped it on the luggage trolley with Trent's. My protest died, though, when Trent smiled that infuriating smile of his and handed both Ivy and me a plastic key. "Ready to go up?" he asked pleasantly.

Ivy closed her eyes in a long blink, then tossed her bag onto the trolley, keeping her smaller computer bag right where it was, over her shoulder.

"Sweet mother of Tink," Jenks swore. "What did you do? Buy the place?"

"Something like that," Trent said, his smooth, suave demeanor slipping back even if he was still in jeans and a casual top. "You don't have a room because I booked the top floor for us. Can we hurry up about it? I have an appointment. I'm already late."

In Seattle, I thought, starting for the elevators when the manager, still blathering at Trent about parking and how to call for a car, pointed them out. The calming spell took hold again, and my tension slipped away.

"Thank you, Trent," I said as I hung my garment bag on the trolley and fingered the little plastic card. It was small for the amount of grief it had just saved us. "I don't know how you do it. I mean, I know, but how? They know we're together."

Trent angled in front of Ivy to push the elevator button, and I smiled. I hadn't known he was a button pusher. Jenks was, too. I couldn't care less who hit the buttons as long as we got there. "I bought the place last year," Trent admitted, then turned to look past me to the lobby. "This is nice. I should come out here more."

Jenks and Pierce were with the bellhop, who was clearly not going to accompany us but would take our stuff up through a secondary elevator. The elevator before us opened to show a lift the size of my closet. *Earthquakes,* I thought, balking.

"Rachel," Pierce said loudly, interrupting my sudden panic attack. "Jenks and I will mind the plunder, er, luggage. There's not enough room in the lift nohow."

I stifled a shudder as I minced into the elevator. "Okay," I said, not wanting two more bodies in here anyway, even if one could fly. "See you up there." *Just get me up there and out of this box,* I thought as the doors slid shut again. I wasn't claustrophobic, and I didn't mind elevators. Where was this coming from?

Trent reached past Ivy to push the topmost button, and I caught a whiff of cinnamon, heavy in the cramped quarters. The car shook as the gears shifted, and we headed up, far too slowly for my liking. I breathed deep, watching the light move.

Beside me, Ivy's eyes flashed black. She edged away from me as Trent chuckled. "I didn't know you were afraid of elevators, Rachel," he said, his voice holding a light mockery.

"I'm not," I said as I gave Ivy a worried look. My thoughts flashed back to Kisten and our first kiss in an elevator, and she pretty much flung herself into the corner, not knowing what I was thinking but tasting the memory of fear and desire flooding me. *Better and better,* I thought as Trent looked between us, amused.

"It's not the elevator, it's the coven," I added when the elevator finally dinged. I held my breath as I waited forever for the doors to open, but it was Ivy who was first out, brushing past me in a spicy wave of vampire incense that made me quiver.

Trent leaned in, whispering, "It's when I'm gone that you're going to have to be careful."

Oh, really? I thought, my attention on the brightly patterned carpet as I stepped from the elevator into the hallway, slowly, so it didn't look like I was bolting.

"We're on the end, there," Trent was saying as he checked his envelope, but Ivy again was ahead of us, steps fast as she strode to the end of the short hall where the big window looked out onto a fire escape. She tried the last door, and I could hear her sigh when it opened. She was inside and gone before Trent and I were even halfway down the corridor. Either she had some intestinal problem she had to take care of or my fear in the elevator combined with the memory of Kisten had hit her hard.

It felt funny walking down the hallway with Trent, both of us carrying the small items we thought were too important to risk coming up on the trolley. I caught glimpses of us in the long mirrors set next to the occasional door, looking like fake windows, and again I was struck by the idea that we were with each other but not together. Like the night on the boat when it had blown up under us, and we were the only two to survive—Trent because I had made a protective bubble around us by using the connection made through his familiar, and then me because he'd pulled my frozen ass out of the Ohio River and kept me from dying of hypothermia.

But now, as we walked down the hallway, there was a new awareness—not of kinship, but an understanding. And it made me nervous even as it was . . . comforting.

"Hey, Rache!" came Jenks's hail from behind us, and the rattle of the trolley as Pierce helped the bellhop at the distant end of the hall. "Top floor," Jenks said proudly. "We're in the penthouse suite. Where's Ivy?"

"Inside already," I said, and Trent ran his card and held the door open for me.

Jenks darted in, and I followed, eager to see what a penthouse suite looked like. Nice. I think the word would be "nice." Or really nice. I'd go as far as friggin' nice.

"Wow," I whispered, stopping somewhere in the middle of what I'd probably call a living room, arranged with two couches facing each other, a coffee table in between decorated with stuff to make it homey and inviting. To my right was a small kitchen, a bar with three stools making a pleasant place to eat if the small table in it wasn't enough. There were fruit and cold cuts laid out, and bread—fresh, by the smell of it. I think the maid had baked it in the oven while she tidied the place.

Looking past the living room, I could see a second living room with a bank of windows. It was on a platform and looked more plush and comfortable. There was a huge TV between the two rooms that seemed to rotate on a swivel. A wet bar took up one side of the upper living room, and it all looked out on a spectacular view of the bay. I hadn't realized we were up so high in the hills, and though it was still foggy, I could see the tops of the bridge poking through. A room with a view— of Alcatraz.

Trent dropped his small satchel on the coffee table. "This is pleasant," he said, gaze darting to the closed doors off the raised living room, which had to be the bedrooms, not closets. "Better than roadside hotels, anyway."

I would have gotten angry with him, but he was smiling, probably remembering that nasty shower I'd dragged him out of, and I couldn't help but wonder what the bathroom here was like. I was betting nice.

Trailing a silver dust, Jenks buzzed out of one room and tucked under the door of another. Ivy's faint shout to leave filtered in, and Jenks darted back into the living room. In an instant, he was at the windows, checking things out. At least we knew where Ivy was.

"I'd just about kill for a shower," I said as the trolley rattled in, Pierce holding the door for it. His eyes widened upon seeing the room, and he stumbled out of the bellhop's way.

In a burst of noise, Ivy's door was flung open. The bellhop's spiel faltered as she strode forward, grabbed her bag, and then vanished behind her door again. I flopped onto the couch with my back to the window, my gaze going to the second bedroom. I'd be willing to bet Trent would claim it even if he wasn't going to be here tonight—off doing his little elf-quest . . . thing.

"She's a little cranky," Jenks said, distracting the bellhop, who looked more than a bit startled as he turned from hanging my garment bag in the front closet.

"Dialing zero will get you the front desk," the bellhop started again, glancing from Trent to Pierce and then to me, clearly trying to match us up before attempting to move any more luggage. Trent's bag was headed in with Ivy until Trent cleared his throat and—sure enough—claimed the second room with little more than a nod.

"I guess I've got a couch," I said, and the bellhop simply emptied the trolley and left the luggage in the entryway. Jenks was still checking the place out, and Pierce had joined him, whistling when he found the bathroom, next to the kitchen.

"Will there be anything else, Mr. Kalamack?" the bellhop was asking when Trent bodily took him by the elbow and delicately propelled him to the door.

"Privacy," Trent said, leaving him at the door and going back for the trolley. "No deliveries. Leave them at the desk. No turn-down service. No incoming calls, except from me. A table for dinner would be pleasant, say about ten. Family style if at all convenient. Chef's choice. Heavy on the vegetables. No deep-fried anything. It's been a long trip."

"Yes, sir," the man was saying, now in the hall with the trolley. "Thank you, sir!" he added when Trent handed him a folded bill. "Welcome home, Mr. Kalamack."

Smiling and nodding, Trent shut the door in his face. He waited until the faint sound of the trolley creaking away came through the door, and then he sighed, his shoulders slumping for all of three seconds before he pulled them back up.

I could hear Pierce trying out the faucets in the bathroom, and I smiled as I draped my arms across the top of the couch. "This is nice."

Trent flashed me a look. Picking up his smaller bag, he headed for his room. "Excuse me," he said, and I would have been hurt but for the reminder that though I could relax for a while, his *quest* was just starting. He'd given himself three seconds to relax. That was it. Three.

From the bathroom, Pierce said, "You could wash a cow in here."

"Look, Rache," Jenks said from the windows behind me. "You can see that bridge they're always yammering about. Huh, it's not that big. The one Nick drove off is way bigger. Hey! Look! There's an island."

Oh, great. The fog had lifted. "Alcatraz?" I said, turning to see, but he'd darted to my bag, landing on it with his hands on his hips, wings moving so fast I couldn't see them. My shoulder hurt from yesterday, and I gingerly felt it. I had a pain amulet in my luggage, but it wouldn't work here. Maybe they had aspirin in the lobby.

"I gotta get changed," Jenks said as he slipped into the pocket that had been designated as his. "Trent wanted to leave, like, five minutes ago."

Pierce came out of the bathroom, immediately going into the kitchen and opening the cupboards to see what there was. In a burst of silver dust, Jenks popped from my bag. "You going to be okay here with Mr. Adventure?"

My gaze slid to Pierce, then back to Jenks. "Go have fun. Don't let him kill you, 'kay?"

Jenks nodded, then tossed his head to get his long, curly hair out of his eyes. In a flash of dust, he had darted into Trent's bedroom with a wad of clothes. I hadn't seen him this excited about a run since Matalina died, and it was depressing in a happy way.

I wasn't too keen on Jenks leaving. Every time he did, I got into trouble. That everyone would think Trent was still in the room might buy me some time—as long as I didn't leave, either. But there were worse places to be a prisoner. The hair on the back of my neck prickled, and I stood, my gaze drawn to the window and the newly exposed bay.

Yep, there it was. I stood for a moment, twenty feet back from the window, and just looked at the dark blob that was Alcatraz.

The small clink of Pierce at the wet bar caught my attention, and I moseyed over to the kitchen. A little sandwich of overpriced crackers and cheese would wake up my appetite, and I made four of them. "Oh, this is 'ood," I said around my full mouth, salivating as the salt and bite of the cheese hit the sides. "Pierce, you've got to try the white cheese. It's sharp."

Pierce gave me a noncommittal *mmm,* and I headed for

Trent's room with my napkin of goodies. I didn't know where Trent wanted to be dropped. If I left it up to Al, he might leave them on top of the needle—the outside of the needle.

Trent's door wasn't shut, and I tapped on it with my knuckle. "Trent?"

I heard a buzz of pixy wings, and then Trent's distant "Come in."

It had come from somewhere deeper in the room, and after brushing the cracker crumbs off, I pushed open the door. "Hey, Trent. Where do you . . . Wow, this is nice."

If the living room and kitchen were well appointed, the bedroom was opulent, with more pillows on the bed than we had in the entire church. Wallpaper and metal appliqués disguised the retrofit for the earthquakes, and I'd be willing to bet the canopy over the bed was sturdy enough to handle more than dust. I ate another cracker sandwich, wondering where Trent was until I heard him talking to Jenks from a room off this one.

"Trent?" I called, not wanting to walk in on him in his skivvies.

"In here."

Having that as an invitation, I crossed the room, feeling the deeper carpet and noticing the lack of even a hint of an echo. It felt nice in here. The first room I peeked into was an office, but the second was clearly a bathroom. "You decent?" I asked, hesitating at the door.

"Depends on who you ask."

Rolling my eyes, I stepped over the threshold, my toes edging the tile work. Trent didn't look up from where he was standing over a sink, leaning toward the mirror to apply something to his face. He'd changed out of his jeans, and I hesitated, drinking him in with my eyes. *Damn.*

He was in a skintight black two-piece of spandex and cotton. Not only that, but he was wearing it extremely well, and I stood for a moment and just appreciated what he usually hid behind his suit and tie, all lean muscle and long lines. His fair hair was slicked back, and the slightly darker color and flat look changed his entire appearance, making him look less professional boardroom and more professional bad boy. A utility belt rested on the counter, holding what were probably thief tools.

Hovering at his eye level and rubbing a dark smear under his eyes was Jenks. The two of them looked remarkably alike—once you dismissed the wings and size difference. Seeing him unaware, I could appreciate how slim Trent was, athletic, with just enough muscle in all the right places. A runner's body. I tried to keep my eyes where they belonged—then gave up, letting my eyes linger where they would—then warmed when my eyes rose to find Trent watching me in amusement in the mirror.

His smile shifted as he recognized my appreciation, the slight movement of his body an invitation to look more. God, he was teasing me, and flushing, I took my eyes off him. *Ellasbeth, your name is fool.*

"What is that you're putting on your face?" I asked to try to move the nonverbal communication away from how good Trent looked and how smug he was that I'd noticed. It smelled like cut grass in here—clean, refreshing, and carrying the bite of chlorophyll. I didn't think it was the toilet-bowl cleaner.

Pulling back from the mirror, Trent capped a bottle and jauntily tossed it to me. I had to move fast, almost dropping my last two cracker sandwiches as I snagged it one-handed. My shoulder gave a twinge as I caught it. "It covers my scent," he said, and I set my napkin down so I could open it. I gave the nondescript white stuff a good sniff to verify that this was where the cut-grass smell was coming from. My shoulders eased as the scent slipped into me, reminding me of summer. *All this, and he smells good, too.*

"You don't stink," I said as I dabbed a bit of it on the back of my hand, and from nowhere, the question flitted through me of what he had wanted to be when he grew up.

"Thank you. I appreciate that." His voice was light, teasing, and I stayed where I was as he reached for the jeans he'd had on earlier, his motions becoming tauntingly slow as he put one foot in, then the other. "I suppose I should have said it will mask any smell I'll pick up in the ever-after," he added, turning to give me a sideways view as he zipped up his pants.

The familiar sound hit me, and I jerked my gaze away, pretending to be looking at the flat-screen TV they had in here. Okay, so he'd been wearing a lot less just a moment ago, and I'd seen him just about naked in the shower, but something about seeing a guy hike up a pair of jeans followed by that distinctive sound of a zipper was so . . . very intimate. And the worst part? It was obvious he knew he was pushing my buttons.

Knowing it as well, Jenks sighed at me and continued arranging his hair. His long blond ringlets were oiled back just like Trent's, and I wondered if there was some kind of hero-worship thing going on. Frowning, I set the bottle down. Trent was putting on his casual shirt over his skintight top, and I didn't dare look at him as he got dressed, but his reflection caught my eye as he stretched, showing every lanky inch of himself. Damn it, seeing him getting dressed was almost more tantalizing than seeing him getting undressed might be.

"You look great," I said, unable to stop myself. "You should wear thief more often."

"How do you know I don't?" Trent teased as he sat on a bench that was in here and began to put his shoes on. No laces. Slip on, slip off. Easy. The casual clothes over a black outfit, the scent-disguising salve, shoes too soft for any real use . . . it added up to a break-and-take. Sure, Trent had the look and the talk, but could he walk the walk? "Ah, Trent . . . ," I started, arms crossed as I leaned into the wall.

Trent looked up from his shoes. "Don't worry. I've practiced this."

"Nothing in that belt pack is lethal, right?" I persisted,

wanting to go look. "Not that I care," I said when he eyed me. "But if you're caught, lethal usually gets you put in jail."

Smiling faintly, he stood up and looked at himself. "And if it looks like a harmless prank, they let you go. I got that part. Thanks." He buttoned another button to hide the black shirt underneath. "If they catch me, I'll be dead, not in jail."

I pushed away from the door frame. "Whoa! Hold on a sec. I told Quen I'd watch you. Just what are the risks here?"

Jenks clattered his wings, but I couldn't tell by his worried expression if this was something he'd known about before or not.

"Quen puts the odds of my being successful at eleven percent," Trent said, not meeting my eyes. "But with Jenks, I think it's much better than that."

"Eleven percent?" I echoed. The same odds Quen had had of surviving that experimental treatment last year, the same odds that Trent didn't believe were really possible.

"My risk, not yours," Trent said as he draped the utility belt around his slim waist and fastened it. I could tell he was nervous somewhere under that facade of calm he had developed in the boardroom. "It's an elf quest, right?" he said, forcing a chuckle. "You're not responsible for me once I hit Seattle. Quen knows that. I've already notified him. What happens to me from here on out is not your problem."

But I'd gotten him here, and I couldn't help but feel responsible for . . . whatever he was doing. *What was he doing?* I licked my lips and lowered my arms, trying to play the "I don't care" game. "You're serious about the dead thing?" I couldn't help but ask.

He didn't answer, and Jenks remained silent as he sat on the TV's remote, his knees almost to his ears. I grimaced, realizing that Jenks had already slipped into backup mode. He never said much when I was on a run with him, either. He wasn't wearing a scrap of red, and it worried me. Damn it, if Trent came back and Jenks didn't . . . I'd make him suffer. If I did nothing else in this world, I'd make him suffer bad.

Seeing me ready to call the whole thing off, Jenks blurted out, "Ready, Trent?"

Trent looked at me, his hair slicked back and his green eyes holding excitement. "Yes."

"You were just kidding about the dead thing. Right? Right?"

Jenks hovered by my shoulder. "Take a chill strip, Rache," he said. "They're faster than the pills and come in convenient dispensers. I've got this covered. He's not doing anything that you wouldn't do."

"That's what I'm worried about." Crap, I was used to beating the 11 percent, but Trent didn't believe it was possible. It was often belief that made the impossible real. *Jeez, maybe I should go with them.*

As if knowing my thoughts, Jenks's expression darkened. Trent took off his watch, leaving it on the counter. His wallet was next, and he took most of the money out of it and tucked it in a small slot in the utility belt before setting the smooth leather next to his watch.

I took a slow breath. If I said anything now, Jenks would be insulted. Trust. I had to trust. But it was hard. "Where do you want to be dropped off?" I asked softly.

Trent was giving himself a last look, fussing with the hair about his ears. "Train station," he said shortly. "Preferably on the platform, not the track," he drawled.

Nervous, I pushed myself into motion. "Okay. I'll call him."

I headed for the living room. Trent followed with Jenks on his shoulder. Pierce was looking through the front closet as we entered, and I couldn't help but wonder if this was what it would be like working for Trent: amicable conversations in penthouse suites in foreign cities, the excitement of a run coursing through me, and the coming satisfaction of knowing I'd done something no one else had before. Very secret agent. Was this why Nick did what he did?

I sneaked a glance at Trent as I sat on the couch, thinking he looked fantastic standing there—his color high and that calm confidence he always had tightened by excitement. Twice he had called on a demon and survived; admittedly it had been a mistake, but he'd done it. He had the guts—or stupidity—to work with wild magic, elven and dangerous. He had a pixy on his shoulder and was ready to do something clever and dangerous—something that, if he failed, would mean his death. I didn't know who he was anymore, and I felt a stirring inside.

Feeling my eyes on him, he lifted his head. "What?"

For a moment, I said nothing, tasting the emotions coursing through me as he tried to read my mind. Was I confusing adrenaline with attraction? Was I losing sight of my desire for independence, distracted by quick, clever people who didn't give a damn about whom they hurt to get what they wanted? Or was I just now seeing who he really was?

Trent's face lost its questioning expression, shades of mistrust seeping in around his eyes. Jenks buzzed his wings at me, and I shook myself. "Nothing. Be careful, okay?"

Not convinced, Trent stood beside a comfortable chair, waiting.

Pierce scrambled to catch the clothes iron as it fell. Jenks flew up and down at the noise, but neither Trent nor I even looked.

"Okay . . ." I breathed as I tugged my bag closer and brought out my mirror. Turning halfway to the back of the room, I shouted, "Ivy? I'm dropping Trent off. I'll be back in five minutes." I thought for a second. "Maybe ten!"

"Okay," came her muffled voice, and I felt a surge of tension.

"Wait!" Jenks exclaimed, "I have to give Ivy my phone. She's going to call my kids for me while I'm gone."

I glanced at Trent, expecting to find a tired exasperation, surprised when I found only a patient understanding. Maybe they'd been talking more than I thought. Jenks buzzed off, Ivy's closed door hardly slowing him down as he slipped through the crack.

Pierce finally got the iron back where it belonged, and he shut the sliding closet door with an attention-getting thump. "Rachel . . . ," he warned me, and my blood pressure spiked, pushed by the adrenaline already coursing through me. His blue eyes were pinched, and his jaw was tight, reminding me of when he had once stood in the snow in a borrowed coat and tried to stop me from helping him with a run. I'd flipped him into a snowbank then, and I'd do the same here. Well, minus the snow of course.

"Don't start with me," I said, and Trent scuffed his foot on the carpet, impatient. "Al owes me for saving his life." The scrying mirror was warming on my lap, and I set a hand on it, feeling a ping of energy equalize. "Thanks for that, by the way. I might be able to milk this for years."

I'd meant it to be funny, but Pierce came closer, sitting on the edge of the chair opposite me, the coffee table between us. The table had expensive-looking picture books on it of the work of local artists, most of which looked too sophisticated for my tastes. "I don't like this," he said.

"I don't like it much myself," I said, almost laughing as I exchanged a look with Trent.

From Ivy's room came an exasperated "I got it, Jenks! Every four hours. Go away and let me sleep!"

Jenks darted out, looking browbeaten, and I turned my attention to my calling circle. It was as beautiful as ever, and I had made it. With a curse.

"Is it going to work?" Trent asked suddenly, startling me. "The salt in the air . . ."

I slid my fingertips to the cave of the pentagram, touching the proper glyphs. "No reason it shouldn't. It's demon, not earth magic." I looked up. "Jenks? Are we clear?"

Jenks landed on Trent's shoulder, shocking the elf. "Give me a break," he said snidely. "I checked for bugs like three seconds after I came in. What do you think I was doing? Looking through cupboards for no reason like a goober?"

Pierce grimaced, scooting to the back of his chair, looking embarrassed.

"Let's do it then," I said and reached for a ley line. My face screwed up, and I swear, my eye started twitching. An awful, metallic taste blossomed in my mouth, and my stomach twisted. "Oh God, the lines here are awful!" I said, finding one that was reasonably clean. It was as if they'd been fractured and were picking up rust and dirt. Maybe it was the earthquakes.

My gaze went to the bolts in the wall, and I forced myself to look away.

Steadying myself, I let the awful ley line fill me, reaching out and touching a finger of awareness into the ever-after by way of the calling circle. "Rachel calling Al, come in, Al," I said sarcastically. "Come in, your immenseness . . ."

Standing across from me, Trent raised his eyebrows in question, and I pressed my hand more firmly, finding it harder than usual to hold the divided awareness. Soon as Al picked up, the interference would vanish, but until then, I was left feeling disoriented.

Abruptly, my focus blurred, and my muscles were suddenly loose. A warm lassitude soaked into me, and I realized that though Al had acknowledged me and made a connection, he wasn't altogether conscious. He was sleeping.

Al? I pushed into his mind, only to find myself surrounded by tiny slate blue butterflies in a field of amber grass, the tips waving at my waist. Al was trying to catch them, but every time he tried, he'd open his white-gloved hands to find them crushed and stinking like carrion. The grass grew tall until it waved over my head and turned into a maze. Al kept trying to catch the butterflies, and they began vanishing through cracks in the walls.

"Al!" I shouted, disoriented, and the dream vanished. Al's panic coursed through me, confusing me even more. I felt him bolt upright, then gasped when a black magic swirled through me, burning my brain. There was a huge drop in the line I was connected to as he pulled on it through me. *Al, wait!* I shouted, but it was too late, and I winced as I felt him throw a ball of unfocused energy at a shadow.

"It's just me!" I shouted as Al cowered, swearing when he realized his mistake.

"Rachel?" Pierce said, leaning over the table to put a hand on my shoulder. Feeling the line burning through me, he pulled away with a disturbed slant to his eyebrows.

"He was sleeping," I said in explanation, dizzy as I tried to see both Pierce and decipher what was going on in the ever-after simultaneously. "I had to wake him up. We're good now."

The hell we are! Al swore, and I felt his surface emotions swirl around and the feel of a soft robe he was draping over himself. *I blew a blasted hole in my wall! Damn it, Rachel, what do you want? I was sleeping.*

"So I noticed," I said, thinking it curious that he was dreaming of butterflies. They looked exactly like the butterflies he'd once made out of snowflakes, brushing them from his sleeve to die in the snow. Except for the chrysalis still on my kitchen windowsill at home. "I'm sorry to wake you, but I have a favor to ask."

Trent cleared his throat. "We drove all the way out here, and you haven't asked about this?" he said, sounding alarmed but not surprised.

"It's not a big deal," I grumped. "If he doesn't, I'll ask Newt. I need to talk to her anyway."

What? Al said, suddenly a whole lot more awake. Ask Newt what?

I resettled myself on the sofa, tucking a strand of hair behind my ear as I noticed my reflection bouncing back up at me, coated in red and silver. "I need a trip through the lines for two. Trent and Jenks." Jenks buzzed his wings, proud to be counted as a person, but I'd never seen him any other way.

Al huffed in his thoughts, sending me the feeling of warm slippers being scooted onto his feet. *I'm not your taxi service.*

"No, you're my teacher," I said. "And I saved your life. I'm not going to bargain for favors in return for saving your life." *I'm asking for some consideration, from one lost witch to a lost demon,* I said silently, glancing at Jenks when he hummed in disapproval, knowing I'd said something, just not out loud.

I'm exhausted, Al thought, and I caught a glimpse in my mind of him looking into a mirror, tweaking the skin around his eyes. *Can it wait? I've been in meetings all day. Yammer, yammer, yammer. And no Pierce to fix my lunch. He makes a marvelous fish sandwich. Ask him, dove.*

He was using pet names—not good. "You made me take him," I said, and Pierce stiffened, knowing we were talking about him. "Al. I need this. It's not a matter of convenience." He made a noise, and I pressed my fingers more firmly until it felt like the ice of the glass was touching my bone. *Look, let me dream a little longer, okay?* I thought silently, not wanting to share with Jenks my low expectations of what was going to happen in the next couple of days. *I know how slim a chance I have to get out of this, but it's a chance.*

Al was thinking—a good sign. I'd saved his ass, and he was going to give this to me. "I need to see this through if only to be able to walk away knowing who my enemies are," I said aloud. I couldn't help it, and my eyes rose to find Pierce's. Not missing a beat, Pierce pointed to Trent.

Trent cleared his throat, affronted, but Al was talking and I had to concentrate. *Growing up is hard, love. Otherwise everyone would do it.*

"Spare me," I muttered. "I need a jump for Trent and Jenks to Seattle and back. I know you're going to do it or you wouldn't have gotten out of bed."

A devious spark lit through Al, making me smile. *One way. It costs too much,* he said.

"There's no inflation in the ever-after, Al."

Call it a recession then. One way.

I looked at Trent and smiled. He relaxed, exhaling as his shoulders dropped. "Okay, one way," I said. "But I want to see them off, so it's one way for them, two way for me."

Deal, Al thought sharply, and Jenks made a burst of gold dust, yelping.

"Holy crap!" the pixy swore, and the fractured disjointedness of San Francisco's ley lines sliced into me, jangling my nerves. I snapped a bubble of protection around my thoughts, large enough to include Jenks and Trent. I could feel Trent's flash of fear dissolve into acceptance, and Jenks readying himself, his steady courage flowing into me like a memory that wasn't mine. Surrounding us like an oily smoke was Al's presence, but I pulled most of his reeking burnt amber and selfishness to me, not wanting Trent and Jenks to have to deal with it. Embarrassed, maybe?

The train station, Al! I shouted in my thoughts, not wanting to show up in traffic. *On the platform,* I added. My nonexistent heart pounded, and I felt the lines grow pure around me again, the taint of salt and rust fading away to be replaced by the taste of ozone, clean, pure, and fast.

A glimpse of an immense, dirty room, not yet formed, sifted through my eyes. The presences of Trent and Jenks were with me, and I dissolved the bubble holding them as I felt their souls slip from my grasp and return to the memory of their bodies. I ached to take a breath, but as soon as I thought I might have lungs, I was yanked back into nothing, my forming body dissolving so fast I swear it hurt.

Al! I shouted, disoriented. And then it was Al sheltering my thoughts. I threw up another barrier between us as he laughed. The platform dissolved, and reality swung around. I waited for the trendy furnishings of the hotel in San Francisco to appear and gritted my nonexistent teeth to endure the fractured ley lines the witches were forced to use here, but the tinfoil-on-teeth feeling never came. Instead, the line grew warmer, comfortable. Familiar.

Crap on toast, I thought as I reached for the top of the leather wingback chair, my fingers ghosting through until I yanked them back and tried again to find them solid. I was in Al's library.

"Trent? Jenks?" I called out as soon as I had lungs. Damn it, had it all been a trap? I should have let Pierce kill him.

"Not here, itchy witch. Safe at the train station as promised," Al said, and I spun to see him in the robe I'd felt him put on, standing by the huge hearth with a bowl of marshmallows on the hearth beside him. "Come sit by the fire," he said, patting the leather seat. "We need to talk."

Seventeen

"The intention was for me to say good-bye," I said, almost setting my scrying mirror down, then changing my mind at the last moment. I wasn't staying—if I had any say in the matter.

Al scooted his chair closer to the fire, sitting on the edge before he shook his robe sleeves to his elbows and carefully wedged a marshmallow on the end of one of his toasting forks. Leaning in, he held the puffed sugar close to the flames. His muscular arms looked almost tan in the firelight. Feet spread wide, he hunched toward the flame, his bare feet showing from under the hem of his brown robe. They were surprisingly normal looking. Behind me, shelves of books were silent witnesses in the dark.

"Your intention was to see that they got there safely," Al said in a low voice, focusing on the marshmallow. "They are. Off to make mischief on an elven scale, which means worldwide and yet somehow . . . totally insignificant. You need a new hobby, Rachel. Something other than nasty little men with visions of world domination."

The marshmallow caught fire, and he pulled it close, somehow looking suggestive as he ran his fingers down the length of the stick to take off the still-flaming puff. "I want to talk to you about magic and sweat," he said, the light from the burning marshmallow glinting in his eyes. "Of good deeds born from stupid ideas. Of honest mistakes leading to dishonest graves." His eyes met mine, and he pursed his lips, gently blowing the flaming sugar puff out.

Oh God. He's talking funny, I thought, nervous as I looked over the dark room. Deciding to stay behind the chair, I let my scrying mirror slide down to rest on the soft leather. I wanted both hands free.

Al stood, and I froze. His movement had been graceful, a studied motion of power that I seldom saw in him. The marshmallow was gone, and he was licking his fingers, watching me from under his lowered brow. My pulse quickened as he went to the fire, taking a second marshmallow from the bowl. *What in hell is he playing at?*

"This trial of yours tomorrow," he said. "Odds are three to one that Pierce will betray you."

"I thought you said he was going to kill me," I said, trying to be flip.

A smile lifted his lips. "Odds are eleven percent there. But the bookies don't know that he lo-o-o-o-oves you," he mocked as he put the puff on the end of the toasting fork. "Stay here. Forget it all, and stay here with me. Let me spare you that."

I felt better with him eight feet away, and my eyes rolled. "Spare *me* the crap, will you? Al, I want to go back to the hotel." *Shit, he was a demon. Why did I keep forgetting that?*

Al crouched before the fire with the toasting fork, looking threatening somehow. His eyebrows were raised when he turned to face me, mocking. "Things have changed."

Stifling a shiver, I scanned the room, but there was nothing here to help me. *Damn, damn, damn! Why had I trusted him?* "Please don't tell me you're making a pass at me," I said, unclenching my fingers from the back of the chair. "It will make the next five hundred years really awkward. Besides, the last guy who said something like that to me while wearing nothing but a robe, I beat senseless with a chair leg."

Al blinked, looking surprised as he glanced down at himself

as if only now realizing the impression he made. But then he smiled. And that smile was cruel.

He stood, and I dropped back a step, heart thudding.

"That demon your familiar let loose? Ku'Sox?" he said softly, poised as I started to sweat. "He's like nothing you've come up against. He wants to play with you. Take you apart slowly while you scream. The collective would throw me naked into the ley lines if I let you run about now. Pierce isn't enough. You're staying here."

"Like hell I am! Is this because I have a shot at getting my shunning permanently revoked?" Angry, I came around the chair so I could glare at him straight on. "I just might win our bet, so you're going to keep me here so you can win by default?"

"Willing to bet your life on it?" Al almost growled as he looked into the fire, his back hunched. "I'm not. Good or bad, my livelihood is connected to your continued existence," he said as his marshmallow burned. "Call me selfish, but you're staying here."

"You might be scared of that thing you all made, but I'm not," I snapped. "His sensitive bits are right where yours are. Ku'Sox is a demon, and I'm getting used to beating you guys off. I beat him off before. I can do it again!"

Al turned from the fire, his goat-slitted eyes landing on me with an unexpected intensity. I felt myself pale. He looked dangerous, crouched before the fire, his eyes glowing as the promise of violence drifted over him. A low sound lifted into the air, and my foot slid.

It was my undoing.

Al leapt for me, the toasting fork clattering, forgotten, to the hearth. Panicked, I turned to run. There was nowhere go. It was pure instinct.

I caught back my cry of terror as his fingers clamped on my shoulder. The world spun as he turned me around. "Al!" I managed, and then I felt myself lifted, shoved into a bookcase.

Hard thumps hit my shoulders and my lungs collapsed as I hit the tomes, little sparkles of energy pinging through me. My breath came in with a rush, and I stared at Al, inches from me, his bare ruddy hand gripping my shirt under my chin. I hadn't even seen him move.

"You think you can beat Ku'Sox off? Let's practice."

"Get off me!" I spat at him, strands of my hair on his face.

His expression became a snarl, and I jerked when his other hand reached behind me and grabbed my thigh. "This should be fun."

"Hey!" I shouted, trying to shove him away; then I shrieked when he pushed me back into the bookcase, his entire body pressing into me. "Get the hell off!"

"I think you've misjudged your strength, itchy witch," Al said, his voice iron hard. "And I'm going to prove it."

"How? By squishing me to death?" I wheezed, and then my eyes widened as Al's mouth covered mine, savage and demanding. The stink of demons assaulted me, hard and fast. A thread of ley line spilled into me from him, diving to my groin and flashing into heat. It could have been ecstasy, but I was too angry. His body was heavy on mine, and his leg forced its way between my knees.

Holy shit! I thought, my arms pinned behind me. I couldn't breathe. Couldn't move. I thought Al was trying to prove I couldn't protect myself. I wasn't scared, I was pissed!

Furious, I tried to get my knee up between us. Feeling it, Al let go of my wrist long enough to punch my rising knee with a heavy fist. I gasped at the sudden explosion of pain, and my knee went numb. My hand was free, though, and I went for his eyes, gouging.

My fingers dug in with a sickening give. Al took the abuse, quickly grabbing my wrist and almost yanking my arm out of its socket as he slammed it back into the books.

"Not nearly enough, dove," he said, smiling as he bent toward me again. My teeth were clenched, and I tasted his blood as he forced his mouth on mine again.

"You son of a bitch!" I screamed, muffled from his lips, and I reached for a ley line.

Al felt it, and I got in a clean breath as he pulled back long enough to laugh at me.

"That's it," he said, breathing heavily, his expression alight. "I think you're pissed enough now. Give me what you've got. I'll slip it back into you so slowly you'll scream in pleasure and beg for more."

It was then that the fear took hold. The ley line he was tracing through me felt good. Really good. I knew what a witch could do to another, and pain wasn't far from ecstasy. This may have started out as an object lesson, but Al could take my abuse and make me writhe for it. I was halfway to climaxing already. This was *not* what I wanted.

Al saw the realization in me and smiled, shifting his weight suggestively, his eyes half closing in anticipation. "You think you can handle me, Algaliarept?" I snarled, and his eyes opened as I used his true name, but his grip on my wrists was painfully tight.

"God, Rachel, you are such a tease," he said, and then he leaned in. His mouth was demanding, rough as he let go of my wrists and grasped the back of my head, crushing himself to me. The line he held sang in me, lighting my synapses in a cascading flash that spilled from my lips down to my groin, and I relished it, even as I despised what he was doing.

I'd fucking had it with men making inappropriate passes at me.

My hands pushed against the books, and we shifted forward, our kiss never breaking as he found the back of the tall chair and stopped. I never could have done it if he hadn't let me, but I wasn't gouging his eyes out, and since what he was doing to me felt really good, he probably figured I was his.

He was still holding my head, and his tongue was making inroads, causing my pulse to pound. A small sound of desire slipped from me, and Al let go of my face, lifting me up so I could wrap my legs around his body, feeling him against me. My hands were in his hair as I drank him in, taking the line through him, learning the paths that the energy took from him to me. God, it felt good, this careful exploration, and I shivered. I knew he was doing the same, and it only made me angrier.

Al broke from me, and we both gasped. "Itchy witch," he said, looking me up and down as he held me to him. "My God. You are . . . Damn. You have no idea how long it's been."

I smiled, my arms around his neck and my fingers running through the hair on the nape of his neck. "I don't think so, Algaliarept," I murmured, leaning in and playing with the corner of his mouth with my own. "I'm not a tease. I needed to know to . . . hurt you."

He sucked in his breath, but it was too late. My legs tightened around him, and I pressed his face to mine. My thoughts dove into his, finding the path among his synapses that he'd first burned eons ago to safely bring a ley line into him. Punching through his thin film of surprise, I grasped the ley line . . . and I pulled.

"No!" he shrieked, realizing his mistake.

My back arched as the power flooded in, painful and delicious. I could hear Al cry out, but it was as if I swam in glory itself, and I pulled him to me, closer, wanting more, arcing it through me back to the line, burning clean and bright, lighting the smut in me with pure fire from the gods.

The soft pop of displaced air almost went unnoticed as my soul chimed, tuned to the ley line I was drowning Al in, but a faint whisper of self-preservation caused me to open my eyes. Everything was bathed in a silvery white light. Everything, that is, but the flat foot in the purple slipper headed for me.

I tried to disentangle myself from Al, and the foot hit me, flinging me across the room like I was a rag doll. I hit a bookcase, numb. My fingers splayed over my chest, and I couldn't breathe. *Shit, I think my ribs are broken,* I thought, and I slid sideways to the floor, my cheek burning on the carpet.

"You lied to me!" Newt screamed, and I tried to cry out in pain as she lifted me up and slammed me against the shelf again. "I killed my sisters for you!"

My mouth was working, but nothing was coming out. My head lolled, and my focus was blurry. The line I'd been connected to was gone, and my gore rose.

And then I was screaming as the line I had yanked through Al was arcing through me.

Tulpa! I thought, trying to spindle it, and I feebly pushed at Newt to get her hands off me.

"Newt! Stop! That's Rachel!" I heard Al croak hoarsely, and the sharp sound of flesh smacking flesh. The world lurched, and I hit the carpet again.

I lay on the floor in a crumpled heap, my fingers rubbing the soft bumps of the carpet. My breath went in and out, and it felt good. It felt good not to be on fire. My head pounded, and I pushed most of the spindled energy out, sagging in relief.

"Newt, it's not Ku'Sox!" Al shouted again, and I heard a bang and smelled ozone and the acrid scent of burnt books.

"I killed my sisters for him!" Newt raged. "Get out of my way, Gally!"

Al's soft hand touched my shoulder, and I jerked, managing to sit up. Al was standing beside me in his robe, the hem trembling. Newt was in front of us, wearing her purple martial-arts robe, her funny, tall-sided hat almost in the fire. She had hair again, the straight black strands cut short in a pageboy style, and her long, ugly feet were bare. It was hard to tell what she was looking at since her eyes were black, but I was pretty sure she was looking at me, hatred pouring from her.

"This isn't Ku'Sox," Al said, his voice shaking, and I wondered why he had stopped her. "It's Rachel. She smells like Ku'Sox because she fought him. It's not Ku'Sox!"

Newt looked at me. Then her black eyes went to Al's. "She survived him? Are you sure? Maybe Ku'Sox is wearing her skin. He does that."

Al took a breath, exhaling long and low. His hand touching my shoulder left me, and I sat where I was, slumped over my knees, my hair in my face. I had tried to hurt Al to get him to leave me alone, and I think I might have gone too far. Drew a line through him like a familiar and almost fried his little kitty soul.

"It's her," Al said ruefully, and I looked up to see him shuffle to the arrangement of furniture before the fire and fall into the chair farthest from me.

Newt's expression became one of familiar confusion. "Have I forgotten something again?" she asked suspiciously. "It appeared as if she was killing you. Or were you two . . . ?" She hesitated, then put a hand to her mouth and laughed. "Gally! You dog! You tried to seduce her?"

"She's been living in my kitchen for almost a year," he said sullenly. "Forgive a man for testing the waters. She wasn't screaming. And my name is Al now. Remember?"

"Testing the waters!" I echoed him, ticked. "You almost had me on the floor." I'd be furious if I hadn't given him back as much as he gave me. God! Men were pigs.

Al frowned, having to look over the couch between us. "You looked like you were enjoying yourself. I know I was."

"And that's why you were screaming like a little girl, right?" I barked, then hunched into myself and held my ribs. *Ow.* Yeah, I had liked it. But not with him, never.

"Is it a pajama party, Gally?" Newt asked, and a wash of black ever-after coated her. My chi ached as Newt shrank until the ever-after fell away, showing her looking like a child in bright red pajamas. Her hair was gone, and her eyes were hollow. She looked ill, and in sudden shock, I realized she was one of the kids in the brat pack at the hospital—the one who had forgiven me for doing black magic. She'd died with one of my stuffed animals clutched to her. And Newt wore her image as if it meant nothing.

"That's not nice," I said, and Newt smiled like a beautiful bald angel with the wisdom of the world in her, hurting me even more.

Newt laughed again, this time with a high, childlike innocence, making me shudder and forget what I was mad about. She was coming toward me with her little hand extended to help me up, and I got to my feet, not wanting her to touch me.

"I was *trying* to provoke you into defending yourself," Al said loudly from the couch. Rubbing a hand over his hair, he looked both sheepish and worried. "I'm worried about Ku'Sox. Newt, since you are here, what's your opinion? Is she reasonably safe?"

"Seeing as she was halfway to killing you, I'd say she has a sporting chance," Newt said in her child voice, and I stifled another shudder.

"That's great," I snarled, limping away from Newt and toward the fire. God, my life sucked. "So I can go back now, right?" I said sullenly as I picked up my scrying mirror and sat down. Crap, I was sore. I was probably going to have to get my ribs wrapped. This was going to look swell tomorrow at the trial.

"Oooh! Marshmallows?" Distracted, Newt almost skipped to the overflowing bowl beside the fire, the visage of a dying child somehow suiting her.

"Al?" I prompted, holding my ribs. I think he'd about crushed my knee, too.

Al slumped in his chair until his butt almost slid off the cushion. His robe had fallen open, and I couldn't help but look. *Dude* . . . He was hung like a horse, his ruddy complexion almost black down there. No way was he getting his tackle anywhere near me.

"Fine," he grumped, oblivious that he was waving in the wind. "If Newt says you're reasonably safe, you can go," he said sullenly. "You'll be back in twenty-four hours anyway."

Yes! I thought in victory. I was going to have to take a long shower to get rid of the burnt-amber stench, but I imagined they'd bring up more shampoo if I called down.

Newt turned from where she was kneeling in her pajamas before the fire, a lightly browned marshmallow at the end of her stick. "Bring a ruler with you when you return," she said, her voice high and childlike. "The ever-after is shrinking. But

I can't prove it unless I have a tape measure from reality. All the ones here are shrinking, too."

Scrying mirror pressed to me, I watched Al cringe. "Shrinking?" I asked.

"Slowly," she said, her pinky sticking out as she tentatively squished the marshmallow to test how done it was. "The rate will quicken exponentially as we have less and less to lose. The ebb and flow of energy between reality and the ever-after has shifted. It's not all coming back. There's a hole somewhere."

She looked at me with her black eyes, and I shivered.

Al sat completely up and tugged his robe closed. *Thank God*. "The lines have been balanced for eons. Nothing has changed," he said, but his voice was too sure, too confident.

Smiling with a dead child's face and beauty, Newt awkwardly sat cross-legged before the fire. "You haven't been to the surface lately." Turning away, she put the toasting fork back into the flames, unsatisfied with the puff's doneness.

"I try to avoid it," Al huffed.

"The buildings," Newt continued as if he hadn't said anything, "are falling at an astounding rate."

Remembering the buildings in Vegas's ever-after, I took a breath, and Al shot me a look to keep quiet. Worried, I felt the bumps of the lines on my scrying mirror. "Buildings always fall," Al said, his eyes darting to his books.

"Yes, Gally," she said, her voice having a childish lisp. "But now they are on *fire*."

Crap, had it been me? I'd made a ley line. Maybe I hadn't done it right. "Um, Al?" I said, scared.

Again Al grimaced, telling me to shut my mouth. "It was probably your brat Ku'Sox," he said, and I clutched my mirror, feeling the cold soak in. Al was lying. He was lying to Newt. It hadn't been Ku'Sox. It had been me, and Al knew it. *Shit. What had I done?*

"Ku'Sox is *not* my *brat*," Newt said as she pulled her marshmallow off the stick, her little-girl pinkie stuck way out. "I was against giving him the ability to hold that much energy. You all vetoed me. Remember?"

Holy crap, Al was outright lying to Newt, and it scared me in a way that Al making a pass at me never could.

"Have a marshmallow, Rachel," Newt said, leaning over the coffee table to hand it to me. "Consider it a prize for almost killing Al."

Numb, I took the perfectly browned puff. *Okay. Let me see if I have this right. Al provokes me into defending myself. I nearly kill him. Then Newt tries to kill me, thinking I'm Ku'Sox. Al stops her, saving my life. And now we're all going to have s'mores together? What in hell is wrong with these people?*

"Thanks," I said softly, sticking the puff into my mouth. The ugly taste of burnt amber hit my tongue, and I gagged, spitting it out into my hand. "Oh my God! What is wrong with your marshmallows?"

His ears red in embarrassment, Al handed me a napkin that hadn't been there a moment ago. I wadded it up with the marshmallow inside, leaving it on the low table between us. "The real ones cost too much," Al said with a sigh. "That's why I burn the hell out of them."

"So if there's a hole in the fabric of time, how do we find it and fix it?" I said, wondering what they were made from if they weren't real. The coffee wasn't any good, either. Brimstone?

"You can't." Pinkie high, Newt plucked a marshmallow from the bowl and stuck it awkwardly on a stick before handing it to me. "Your turn."

The toasting fork was warm in my hand. "You can't pinpoint it, or you can't fix it?" I asked, thinking that was an important distinction.

Newt didn't say anything, kneeling on the hearth and running her fingers through the fire as if it were a kitten's fur. Al's slippers shifted a hair's breadth, and I realized he was more than a little nervous. At the sound of the soft scuffing, Newt glanced at him, a sly look on her face as she smiled with her black eyes. My gut hurt as a second haze of ever-after sifted over her, leaving her looking as she had when she slid into Al's library and sucker-kicked me. "You're sweet," she said as her intent expression turned to me and I shivered. "Don't you want your marshmallow?"

"I just want to go back," I said, and then I stiffened when she got to her feet with a boneless grace, coming to sit on the couch, angling herself so her knees almost touched mine.

"And back you will go," she said, her hand touching my hair.

"If the ever-after is shrinking, maybe she should stay here," Al said, and I stiffened. Newt saw my anger, and my hair slipped from her hand.

"I proved I can hold my own against Ku'Sox," I said. "Besides, Pierce is there in case I do something really stupid. You owe me this chance. If I can't survive the next twenty-four hours, then I'll never survive here."

Newt's thin eyebrows were raised in question. She saw my scrying mirror, and I stiffened when she took it from me. "Such a pretty little triangle," she said as she gazed at her hazy reflection in my mirror, then shifted her appearance to look like me. "Al wants to kill Pierce," she said, tucking a strand of her now curly red hair behind an ear, making me shudder. "But he can't leave Rachel alone and vulnerable in the sun. And Pierce"—she handed my mirror to me—"well, he is going to destroy you whether he wants to or not. Scheming, scheming. Such little men's desires flow around you."

It was more than a bit disturbing to see myself dressed in Newt's clothes. This was one of her bad days, I think. "Pierce doesn't want to kill me," I said, my thoughts flashing back to our night under the earth, then his sullen temper when I'd saved Al. Maybe he'd forgive me if I told him I'd almost killed Al, too. "He had a moment of pique, is all. He'll get over it."

She was nodding, looking like me as she sat on the couch.

"They all get over it, don't they? And then he'll destroy your hope, kill your soul. He won't even know what he's doing until it's too late. I can tell the future because my days are always the same." I stiffened as she touched my hair again, head cocked as she studied it, feeling it between her fingers that looked like mine, right down to the wooden pinkie ring and the chipped red nail polish. "Between you and me, you'd be better off with both of them dead," she finished.

Al cleared his throat. Newt's gaze shifted to him and she made a soft noise. "Al, you are a fool," she said as a sheet of black ever-after coated her and she turned back into her usual androgynous self. "You might have more than two curses to rub together if you didn't allow both your familiar and your student to run about in the sun, plotting against you."

"Then she should stay, yes?" he said, and she threw her head back and laughed.

"No. Rachel goes back," she said, and I sagged a little in relief. "There's more than one bet to be settled tomorrow, and they made me the referee again. They never let me bet anymore. Not since I won Minias. Where is he, anyway? Oh, that's right." She eyed me speculatively. "I killed him."

Great. Newt was a demon bookie on top of everything else. "What are my odds of getting my shunning permanently revoked?" I asked, having to know.

Newt smiled and handed me my scrying mirror. "You're going to lose because of Pierce. Didn't you hear me? Or do you forget things, too?"

I couldn't answer, trying to find enough air to breathe. *Do I have a shot at this or not?*

"That's my girl," she said, her eyes holding a shared pain as she saw my confusion. "Al, where are you going to put her? Not in your room. She'd pull a line through you and kill you when you hog the blankets. I'll take the waif in. I promise I'll bring this one up properly."

Newt patted the six-inch space beside her thigh, and my face became cold. *Oh God. Anything but that.*

Al stood, tugging the tie on his robe tighter. "I have everything under control."

Newt waved a thin hand in dismissal. "And that's why she was arcing a line through you, yes?" she said, then vanished. The seat cushion rose slowly, and the fire flared as new air was sucked down the chimney to replace her mass.

I forced my teeth to unclench, and I shifted my grip on my mirror. "Now, Al?" I prompted, and Al slumped back in his chair again.

"Al?" I said again, louder, and he glanced at me, his fingers searching the chair cushion until he found a little tin of his Brimstone. Opening it, he sniffed a pinch up each nostril, his head going back as he closed his eyes and sighed. Great, now I was going to set the Brimstone dogs off at the coven's meeting tomorrow.

"You do like doing things the hard way," he said, eyes still closed.

"You said you'd send me back," I warned him, and his head came down, his eyes looking a little redder than usual.

"I am, I am," he said, but he was just sitting there, pinching the bridge of his nose. He did that only when I really screwed up. Like the time I used foxglove instead of peppermint, and the curse I was working on turned his ink into stone. "I don't know if I should hope you win your bet or lose," he finally said.

"Huh," I said. "I thought you wanted me to lose."

"I do," he said, "but if you're in reality, it will take longer for anyone to figure out that *you* were the one who made the hole in the fabric of time. Nice going, Rachel."

Worry clenched my chest, and I set my mirror across my knees. "Why are you assuming it was me? Maybe it was Ku'Sox. He did make the arch fall down. I didn't do anything that you didn't do when you made a ley line."

But Al was shaking his head. Sighing heavily, he let go of his nose. "I made my ley line while jumping from the everafter to reality. You made yours jumping from reality to reality. It's leaking."

I licked my lips. "I guess the collective is going to be pissed, huh?"

His bark of laughter startled me, and I tried to hide my jump. "Yes, the collective is going to be pissed. I just hope I can find out how to fix it before they listen to Newt and realize she's right."

"U-uh . . . ," I stammered, and Al frowned at me.

"U-uh . . . ," he mocked, then reached beneath his chair to the bundle that hadn't been there a moment ago. "Here. You're going to need this for your hanging tomorrow."

I caught the cloth-wrapped package he threw at me, scrambling so as not to lose my hold on the mirror. "What is it?" I asked, thinking it was too heavy to be someone's head.

His red eyes landed on me, seeing me scared, cold, and disheveled. "You are a mess. Wear it. I'm not picking you up tomorrow in rags."

"Hey! I have a chance here, you know. This is supposed to be a formality!"

He grinned at me with his blocky teeth. "You don't have a rainbow's chance in hell to get your shunning revoked," he said, fingering a marshmallow before dropping it back into the bowl. "You just traipsed across the continent, black magic spilling in your wake, freeing demons and destroying a national monument. You knocked out a coven member. Kidnapped her. Let her watch you use demon magic to fight off said freed demon. Twice. Hell, girl, you burned down Margaritaville!" His smile widened. "You are so screwed," he said, hitting his Brit accent hard.

"Shut up!" I shouted, holding my scrying mirror close between me and the package. A puff of burnt amber wafted up, and I winced. Whatever he had given me was going to need to be dry cleaned.

"All right, all right," Al said as he sat up and rubbed his hands together. "You can go home. Or to your pathetic little hotel room. Whatever," he added when I made a noise of protest. "I'm going to have a busy day today, and you'll just muddle it up if you're whining about here. I've got to make reservations at Dalliance. It's a little tight, but if I drop your name, something will open up. And there are your quarters to arrange." He looked up at me. "Are you sure you don't want to be roomies? You can have the soft pillow."

I closed my eyes and tried to find strength. "Please don't start." *I had a chance, didn't I?*

"Go, go, go . . . ," Al said quickly. "And here. Sorry for being so rough. I didn't think you had it in you."

My eyes opened, and I saw him make a tiny ley-line gesture just before the ley line took me. Warm and tasting of salt, it slipped into me, dissolving me into nothing but memory. I tried to listen to the line like Bis said he could, or sense an auratic color, but nothing could get through my protective circle. Al even took the smut for the trip, which I thought was odd, and with very little disorientation, I caught my balance as the curse touched my thoughts and rebuilt myself from my memory. My jeans still stunk of ever-after, but my aching muscles, sore back, and pulped knee felt perfect. That small gesture Al had made before sending me home must have been a healing curse, because traveling the lines wouldn't do that to a person. I'd tried.

The walls of Trent's penthouse suite shimmered into existence, and the soft sounds of music. Apparently Pierce had figured out the MP3 player. My dusty boots pressed into the carpet, and I shivered as I suddenly had a body again and the cool, dry, air-conditioned air hit me.

Pierce was standing at the windows, watching the light of the unseen sunrise spill over the bay. His stance was worried, and he clearly didn't know I was back. The fog had lifted, and Alcatraz was visible. I took a breath, and he turned.

"You're back," he said, his voice giving me no clue to his mood, but his features . . . It was all there to see. His blue eyes held thick worry, anxiety, and relief, all mixed up. He didn't move toward me, and I didn't know where we stood anymore. Obviously he was glad I was back, but not enough to touch me.

He wasn't confident enough of the future to cross the room and tell me today was going to be okay, that I was going to see midnight come and go—and be better for it.

"I'm back." Not looking at him, I carefully set the scrying mirror down and dropped the package on the coffee table behind me. God, I stank. I didn't think the hotel soap was going to cut it. A fifty-five-gallon drum of tomato juice might.

Pierce hesitated, then went to the chair by the window, taking up his long, heavy cotton coat and shrugging into it. "What took so long? Kalamack giving you trouble?"

Why did I care what he thought? "Al was messing with me," I said shortly, not wanting to get into it.

Pierce hesitated in his motion to adjust his collar, and he looked at me from under his shaggy bangs. "Are you okay?"

I nodded, and he turned away, watching his reflection in the mirror as he arranged his sleeves. "Where are you going?" I asked, as it was obvious he was leaving.

His eyes met mine in the reflection. "To converse with Vivian."

About me? "Pierce . . . ," I started, remembering what Newt had said about my odds. Having a shunned witch speaking for me wouldn't help.

"Not about you," he said as he took his hat from the stand beside the door and arranged it on his head. "I'm wanting her opinion concerning me trying to reclaim my spot before they fill it. It will give you another positive voice."

My lips parted. "But you were dead!" I said, and he turned to me, his dark eyes smiling.

"I was," he said, inclining his head, almost hiding his face behind his hat. "That's a tricky word, 'was.' Once a coven member, it's for life, and I'm alive." His smile deepened as his gaze became unfocused. "Wouldn't that beat all creation? A coven member who is also a demon's familiar? It would make you look rather . . . tame." Gaze sharpening, he took a step to the door and stopped. "Do you have your phone? Call me if you have trouble."

I bobbed my head. He was going to try to reclaim his spot in the coven. I bet that would shift the odds in the ever-after if anyone knew.

"Good then," Pierce said, and I did nothing, completely shocked when he leaned into me and gave me a quick, almost-not-there kiss. On my mouth. And then he was gone before I could even find the scent of redwood in my soul.

"Wish me the luck of the dead," he said, half in the hall, half in my life.

"Good luck," I whispered, and the door shut. *He had kissed me?*

He had kissed me, and like an idiot, I'd done nothing. It wasn't as if he'd never kissed me before, but clearly something had changed in his thoughts between my taking Trent to Seattle and now. When I'd left, he had been cold and broody— angry with me for having foiled his attempt to kill Al, and rightly so. I'd done nothing to apologize, and he knew I'd do it again in a heartbeat. And yet he had kissed me and left to claim his old position to *help* me?

I wanted to mistrust this. I wanted to believe that it was a trap to further his own standing and perhaps find a way out of his servitude with Al, because with mistrust came distance, and my heart would be safe. But a small, wiser part of me knew that for all his dark power, for all the crap he had made of my life, Pierce was true to his beliefs and wouldn't stoop that low. If he was trying to help, it was genuine. He had set his own desires aside to further mine, and the knowledge of that was scary. His sacrifice made it far too easy for me to put him in the position of hero, inviting me to turn a blind eye to the darker side of his psyche so I could feel the rush of falling in love again.

Not this time, I vowed, my hands in fists as I wiped off the lingering taste of redwood from my lips. He was a black witch who would use forbidden magic to kill those who threatened his life or the lives of those he cared about.

So was I, but that didn't mean I had to love him for it.

Eighteen

I'd already used the glass-and-tile shower in the front bath-room, scrubbing my scalp until it hurt as I worked to get the last vestiges of the burnt-amber stink from my hair. The hotel shampoo smelled far too masculine for me, and I thought it irksome that the management assumed only men would be renting the top floor. But then again, they probably hadn't expected Trent to blow into town with two women. Fortunately I had some of my own shampoo and detangler, and I was again smelling like strawberries and oranges.

I smiled, settling myself deeper into the bubbles. Yes, I had already showered, but there was nothing like a long soak to prepare oneself for a lynching. Especially when you could watch TV while doing it.

Clicking from the Weather Channel to the news, I set the remote next to my plate of crackers. A half-empty bottle of water stood beside it. The scent of coffee slipped in under the door, telling me that Ivy was up. I felt like a prisoner, even after having been a guest at Alcatraz and knowing what true incarceration felt like. *Never again,* I thought as I adjusted the towel wrapped around my hair. If I couldn't beat this, I'd go live with Al.

But I didn't want to.

My gaze drifted to my heavy-magic detector, the disk a flickering, sickly green. It wasn't working well, and I couldn't trust it. I felt like Jenks at five thousand feet. Ley-line magic, too, was messed up because of the ley lines, fractured and broken by the seismic activity. This was why the coven had their convention here. Unless you lived here, you were at a disadvantage and didn't dare use your magic in a pique of anger or implied insult. *Demon magic worked, though,* I thought bittersweetly as I extended an arm up and looked at the lack of bruises. That curse Al had given me before sending me back had rubbed out every ache.

The TV detailed California's latest wildfire, and I stretched out all of my five foot four in the water with room to spare. Fires, mudslides, earthquakes, smog, broken ley lines . . . Why did anyone live here?

I breathed deeply, my eyes flicking to the short dress that Al had given me. I could still detect a whisper of burnt amber drifting from it as it hung on a wooden hanger on the back of the door, and I was hoping that the moist air might help. Apart from the purple scarf, it was all-white leather from the cap to the boots, supple like butter and having a luster that would show off my curves. I knew without trying it on that it would fit. I didn't want to know how Al knew my size. Apart from the color, I'd look like Catwoman. *Me-ow.*

My first reaction when I had shaken it from the paper wrapping had been "Is he kidding?" No one wears white leather, especially not head to toe. But now, after I'd been looking at it for over an hour, I thought why the hell not? Skimpy as it was, leather did have a small resistance to thrown potions.

There wasn't a clock in here, but the ticker on the bottom of the news said it was getting late, and I sat up. The water fell from me, creating bubbles, and I stood and reached for a fluffy towel. It felt good not to hurt, and I dried myself off, going over every inch of my smooth, unblemished skin that should be aching and purple from fighting first Ku'Sox and then Al. Demon curses. Better than Band-Aids, and they didn't wash off in the tub, either.

The TV switched to an on-the-scene reporter, yelling as she

tried to be heard over the fire trucks. It was a small warehouse fire on the docks of Seattle. *Jenks?* I wondered. God, I missed him, and I hoped he was okay. They were supposed to be back by midnight, but I doubted they'd make it. So much for Trent's promises. I was sure he'd have a pixy dust of an excuse.

Wrapped in a white robe embroidered with the hotel's initials, I undid my hair and tried to go through it again. I could see the TV in the mirror. The woman was going on and on about numerous minor problems all over Seattle, from an elevator becoming stuck in the needle, to a catfight at the international cat show Seattle was hosting, to hundreds of fender benders that seemed to happen simultaneously across the Seattle area. She was asking everyone to be patient. Apparently the 911 system had been scheduled for maintenance, and the load of calls had crashed the backup.

Jenks, you little devil, I thought with a smile, but then changed my mind. Jenks was good, but he couldn't be in more than one place at a time. This had all the earmarks of a demon.

My motions to comb the detangler through my damp hair grew rough, and I frowned. All this for a wedding band? I didn't want to believe that Trent had released a dangerous, day-walking demon to be a friggin' distraction—even if it was to control the direction of the next elf generation. And since elves had their fingers in everything, everyone was going to feel it. *Damn it, Trent, you'd better know what you're doing.*

The knock at the bathroom door made me jump, and I set the comb down with a clatter when Ivy's voice came through the thick door, saying, "Rachel? Can we talk?"

What did she want? "Give me a minute to get dressed?"

"Sure." There was a moment, then from deeper in the room, louder but muffled, "Do you want something to eat?"

I reached for my underwear, then hesitated. "You mean like room service?" God, I felt like a prisoner, and in a sudden decision, I took Al's outfit off the hanger instead. Might as well make sure the dress fit.

"No," she said, voice softer. "I wouldn't eat anything they bring up now that they know we're here. If you don't want cold cuts or fruit, I've got Milk Duds."

Ivy is the one buying the Milk Duds? "Uh, no thanks." I zipped up the side zipper on my hip, gratified that nothing pinched or bunched when I bent to put on my socks. "You want to see my go-to-trial outfit?" White. Was he serious?

"Sure."

She sounded depressed, even through the door, and I became worried as I adjusted the sleeveless top over my bare skin. It laced up the back and had a neckline that would show off what little I had to my best advantage, accentuating instead of hiding what wasn't there.

"I, uh, had three gallons of syrup sent out to the Petrified Forest," she said, standing by the door by the sound of it.

"You're kidding! How?"

She was silent, and I imagined her shrugging. "Internet," she said shortly. "Jenks's freedom cost us $275, but most of that was to pay for someone to deliver it."

I couldn't help my smile. I hadn't forgotten my promise to the pixies, but leave it to Ivy to know how to arrange it online.

"Have you given any thought to tomorrow?" Ivy asked, her voice hesitant.

I posed in the mirror, stuck out my chest, then slumped and reached for the boots. They were white, too. "All the time."

"No, I mean really. Have you thought about tomorrow?"

Sitting on the edge of the tub, I slipped the low-heeled boots on. They fit perfectly, and the zipper was well oiled. My estimation of Al knowing what a girl likes went up. I thought of that kiss of his and squinted. "Ivy, I'm just trying to get through tonight. If I don't make it, then I'm . . ." I took a breath as I stood and looked at myself. Damn, I looked good. Like a leather teardrop. "Then I'm in the ever-after," I finished, slightly depressed.

Fear flared up, and I squashed it. I didn't want to come out of the bathroom wearing leather and stinking of fear. Ivy was good at resisting temptation, but she wasn't above taking a lick of frosting from the cake before it was served.

Putting the cap on my head, I looked at my reflection, my hair still damp and my skin still holding the glow from the bath. Maybe I shouldn't call it fear. Maybe it was dread. My throat became tight, and I sent my gaze to the purple scarf. Purple was how a demon showed pride or favor to its familiars, and it made me feel like it was the first day of school, when you know you're too chicken to stand up for yourself and you don't have any friends to rely on—all alone and your mother telling you at the car you'd be okay.

My hand ran across the scarf, feeling it cool and smooth against my fingertips. I couldn't make myself put it on.

"I've been thinking about it," Ivy said from the other side of the door. "If you have to go, I'm going to shut down the firm."

Whoa. I pointed the remote to shut off the TV. Flinging open the door, I found Ivy sitting beside the window in the bright light, her back curved and her shoulders slumped. She looked tired. "Why?" I asked as I crossed the room. "You're great at this. What about Jenks? You just going to leave him alone in the church?"

Ivy's head came up, and she tossed her hair from her eyes, smiling faintly. Her gaze traveled over me, taking in the leather dress. "I like that," she said. "You look good in white. And before you get uptight, Jenks will be fine. He's thinking about going to work for Trent if things go wrong tonight."

I looked at her, shocked. *Work for Trent?* "He told you this?"

Shrugging, Ivy pushed back into the chair, every motion screaming of an inner pain. "We've talked," she said, her voice low. "One of the reasons he was so hot to go with Trent today is because he's trying it on." Her eyes flicked to mine and held them. "There's nothing for him in the garden anymore. Especially if you're gone."

I was not believing this. "Trent? Are you kidding me?"

Ivy looked out onto the bay. "I know you're focused on tonight, but in case there isn't any time to talk before you go . . . I wanted to let you know that I enjoyed being with you."

Oh my God. She was saying good-bye. Agitated, I came to stand before her, not knowing what to do with my hands. "I am not dying!" I said, finally sitting down on the edge of the nearest chair and taking my hat off. "I can come back for visits and stuff."

Her jaw was clenched. "I know."

She looked at me, and I suddenly realized that this was for real. My eyes filled, and there was a sudden lump in my throat. I wanted to touch her shoulder, but her body language said not to. "I can visit."

Ivy's eyes were just as full, but neither of us would let a tear fall. "Let me say this," she whispered. "Will you just let me say this?"

I put a hand to my middle to try to get it to stop hurting. "Why are you saying good-bye?" I whispered.

She lifted her hands and let them fall. "Because I can't follow you," she said suddenly. "I started on this trip two days ago, and it wasn't until Arizona that I realized I wasn't doing a damn thing. I was driving, sure, but you don't need me. You never really did!"

"Yes, I do," I said quickly, but I shut my mouth when she shook her head.

"Not like I want you to. You're moving fast, Rachel. And vampires are slow. It's like you're from the future, and you're here trying to yank everyone forward so some of us have a chance to survive what's coming. You're leaving Jenks and me behind."

Anger flared, but it was at the universe, not her. "This demon thing wasn't my idea!"

"I'm not talking about the coven and shunning. I'm talking about you changing everything." Ivy crossed her legs and gripped her biceps, looking vulnerable. "The Weres, the elves, the vampires. You're stirring everything, like a catalyst, and you're leaving us behind. It's okay. We're not mad. Sad maybe, but not mad." She let go of her arms and met my eyes. "I knew ever since you sealed that room in the tunnels that you and I weren't going to work even if you woke up some morning and wanted it to. I felt the power of what you could do. I saw it. I saw the fear in Edden's eyes. It only made me love you more."

I blinked fast. "And you don't think I need you? After that? Ivy, it was your soul that protected me."

She nodded, hiding her face as she wiped her eyes. "You'll do better once you let us go. Jenks and me both. We'll be okay."

My head was shaking in denial. "I'll beat this, Ivy. I always do."

Her chin came up. Eyes black, she snapped, "What if you do? You think we can drive back to the church and go on like nothing happened? It won't work. I can't pretend anymore that one day you're going to wake up and be anything different from what you are right now. I'm not talking sex and blood. I'm talking about you and change. How you make it happen and how you adapt to it. Your mind lets you. Jenks and I . . . we can't."

"Ivy."

"I never had a chance," she whispered.

"Ivy!" I said louder, and she focused on me.

"I never had a chance," she said again. "But thank you. I've seen what it's like to be normal. Been a part of a family, even if I was on the fringes."

I reached over the space between us, touching her. "You've never been on the fringes."

She looked at my hand on her, smiling almost. "I've never been in all the way, either, and don't start thinking that you did me wrong. Hell, Rachel, if I'd gotten all the way in, I would have self-destructed, destroyed myself. You knew that," she said, and my hand fell away. "I don't . . . I didn't have a way to cope, to accept that I deserve good things. But I feel good right now."

She smiled, looking at the ceiling as she wiped her eyes

again. "Do you know I'd never remembered feeling good before you? Kisten was safe, but you felt good, even when you weren't around. Even when you were out doing stuff. Even when I was out with one of my blood partners, and I knew that when I came home . . ." She hesitated. "I knew that you would be there, or would be back soon, and you wouldn't look at me and hide your disgust at what I am but would let me work it out. You were like a warm finger touching my thoughts, pushing the black down and not letting it rise up. Keeping me sane. I've felt good so often that now I can recognize it even when it doesn't come from you. I can feel good about other people."

My chest was tight, and I could do nothing but look at her miserable, happy face. Maybe I should let her go.

My expression must have shown my thoughts, because Ivy smiled even as a tear leaked out and she wiped it away. "I wanted to say thank you before Jenks and Trent get back and things start to happen. I know I can find the good again, now that I know what it feels like. I can recognize it. Keep from destroying it." She touched my knee, and I blinked back my own tears. "I can't ever repay you for that. It's more than I ever thought I'd find. Thank you."

"You're killing me, Ivy," I croaked, throat so tight it hurt.

"Payback is hell, isn't it?"

I tried to say something, failing.

"Just say you're welcome," Ivy said, standing up to look out the window at nothing.

There were lots of things I wanted to say, and none of them was "You're welcome." I wanted to say that I was going to lick this. That nothing was going to change. That this was just a bump. But when my gaze focused past her and found the blocky gray shape of Alcatraz, I didn't know if it was true. Feeling a sense of mild panic, I stood.

Ivy turned. Looking at me, she leaned in and gave me a hug. I held my breath so I wouldn't start crying, so I didn't breathe in her soothing vampire scent, but I knew it was there. My arms went around her, and I had a fleeting thought that she felt small for such a big person.

Reluctantly Ivy let go and dropped back. "I hope you get your shunning rescinded. I hope we drive back, taking our time and actually sleeping. I hope that nothing changes. But even if we can make all those things happen, let me go. Right now. I need to move on and find something good that I can hold on to."

I stared at her black eyes. She'd come a long way. We'd never have been able to have this conversation last year. "But—"

She leaned in, taking my face in her cool hands. "This is good-bye, Rachel."

Oh, shit.

I knew what was going to happen, and I let it. Ivy's lips met mine, and my eyes closed. My heart gave a thump. Her lips moved against me, tasting lightly of coffee. All the tension that had been winding up in me unraveled in a rush of endorphins, followed by a spark of adrenaline, glowing through me like pixy dust.

For the first time, there was no fear from her vampire teeth, no worry of the promise of ecstasy and danger she held. She was just Ivy, and her hand slipped to my waist, pulling a ribbon of feeling through me. My blood rose, pounding, responding to her touch. She smelled like incense and soap. She held me to her without binding, without promise, only passion in her embrace. Her mouth was soft, unbelievably soft.

Blood humming, I felt her tongue whisper against me and her grip quiver against my jaw as the scent of her tears lit through me. Salt and blood. Oh so close, and my own closed eyes spilled over as my body ached. She began to pull away, I realized I was tasting what I could have had—but now was gone. And it hurt.

Feeling it, Ivy let go. I blinked, trying not to cry. Even as she stood there, I'd lost her. Even though she'd never been mine, now she was gone. I didn't want anything to change, but

I couldn't stop it. She was right, even if everything went perfectly tonight, nothing would be the same tomorrow.

"You're not leaving me," she said, her eyes damp. "I'm leaving you."

The knock at the door shocked both of us, and I stifled my jerk when Ivy turned to it with her vampire-quick reflexes. I wasn't thinking, the heat of that kiss still aching. She looked at me, her soft smile the last thing I would have expected from her right now.

"I'll get it," she said, motions like an old jazz song as she drifted past me in a wave of happy vampire.

"Damn it, what's wrong with you, Ivy?" I said, shaking.

"Nothing. I feel good. Hell of a good-bye kiss."

Good-bye kiss. God, she had me in the ever-after already. "Whoever it is, don't let them in," I said, wiping my eyes. "And we're not done talking here."

"Yes, we are," Ivy said as she looked through the peephole. "It's your mother. And some guy with red hair."

"Robbie?" I jumped up and started for the door. "Let me see," I said as I got close, and she shifted away.

In the hallway, looking anxious in a yellow sundress and a straw hat, was my mother. Beside her was Robbie, his hair slicked back and a pleasant expression on his face. "It's my mom!" I said, reaching to open the door. It cracked open, and then it slammed shut, slipping right out of my grip.

I turned to Ivy, and I heard my mother huff through the door. "Ivy!" I protested, her black eyes setting me back a step.

"That's not your mom," she said, and I got cold.

Nineteen

I stared at the closed door, hearing a muttered conversation behind it. "What do you mean, that's not my mom?" I asked Ivy again, my voice hushed, and she shrugged.

"How would she know you're here? You call her? I didn't."

No, I hadn't, and I looked through the peephole to find her and Robbie discussing things. "She knows I'm somewhere in the city," I said. "She's crazy, not stupid, and the press probably knows where Trent is staying."

"Rachel?" my mom called. "I want to talk to you before your trial, sweetie."

Ivy shook her head. "She's not swearing. And when has Robbie *ever* been happy to see you?"

I frowned, squinting through the peephole to try to see my mom better. Her shoes didn't match her dress, and Robbie was still smiling. It was the last one that did it. "You're right." Raising my voice, I shouted, "Nice try! Go away!" I dropped down to my heels, feeling like the little goat who didn't let the big bad wolf in to eat her.

"Is Trent there?" the man who wasn't Robbie asked, his voice off.

Ivy leaned toward the door. "No," she said belligerently. "Whatcha going to do about it?"

I smacked her shoulder with a huff, and she blinked innocently at me. The growing rim around her eyes vanished, and I backed up a step. "What did you tell them that for?"

"To hurry things up. I want to see the sunset over the bay this evening."

I sighed, leaning to look out the peephole again, but I only got a glimpse of them, their heads clustered over a glowing leyline amulet, before I flung myself away, pulling Ivy with me.

Her shout of protest was drowned out by a loud bang, and the heavy steel door burst inward, landing askew on the front couch in the lower living room.

"Holy crap!" I exclaimed, struggling to find my balance as I held Ivy's arm. I reached for a ley line as the door frame smoked, but the energy source oozed through my mental fingers like slivers of broken mirror. It hurt, and I scrambled to fill my chi with the nasty stuff.

The smoke cleared, and I let go of Ivy when my mother and Robbie came in. It was obvious it wasn't them, and I frowned when I recognized Wyatt and that young coven witch behind them. Son of a bitch, Trent had been right. They were going to try to off me.

"You!" I exclaimed, then yelped, ducking and trying to set a circle when Robbie pulled a small air gun from his jacket pocket and pointed it at me. Holy crap, they *all* had air pistols!

The circle around Ivy and me gave a hiccup and died. It just flickered and went out. Shocked, I just stood there as Ivy snatched the serving tray from the coffee table. The last of the crackers and cold cuts went flying as she pulled it up to intercept the splat ball. It hit with a ping of sound and a hiss of magic. Yellow foam bubbled, quickly turning black as the salt in the air interfered. Her lip curling in a sneer, Ivy threw the tray like a lopsided Frisbee at my not-mother.

Drawn gun dropping, my not-mother jumped out of the way, knocking into Robbie and ruining his aim. His splat-ball shot hit the ceiling. Trent was going to be ticked. The tray thunked into the wall and stuck, quivering. It would have broken a couple of ribs easily. Whatever was in those splat balls Robbie was shooting was nasty. Robbie, hell. It was Oliver. I could tell by the way he snarled and shouted, "Shoot them both!"

"Down!" Ivy hissed, jerking me up the steps into the upper living room and behind the couch.

"My circle didn't hold!" I said, feeling betrayed as I took them in. There were four of them. Oliver looked like Robbie. That was probably Amanda posing as my mother, seeing that I recognized Wyatt with his steely brown eyes and stern expression, and the last geeky-looking witch—Leon, if I remembered the papers right.

"You couldn't wait until tonight, huh?" I shouted, then ducked down behind the massive swivel TV that was almost a room divider. Yellow froth bubbled where Ivy and I had stood, and four new splatters outlined the angle of their reach. Ivy smelled of excited vampire as she crouched beside me, her eyes going blacker by the second. My bag was on the couch. There was nothing in it to help me anyway.

"I thought you said earth magic didn't work on the coast," Ivy said breathlessly, and I yanked her back down when I heard twin puffs of air.

"It generally doesn't," I said, running through my repertoire of magic tricks and coming up short. They had timed this perfectly. No wonder they hadn't tried to kill me on the way. This was the only place I'd be helpless. "But they're coven," I said, eying the mass of black bubbles and trying to guess how long it took for the salt in the air to naturally break the charm. "You know, best of the best. All they need is for the charm to work long enough to get close enough to kill us." I looked at her, starting to get worried as I listened to Oliver's demands for us to come out. "How long does that take?"

"Three seconds if you're not resisting," she said grimly.

Yeah. That was about what I thought, too. Damn it, where was Pierce when I needed him? Mr. Black Magic Man would be helpful right about now.

The splats had stopped, and I wasn't surprised when I heard

Oliver say, "She's not coming out. You go that way, and I'll go the other."

Ooh, they were going to split up. Bad life choice. I looked at Ivy, thinking we might be able to salvage something. "I'll take the two guys. You take my mom and Robbie."

Ivy's focus became distant as she used her ears to place everyone. "No offense, Rachel," she whispered, "but your mother is going down."

I nodded, but Ivy was already moving, a scream coming from her as she dove over the spell-tainted carpet and back to the broken door. I rose, seeing her stand from a roll right in front of my shocked mother. Kicking at Wyatt, she backhanded my mom, sending her sliding into the wall beside the quivering tray. Amanda's arms splayed awkwardly, and the gun slipped from her grip and hit the floor. Ivy snatched it up, grinning as she turned.

The men had scattered, the more levelheaded Wyatt going for the bathroom where he could get a better shot at me, the less experienced Leon diving into the kitchen to hide behind the eat-at peninsula. Oliver, seeing that gun in Ivy's hand, dove for the kitchen as well.

"Hey!" I shouted, standing tall and then ducking to evade Wyatt's shot. Oliver peeked above the counter, shooting wildly, almost hitting Ivy. Grimacing, she grabbed Amanda as the poor woman struggled to find her feet, still dazed from hitting the wall. Oliver's next spell hit her square on. Amanda's eyes widened, and then she slid into oblivion, her anger at Oliver dissolving into a spell-induced coma.

"Shoot her! Shoot the vampire!" Oliver demanded, and Wyatt peeked from around the bathroom door. His range wasn't as wide as he probably liked, and he needed to expose himself if he wanted to get a good shot at me. But it wasn't me he was aiming at, and I threw a vase at him. My eyes narrowed when it bounced off a quickly invoked circle and broke on the tile. Either he was used to the crappy lines here or he was using a familiar.

Peeved, Wyatt shot at me, and I ducked back, but it gave Ivy the second she needed to find cover. She was beautiful with adrenaline as she slid back to me, rocking to a crouched halt in the lee of the TV. "I got you something," she said, smiling as she handed me Amanda's gun, and my gaze darted to Amanda, out cold. The spell wasn't breaking as fast as I thought it might. Must be strong stuff. I bet she'd be ticked for having been taken out by one of Oliver's spells. Again.

"Thanks," I said as I hefted the weapon, then squeezed off a couple of shots in the general direction of the kitchen and bath, just to let them know I had it. "Hey!" I shouted, still eying Amanda. "What you got in these splat balls, boys?" I asked. "Is Amanda going to be okay, or should we call a time-out?"

"Cover me!" Oliver screamed at Leon, and Ivy snickered at the young witch's refusal. Just because you're good at magic doesn't mean you like to risk your life. Wyatt poked his head out, and I shot at him, the flash of his bubble deflecting it to the ceiling where it dripped to the carpet. It gave me an idea, and I aimed for the ceiling in the bathroom. Two quick puffs of air and there was an evil-looking, foaming mass hanging over the threshold and making a venomous stalactite. With any luck, it would drip on him.

"How come his magic is working?" Ivy asked.

I pressed deeper into the shelter of the TV. "He's used to the lines here." I wished I was. But in all fairness, his bubbles weren't lasting long, either. Maybe that was the trick to it.

"Hey, Ivy," I said, a sudden thought coursing through me. I couldn't tap a line worth a damn, but I knew a spell that used just quick bursts instead of long, drawn-out pulls like a circle. Maybe if I kept spindling power, filtering it, as it were, I could do something. "I've got an idea," I said, turning the gun over and opening the hopper.

Ivy's confused expression softened to one of amusement as I shook a little yellow ball into my palm, clearly remembering our games in the graveyard where I deflected splat balls shot by Ivy and thrown by the pixies. All I needed was some ley-line energy and a focusing object. "But you can't tap a line," she protested as I jammed the hopper back into place and handed the gun to her.

"I can. I just can't hold on to them for very long," I said, shifting my shoulders as the broken energy seeped in, filling my chi and spilling over to be spindled in my head. My damp hair would stay flat, not giving me away. "Here, you take the gun, I'll deflect what they shoot." I didn't need Pierce. We could do this together, like we always did. Relying on him had made me soft.

Ivy's smile grew. "Ready?" she asked, ducking as a splat ball zipped inches over her.

I wasn't, but she had already leapt into motion, the little *pop-pop-pop*s of compressed air joining her howls as she made the jump to the broken door and propped it up to hide behind. I stood, the splat ball lightly held in my left hand. "Hey!" I shouted, and heads turned.

His eyes alight, Oliver shifted to aim at me. My heart pounded. Four puffs of air sounded loud, but my hand was moving already, the thumb and pinkie showing direction and distance, the three middle fingers giving my spell strength. *"Iacio!"* I shouted, feeling a drop in my chi.

My ley-line spell hit the splat ball headed toward Ivy, and the yellow plastic bounced as if hitting a wall, deflecting back to Wyatt. His eyes widened as he pulled back, and the ball vanished somewhere inside the bathroom. I could do this. It would work!

"Iacio!" I shouted again, and I bounced a second ball at Leon. The man ducked back behind the kitchen peninsula, his brown eyes wide in fear.

"Rhombus!" I shouted, and the two shots from Oliver simply hit my bubble as I ducked, not willing to trust it. The balls slowed, as if hitting cotton, then fell unbroken to the carpet.

"Rachel!" Ivy shouted, and I spun, hand raised to ward off Wyatt's next shot. I didn't have enough time for a spell, and my circle was sputtering out its existence. I dove for cover. His shot went wide as he pulled back too soon, ducking behind his own circle for an instant. Crap, this wasn't working, but even as I prepped to deflect another charm, I watched the glob I put on the bathroom ceiling *finally* drip.

Wyatt jerked as the spell hit his head, reaching up to touch the cold spot, his expression shifting to alarm. His eyes met mine, and I stood, hearing Ivy shooting at Oliver and Leon. "Son of a bitch," Wyatt said, hatred in the expression he directed at me, and then his eyes rolled back and he dropped.

Two down. At least until the charm broke from the salt in the air.

Grinning, I pulled heavily on the shattered lines, spindling energy that tasted like broken rock deep in me. Ivy was out of ammo, and she threw her gun down in disgust. Still, she didn't hide behind the door, but boldly strode forward to the kitchen, beside me.

My brother's thin face that Oliver wore was red and ugly as he stood in the kitchen and shot at me, backing up as I came forward. His eyes became more and more frightened and his shots wilder as I absorbed his magic in quickly invoked bubbles I took down as soon as his magic hit them. I felt like a demon, unstoppable, and a part of me was worried even as I enjoyed the sensation.

"Why won't you die!" he yelled at me, and I backed him up past Leon. The young witch was crouched in the corner, his gun shaking. But Oliver still didn't get it. Four coven members reduced to two, soon to be one, all because of a little more knowledge, and it wasn't even black. I could spindle ley-line energy, and they couldn't. It had made all the difference.

"You need to shut up," I said, and feeling Ivy behind me, I swung my foot in a wide crescent kick. That Oliver still looked like my brother was going to be a bonus.

Oliver's eyes widened, and his mouth opened in protest as he saw my foot coming. "No!" he managed, and then it connected with his jaw.

The shock reverberated up through my leg, and I jumped back, hopping on one foot as the other throbbed, the pain a sharp stab. This was exactly why I hadn't used my fist, and I staggered. Ivy gripped my arm, and together we found our balance. "You really need to just shut up," I whispered, my weight on my good foot as I looked down at Oliver, out cold and slumped into the cupboards. Spots of potion hissed and subsided, and I looked up to be sure there was nothing on the ceiling ready to drip on me. I felt drained, and I frowned as Ivy let me go.

My eyes went to Leon, pressed against the cupboards. Scared, he dropped his gun and kicked it across the tile toward us. Seemed like it was all over but for the lawsuits.

As Ivy smiled at the frightened witch, I crouched before Oliver, fingering the cord to the questionably legal ley-line charm that turned him into my brother. *Expe-e-e-ensive.* Giving it a yank, I broke the chain and tossed the amulet into the sink. The image of my brother wavered and shifted, and Oliver took shape, still out cold and drooling. I rose, wishing I had some zip strips. There was a red mark on his cheek, swelling already. Damn, my foot hurt.

"You going to be good?" Ivy asked Leon, and when he nodded, she sauntered out of the kitchen. I watched her, slightly concerned. She had taken care of herself yesterday and so wasn't hungry, but fighting brought out the worst in her.

"Watch out for that dripping potion," I warned her, and she dragged Wyatt onto the carpet before hoisting him up and dumping him unceremoniously next to Oliver. Amanda was next. At least I thought it was Amanda.

"What are you going to do to us?" Leon whispered, and my eyes flicked to his, holding his gaze. "We will be missed. You can't just kill us."

"My God, do you really think I want to kill you?" I said, disgusted, though chucking them out the window had occurred to me. They would just send assassins after us until I fled to the ever-after and everyone I ever knew was in jail. But he had brought up a good point. I had them. Now what?

"Why couldn't you just leave me alone?" I said, irate. I slid aside to give Ivy more room as she pulled the image of my mother into the kitchen and let her slump over Wyatt. The woman's eyes were twitching as the charm began to break. Oliver, too, was stirring, his wincing eyes shut as his fingers fluttered up and over his swelling cheek. Good. I had a few things to say to him. That the potions had lasted this long was a testimony to coven magic. Oliver might look stupid and slow, but he wasn't. He was just backward as all hell.

"Do you have an anticharm for this?" I asked Leon, wanting to hurry things up.

He was still pressed into the corner, and his eyes darted to the front pocket of Wyatt's jacket. "S-salt water," he stammered.

"Thanks," I said, gingerly searching the spelled witch until I found a couple of the little vials.

Only now did I take the amulet off my not-mother, smirking as the slightly chunky blond earth witch shimmered into existence. Yeah, it was Amanda. I flicked the top off a vial of salt water and dumped it on her. She came to, sputtering as she pushed herself off Oliver and sat with her back to the cupboards. Wyatt was next, glaring at me as soon as he could focus.

"If you move, I break your fingers," I told the ley-line witch, then turned to Amanda, crouching to look in her eyes. "Hi, Amanda," I mocked, and her lips moved, but she didn't say anything, terrified. "Don't worry," I said as I straightened and backed up. "I'm not going to eat you. At least not today. If you make me go hide in the ever-after, I might have a different answer for you."

Ivy silently handed me one of the two remaining guns before she took up a position near the wide entryway to the kitchen, blocking their exit and still having a good view of the hallway through the blown-off door. Her feet were spread wide, her hands were on her hips, and her eyes were dark. The fear and anger weren't dissipating nearly fast enough. Sure, the coven was down, and we had their guns, but what was I supposed to do with them now? Trent would slap a forget curse on them. Pierce would probably want to give them to Al, seeing that those of their ilk had buried him alive. I wasn't going to do either, and I was the one they called black. It just wasn't fair. Frustrated, I tucked the splat gun in the small of my back.

"You'll burn for this," Oliver snarled.

I'd had enough. Angry, I grabbed his shirtfront, shaking him as he tried to get his eyes to focus. "You should have listened to Vivian!" I said, then shoved him back against the cupboard. Wincing, he felt the back of his head, not nearly scared enough.

"Well?" Ivy said. "You want me to find some friends and drain them?"

She was joking, but Leon paled.

I scowled, wondering if Vivian knew they were here and if she was okay. Maybe they just didn't tell her what they were doing. "I have to make a call," I muttered, rocking back to get my phone out of my bag. "If any of them move, break their fingers. If any of them speak, make it their teeth."

Ivy smiled to show her fangs, and Amanda shrank back. Unspent adrenaline made me jittery as I found my bag and pulled out my phone. On impulse, I flipped it open and scrolled to the camera function. "Smile!" I said, snapping a picture of the four of them slumped against the cupboards, then carefully punched in Vivian's number. Not that the press would believe a photo, but I wanted it for my scrapbook.

Oliver glared at the fake sound of a shutter clicking, and he almost got up, settling back when Ivy cooed at him. She was doing remarkably well, only the faintest widening of her pupils giving away her bloodlust.

I sat on the arm of one of the chairs where I could see out into the hall and them. The propped-up door was nearby, and I kicked at it. I hadn't let go of that broken ley line, slowly replenishing my chi and spindling it in case they tried something else.

Finally Vivian picked up. "Hey," I said before she could

even say hello. "Did you know about your friends crashing my hotel room this afternoon? They made a bloody mess."

"No, but that explains a lot." She was on the conference-room floor if the background noise meant anything, and I held the phone closer when I heard Pierce's low inquiry of my state of being. "Everyone still alive?" she asked.

"For the moment. And only because they stocked their splat balls with nonlethal charms. They blew the door right off my room, and I'm not paying for it. Aren't coma spells a little too close to black magic for you guys?"

"Your word against ours," Oliver said snidely, and Ivy moved, threatening to hit him.

His voice was far too confident. I took a breath to tell him to shut up, but his eyes narrowed in victory and he smashed the back of his hand against the cupboard. There was a snap of glass as the stone in his ring broke.

"Down!" I shouted, and Ivy dove for cover. I cowered behind the propped-up door, but nothing happened.

Oliver was laughing, and slowly I got to my feet, embarrassed. Vivian was yelling through the phone, but Ivy was staring at me, her eyes a scared black. A second later, I knew why.

"Earthquake!" she exclaimed, and I staggered for balance as the floor suddenly became Jell-O.

"Get under a table, Rachel!" Vivian was yelling. "Get in a doorway!"

A chunk of ceiling fell between Oliver and me. I froze, not knowing what to do. As one, the four witches ran for the door. It was all I could do to stay upright, and I fell into the couch as they found the hallway and vanished. Pictures were falling, and one of the windows cracked, sounding like a gunshot.

"Rachel!" Ivy cried, then grabbed my arm and yanked me into the threshold of the door to the hallway. We stood there, holding the doorway to remain upright as the ceiling flaked and bits of plaster covered the burn marks. Finally it stopped, but I was still shaking. My eyes went to the empty hall. They were gone.

"Why do people live here?" I asked, looking at the room as if I'd been betrayed as I took the gun out of my pants and dropped it on the couch.

"Did they do that? Make the earthquake?" Ivy asked.

"Probably." Her pupils were still black, and I shifted away from her, not wanting my own fear to tip her over the edge. I put my ear to the phone to find that the connection had been lost. Pierce was probably on his way back already, a day late and a dollar short. The damage to the room from the quake had been minimal, and the broken door from their attack could be dismissed by a paid-off insurance adjuster. I still had my photograph, though.

"And they call me a black witch," I said as I closed my phone and gingerly picked my way through the burns and plaster dust to the window to look down and see if I could spot them leaving. I couldn't help but wonder how many of the smaller quakes that the coast sustained were from the coven. This was just nasty. But at least I was alive.

Ivy had gone to the wet bar, and the hiss of something full of sugar and bubbles opening was loud. We *both* were alive.

"Thank you for helping me," I said.

Ivy exhaled long and loud as she came up from her drink. "You're welcome. Any time."

I smiled, but my thoughts were on her last words before the coven had shown up. Ivy and I worked well together. We always had.

Too bad I'd totally screwed it up.

Twenty

I leaned forward over the backseat to look up at the tall conference hotel we were trying to turn into, feeling lost as we waited for traffic to clear. We weren't in my mom's car since it would be impossible to find a parking spot. No, we were still cashing in on Trent's hospitality, and we'd ridden across town in the car his hotel had on reserve for when their most important guests wanted to go somewhere. The car was long, black, and shiny, and came with a driver. Only problem was that Trent wasn't in it. No Jenks, either. To say I was worried would be like saying pixies were a tad mischievous.

It was getting close to midnight and the conference was starting to kick into high gear. Lights from the oncoming traffic were nonstop. Pierce sat beside me, his feet spread wide as he tried to look unaffected by the crowds, but I could tell they were getting to him. He wasn't happy that the coven had used his chat with Vivian to take a shot at me, and he'd apologized several times, thinking I blamed him. I didn't, but the odds the demons had given me were sounding more realistic than they had.

Pierce was wearing his long coat despite the weather being too hot for it, and he held his hat like a life preserver. Dressed in brown slacks and a brightly colored vest over a white shirt, he made an odd statement—one that was probably going to go unnoticed. Just from the car, I could see three witches in traditional robes and hats. Behind them was a woman wearing wings for the ball tonight, and behind her three guys dressed like Neo from *The Matrix*. To be fair, though, there were just as many people wearing business suits as pointy hats, and the clothing of choice seemed to be jeans. Goth was still in, and almost every fifth person had a glowing bracelet with SAN FRANCISCO—2008 blinking from it, this year's knickknack of choice, apparently.

Ivy is going to fit right in, I thought as I glanced at her, up with the driver. The turn signal of the car ticked as we sat in silence, waiting for someone to move so we could pull into the drop-off area. I leaned back into the cushions, my curiosity rising when Pierce reached into his coat pocket and pulled out a badge with SECURITY on it. "When did you get that?" I asked as he looped it over his head. The name on it was Wallace Smyth. Holy crap, Pierce stole it?

He smiled, teeth glinting in the light of the oncoming traffic. "This afternoon," he said, shuffling through his pockets again to bring out two more. "Before the cowardly dogs attacked you. You can't get past the first floor without a badge. Ivy, here is yours. I thought you'd like the black."

Ivy took the black lanyard, looking bemused. Her badge had her name on it. "Thank you, Pierce," she said, looping it over her neck, and he smiled.

"And, Rachel, I picked up yours, as well. It was good I did. You may have paid for it months ago, but they'd lost it and it took three people an hour to produce another."

"I'm not surprised," I said, feeling the cool plastic in my fingers. Mine said PRESENTER. Great. I was part of the entertainment.

"Thanks, Pierce," I said as I attached it to my bag, hoping there wasn't a bug or a charm on it. If we got stopped because Pierce had stolen a badge, I was going to be mad, but I really appreciated his picking them up. I didn't give him enough credit, and a pang of guilt twanged through me.

The hum of my phone from my bag made it worse, and my

foot started to bob as I ignored it. I knew who it was without looking. Ivy turned from the front, eying me. "If you keep avoiding him, he will think you are mad at him," she said, clearly able to hear it as well.

"I know," I said, wincing, thinking it curious that she knew who it was, too. Maybe I was telegraphing my body language louder than I thought.

"Who?" Pierce questioned, looking up from arranging his badge.

Ivy smiled softly. "Bis is waking up in the daylight when Rachel pulls on a line."

The man made a surprised grunt, and I flushed. "How do *you* know?" I asked her, wishing the traffic would clear so I could avoid this conversation. In my bag, my phone continued to hum.

"*I* take his calls," Ivy said dryly, then turned to face me fully. "Rachel, he's older than you think. He's not looking for a date, he's just confused. Talk to him!"

"I'm confused, too," I exclaimed softly, my guilt growing stronger. "I never asked him to be my gargoyle. It's wrong. It's slavery!"

Exhaling in exasperation, Ivy rolled her eyes to the car's ceiling. "I know what slavery is, and this isn't it," she said. "He does have his own life. And don't forget, he sought you out, not the other way around. You are something he needs, and I don't think you have a say in it. Talk to him. He thinks you don't like him," she added, and I bit my lower lip, even more concerned. That was not at all what I had wanted to happen.

"He's bonding with you? Already?" Pierce said, his eyes wide. "He's just a kid!"

"See?" I said, and Ivy turned around in exasperation. "Even Pierce knows it's wrong."

She was silent, but I could see she was clenching her jaw. Frustrated, I took out my phone. It wasn't humming anymore. A soft depression had taken me, not all of it from the upcoming trial. "He is, isn't he," I said softly as I looked at the tiny screen, more of a statement than a question.

Pierce's hand touched mine, and I jumped. "There is nothing improper about this relationship," he said seriously, making me all the more uncomfortable. "This is not a bond of love, but of necessity. You need a gargoyle to teach you to jump the lines, and in turn, you will give him a holy place to live, safe from demons."

"Safe from demons," I said, and the driver shifted uncomfortably, the back of his neck stiff. "Yeah, right."

But I slipped my phone into a tiny pocket in my bag, hoping I didn't miss his next call. Hell, I should just grow a pair and call him back while I still had a chance. I was running out of time. My stomach hurt, and I ran my hand over the smooth bumps of the French braid my hair was now in. Outside the car, people were moving quickly, their excitement making their pace fast and their words high-pitched. A spot finally opened up and the car pulled into the drop-off area. Pierce was out of the car even before it stopped moving, coming around to open my door. Ivy dropped her head and searched her purse for a tip, and I gathered myself to get out, glad to put off my chat with Bis for a few minutes more. The scent of exhaust-tainted wet cement mixed with the sound of hushed tires and loud conversations over engine noise.

Was Bis bonding with me? It sounded so . . . demonic.

"Rachel?"

It was Pierce, and he had his arm out to escort me. Giving him a worried smile, I looped my arm in his and together we went to the curb. I felt like I was in a spotlight, but no one was looking at me despite my wearing enough leather for a small cow. I'd left Al's purple sash at home—and the cap. I didn't care if I was the only one who would know purple was a sign of demon favor. It felt like a leash.

Ivy's door shut with a solid *thunk,* and the car took off, immediately replaced by another just like it. "Ready?" she said as she joined us, her eyes bright and her motions quick.

She was wearing her boots, and they clicked smartly on the pavement.

"As much as I'll ever be," I said, turning to the twin set of double doors. Pierce's hand landed on mine, and with him on one side and Ivy on the other, we went in, my high-magic-detecting amulet sputtering a hazy red. I wasn't surprised when every last erg of painstakingly gathered ever-after washed out of me. Hotel security. You can't have a group of witches this size without some kind of leveling field. Pierce's hand left me, and he shifted his coat on his shoulders as if trying to fit into a new skin.

Our pace slowed, as much for the people clustered near the door as for the sound of a hundred conversations beating on our ears. Single file, we passed among the groups of people gathering here to either step out to make a call, have a smoke, or just use the front as a place to meet their friends. I followed Pierce with half my attention, more interested in the huge chandelier that stretched up six stories, dominating the entire interior cave. The ever-after draining out of me when we had crossed the threshold had been caused by something and I was betting it was this. It looked a lot like the device Lee had had on his boat, but a whole lot bigger.

My dropping gaze landed on a black-suited man with absolutely no expression on his face. He was wearing sunglasses and staring at me. Nervous, I set a hand on Pierce's shoulder, anxious not to lose him in the crowd.

"I see them, too," Ivy said from behind me.

Them? There was more than one?

Pierce turned as we finally got through the worst of the crowd. "I walked the place this afternoon," he said, glancing first at the man I had noticed, then to another by a bank of elevators. "Registration is that way. Food is that way. Rest areas are on the first and third floors."

I was guessing he meant bathrooms, and a sudden urge to cross my legs and do the little-girl dance took me. *Relax, Rachel.*

"I should have been doing that," Ivy muttered, and Pierce nodded, ticking me off. Ivy had been there to help me beat off the coven. He had no right to make her feel guilty.

Still not undoing his coat, he led us across the lower floor. "You were a mite busy keeping Rachel's body and soul together," Pierce said, then pointed up to the overlooking second story. "The common entry to the auditorium is up there. There is an entrance on the ground floor, but it's guarded. Coven members only."

"Good, an escalator," I said, stifling a shiver.

"Since when are you afraid of elevators?" Ivy said as she got on before me and Pierce got on behind me, his hand on the small of my back, steadying me. I'd take offense, but I was ready to bolt and my knees felt like rubber.

"I'm not," I protested, pulse quickening. *God, it's about to happen. My entire life is going to change in the next hour.* "I'm—"

"Thinking about the coven taking a last potshot at you. I know." Ivy came back even with me as we passed a group of harmless-looking witches on their way down. I dropped my gaze so I didn't have to make eye contact, adjusting my badge on my bag. If I held my arm just right, it would be obvious I had a badge without making it easy to read my name. I didn't want to be recognized, but I think I was by the amount of whispering and pointing going on. Unless it was my dress.

Ivy was first off, and I found myself exhaling as I followed. Pierce bumped into me, and looping his arm in mine, he almost pulled me to the set of double doors across from the wide, low-ceilinged, lobbylike area. People were clustered here, too, and I felt myself pale as the conversations stilled and faces turned to us. I heard the click of a phone camera, and I shook myself.

"Chin high," Pierce said softly, but I was nauseated. I'd been running from this for what seemed like a lifetime.

His fingers touched mine, and I felt a tingle. He was wire tight, but it was the faint pulse of cracked ever-after in him that caught my attention. "How are you tapping a line?" I said as we settled in at the back of a short line to get in. They were checking badges, and I was doubly glad Pierce had picked up mine.

Pierce curled his fingers to take a stronger grip on me, and my shoulders eased when I felt the warmth of a masculine-tasting energy fill me. "I borrowed an amulet from a security member," he said, shooting me a sly glance, then looking dead ahead. "And his badge. Don't worry. Wallace never reported it. He's being entertained."

From Pierce's wry expression, I had a pretty good idea of how Wally was spending his evening. *Oh, man. That is going to look great if they find out.*

Beside us, Ivy chuckled, and I felt tons better as Pierce funneled energy into me, slippery or not. It would leave as soon as I let go of him, but in the interim it was nice. "You are a cad," I whispered, leaning in to smell his redwood scent mixing with a woodsy cologne. *When did he have time to shower?*

"But a smart one," Ivy said. "Good thinking."

Pierce pulled his gaze from the head of the line. "I won't let harm touch you. If there's trouble, I'll be there, and as soon as we get through security, I'll give you the amulet."

I could see the sense in that, and I nodded as my headache began to ease. The line moved forward, and I took the pen after checking my lethal-amulet detector. It wasn't working, but old habits die hard. As the bored woman behind the table talked to her neighbor, I signed the paper, adding a period at the end of my name to break any psychic connection. I handed it to Pierce, who immediately gave it to Ivy.

"I'm her security," he lied to the woman, taking my bicep a little more firmly.

I eyed Pierce, letting him manhandle me since he seemed to enjoy the excuse and I couldn't protest without causing a stir. A flash of interest broke across the woman's face, and she looked from the paper Ivy was signing, to the badge pinned to my bag, to me. In one breath, her expression went from pleasant to disgusted. "Oh, it's you. You have a reserved seat up front."

Oh, it's you? Nice. "Thank you," I said pointedly as Ivy pushed the paper back toward her. "Do you know if Trent Kalamack is here yet?"

"No." She was breathing fast, and the ladies to either side of her were silent.

My gut twisted. Black witch. They thought I was a black witch, and they could hardly stand me. "We're going to need one more place," I said, indicating Ivy, and the woman shook her head.

"She can't go in."

I'd had it with women who thought they had ultimate power because they'd been given a tiny task, but I exhaled, trying to relax. "Why not?" I asked, voice level as I hitched my shoulder bag higher.

"Witches only."

Pierce looked up, scanning the crowd behind us as someone began calling "Yoo-hoo!" in a loud, demanding voice.

"Trent Kalamack isn't a witch," I said, my temper rising.

Pierce let go of me to wave at someone, and the power that had been seeping through me drained away. A headache slammed into me, and I stiffened.

"Mr. Kalamack is part of the proceedings," the woman said. "*She* isn't."

Angry, I put my hands on the table and leaned into her slightly. Ivy drew me back, her eyes holding a surprising lack of anger. "I'll get in another way," she murmured.

"No." I pulled from her, and the woman looked frightened that Pierce wasn't paying attention to me. "I've been shot at, bugged, and attacked. I want you there, and there's no reason you can't come in!"

The woman fidgeted nervously, glancing first at Pierce, then the people starting to pile up behind me. "It's for security reasons," she said, and I nodded dramatically.

"Uh-huh. Which is exactly why I want her with me."

"Rachel!" a familiar cheerful voice exclaimed at my elbow, and I spun. Pierce was grinning. Beside him was my mother, a shopping bag under her arm, a big yellow hat on her head, and a broomstick in her hand. She was beaming, and every thought went flying out of my head.

"Mom!" I exclaimed, eyes wide as I gaped at her. "What are you doing here?"

"Damn, you make even white leather look good!" She gave me a huge hug, dropping her bag and pulling me close. The scent of lilac and redwood filled my senses, and the broomstick pressed into my back. She stepped away with a hand on her hat to keep it from falling off, and her eyes glinted with unshed tears.

"I flew in this morning," she said, glancing down at her badge. "I wanted to see you. I knew if I waited around, you'd show up in the middle of trouble. And here you are!"

I gave her another hug, not believing this. The woman at the table gestured for the next person in line, and we moved to the side.

"Mom, I'm glad you're here," I said, thinking she looked great, her red hair cut in a bob and her jeans and T-shirt showing off her figure. Now that she wasn't dressing down, we could almost be sisters. Dread hit me, though, as she started moving us to the double doors. If things didn't go well, this might be the last day I'd ever see her.

"Come on," she said, taking my arm and leading me forward as if we were going for coffee, not finding seats at my trial. "Trenton got us seats up front, but if you wait too long, numbnuts start trying to sit in them." She turned to look behind us. "Hi, Ivy. It's good to see you," she said, and Ivy murmured something back, never quite comfortable around my mother.

My mom's pace faltered as she gave Pierce the once-over. "Wallace, eh?" she said 'dryly. "You must be Pierce. Nice to finally meet the man who got my daughter her first I.S. record. You'll do, I suppose. I hope you're good in bed. It's a pain in the ass trying to train you men to do what pleases a woman."

I caught a glimpse of Pierce's shocked expression, but my last fear had been banished. It was my mother, not a look-alike. If it came into her head, it came out of her mouth.

"Mom . . . ," I protested, but she was off again, saying it was good to see me and that she liked my hair like this, asking me if I'd been in St. Louis when the arch fell down, and what about that earthquake this afternoon? Wasn't that something? I knew her chatter was her way of coping, and I said nothing but made the odd noise at the right moment.

The double doors opened before us as someone went in. My eyes rose, and my feet kept moving. The muffled noise hit me first, and the smell of foam and the cotton fabric on the chairs. It was all blue and gray, and they were piping in music. It was nearly full already, and the sound of a hundred conversations was daunting, even if the acoustics had been arranged to soak it in. The stage was a good fifteen feet below where we'd come in, well lit, with a podium in the middle and an oval table holding six chairs facing the audience. Oliver and Leon were already there, ignoring the mass of people as Oliver talked and Leon listened.

My heart thumped, and I froze.

"Is that your mother?" Pierce whispered.

I started to answer, and the door attendant moved in front of us. "Ma'am, you can't go in," he said to Ivy, and my head snapped up.

Already inside, my mother turned, her chin up and her eyes glinting. "Get the hell out of the way," she said loudly as she shoved her way back to us and claimed Ivy's elbow. "Don't you know who this is? Move, or I'll jam this broomstick up your ass."

Pierce stood speechless, but I was grinning. "Yep, that's my mother," I said, then followed Ivy when my mother yanked her over the threshold, glaring at the man as if ready to make good on her threat if he made so much as a peep. The door attendant was way outclassed, and he gave up, cowed.

Ivy glanced over her shoulder at me as my mother led her down the steps to the floor of the amphitheater. Slowly my smile faded. There were too many people in here, and the stage looked huge.

"Your mother isn't afraid to speak her mind," Pierce said, and my shoulders eased as he took my hand and the ever-after seeped in. I knew it wouldn't last, and I gripped his fingers, afraid to let go.

"She's like that," I said, head down as I watched my step. People had noticed our entrance, and the conversations were shifting. More whispering, more bitter gossip.

Pierce's grip on mine tightened, and I looked up, feeling a warning in his touch. Vivian had come from the back, looking confident and unique in a flowing, princesslike robe of tie-dyed colors, all purple, blue, and green. Her hair was arranged off her neck, and she looked like an upscale San Francisco hippie, as far from my white-leather-clad sleekness as a bird was from a frog. Worry flashed through me. Robes flowing, she strode to the podium, bending to pull out an amulet. She looked good, rested and ready. I wished I was.

"Test," she said simply as she held the amulet, and when her voice rose with a pleasant volume over the babble, she dropped it into a pocket and went to talk to Oliver. The entire auditorium had the feeling of preparation and excitement, and I gave Vivian a stupid little hand wave when she looked up, following Oliver's finger pointing to me. He was wearing an impressive suit, and again I felt nervous in my outfit. *White? Thanks a hell of a lot, Al.*

Vivian straightened, breaking eye contact with me before I could get any sense of what she was thinking. Oliver was supposed to vote for me, but after this afternoon, I doubted that would happen despite the agreement we'd come to in an FIB interrogation room two thousand miles away. I was hoping I wouldn't need my gentle four-word reminder that I could bring witch society down. *We came from demons.*

Finally we made it to the ground floor and the small space

before the stage. My mother and Ivy were waiting at the head of an empty row of seats. Actually, the three rows after that one were empty, too, no one wanting to get too close to us. Nerves wouldn't let me sit, and we clustered together in the aisle. As Pierce and my mother made small talk, I scanned the rising rows for Trent.

Ivy leaned in, smiling with her lips shut. "You look green. You want me to go up there with you and hold your hand?"

"Can't you be nice to me for once?" I said, and she laughed. "Trent isn't going to show," I added, wondering what my mother was telling Pierce. His eyes were wide, and my mother's expression was intent.

"Is that necessarily a bad thing?" Ivy asked, and I tried to decide if she was joking.

"I'm worried about Jenks," I said, and she nodded. "Has he called?" I asked for the umpteenth time, and she shook her head, eyes falling from mine.

I thought of my phone, in my bag, wondering if I should turn it off. I didn't want to miss Jenks's call if it should come in. A flash of guilt hit me. It was too late now to call Bis, too.

A stir at the door we had come in caught my attention, and I turned away when the man my mom had threatened came in, pointing our way. "Don't look," I told Ivy, thinking that they were going to haul her out, but my fear vanished in a wash of elation when the familiar clatter of pixy wings sparked through me.

"Jenks!" I exclaimed, suddenly feeling ten feet tall as I saw the glint of pixy dust. I didn't care if people were staring and whispering loudly. I waved like a fool, grinning when a bright sparkle at the top of the theater dropped to us.

"Oh my God, Jenks!" I said, elated and feeling the size difference between us keenly as he came to a pixy-dust-laden halt in the center of our group. He was smiling, a long tear in his black sleeve and his hair matted, but he was okay. "How did it go? Are you all right? Where's Trent?" I asked, wanting to give Jenks a hug but having to settle for extending my hand for him.

Jenks nodded to everyone, zipping around Ivy to wreathe her in silver sparkles. "I'm good," he said, wings moving well and clearly overflowing with energy. "You'll never believe it, Rache," he said, eyes sparkling with news. "Trent's here. He's in the bathroom with Lucy."

"Lucy?" I asked, wondering if Ellasbeth had a younger sister. "What did you do?"

Jenks landed on my hand, then sprang into the air, unable to contain himself. "You'll never guess!" he said, darting back and forth. "The guy is slicker than toad snot. Trent is—"

"A daddy," Ivy interrupted, her gaze fixed on the door we'd come in.

I spun as Jenks yo-yoed up and down, shrilling so high and fast I couldn't understand him. My eyes bugged out, and beside me, my mother swore. "No. Friggin'. Way," I said.

Trent was on the threshold in his usual thousand-dollar suit, rearranging his badge and surrounded by too many women. One was jiggling a fussing infant. A girl from the looks of the sweet little bonnet. *Lucy?*

"No. Friggin'. Way!" I said again, touching gazes with Ivy before I looked back and saw Trent take the baby. My eyes widened. She was his?

"Yes, way!" Jenks was saying, and Pierce sighed, dropping back a step. "I about crapped my pants when I found out. No wonder Trent wouldn't spill. That's his kid. His and Ellasbeth's. That's what he was doing, Rache! We were baby snatching! Like elves used to in the old days!"

Trent had done the nasty with Ellasbeth? Ewwwwww.

Pierce seemed bored by it, but my mother was melting into a puddle of anticipation, her hands almost outstretched, as Trent made his way to us.

"It was some ancient elf quest to prove himself and become a man. He had to steal a baby and not get caught," Jenks said, still too excited to land anywhere, and I couldn't look away. *No. Friggin'. Way. Trent had a kid?*

"He stole her!" Jenks said, finally landing on my shoulder.

"Right out of her crib. Like in the old days when they would leave changelings, but Trent only left a crumpled bit of paper in the crib. Rache, he sang this weird little song, and she just woke up and loved him."

I had to admit that Trent seemed to know what he was doing as he patted the little girl to make her stop fussing. He looked up, his eyes meeting mine still holding a blissful happiness tempered with a severe protectiveness. "He traveled three thousand miles to steal a baby?"

"*His* baby! Not just any brat," Jenks said, wings fanning my neck. "His and Ellasbeth's. You got fairy farts in your ears? She was pregnant when you broke up their wedding. Lucy is the first elf baby to be born perfect, even before Ceri's. The first without the demon curse, and every baby born after her will be perfect. Because of you."

I licked my lips, and Pierce moved to make room for Trent. The next elf generation. Lucy was the beginning. That's what Trent had meant. And it was because of me? No, it was because of Trent, Jenks, Ivy, and me. We'd done it together.

The noise of the auditorium seemed to fade as Trent scuffed to a halt before us, his ears red as he met everyone's eyes. "Trent?" I managed, and then my mother broke down.

"Ohhh, let me hold her!" my mom exclaimed, hands reaching out.

Immediately everyone relaxed. Trent's attention fell from me, focused entirely on his little girl as my mother came close. "Ms. Morgan," Trent said, his hands changing position as he carefully moved his . . . daughter? "She's a temperamental little thing. She might not like you."

"Of course she'll like me," my mother huffed. People were watching, and onstage, the last of the coven members had assumed their places. My mother took Lucy, and the little girl began to cry, green eyes spilling over as she refused to look at my mother, searching until she found Trent, then making a face as if she'd been betrayed.

"Oh, dear," my mother said, jiggling her carefully, knowing

that it was a lost cause. "Such a beautiful thing you are. Don't cry, sweetie. Your daddy is right there."

Jenks was laughing—not at my mother, but at my and Ivy's shocked expressions. "You're a dad?" I tried again, and Trent shrugged, his attention lingering on my dress.

"It happens."

"Rachel, you take her," my mother said, clearly uncomfortable. "She might like you."

"No. Mom, no!" I protested, but it was my mother we were talking about, and it was either take the baby or have her hit the floor. I had no choice, and as Trent stiffened, I found I was holding another person in my arms. I couldn't look at her as her blanket fell away, scared almost as she cried, but I held her against me, and burn my toast if I didn't jiggle a little on my feet. She was kind of soft and squishy, but she fit nicely against me. I gave another hop, and when I looked into her eyes, she quit crying.

Trent's hands dropped from where he had been going to snatch her away. Pale eyebrows up, he said, "She likes you," as if he didn't believe it.

"Of course she likes Rache," Jenks said belligerently, leaving me to hover before the baby and make her sneeze from his silver pixy dust. Cooing, Lucy flung her hand out—searching for Jenks, probably—but latching on to my finger instead.

Shit.

Her tiny hand gripped mine with a surprising warmth, and in a shocking wash of emotion, I felt everything I knew shift. The scent of cinnamon and baby powder hit me, and as my eyes widened, my heart melted, making room for her. As I gazed into Lucy's green eyes, and seeing her pale hair and perfect face, it was as if something had flipped a switch in me. I'd held babies before. Hell, I'd babysat for my old friend at the I.S., but this small person holding my finger had looked to me for protection from the noise, the crowd, and the frightening sparkles of pixy dust. All of a sudden, I didn't want to give her back.

My gaze came up, fastening on my mother. Unshed tears made her eyes dark. She was gazing at Lucy with longing, remembering Robbie and me. When she glanced up, I gave her a rueful smile. Damn it, she'd given me Lucy for just this reason. It wasn't an elf thing, it was just . . . life.

"She likes you," Trent said again, but he was reaching for her, jealous maybe.

"Perhaps she knows you helped her survive," Ivy said from the background.

"Look at her ears, Rache," Jenks said as he returned to my shoulder, and I moved away from Trent. "You gotta look at her ears."

Her ears? Pulling her back to me, I leaned closer, breathing in cinnamon as I peeked under her bonnet. Trent's jaw was clenched, but he let me do it. Lucy just cooed, and I stared as Ivy leaned close to me to see as well.

"You've got to be kidding," I whispered, my attention darting up to Trent as he frowned. "They're pointy." Trent was annoyed, but I was almost laughing. "You guys have to dock your ears to fit in?" I said in a hushed voice.

"Not anymore," he answered, reaching to take her.

Lucy gurgled as I felt her almost-not-there weight leave me, kicking in frustration until her father—*oh my God, Trent had a baby*—took her. My shoulders slumped, and I felt her loss. On the stage, they were making motions to start the meeting, and Pierce was trying to get my mother and Ivy to sit down. "Is she really yours?" I asked Trent as they took their seats in the second row while he rearranged Lucy's blanket around her.

He wouldn't look at me. "In about six different ways," he said, and remembering how I'd felt after holding her for just one minute, I knew what he meant.

"Trent, why didn't you tell me you were after your . . . child?"

All around us, people were settling in, hushing themselves, getting ready for a show. But he was oblivious to them as he looked at me, a mixture of embarrassment and reluctance in him that I'd never seen before. "I don't know," he admitted, seeming more honest, more bewildered than he'd ever been before. "It sounded lame. Me? Going three thousand miles to steal a baby? I'm a product of the twenty-first century, not some elf with a title living in a castle with servants."

"Yeah, but it was your kid," Jenks said, having finally parked it on my shoulder.

Lucy was kicking at her blanket, and Trent tucked it back not even knowing he had done it. "She wasn't mine until I saw her." His gaze was unfocused as he remembered. "She's . . ." He stopped, unable to put it into words as he looked at her. She was entirely her own person but needed him for everything.

"She's beautiful," I said softly.

Trent's attention flicked to me, and his grip on her grew possessive. "I'd do anything for her. Risk anything. I never got it until now. I never understood true sacrifice."

Huh. Maybe Lucy was going to save us all.

Jenks clattered his wings, going to distract her and make her squirm. "Just like any parent, Trent," he said as he hovered over her, reminding me of who he was. "Think you can *do anything* for Rachel for the next hour? You owe her. I may have helped you get Lucy, but Rachel got you here alive to do it. Even with your *help*."

My chest tightened, and where I was came rushing back. Trent was nodding, and Vivian began tapping her amplifying amulet for attention. "Just about anything," he said, smiling with half his face. He looked at me, and even that vanished. "Rachel, it's going to get bad. You're going to have to trust me. You've got to lose before you can win."

"Oh, that makes a lot of sense," I said darkly. "You aren't old enough for wise-old-man crap. Even with a three-month-old in your arms."

He leaned close as Jenks zipped off to talk to my mother. "I mean it," he said, Lucy reaching up for my face. "Oliver is going to weasel out of his promise no matter what I say. He knows you're not going to tell anyone that witches were born from demons. If you do, witch society will crumble in a century of witch hunts that will make Salem look like a puppet show."

"No," I said, but he wasn't listening.

"You're going to lose," he said firmly. "And when you do, I'm telling you, don't do anything stupid. Go with it. Go to Alcatraz. Go with Al. I don't care, but just go with it. It's not over when that bell rings."

Trent's gaze went to the silver bell on the coven's table, and fear slid through me. I heard what he was saying. Oliver was scum. Trent didn't see me walking out of here. He had me lost and was planning a comeback. I looked at Ivy, and her eyes dilated at my fear.

"Take your seats, please," Vivian said loudly from the podium, her words bouncing through the auditorium and silencing 90 percent of the noise.

Pierce was at my elbow, and he pulled me down the empty aisle of seats, putting us right in front of my mother and Ivy. Trent edged in next, and we all sat. On the stage, there were two empty chairs at the coven's table, one for Vivian, one for Brooke. I could not lose. I couldn't. I'd be in the ever-after, taking my sun in thieving snatches.

Vivian gestured at the silver bell, and it chimed, making me jump. A wave of force had echoed out of it, having the feeling of a bubble going up. The auditorium was closed for the duration. No one in or out. It had begun.

Twenty-one

I said pipe down!" Vivian said crossly when the room reacted
to the doors locking. Trent tried to quiet Lucy with an offered pinkie, and she protested, refusing it. Behind me, my
mother piled her stuff on the empty seat next to her and settled
in, completely unfazed. Pierce took off his hat, ran a nervous
hand over his soft curls, and dropped his hand to finger his
stolen badge.

"You will *shut up!*" Vivian shouted, cheeks coloring when
Oliver said something only those on the stage could hear. "As
the junior member of the coven, it's my responsibility to maintain order at these proceedings, and you will be silent or I'll
gag you myself!"

My mother leaned forward, between Pierce and me. "She's
a bit of a hard-ass," she said, and Jenks buzzed his wings.

"You've no idea, Ms. Morgan," he said. Then he sat on my
shoulder, his wings tickling my neck. It was good to have him
back.

Vivian put her hands on her hips and waited, frowning.
Slowly the witches grew silent as she used a sixth-grade-
teacher stare on them. I put a hand on my stomach, feeling
sick. Everyone I cared about was around me. Oliver had promised to clear my name if I publicly apologized for using black
magic and never went to the press with the fact that witches
were stunted demons. I had held up my end of the bargain,

even when the coven had tried to off me, but Trent, playing peekaboo with Lucy, believed they'd back out of it, scared I'd go to the press with the ugly truth anyway. If Oliver called my bluff, I didn't know if I could do it. Not only would it destroy our society, but it would upset the balance of everyone else's. *I'll hurt him. I'll friggin' make Oliver sorry if he screws me over.*

I jumped when Pierce touched me, a slow trickle of broken ever-after turning into a rush that made me feel ill once he had my attention. "You need this," he said, slipping me the security amulet.

"Pierce, no," I whispered, not taking my eyes off the stage as I tried to shove it back into his hands, but he only dropped it in my pocket. Neither one of us was touching it, but it was a ley-line charm, and I tried to dampen the flow to something that didn't feel like tinfoil on teeth. My headache eased, and I was starting to wonder if I needed to be in touch with a ley line to feel good.

"Thank you," I whispered, and he sat in his chair, totally happy with himself.

"It's a trifle," he said, and I touched his hand with my free one, completing the circuit and giving him a taste.

"I mean, for being here with me," I said, and he smiled.

"I know." From my other side, Trent sighed dramatically, and Pierce pulled away, turning his attention to the stage.

"Thank you," Vivian said sarcastically, not a hint of over-done dramatic flair in her speech. "This is going to be a long night, and I want it done before sunrise so you princess wannabes can hit the fairy ball on the beach, so I'm going to throw out all the dramatic crap you're all used to from Oliver and cut to the chase."

The casual, matter-of-fact manner in which she was conducting herself had caused a stir, but I was relieved. Vivian was a bit of fire and spit, and I didn't think I could stomach seeing her standing before us in robes and speaking with the airy distance of pomp and circumstance.

"This doesn't mean I will be dispensing with the *rules*," she said, accentuating the word as if talking to Oliver alone. "And since we can't do anything without a full quorum, we're going to take five minutes and swear in a new coven member."

Beside me, Pierce trembled. His hands formed fists, and then he opened them, setting them on his pants with his fingers spread wide. There was an excited reaction from the crowd, and my attention went to the five hopefuls sitting in the same row we were but on the other side of the theater.

"Initiates?" Vivian said, her mood shifting to one of ceremony.

"Excuse me," Pierce said as he stood, causing a stir among the people who noticed him.

Trent looked up at him in surprise. "Where is he going?"

I didn't answer, instead leaning back when Ivy touched my shoulder and whispered, "This should be interesting."

Vivian hadn't noticed him crossing to the second set of stairs, focused on the other five hopefuls coming up the left side. "After much deliberation . . . ," she began, then hesitated as the crowd reacted to Pierce taking the stage and walking steadily forward. Vivian turned to him, and I swear her eyes held amused anticipation.

Pierce halted, just shy of center stage. "May I approach, Madam Coven Member?" he asked, voice booming so he could be heard without an amulet.

Oliver reached to touch his own amulet. "No," he said flatly, and Vivian gave him a withering look.

"You gave me this job, Oliver," she said sharply. "Let me do it." And as Oliver frowned, she turned and dramatically crossed the stage to hand Pierce another amulet. "The coven recognizes Gordian Pierce."

Pierce fingered the metal ring, his eyes going everywhere but to me as he took off his coat and went to set it over the podium. Slowly he took over the stage without saying a word. His head came up, and the crowd became still. He wasn't wearing anything unusual, just brown slacks, a white shirt, and that flamboyant vest, carefully buttoned and holding a pocket watch. The way he carried himself evolved as he stood there, and I stifled a shiver as Trent grunted in surprise. He was different, dangerous. And I had no idea what he was going to do.

"I'm of a mind to beg your pardon, Madam Coven Member," he said softly, his words going out perfectly with the help of the amulet. "And with all due respect to those fine witches you have assembled here, sworn in and ready to commit their lives to service, there is no coven opening. I am here. I am the sixth. And that's all the pie there is."

The crowd stirred, most of the noise swallowed up by the space. With a sliding sound of wood, Oliver stood. "Get him out of here!" he roared, stirring the people into a buzzing whisper.

Pierce didn't recognize him, fixed on Vivian, waiting out the noise.

"You are a black witch!" Oliver shouted. "Shunned and—"

Pierce spun, and Oliver's words choked off. "Bricked into the ground, aye, where I gasped out my last, six feet under, buried alive and breaking my nails to bloody stumps as I tried to claw my way free. And I died despite it. But I'm a coven member nonetheless, and I have returned to claim my position. And 156 years of back pay."

Ivy leaned forward and tapped my shoulder. "I take back everything I said about your sleeping with him."

"Gee, thanks," I said dryly, and Trent stifled a guffaw. Jenks, though, clattered his wings for us to shut up so he could hear.

The other coven members put their heads together, and I waited, watching them. Amanda looked scared, Oliver full of bluster, Wyatt peeved, and Leon like he wanted it to be over.

It took only a moment, and then Oliver said, "You are a black witch, tried and condemned. You have lost your claim. Security!"

Dropping back a step, Pierce took a stiff stance. I knew he

couldn't tap a line, but it was dramatic, and the approaching men halted before they even hit the puddle of light.

"I will be heard!" he shouted, eyes angry. "This meeting, called for Rachel Morgan to apologize for using black magic in her effort to save lives, is a farce. The goal here is to validate or deny the use of black magic for the greater good, not apologize for using it. I opine that until you make a fist of the issue, I have a claim!"

Vivian waved security back, and Pierce relaxed. From the audience rose a nervous murmur. Oliver, though, seemed too catty for my comfort. He looked to his left, then his right, to get everyone's opinion and their nods, and sat back down with a magnanimous gesture.

Crap, it was all or nothing now. Apologizing wasn't going to do it. I had to justify myself. Thanks, Pierce.

Vivian's smile grew wide, as if that was a good thing, and I let out a breath, unaware that I'd been holding it. "The vacant coven membership remains in question then," she said, glancing back into the wings to someone on the support staff. "All in favor of exploring the validity of legalizing black magic in specific people for the intent of the greater good and using the case of Rachel Morgan as the cornerstone?"

As one, they all muttered their ayes.

"Opposed?"

It was simply a formality, but no one breathed as she waited to the count of five. Clearly pleased, Vivian looked down at me, and my heart stopped. "Rachel, is this okay with you?"

"S-sure," I stammered when Trent jabbed his elbow into me.

"Can we have two more chairs up here?" Vivian asked someone in the wings, and a skinny, tall man in black slacks and shirt emerged with two plain brown folding chairs.

"Well, get your ass up there," Jenks said, and I had a moment of panic.

"Wish me luck," I whispered as I set my bag on my chair and stood. I was feeling Jenks's loss already as he stayed, perched on the back of my chair, beside Trent, where his dust sifted over a cooing Lucy, reaching for him with her little hands.

I felt unreal as I watched my steps, head down and looking at the red-and-silver pattern in the carpet as I made my way to the stage. The stairs had treads on them, but I still held the railing as I went up, my palms starting to sweat. Someone in the crowd hissed as I found the light. It was warm up here, but I shivered. Pierce stood beside the podium where the two new chairs waited. He wasn't smiling. And I was so friggin' scared.

"Come on, Rachel!" Jenks shrilled. "You're a badass, not a bad witch!"

My head came up, jaw clenched. He was right, and I gave him a bunny-eared kiss-kiss. Someone laughed. I couldn't see who it was through the lights, but I breathed easier.

Vivian's Möbius-strip pin caught the glint of the spotlight, and wisps of her blond hair that had escaped her elaborate coiffure drifted in the heat as she approached me. Confident and sure, she looked miles away from the tangled mess in the back of my car. Handing me my amplification amulet, she gave my shoulder a squeeze to publicly show her support. It was a bold move on her part, and I appreciated it. She couldn't be fired, but as Pierce had proved, you could be retired.

"It's a ley-line charm," she said. "But you have to touch it for it to work. Good luck."

"Thanks." I looped the amulet over my head, making sure that the small disc wasn't touching skin. I didn't want anyone hearing my private words to Pierce.

He sat a moment after I did, and I tried to look attractive but not slutty in my leather dress. I had a moment's thought for the cap I'd forgotten, on the couch back at the hotel, and then I turned to Pierce as he said, "Are you well?"

"I'm okay. Yourself?" I was going to puke. I knew it.

Pierce sent his gaze into the glare. "About the same. Having died once, the outcome of a public trial has lost much of its threat."

"I'd think it would be the other way around," I said, then

jerked when Vivian called my name. She was back at the podium, waiting.

"Rachel? I think everyone knows why you're here. Would you like to say anything?"

Some of the crowd muttered, and I thought I heard "black witch," but I stood, trying to gather everyone's attention with a moment of silence. I picked out Trent through the glare, thinking he looked worried as he tried to keep Lucy quiet. I daren't look at my mother or Ivy, and Jenks was too small. This would be tricky. If I lied, the silver bell on the table would ring. I had come here under the lie of having been forced into black magic to test Trent's security systems. That wasn't the issue anymore, and I'd have to be careful with what I said.

Finally there was silence. I took a breath. Feeling dizzy, I reached to touch my amulet. "I'm here because of manipulation by both the coven and outside forces, and I'm claiming my shunning should be permanently annulled."

You'd think I'd dropped a bloody vampire into a sweet-sixteen pajama party. The crowd burst into noise, and I felt sick when from up in the balcony, the chant "Burn her, burn her" drifted down.

"Steady, Rachel," Pierce said, his eyes narrowed as he sat beside me. "They're ignorant and frightened."

"Yeah, but they can still kill me," I said, thinking longingly of my kitchen.

"Enough!" Vivian shouted. "You want me to clear the auditorium and do this behind closed doors?"

Fear tightened my shoulders, and I almost panicked. A private "trial" would be my end. The threat of my going public with our origins would be gone. I'd never even get my say, but would be shoved on a boat and be on my way to Alcatraz on the midnight run. But Vivian was only trying to get them to be quiet, and it worked. Still holding her frown, aimed at the crowd, she gestured for me to continue.

"I was forced into learning black magic in order to survive," I said truthfully, nodding to Trent, in the first row. That a hundred circumstances had forced me, not Trent, was beside the point, and I couldn't help it if they thought I was talking about him. "I know black magic, but I've never hurt anyone but myself. And I'm not going to apologize for it." My eye twitched as I thought of the fairies, and from the coven's table, there was a tiny ping of sound as the silver bell rang, giving evidence of my lie.

"No, that's a lie," I quickly amended as the crowd stirred. "I killed fairies to keep them from burning down my church and massacring my partner and his family when the coven started taking potshots at me. But I've never hurt anyone who wasn't trying to kill me first."

The crowd responded with an almost disappointed ferocity. I felt my face pale when I realized that these people, whom I counted as my own, were actually *eager* for my blood. They reminded me of Trent's dogs, and my knees became weak.

"I'm sorry, Rachel," Pierce said, touching my hand. "I'm so sorry."

"Fairies aren't real people!" Jenks shrilled, his familiar voice cutting through the noise. "That doesn't count."

Oliver leaned forward to pour himself a cup of water, looking too satisfied to live. "But Rachel believes they *are* people, and she used black magic to kill them," he said as he touched his amulet. "I say it stands."

I could see the rest of the night with crystal clarity. Vivian would be on my side, but Oliver would pick holes in everything until there would be nothing left of my defense. I found Trent in the haze, and he shrugged, having known it already. Frightened, I took a breath to refute the statement, though I didn't know how.

Pierce stood, surprising the crowd into soft whispering. "I was there when Rachel twisted the curse to burn the fairies," he said. "I was part of it as much as she was. More so. There was no way to survive but for burning them. Rachel took part, but she drew the curse back into herself at great cost before it was fully invoked, turning a deadly curse into a nonlethal one, saving most of the fairies at great hurt to herself."

"She drew a curse into herself and survived?" someone shouted. "She's a demon, that's what she is!"

My eyes widened, and I swear, my heart stopped. I looked to Trent, panicked. I hadn't told. *I hadn't told anyone!*

Everyone in the audience started talking, and Oliver just sat back and enjoyed it, arms crossed in confidence. I was going to be branded a black witch and sentenced to Alcatraz. There was no way around it. Damn it, Al was going to win.

"The issue at hand is not whether killing fairies is lawful!" Trent shouted as he stood, and those around him quieted. "Who here hasn't accidentally killed one of the winged folk? It's a tragedy, but should we all be considered murderers for it?"

I exhaled and let go of Pierce's hand, then winced when he shook it, trying to get the circulation back. I hadn't even known I'd taken it. Jeez, I probably looked like a scared little girl. *And Trent had spoken for me?*

Vivian walked to the podium and pulled another amulet from under it. "The coven recognizes Trenton Kalamack."

I'll give Trent one thing. He knew how to make an entrance. He was already halfway to the stairs, and Lucy babbled as he took them. The crowd's noise rose and fell, and I detected a softening. It was hard to think ugly thoughts when you were watching a highly successful businessman with a happy baby in his arms.

Trent and Vivian murmured a few words, their heads almost touching, and then he took the amulet. Lucy's cooing rang out, and then Trent disentangled her little fingers from the amulet, whispering to her in what sounded like another language. The crowd liked that, and I wondered if he'd done it intentionally. Trent gathered himself, and when he looked pointedly at me, I sat down, my chair scraping. That same guy brought a third chair out, placing it between me and the podium.

"If I may continue," Trent said, not sitting, and Pierce touched my knee, stilling my bobbing foot. "Should Rachel Morgan be held accountable for her actions when she was manipulated by outside forces into a place where to survive she had to learn a dark skill? Forced to learn and utilize black magic at the whim of another? I don't know. My intent would have been twofold. First, to see if my security systems could stand against the worst a witch can produce, which I think we can all agree is the magic done by a black witch. And second, a minor question of mine, curiosity, really. I wanted to know if a good witch could use black magic and not be . . . wicked."

The crowd buzzed, and I wasn't pleased. That little silver bell wasn't ringing. Had Trent taken advantage of the situation to find out if I was trustworthy? *Son of a bastard . . .*

"Is this to be a morality trial?" Oliver asked, and I swallowed hard. With the room out for my blood, there was no way I could win, and telling them of our beginnings would make things doubly worse. *Damn, damn, and double damn.*

"Perhaps," Trent said, his soft, melodic voice spilling out to fill the room with confidence. "What would have started out as an experiment in security has left me racked with guilt. This is my fault," he said, and people started to listen. "I was blind to how seriously the witch community would respond to black magic. If I'd known, I would certainly have chosen another method for testing my security."

Why in the hell wasn't that bell ringing? I asked myself, unless Trent was confident that his wording put everything into the theoretical. I couldn't have gotten away with it, but I wasn't a bloody politician.

"I feel remorse for having manipulated such an honest person into a bad place," Trent was saying, his words hitting me hard. "I want to make reparations. Rachel doesn't deserve imprisonment for the things she has done." He turned to the coven's table, holding Lucy's hand away from his face. "There was an arrangement, Oliver. It went too far. She should be pardoned, and you know it."

Vertigo was dancing about my brain, and I was glad I was sitting. Trent was referring to the deal we'd agreed to in the FIB interrogation room, and with sudden clarity, I realized I was lost. If Oliver called my bluff, I was lost. My gaze found Ivy and my mother, both dealing with the stress in their separate ways. I couldn't turn society upside down by telling them where witches had come from—and Oliver knew it.

Vivian invited Oliver to speak, and he laid a hand on his amulet as if covering his heart. "You offered her a job, if I remember correctly," the highest-ranking member of the coven stated. "Perhaps this is a ploy to get yourself a black witch on your payroll, Mr. Kalamack. A legalized black witch who you think is . . . good at heart."

The auditorium buzzed, and from the front row came Jenks's high-pitched "Go to hell, Oliver! Rachel isn't working for no scummy politician!"

Vivian gestured to the bell, sending a clear pinging out to silence the crowd. "If I may bring the conversation back to what we're here for?" she said when they quieted.

Oliver leaned over to look at her. "And just what is that, Vivian, if not holding witches accountable to our laws? Laws that have kept us safe for thousands of years?"

Trent was walking toward me, a faint smile on his face as he sat in the rickety folding chair beside mine. His expression was both confident and satisfied, and not any of it was from Lucy babbling in his arms. Something was up, and I probably wasn't going to like it. "You took advantage of this to find out if I was a good witch?" I said softly. "And you wonder why I don't like you?"

"See the course through," he said, careful to keep from touching his amulet. "There will be hell to pay, but I will see you back on this side of the lines before I'm done. Trust me."

Frustrated, I sat and crossed my arms over my chest.

Vivian had taken the floor, and slowly the crowd became quiet. "Rachel Morgan and Gordian Pierce knowing black magic is only part of the issue here," she said, head rising to take in the edges of the room. Her voice had taken on the cadence of a storyteller, and I fidgeted. "This is more than a trial of black witchcraft, but a question of how far we allow accepted morality to stretch to maintain the public safety. Two days ago, I was sent to watch Rachel on her journey here. Two days ago, I was certain that black magic, under any circumstances, was grounds for shunning."

Oliver leaned forward, eager for the kill. "And now . . . ," he drawled.

She hesitated, took a breath, then let it out. "Oliver, we're in trouble," she said, her voice heavy with concern. It was as if she was speaking to him alone, and I felt a stab of alarm for what might come out of her mouth. "Rachel wasn't the reason the arch fell," she said, then, for all the good it did, held up a hand against the rising crowd.

"It fell because of salt-dissolving adhesive?" Oliver muttered, but his voice was completely overwhelmed by the crowd's noise. Beside me, Pierce grimaced, trying to look positive but coming across as ill. To my other side, Trent was stone faced. I couldn't tell if this was part of his plan or not. On his lap, Lucy was falling asleep, the bright lights and heat hitting her hard.

"Silence!" Vivian yelled without the aid of her amulet, and most of the crowd shut up. "Let me tell you what happened."

My foot quivered, and I looked down, then up into the faceless crowd.

"I traveled first behind Rachel, then with her," Vivian said, only to be interrupted by Oliver.

"And you expect us to believe that you are seeing things clearly?"

Vivian spun to him, her tie-dyed robe furling. "You know I'm not spelled, Oliver," she said tartly. "Disagreeing with you does not equal having one's judgment impaired, and if the rest of your bootlickers would grow a pair, we might have some justice here and maybe save our asses! We are in dire danger, and it's not from Rachel!"

The crowd became silent. Pierce leaned over to me, and with his pinkie just touching the amulet, he whispered, "I like her."

Someone laughed, and Vivian shot me an encouraging glance. "I stand before you in the sphere of the coven's truth charm, and I say that I traveled with Rachel, drove her car after she fought off a demon. *A day-walking demon,*" she said loudly when the noise rose. "She didn't call it, it came of its own volition. I stand here now because she bested it. It was beyond me."

Not a sound came from the audience as they took that in. "A day-walking demon?" someone shouted. "That's impossible!"

Trent scuffed his feet to pull eyes to him. "They exist. A demon possessed one of my associates and was able to stay on this side of the ley lines, in the sun. It was Rachel who banished the demon and freed my friend. Day-walking demons are here. Your safety is severely compromised. The rules are evolving!"

He had to shout the last, and Vivian looked worried. I could well imagine the fervor going on past the doors, where this was being piped out. Vivian twitched her dress to gather the crowd's attention. "Unfortunately, Mr. Kalamack is correct. Demons are finding ways around the rules. Something has changed, and they can walk in daylight unsummoned. As we are now, we can't stand against them."

Oliver cleared his throat nervously. "Of course you couldn't stand against a demon, Vivian. You may be coven, but you were also alone."

"That's what I'm saying, Oliver," she said sarcastically, anger at her own lack of ability bleeding through. "I was alone, but so was Rachel, and she beat him back. My drawn circle fell as if it wasn't there. Rachel's didn't. It held firm. I'm not saying that black magic is stronger. But her magic has the strength of earth magic with the speed and flexibility of ley-line charms, and by continuing to ignore all of it because of the fear of some, we will condemn ourselves along with a good woman."

I was going to cry. Pierce took my hand, and I squeezed his. Even if I didn't make it out of here, someone had said I was a good person. It was worth the two thousand miles of bad food, dirty restrooms, and two nights without a bed just to hear someone say it.

"Vivian, stop inflaming the issue," Oliver stated when he could be heard again, and Vivian turned to the crowd, talking to them.

"I have seen my skills brushed aside as if nothing, and I am scared. Ignorance and denial will get us enslaved or dead. Don't let fear blind you. Don't let fear cause you to destroy someone who can stand against them. Rachel fought off a day-walking demon that was released when the arch fell, and you want to shun her?"

She was shouting, but most people were listening. "We all saw the news!" she said, gesturing. "We all felt the tragedy, saw the lives ended. I can't stop it! The coven can't stop it. She can!"

"I think she freed it!" Oliver shouted, standing to point a finger at me. "She was there!"

The crowd held its breath, and in the silence, I sat straighter. "I didn't release the demon from under the arch," I said, and there was no ping of the bell.

Oliver grimaced as his trap sprang with me safe outside it. The auditorium quieted beyond the haze of the lights, and Oliver's chair squeaked as he leaned back.

"What scares me," Vivian said, softer now that she had everyone's attention, "is that my circle, well drawn and able to handle anything, was nothing to him. This day-walking demon brushed through it. Rachel saved my life at great risk to herself—knowing that I had been sent to spy on her."

"With black magic," Oliver muttered.

"Are you that stupid, Oliver?" Vivian belted out, and I realized that most of my trial was going to be a fight for power between these two. The rest of the coven would vote with the winner. My life hinged upon a narrow-minded man and his fears.

"Of course she used black magic!" Vivian said. "Demons

are *laughing* at us for our self-imposed ignorance. Rachel used black magic against a demon. It hurt none but herself and saved my life. I have a hard time finding wrong in that."

Vivian dropped back a step to let people think about it.

"What about Las Vegas?" Oliver stated, too confident in himself to get up. "Property damage and lives ended. The same demon, yes? The same black magic."

Vivian nodded. "Yes. It took both Pierce and Rachel that time, and the curse they used unfortunately set the building on fire. The bodies found therein were ended by the demon before they could banish it. I can truthfully say that Rachel and Pierce both used restraint in twisting curses. Rachel uses more restraint, actually," she said as she glanced at me. "And while the demon was not destroyed, it was successfully banished."

Oliver chuckled. "To do more mischief."

"Hey!" I blurted out, making Lucy jump in her sleep. "We were trying to survive!"

"And the demon just showed up?" Oliver asked, looking from me to the bell.

"The demon just showed up," I said clearly, daring the damn bell to ring.

"You are a menace," Oliver said loudly when it didn't. "I say we give you to this demon, and maybe it will go away."

My mouth dropped open, and from the higher seats, a few people clapped. Nearer, through the haze, I saw frightened expressions and heard a soft murmur rise. *Give me to a demon? Was he serious?*

Vivian strode dramatically across the stage, gathering eyes to her and taking them from me. "Do you even hear yourself?" she said, putting a hand on the table and leaning toward him.

Oliver drew back, but he was clearly unrepentant. "If she's a black witch, then giving her to a demon isn't a crime."

No, it would be a joke, I thought.

At the end of the coven table, Leon raised his hand for everyone's attention. "I'm not going to agree with any plan that gives a person to a demon," he said, shocking Oliver. Amanda and Wyatt nodded, looking less sure, but agreeing with him. Emboldened, the timid man took a firmer grip on his amulet. "I *am* willing to consider that legalizing black magic in certain individuals might be permissible," he said, and the crowd buzzed. "I'd like to explore this in greater detail, that perhaps a coven member might be allowed to become skilled in black magic if the ends are good."

Pierce exhaled, and I smiled at him. If his claim to the coven was accepted, then I'd have two strong votes for me. Trent, too, looked less stressed, and the soft clench of his jaw eased. Maybe this was how they planned on getting my shunning permanently revoked. Working for the coven to fight a demon was a hell of a lot better than living in the ever-after or being Trent's witch. I relaxed, seeing an end I could live with, even if it would cramp my style. Working for the coven. Ha! But at least I'd get paid for doing something I'd probably have to do anyway.

Seeing his victory dissolving in a wash of common sense, Oliver stood. "We should adjourn and discuss this in private."

"Whoa, whoa, whoa," I said, grabbing my amplifying amulet, uncrossing my legs, and leaning forward past Trent to see Oliver better. "I was promised a trial before my peers." Along with my shunning being removed and an end to this, but first things first.

Pierce stood, tugging his vest straight and reaching for his amulet. "A private council is how I ended up in the ground," he said. "I won't accept going behind closed doors."

A hole in the ground, a cell with no windows. I could always call on Al, but if I did, there'd be no way I'd get my shunning removed. I fidgeted as the crowd buzzed and the witches at the table discussed the issue. Finally Wyatt rang the bell for silence. "I want to do this here," he said, and Oliver fell back in his chair with a dramatic expression of irritation. "I don't want to spend days on this. I have just one question." He looked at the other two witches, silent, but clearly as interested as he was. "Perhaps this is a morality trial after all."

Morality, I thought, starting to sweat. I could do this. I didn't know what to do with my hands, and I envied Trent, who was holding Lucy. He could suggest running me through with a flagpole, and as long as he was holding that baby, all they would say would be "Awwww."

Vivian looked questioningly at me, and after glancing at Pierce, I nodded. Seeing my acceptance, she inclined her head at the witch, and he reached for his amulet as he leaned forward. "I want to hear why they each risked shunning to learn black magic."

The crowd quieted, and I felt a wash of hope. Survival. I'd done it for survival. And I could say that without that stupid bell ringing. Who would blame me for that?

"Very well," Vivian said, a faint worry line on her brow giving me pause. "Rachel, why did you learn black magic?"

Pierce sat down and I stood, nervous as I took a step forward. "By necessity," I said, thinking of all the curses I'd used and the soul-searching that had come before them. "To stay alive, and to save the lives of those I love."

The audience was silent, waiting for the bell that never rang. Even as the truth came out, I was saddened. They had truly believed I'd done it because I was a power-hungry monster.

"Gordian Pierce?" Vivian said.

The chair creaked as he stood, and I watched him step a little past me. "I learned black magic to kill demons."

A wave of soft sound rose and fell from the people beyond the haze, and Oliver leaned forward, his little eyes glinting. "And have you . . . killed demons?" he asked. "With your black-arts skills?"

"I have had moderate success," he said, and from the corner of my sight, I watched Trent bow his head, holding Lucy close as if he were hurt. "I have tried," Pierce stated loudly as the crowd showed their disbelief. "Just two days ago, I almost killed a demon."

Al, I thought, grimacing. Then I went cold, turning to look at Pierce in horror. *Shit.*

"But you failed," Oliver needled him. "Why should we allow you to rejoin the coven if you're not skilled enough?"

Shit, shit, shit! I thought as I silently begged Pierce to keep his mouth shut, but I couldn't move. If I moved, it would look worse.

"I would have succeeded," Pierce said hotly. "The hell spawn would be dead but for—"

Pierce stopped. His eyes wide, he looked at me in fear. "I'm so sorry," he whispered, knowing what was going to happen. "Rachel, I didn't think . . ."

I swallowed hard as his words went out to the hundreds assembled, waiting.

"But for what?" Oliver said. Standing, he gestured. "But for what, Gordian!"

Trent's head was bowed, and Vivian looked pained. She knew. She had heard us talk.

"I failed," Pierce stated. "It was my failing. I'm not good enough."

"Why?" Oliver's voice was demanding. "If you're not good enough, then this claim of learning black magic to save ourselves is a load of crap and you should be buried alive again!"

Pierce's eyes closed, his jaw clenched, refusing to speak.

My chest hurt, and I said the words for him. "Because I stopped him."

Twenty-two

Trent bowed his head as the auditorium erupted in noise. In Trent's arms, Lucy woke and began to wail. I knew how she felt.

"Rachel," Pierce said, and I pushed his hand from me, standing with my chin high even as I felt my one chance slipping away. *Damn it. Damn it back to the Turn and hell again.*

"You'd have us pardon the black witch who stopped another from *killing* a demon?" Oliver was shouting, and I cringed. "If you're afraid and want the taint of black magic among us, the choice is simple! We should choose a demon killer, not the one who saved him! All in favor of Pierce regaining his position?"

My head came up. They wouldn't vote for me; not now. The crowd became even louder, and as security came forward to keep them back, a bubble snapped into place over the stage. At the coven table, grim-faced people raised their hands. One, two, three, four.

"Trust me," Trent said, standing with his lips inches from my ear as Lucy howled. "You saved me from demons, and I will save you from the witches. Just play it out. *Trust me.*"

"I don't understand," I said, feeling his grip too tight on me. "Trent . . ."

"We are voting, Vivian!" Oliver stated, and the woman

spun to him, her face tight in worry. "Either say yea or nay or your voice won't count."

"I vote against Pierce," she said quickly. "Oliver. Wait."

But Oliver was striding to the front of the stage. The noise was loud, and he shouted, "That is four for Pierce, one against. Pierce regains his position, exonerated from his past crimes of black magic, and is given leave to use such skills to destroy demons and save lives."

This was a good thing, but my stomach was tight, and Oliver was far too happy. Pierce was being pulled backward to the table, absently shaking hands with nervous people now sworn to protect him by a brotherhood only broken in the direst of situations. And he in turn would protect them. *From me?*

"All in favor of permanently rescinding Rachel Morgan's shunning and reinstating her as a white witch capable of doing black magic?" Oliver stated.

"Wait!" I said, then fumbled for my amulet. It was going too fast. And Trent was backing away with a crying Lucy— abandoning me.

"Oliver," Vivian said loudly over the clamor of a hundred voices. "This is not fair, and you know it!"

He grinned at her, looking evil. "For or against, Vivian."

"I vote for Rachel," she said breathlessly.

"As do I," Pierce said, but there were four hands raised against me, and my heart seemed to turn into a black stone.

It was over?

It was over that quickly?

"You lose," Oliver said, smiling.

I fell back, stumbling until I put the three chairs between me and them. I had that security amulet, and I wasn't helpless. "You promised me a fair trial!" I said, but no one was listening. "Oliver, I swear, you'll give it to me, or I will talk. I'll tell them everything!"

"No, you won't." Oliver wasn't using his amplifying amulet, his back to the assemblage, and I felt myself pale. I looked past him to the crowd, visible now that the house lights had come up. I found my mother, clutching her hands to her chest and crying. My gaze fell then to Ivy, who was ready to live at last—without me. And then I found Jenks, looking aghast and unable to reach me because of the bubble between us. He'd be fine. He'd go live with Trent, the bastard, and his children would play with Lucy.

They'd all be fine without me, I thought, my throat closing as I fumbled in my pocket for the amulet that Pierce had given me. I was *not* going to Alcatraz. I'd call Al first.

"I did no wrong," I said, reaching out and tapping a line, feeling my hair start to float as the broken jaggedness filled me. "I know black magic, and I will use it when threatened. I'm not a black witch—"

"Take her," Oliver said, motioning for security, and Pierce stiffened, surrounded by his new peers.

I motioned for him to relax. Al was waiting for me. I could hide out in the ever-after until things cooled off, and then come back. I could always do a disguise or something. *Who was I kidding? They'd know it was me.*

"Oliver, you already tried Alcatraz," Trent said, his voice calm and smooth. "As I recall, that was a dismal failure. You need something more permanent."

I turned toward Trent, livid. *Like a lobotomy?* "What are you doing?" I all but hissed, and he retreated, putting more distance between us as Lucy howled.

"There's nothing to stop her from escaping again," Trent said matter-of-factly. "I've a better idea."

Someone grabbed my arms from behind me, and I struggled, grunting when a zip strip was slipped over my wrists. As Pierce stood, made helpless by his new position, the jagged ley line left me.

"What do you have in mind?" Oliver asked as I shook the security off and stood in the hot spotlight, hearing some people cry for my blood and those I once trusted either silent or plotting against me. Trent had said to trust him, but every instinct I had said to fight.

"I can curse her," Trent said, and Vivian's eyes widened. "Send her to the ever-after, which is where she'd flee anyway, but curse her so that she can't return unless summoned."

"You son of a bitch!" Jenks shrilled, a hot red dust spilling from him.

"Like the demon she is?" Oliver said, smiling wickedly, but I could do nothing except stare. Was there such a thing, or was this part of his plan? Put some fake curse on me so I was off the coven radar? Brooke had offered me something similar. What would my life be like now if I had accepted?

"Well, she is a demon, isn't she?" Trent said with a nasty boys'-club smile on his face.

I didn't know what to do. He had said trust him, but this . . .

"Oliver, we can't," Vivian exclaimed, aghast enough to tell me she thought it might be possible. "That's inhuman!"

"She's a demon!" Oliver shouted. "Human morality doesn't apply to her!"

A thump reverberated across the barrier sheltering the stage, and everyone cowered as the shimmering ever-after pulsed. Ivy had ripped a chair from the floor and thrown it. She looked wild, eyes black, shaking with anger given free rein. Oliver gave the incensed vampire a disparaging glance. "Can you do it?" he asked Trent.

Pierce was being restrained. I knew he could break from it and was following my lead of wait-and-see. Trent glanced at him before nodding. My heart thudded. *Trust him?*

"I need a collective," he said, and I could imagine my life ending. I'd never be able to return, I'd never see the sun— unless this was part of his plan. *How bad had it been,* I wondered, *when he had been a demon's slave? How much hatred had he hidden from me? Was he going to laugh at me now? Hurt me?*

"You putrid elf! That's my daughter!" my mother screamed, and Trent twitched. He'd been named. His secret was out. But I didn't think it mattered. He had left his daughter's ears undocked. The elves were coming out of the closet with her. The directive of the next generation. He'd given me a say in it. Or had it all been a lie?

Oliver shifted into motion. "Isolate them," he directed, pointing at my mother and Ivy, now struggling violently. "Form a collective! We do this now!"

"Oliver! We need to think about this!" Vivian demanded as she confronted him, but Oliver motioned for security, and she was restrained.

"You are outvoted," Oliver said with satisfaction. "Put her with coven member Pierce."

I felt sick, unable to move. It wasn't the plastic straps with the charmed silver at their core that kept me from reacting; it was Trent. He had said to trust him. He had said I had to lose. He'd told me to go quietly, but I didn't know why!

The light from above was eclipsed as security shoved me into a circle one of the junior coven members had sketched and I fell to my knees. Trent's shadow lay heavily on me. I looked up, his stone-cold face scaring me. Lucy was bawling in someone else's arms—her wailing giving my unvoiced fear a sound. "T-Trent?" I stammered. He could do it. He said he had a curse, and I believed he could do it. He'd been dropping elven wild magic the entire trip, and apparently he had a new trick to show me.

"Betray me, and I'll never rest until you're dead," I vowed, my hands bound behind me, kneeling before him and the entire witch council.

He grabbed my shoulder, hauling me up as the crowd shouted its approval. Not as far from our witch-burning past as I had hoped, I guess.

"I've got a demon curse to give you," he breathed for me alone, green eyes turbulent as his wild magic seeped from his fingers and sent tendrils of power I couldn't use through me, tingling, warming, seductive. "I've been carrying it since the arch fell. Ku'Sox gave it to me. I had to take it to free him. It doesn't do anything to me but give me a headache. You, though, I think it will work on."

Ku'Sox? I went cold, the memory of an elven assassin singing me to death rising high in me, pulled into existence by Trent's magic seeping through me like a soporific, soothing even as excitement sparked from his touch. I'd almost died under wild magic. And now he wanted to give me Ku'Sox's curse with it? I was a fool. Elves fought demons. He'd used me again.

Trent leaned in closer, his hand light on my shoulder. "Once I give it to you, you can—"

"No!" I cried, my bound hands coming up to shove him away, but Trent had grabbed me, his eyes looking behind me. "I'd sooner get a lobotomy," I said, scared. "You son of—"

Agony exploded in my knees as something hit me from behind, exactly where the guards in Alcatraz had gotten me. Gasping in pain, I crumpled, my knees exploding. I looked up, finding Trent staring down at me, his brow pinched, his unsaid words swallowed in frustration.

"Curse her," Oliver said as I tried to breathe. "And hurry up about it," he added.

Squinting in pain, I looked up when Trent's shadow fell over me. "You not trusting me is going to get you killed," he said, his expression grim as he bent to lift me up, failing when I refused to cooperate. "As I was saying, take the bloody curse and give it back to Ku'Sox."

My muscles went slack, and my mouth opened in an O of surprise. Give it to Ku'Sox? That would mean I'd have to, like . . . touch him!

Seeing my understanding, Trent stopped trying to get me to stand up and turned to the audience. A gold-tinted wash of ever-after sprang up around us, and as the watching people chanted in unison to show their collective spirit, I felt the tingle of wild elven magic spark through me again, making me tremble. Ku'Sox wanted to dissect me. And Trent thought I could hold him still long enough to curse him? Was he nuts, or just tragically overestimating my abilities?

Trent was inside the circle with me, and I tried to get up,

falling back against it when he shoved me back down. "No," I pleaded, my hands bound before me, but he began to chant, low and under his breath as he gathered his magic. I took a wild breath, collapsing slowly when a wave of lassitude spilled into me, carried by his music, circling over and over in my mind, becoming my world. Wild magic. *Oh no . . .*

It promised peace, and even as I tried to fight it, my eyes slipped shut against the harsh glare. My soul hurt and needed to heal. Too much had happened, and I wanted it all to be over. That's what the magic promised, and I wanted it even as I fought its peace.

My head bowed, and Trent knelt before me, singing in words I couldn't understand, his beautiful voice rising and falling so softly, it was only for me to hear. A tear slid down my face, a tear for all that I hadn't done, that I should have done differently. Regret. But it didn't matter now.

Trent's energies prickled against me, and I suddenly realized he wasn't singing anymore.

"Rachel?" he breathed, and I lifted my head, numb. *"Si peccabas, poenam meres,"* he said softly, putting a hand on my shoulder, and I shivered as the curse slid gently from him to me, settling like tattered silk atop my aura.

"Why?" I pleaded, thinking I'd been stupid to trust him. My eyes met his, begging for mercy. It was just us, though we were surrounded by hundreds bearing witness to the event.

"Because you're the only one who can," he said, and I stiffened as the curse began to soak in, making me want to scream. Like a thousand beetles boring into my skin, I felt the curse burrow into me, finding a place among my cells, wiggling, squirming maggots embedding themselves in my soul. A smut-tainted wash of ever-after coated me, and as I heard the howls of the crowd become muffled, I knew I was being pulled into a ley line. And yet Trent gripped my shoulder, not done with me yet.

"She's still here!" Oliver shouted, his ugly face shimmering behind Trent's circle.

"The first part shifts the curse," Trent said, talking to Oliver, but looking at me, his fingers pinching my shoulder so hard it hurt. "It's the second one that severs it from me and banishes her."

He was telling me how to do the curse, but I could hardly focus on him, my drive buried under wild magic and my senses dulled. Somehow my gaze found my mother in the mass of howling people. She was crying, leaning on Ivy, who stood stoically as her heart broke. Seeing me look at her, my mom rallied, pushing away the man blocking her and striding forward.

"Give them hell, Rachel!" she shouted at the edge of the bubble, tears streaming down her face. "I'm proud of you!"

Trent yanked me up by the shoulder, and I staggered, my knees barely able to hold my weight. "I curse you, Rachel Mariana Morgan, to be fixed to the reality I banish you to. There you are cursed to remain until summoned, be it day or night, forever bound as a demon." His eyebrow lifted, mocking me. "You got all that? Want me to write it down for you?"

The curse. He wanted me to give it to Ku'Sox. Should I be pissed or marvel at his foresight? "Okay," I said numbly, and a hint of a smile flickered in his eyes. My jaw trembled, and doubt hit me. Why was I trusting him! "Trent? Wait!" I cried out, knees throbbing.

"Just so you know, I've trusted you since camp," Trent said, then shouted dramatically, *"Facilis descensus Tartaros!"*

His hand let go, and it was as if I was sucked into myself, yanked backward into nothing. The jagged disjointedness of the San Francisco lines took me, dissolving me to thoughts and memories, and dropping me into the infinity of time.

He trusts me? I thought. Trust me, Trent had said. I wanted to. But to risk death to curse Ku'Sox? Why should I even bother?

The world had turned its back on me. I should turn my back on it.

Twenty-three

Sliding, I hit the red soil face-first, eyes clenched shut and teeth together so I wouldn't bite my tongue as I scraped against the ground for several feet before coming to an ungraceful stop. The shift here had been rough, almost as if no one had been assisting, the subtle calculations that brought one back into reality standing and stable completely absent.

My first breath was choking, and I sat up, babying my knees and wiping the dirt off my bare legs and trying to figure out where I was. Yes, I was in the ever-after, but where? This wasn't Cincy. The ley lines were too jagged and the skyline wasn't right.

It was dark, the moon unseen behind boiling red clouds, the surrounding buildings slowly melting, slumping into themselves and burning as they collapsed. The thing was, they never seemed to fall completely. The best way I could describe it was that it looked like the world when you've been on a merry-go-round for too long—everything a jumping mess.

Knees throbbing, I tried to find the moon or some gravestones to fix on. If it was like Cincy, then they would be solid, free of the nauseating red sheen on everything. But there was no moon, and if there were any graves, they were unmarked. Not only was I two thousand miles from home with my knees busted again, but I was on the wrong side of reality. At least I had gotten rid of the charmed silver, though, and I rubbed my wrist, glad I could tap a line again, even if they were nasty, broken things.

On a whim, I tapped a line, wincing at the ugly taste of it but holding on all the same. Al could usually feel it when I tapped a line in the ever-after and would come and fetch me; otherwise, I don't know how he'd know I was here.

"Stupid elf," I muttered, wrapping my arms around myself and shivering in the same, nerve-grating wind. God! I hoped I wasn't being more stupid than usual. Had I really sat there and let him curse me? Because I *tru-u-u-u-usted* him?

The earth shook with one of the West Coast's frequent tremors, and the building across the street collapsed. And collapsed. And collapsed again. For an instant, I saw a flash of black sky with stars, and a hint of peaceful gray water, and then it was gone and the red-sheened glow was back. Shivering violently, I took a step toward the fleeting image as a breath of salt-laden air pushed aside the burnt-amber stink for the briefest of instances. Did heaven lay just underneath the hell surrounding me, visible only on the farthest arcs of the pendulum swing?

A rock fell behind me, and I turned, my welcoming snarl freezing. It wasn't Al. Heart pounding, I licked my lips and squinted in the reddish glow at the top of a small slump of rubble. "Oh, hey. Hi," I muttered, seeing the thin, raggedy figure standing belligerently above me, a bent stick in his grip. His bare foot moved, and another rock rolled clunking to where I was sitting.

"Yeah, I see you," I said as I painfully got to my feet, and then I yelped, ducking when he threw his stick at me.

"Holy mother pus bucket!" I yelled, dancing back as the surface demon jumped from the rubble to land ten feet in front of me. The slump of debris behind him slowly melted into dust and blew away, and a park bench took its place, only to crack and crumble as the demon inched closer.

"Look, home slice, I got no beef with you," I said as I hobbled backward, tugging my dress down. "I'm simply in the wrong place at the wrong time. Give me a minute, and I'll be out of your hair. Off your turf. Outta your . . . crib."

He snarled at me. Honest, what had I ever done to him? But when he picked up his stick and his black-eyed stare went behind me, I had to look.

"Swell, you got brothers," I said, rising out of my crouch and putting my hands in the air as if giving up.

Bad decision. One of them threw a rock, and I ducked, pulling heavily on the ley line and wincing as a lame-ass circle wobbled into existence. The chunk of concrete hit my bubble inches from my head and slid down, and the surrounding surface demons edged closer. There wasn't any salt water around to interfere with my magic, but the more heavily I pulled on the broken ley lines, the harder they were to work with, until it felt as if I were trying to hold a cat going boneless and slipping out of my grip.

The surface demons were wincing even as they crept closer, and I wondered if they felt the line I was trying to hold. It was giving me a headache, too. "Let's all be friends, okay?" I said as I backed up. "I don't want to be here any more than you want me to."

I jerked when two more rocks hit the bubble behind me, but a third one got through, and I gasped when my circle fell and the rock hit my shoulder. "Hey!" I exclaimed, popping my circle back into existence as I rubbed my arm. "Look, I'm not a demon, okay? Well, maybe I am, but I'm not like the rest of them. I can walk under the sun." Wincing, I added, "At least, I used to be able to. Maybe we can come to a mutual understanding. I help you, and you don't stone me to death."

The first surface demon raised his stick, yelling, and they ran at me.

"Maybe not," I whispered, wide-eyed, and I pulled harder on the ley line, shoring my wobbly circle up. "Al!" I shouted, wondering where he was. I hadn't wanted to admit defeat, but hell's bells, I needed some help.

The surface demons barreling toward me suddenly skidded

to a stop, their black eyes wide as they tasted the night. "Now you're going to get it," I said, guessing Al was coming when the ones in the back scattered. "You should have been nice."

With a weird cry, the closest surface demon fell back, but it was too late. A flash of red light exploded overhead, smashing the buildings away as if I were at the center of an atomic explosion. The surface demons scattered like brown leaves, the remnants of their clothes and auras fluttering. It was Al, and he burst into existence in a grand mood, an old-fashioned lantern in his hand and a walking cane at his side.

"Rachel Mariana Morgan!" he shouted enthusiastically, raising the lantern high, and I painfully rose from my crouch, breaking my bubble with a small thought. "I've come to save you, love!"

I winced, even as I was glad to see him. He'd won, and with a cheerfulness that made me sick, he strode over the rubble between us, kicking rock and rebar out of the way. I couldn't help but notice that the buildings he had destroyed with his entrance were back again. This was unreal. No wonder the surface demons were crazy.

"Done already?" he said, his mood expansive. "From witch to demon in less than an hour. It must be a record. And what are you doing in the badlands? They're somewhat . . . unnerving, are they not? Especially now."

I was scanning the edges of the ragged horizon, looking for heads, sticks, rocks, whatever. "Yes. I'm done. You were right. Oliver lied. Pierce is an idiot. They should all eat toads and die. Can we go home?"

Oh God. The ever-after was my home.

Al blinked, tucking his cane under an arm and a white-gloved hand turning my chin to him as he peered into my eyes. "Rachel, love, what did they do to you?"

I blinked, shocked to find that tears suddenly threatened. "Nothing."

"They cursed you . . . ," he whispered, flinging his walking cane at a surface demon. The creature squealed, and a putrid puff of green smoke was torn apart by the gritty wind. "It was that elf, wasn't it?" Al said. "I smell the stink of wild magic on you. You can't go back unless summoned."

"No, I can't," I admitted, feeling stupid. "But Trent has a plan . . ." My words trailed off and I felt even more like an idiot. What was the point? I was here. Even if I cursed Ku'Sox, I was still shunned, a virtual exile.

"I told you to take that piece of elf crap firmly in hand," Al said, pulling himself to his full height and frowning sternly at me. "Now look what he's done. You were a day-walking demon, free to come and go as you please, and now you're chained like the rest of us. What a waste. Stupid girl."

I said nothing, and Al stepped back, his lantern making a hazy gold glow around us. "He has a plan, eh?" he mocked.

Bless it back to the Turn. "Yeah," I said, yanking a strand of hair out of my mouth where the wind had put it. "But it doesn't matter anymore. Can we get out of here? It stinks, and my knees hurt."

Shaking his head, Al tsk-tsked, making my face burn. I suddenly felt small beside him, and I shrugged out of his arm, trying to go companionably over my shoulder. "This is why we don't live on the surface," he said as he tried to cover up my rebuke by tugging his frock coat straight. "I've never seen it this bad, though. Usually the buildings don't fall like this." He sniffed and adjusted his smoked glasses. "Shall we go?"

Shivering, I hobbled up to him, feeling his warmth. I was starting to get depressed. I was never going to see the sun again. "Thank you for picking me up," I said, and Al beamed.

"It's what I live for, Rachel. I have a treat for you."

"What?" I said, cringing at the idea of another one of his parties.

"Dalliance," he said, dissolving me into a memory and pulling me into a line. *I'm taking you to Dalliance.*

Twenty-four

The transition was smoother this time as we crossed merely the ever-after, not realities, and my feet barely stumbled as the stink and grit of the surface echoed once and died, replaced by a heavy bass thump and the sound of clinking glasses. Laughter mocked me, and I looked up, numb as we misted into existence. *Damn it, Trent.* Trust me. He had said *trust me.* Did he have any idea of what he was asking?

"Right on the tick," Al said jovially, his arm in mine as he checked his pocket watch. "Clean yourself up, Rachel. Dalliance is a respectable establishment."

I didn't know whether to cry or scream. I'd put my trust in a scheming elven drug lord. Al was right. How stupid could I be? I'd lost. I'd lost Jenks, Ivy, my church . . . everything, cursed to remain on this side of the lines unless summoned. If that didn't make me a demon, what would?

A bar was to my left, full of demons in trendy clothes reaching over one another to get their drinks. The music was so loud that shouting replaced talking. In front of me was a much more refined restaurant, sedate but borrowing from the energy at the bar. The theme seemed to be Art Deco, with a lot of thick glass etched with circles and triangles. Gray-and-white-patterned carpet mixed with tile, again using the circles and triangles theme. It was modern, expensive, and looked mildly excessive. The smell of food made my stomach growl, which ticked me off. How could I be hungry?

A host wearing a tux was talking to the three people ahead of us, his goat-slitted eyes telling me that they used demons as workers here, not familiars. Trendy and expensive, indeed. The music thumped, and laughter broke out from the wide-spaced tables where waitstaff eased through like boats in the fog. The restaurant was only half full, and the host led the demon trio ahead of us to a table, their clothes and manners making them look like CEOs out for a night of schmoozing on the company's account. Men. Everyone here was male. Behind the host's mahogany desk, DALLIANCE floated in mist, sparkling like Jenks's dust.

Jenks . . .

I blinked fast, my jaw clenched. A tingling at my shoulder pulled my attention to Al. He'd changed from his crushed green velvet coat and lace into a three-piece charcoal gray suit. A red handkerchief peeped from the breast pocket, and his hair was slicked back. He looked like a professional businessman, right down to the eight P.M. stubble.

"Cheer up, Rachel," he said, shifting his shoulders as if fitting into a new suit. "This is Dalliance. You're not still moaning about Pierce, are you? We'll pick up your little pet tomorrow. Tonight is for celebration!"

"Where did you get that?" I asked, not caring about Pierce.

He looked at me, new lines in his face as he played the part. "My closet. You don't think I am a one-trick pony, do you? Hold still. First thing tomorrow, I'm teaching you a brush-and-wash curse."

I took a breath to complain, even as I felt a wave of his energy cascade over me, easing the pain in my knees if not the ache in my heart. Yes, I was depressed, and yes, I'd just lost everything, but I felt like a slob with the grit of the surface on me, and if it would clean me up, then all the better.

I shivered as the curse slipped away, looking up as Al took out a pair of modern wire glasses and perched them on his nose. They had a bifocal line, and I knew he didn't need them. "Much better," he said with a sniff. "No one takes you seriously if you're in rags."

I jerked when his energy flowed over me again, and my tight leather melted away into an uncomfortable gray business suit. A purple Gucci bag was in my hand, and a Palm Pilot on my hip. "Hey!" I exclaimed, my hand going to my hair to find that it was back in a bun. My shoes were so tight they hurt. "What was wrong with the leather dress? You picked it out for me."

The host was coming back, and Al pulled me forward as if I was his arm candy. "This is Dalliance. If we don't fit the theme, we can't stay."

The thought of Bis made my brow furrow. I should have called him when I had the chance. "I just lost everything in the world that means anything to me, and you're taking me out to eat?" I protested.

Ignoring the host now looking at us, Al waited until I brought my gaze up to him before saying, "You just gained everything in two worlds, and I'm taking you to Dalliance. You don't eat here, you network."

My shoulders slumped. Networking. I was sick of demon networking/partying.

The host sniffed at us, and Al turned, his jaw a little heavier than he usually had it, his hair a little thinner. *What do you really look like?* I wondered, thinking of that black-skinned demon with the tail he'd scared his gargoyle with.

"Reservations for two. You'll find it under Algaliarept," Al said, hooking his shiny dress shoe behind my leg and pulling me forward.

The man looked at the folder open on his desk. "You've been declined," he said distantly, his voice clear over the music thumping around us.

A growl escaped Al, and the skin around his eyes tightened. "There's been a mistake."

Looking Al straight in the eyes, the demon said, "Your credit sucks, sir."

"Ah." Al poked me in the ribs, making me jump and stick out my chest. "How long have you worked here . . . Calvin?"

Calvin closed the file. "Long enough to know that Dali is not your personal friend but your parole officer. No table."

Dali? What did Dali have to do with this? Al was starting to look ticked. True, I didn't want to be here, but I wanted to be at Al's little four-room palace even less. "Al, I'm tired," I said, wrinkling my nose as if I smelled something rank. "This slop will likely give me the runs. Can't we just go home for a cheese sandwich?"

The host turned his attention to me, sneering. His expression became empty of emotion, and then I gasped when he reached across the desk, grabbed my arm, and yanked me closer. "You're not a familiar," he said, his face inches from mine. "You're that—"

I yelped as I was jerked back, Al having taken my other arm and reclaimed me. "She's not a *that,* she's a *whom.* Hands off the lady."

"Hey!" I said, my arms out like I was being crucified. "If you *both* don't let go of me, you're *both* going to be singing soprano!" Just because I was in heels and carrying a Gucci bag didn't mean I didn't know how to use them in new, creative ways.

The two men looked at each other and let go simultaneously. Regaining my balance, I snatched my bag from the floor and tugged my uncomfortable skirt straight. God, this suit made me look like a dullard.

A heavy, balding man in a tux strode from the kitchen looking bothered as he started for us. Eyes fixed on us, he gave a final bit of instruction to one of the waitstaff and continued forward. My eyes widened. I knew this demon. It was Dali, and suddenly the name of the place made sense. Demons could look like anything; why Dali wanted to be an older, overweight civil servant who ran a restaurant was beyond me.

"You got her?" he said to Al, his bushy white eyebrows bunched as he took me in.

"She's with me," Al said as he beamed, taking my arm in warning.

Dali flicked his eyes over me. "And you're sure she's . . ."

Al's smile grew even wider. "She is."

I felt like a cow he'd traded a handful of magic beans for. "I'm what?" I asked, and Al inclined his head at me, his expression becoming decidedly—worriedly—fond.

"A demon," Al said, and Calvin sniffed his disbelief. "We are here to celebrate, and this pile of crap won't seat us."

The host stood firm, and Dali looked at the list as if he didn't care.

"Dali! She is!" Al protested. "I know it! They cursed her and everything!"

"Dali, she isn't," I muttered, and the older demon sighed, tapping the paper with a thick finger. Behind him, six tables sat empty.

"I suppose I could give you a table by the kitchen," he finally offered.

"The kitchen?" Al echoed, appalled.

Dali let the folder hit the desk with a smack, and Calvin looked vindicated. "I've seen nothing from her that warrants anything better," Dali said, and Al huffed. "Cursing her doesn't make her a demon."

"I'm telling you, she is!"

Leaning in, Dali said calmly, "You're a scam artist on the skids—"

"I am a procurer and instructor of fine familiars for the discriminating palate," Al interrupted. "You've bought from me yourself."

"—and I'm not about to fall for one of your Henry Higgins cons," Dali finished.

Affronted, my mouth dropped open. "Hey!"

Al lost some of his confidence, hunching slightly. "Dali . . . Give me this one thing. A table. That's all I'm asking. How can I prove her birthright if no one *sees* her?"

The music shifted to a faster pace, and Dali frowned. "Sit

them in the corner," he finally said, and Al straightened, beaming.

"I'm not a demon," I said as the host moved to show us to a table.

"That's what I'm thinking, too," Dali said, his head down as he scratched something in that folder of his.

Al pinched my elbow. "If you can't say something nice, keep your mouth shut, Rachel. You are *not* helping."

Mood ugly, I followed Al's not-very-subtle push to go first. My feet hurt in the gray pumps, but at least my knees were okay. Beside and a little behind me, Al nodded to the demons we passed as if they were great friends, only to get a lackluster response. Unlike most of the places Al had taken me, there were no familiars, and I didn't like being the only girl in the place.

"Al," I whispered as he led us to the back. "I'm not a demon. I know I said I was, but that was for the coven because I was mad. I'm not really one."

Smiling at someone, Al waved. "I believe you are, and the sooner you accept it, the sooner we can get out of a four-room apartment and into something more suitable."

Okay, I was more than arm candy. I was his ticket to solvency. "Al . . ."

"Relax, itchy witch. Smile!"

"I have a name," I grumped, my stomach pinching me harder.

"Yes, but it has no pizzazz. *Ra-a-a-a*-chel. Rach-*e-e-e-eel*," he said, trying it out in different ways. "No one will tremble in terror at that. Oh my God!" he said in a high falsetto. "It's Rachel! Run! Hide!"

I'd had boyfriends who might differ with him, but I was silent when the host stopped before a booth behind a pillar. Al smoothly pulled out a chair from the adjacent empty table. "Relax," he said as he invited me to sit. "You're the only female demon besides Newt, and she's fucking crazy. Let them look at you."

Uncomfortable, I sat, amazed when Al expertly scooted my chair in without a scuff on the carpet. "They've seen me. Can we go home now? I've had a hard day."

Home. His home, not mine. A pang hit me, making it hard to breathe. Ivy. Jenks. My mother. Trent better not have screwed this up. I was going to freaking kill him.

Al sat beside me, both our backs to the wall, and the host sniffed before he walked away. "A bite of supper is just the way to end a trying day," Al said as he snapped out my napkin and draped the black cloth over my lap. "Don't you think?"

Not saying anything, I settled back, trying to figure out what was going on. I mean, I knew I was at a restaurant and was on display, but Al wasn't being lewd, lascivious, lustful, or any other nasty *l* word. I didn't know where I stood, and that made me uncomfortable.

"Al," I said suddenly as I looked over the table. "He didn't leave us menus. How am I supposed to order if he didn't leave menus?"

Al was fiddling with the lit candle, playing in the curl of heat like a five-year-old. "You eat what you're given. It doesn't get better than that."

I frowned, not liking not knowing what I was eating. "No wine. No eggs. Nothing with a sulfur-based preservative. It gives me headaches."

Sighing, Al looked at me over his new bifocals. "Rachel, Dali himself doesn't get real eggs or wine. Chill and enjoy yourself, will you?"

Chill? Had he told me to chill? Al looked funny, still himself, but older as he played the part of the successful businessman taking his main squeeze—that'd be me—out to eat.

One of the waitstaff set twin glasses of water before us, her aggressive "Welcome to Dalliance. Can I get you something to start with?" bringing my head up.

"Brooke!" I exclaimed, and the older woman snarled at me, her eyes tired and her hair slicked back in an unflattering cut close to her skull. "You sold her as a waitress?" I stammered at Al. She was coven quality, and they had her slinging orders and clearing tables?

Brooke's grimace curved up into a weird semblance of a smile. She was wearing a tight gray uniform that went with the décor but didn't look good on her, the starched white collar and the cut making it second-class subservient. Her Möbius-strip pin still decorated her lapel, but it looked like a joke now, spotted with something. *Spit?*

"What would you like, *Madam Demon*?" she said, looking extremely pissed.

"See, even Brooke knows what you are," Al said as he moved his empty glass. "Tell the piece of witch crap what you want to drink. Hurry before there's a shift change."

I stared, my heartbeat fast. "She's a coven member, and they made her a waitress?"

Brooke waited, her face becoming red.

"What do you want me to do?" Al said, not looking at all embarrassed. "If I sold her as a skilled familiar, I'd get her back in a week. To tell you the truth, I'm a little disappointed."

Brooke's jaw clenched. "Can I interest you in the specials tonight?" she asked, the hatred in her voice coming in clear over the thumping of the music.

My head was shaking in disbelief. "Brooke, I'm so sorry. I tried. I really did."

"Can I start you off with a drink?" she asked tersely. "The Brimstone Bomber comes highly recommended."

Al gestured flamboyantly and leaned back. "Two of those, yes. And whatever the chef suggests. Something sweet for the lady, and something earthy for me."

"As you will it," she said, and turned to leave, her pace slow and giving the surrounding demons a wide space. I saw why when one reached to grab her ass, laughing when she scooted to avoid him.

I felt sick. Why hadn't she listened to me? I'd told her not to summon Al. Hand to my middle, I looked away. "She's too expensive for me to buy back, isn't she?"

Al nodded, watching her walk away. "Very much so. Dali has wanted to bring familiars onto his waitstaff since he started dabbling in the entertainment field, but he hadn't found any able to handle the shifts. As I understand it, she's been good for business. Who wouldn't want to have their ass kissed by a coven member? Relax. Enjoy yourself."

That was the third time he'd told me to relax, and I was getting tired of it, but I froze when he took my hand, his usual white glove gone as he lifted my fingers to kiss them. Uncomfortable, I pulled away, ignoring his snort of amusement as I looked over the arriving people. The tables were starting to fill. *Because of me?*

My feet hurt, and I wanted to take off my shoes. Demons were looking at me, and I didn't like it. "Al, how old do gargoyles need to be before they bond with a, uh, witch?" I asked him, thinking of the little guy.

Al was making the "phone me" gesture to someone. "Several centuries. Why?" he asked, seeming uninterested. "Once bound, they live as long as we do."

I played with my silverware, feeling guilty. Several centuries. Bis couldn't be that old. He acted like a teenager, and I remembered him saying he was only fifty.

With a soft sound of linen, Al turned to me, his strong features bunched up in question. "I said why, Rachel. Is Bix getting clingy?"

Like falling asleep in my kitchen? "No," I lied. "And it's not Bix, it's Bis."

Al rubbed his hands together in delight. "I thought as much. They don't bond well until they can remain awake during the day. Bis is too young yet."

My expression went flat. Oh my God. It was happening—whether I wanted it to or not. Bis was going to tie himself to me, and then we would both be stuck here. No. I wouldn't allow it. "Hey, there's Newt," I said to change the subject, and as if my speaking her name caught her attention, her gracefully long neck turned our way.

"Don't look at her!" Al exclaimed. "Don't—" He groaned as the crazy demon smiled and changed her path to us. "Shit," he added, slumping. "She's coming over."

"What?" I said, uneasy, but seeing two empty places at our table. "She's the only person I know here besides you."

Al looked at the ceiling as if in pain as Newt made her way to us, her pace both provocative and flat, her motions feminine but her figure androgynous. She was wearing a man's business suit, and it changed to match mine as she approached.

"Well, that's an improvement," Al muttered as he brought his gaze from the ceiling. "See, Rachel, you're having a positive impact already." Pasting a smile on his face, he stood. "Newt! Love, I'm so surprised to see you here! Please join us!"

"Sit down, Gally," she said, turning her cheek so he could give it a perfunctory kiss. "I know you loathe me down to my mRNA."

My eyebrows rose, and I met his gaze glancing to me as he helped her with her chair.

"You seem unusually cognizant tonight," he muttered, taking the purse that appeared as she handed it to him.

Newt, now wearing a blond pageboy cut, sniffed. "It's amazing what one remembers given time." Hand long and thin, she gestured for Brooke to bring her a drink, then focused on me, black eyes wide and wondering. "Did you bring me my ruler, Rachel?"

My mouth opened, then shut. "Um, I forgot," I said. "Sorry."

"Newt, love." Al took her hand and gave it a kiss. "Let's not talk business. Not tonight."

Newt pulled her hand from him with a little tug, looking disgusted. "No, let's talk of the future. Did I not say I could see the future? I'd like to hear of your day, Rachel Mariana Morgan."

My gaze fell, and I remained silent. She saw the future, all right. But seeing that I had a pattern of being screwed over, it wasn't hard to predict.

Al cleared his throat as if bothered that I was unhappy, and Newt tried again.

"Rachel," she said, leaning back in her chair with her glass, "do you enjoy looking like a rung-climbing peon who has to sacrifice the fruits of her ovaries to have status in a man's world?"

"No," I muttered.

"Then go put on something new in the jukebox," she said, handing me a coin. "My treat. Something exotic and old, when women were recognized for the goddesses they are."

Al's eyes widened in wonder as I took the tarnished gold coin she slid across the table to me. It felt slimy, almost, and I glanced to Al for guidance. Was I being gotten rid of?

"Go," he encouraged, indicating what looked like an accurate representation of a jukebox, complete with colored bubbles and 45s. It didn't fit the décor, but it still looked as if it belonged there in the corner.

I stood, not appreciating that Newt's smile was probably because I'd looked to Al for direction. My shoes hurt me, and I kicked them off, leaving them under my chair as I padded across the carpet, my head up and not looking at the demons watching me as I gave them a wide birth.

"She's sweet," I heard Newt say as I left. "Look, she's afraid."

"No, she isn't," Al grumbled. "That's the problem."

"Mmmm. If she ever has sex with you, I'll kill you."

"You don't think I know that?" he muttered.

"So give her to me now and be done with it. You can't handle her," Newt coaxed.

"Yes, we all saw how well you did with Ku'Sox."

And then I was out of easy hearing range, with a whole lot more to think about.

I came to a halt before the jukebox, fingering the greasy coin in speculation. I'd never held a chunk of demon smut given real form before. And I was going to buy a song with it?

Everyone in the place was watching me. I could feel them taking in my knee-length skirt and the blah nylons, my hair in that ugly bun, and that I was barefoot thanks to Al putting me in too-small shoes—I think they might have fit Ceri. My back to them all, I forced my shoulders down and looked over the titles. None of them was remotely familiar. Not a single Barry Manilow or Rob Zombie. The titles seemed to be places and dates, only a smattering in English.

"Cuneiform?" I mused aloud, never having actually seen it in use, but that's what that weird writing among the French, German, and Latin had to be. Immediately I dropped the coin in, hearing it clunk through the machine before I pushed the proper button.

Behind me, the lights dimmed. A wave of conversation rose along with masculine groans from the bar as the modern, loud thumping shifted to an ancient set of drums and flutes. I wrinkled my nose, thinking someone's dinner smelled like a barn, and when I turned, I could do nothing but stare. *Wow.*

"Most familiars can't handle the shifts." Now I understood that Al hadn't been talking about lengthy hours but shifts of reality. The restaurant had changed. There were reed mats on the dirt floor, and the tables were made of rough wood and were lit by candles and tarnished metal lamps filled with flaming oil and hanging from an overhead shade. We were outside, and a breeze shifted a strand of hair that had escaped my bun. It was night, and beyond the glow of a central cooking hearth, more stars than I'd ever seen stretched in a sparkling wash, brilliant all the way to the horizon because there were no city lights to dim their glow. The wind carrying the scent of salt to me was warm. It was incredibly realistic, reminding me of Dali's seaside office on casual Friday. The grit of sand was beneath my feet and the reed mats, and the muggy air smelling of horse and wet wool was hot.

One by one, the clientele sitting at the rough-hewn benches was changing, flashes of ever-after cascading over them to leave the much skimpier attire of homespun robes and sandals. Dressed in a business suit, I was totally out of place.

"Oh for the two worlds colliding!" Dali shouted as he burst from a maroon tent that had once been the kitchen, his new black robes flapping. "Who the hell put in Mesopotamia? You know how hard it is to get lamb to taste good?" he finished, sputtering to a halt when he saw me standing before the jukebox in my nylons and machine-made fabric.

Embarrassed, I looked at Al, seeing that he'd changed into sandals, his chest and much of his legs bare but for a draping gold cloth. Regal and confident, Newt reclined beside him on a cushion with a silver goblet that she distantly toasted me with. Her hair was in beaded dreadlocks, and she'd ringed her eyes with a dark pigment.

"Al!" Dali said, red faced. "She fits in, or you go."

Al grinned and blew me a kiss. I shivered as the wind brushed me with his intent, and my uptight gray suit melted into a robe of rich golds, purples, and reds. Little green rocks had been sewn into the fabric, and I felt the new weight of it settle comfortably on my shoulders.

"Nice," I said, my hand jerking up to keep my headdress on when I leaned over to see my new sandals. Yuck, my hair was oiled flat to my head. That was going to take forever to wash out. But I fit in now, and grimacing, Dali turned and vanished back into the cooking tent, his voice raised as he yelled at the staff.

Okay, I'm a Mesopotamian princess. Pulse faster, I headed back to the table amid whistles and a few complaints from where the bar had been. Everyone there was now sitting on the sand around a huge fire pit in the open air. Instead of a kitchen, waitstaff brought wooden bowls and platters from a second cooking fire, and apparently lamb wasn't a favorite.

"Interesting choice," Al said dryly as I wove my way past the benches and cushions the upper echelon were seated on and eased onto a smooth, tooled chunk of wood.

Newt set her tarnished silver goblet down. "I rather like Mesopotamia," she said airily. "It's so easy to distinguish the haves from the have-nots." Smiling, she regally motioned for Brooke to bring us a plate of cheese and flat unleavened bread. "And the wannabes."

"No need to be catty, Newt," Al replied, then nodded at Brooke—who was now in rags. "See, I told you she was good. It takes an unusually skilled familiar to stockpile all the changes needed to run this place. On a busy day, there might be three shifts an hour."

"Three shifts?" I said, now understanding why you didn't bother to order from a menu. You got what you got. "So Brooke has to change herself? It doesn't just happen?"

Al grunted his answer, grabbing a handful of bread as Brooke set it down. "Newt, can you remember the last time you saw Mesopotamia?"

"I can't remember the last time I was here," Newt shot back, and I smiled nervously, not sure if she was kidding or not.

"So all those buttons are different restaurants?" I asked, looking at the jukebox, now totally out of place, like a British police call box on the deck of the *Titanic*.

Al bobbed his head and downed a glass of red wine. "They are memories," he said, looking at Newt. "Apart from the last one, we've not had a new one for thousands of years."

Newt's brow furrowed, and she flicked a grape at him. "I apologized formally for that," she muttered. "It was Ku'Sox's fault."

"Ku'Sox." I breathed in, wondering if Al had made this memory as I snatched up something that might be a cracker after a few thousand years of civilization. How Ku'Sox had anything to do with the lack of new memories at Dalliance was beyond me. Maybe he'd broken the machine. He certainly had broken my life. He and Trent. Stupid elf. *You can summon me back any time now, Ivy.*

"Stay away from Ku'Sox, Rachel," Al offered as he filled my empty glass from a flaccid wineskin.

My nose wrinkled. No way was I drinking anything that came out of a bag with fur still on it from its previous owner. "Not a problem," I said. "Besides, last I saw him, he was hiding out in reality, and what are the chances that he'd come back here?"

Newt sipped from her silver goblet, her fingers playing in the candle flame. "Everyone finds his way home eventually," she said, and as I watched, her eyes changed. Though she made no move as she reclined in idleness like a goddess on a throne, the light behind her black orbs went from complaisant to virulent hatred.

Al noticed, too, and he motioned for me to shut up.

"You want to kill him?" Newt asked me, her mild tone a stark contrast with her hidden anger.

"Yes!" I blurted out, then hesitated when I saw her fondling a knife on her hip. "Uh . . ."

"That's two of us, then," she said, interrupting me. "Give me enough time, Gally, and I'll have the majority."

"No one likes the little genetic designer dump," Al said, trying not to look at her, but it was hard not to. "But we can't kill him. Same as we can't kill you, love," he said to Newt, clinking his glass to hers. "Genetic material is genetic material."

"Al," Newt pouted as I puzzled over the designer-dump comment. "Is that what I am to you? Genetic material?"

"Of course not, love," he said, playing with her. "I want your library, too."

I watched Newt's mood sour as she stabbed a grape and ate it off the point of her knife. "I despise the bastard even more than you do, Rachel, though that might change as he takes everything you love. You need to be clever to best him. Are you clever, Rachel?"

Oh God. She wants to know if I'm clever. I glanced at Al, and he stared at me, then shrugged. Licking my lips, I said, "It's the shiny pot that puts a hole in the sky."

Al's mouth dropped open, but Newt thought about it, her

expression thoughtful and her fingers finally leaving her knife. "Very true," she said as she eased back into the cushions.

With a soft click of his teeth, Al's mouth shut. His eyes were cross, and he seemed peeved that I'd found a way to satisfy her without compromising myself at all. Hunching into his drink, he muttered, "Dali is headed this way. Newt, I swear, if you get me kicked out of here tonight, I'll never sell you another familiar as long as I live."

"Boohoo," Newt said, a wiry arm rising delicately to the demon approaching behind her, an invitation to take it, I suppose.

Sure enough, the robe-bedecked, extravagant civil servant gone tent restaurateur elegantly touched his lips to her fingers before gesturing for more fruit and cheese. "Is everything to your liking?" Dali said, only the slightest hesitation hinting at his annoyance with Newt being here. Inside me, a feeling of warning coiled tighter. There were too many eyes on our table.

"As always, Dali," Al answered, and the demon frowned at him.

"I was asking Newt."

Newt beamed, fully aware that she wasn't welcome and relishing the fact that they had to put up with her. "I can truly say I don't remember a more perfect evening, Dali. As Algaliarept says, it's as wonderful as always."

A brief flash of teeth, and Dali turned to me, his veneer of pleasantry becoming transparent. "And you, Rachel? Enjoying Mesopotamia?"

"U-uh," I stammered, not liking being put on the spot. *Crap, the demons watching us were pointing now.* "I can honestly say I've never had an evening quite like this." Dali was hunched a little too close, his mood a little too aggressive, even for a demon. If everyone in the place hadn't been watching us before, they were now. *Why is he over here?*

Al seemed to be thinking the same thing as he set his cup down and pointedly looked at Dali. Newt, too, cocked her head, clearly waiting. "It's not me, of course, but others," Dali said, a thread of his eagerness to cause trouble coloring his voice. "Some of the clientele feel that a member of your party is not a demon and therefore should wait outside."

"Rachel not a demon!" Al shouted dramatically, and I twitched. "Who dares?"

"I do!" exclaimed a strong voice, and my head turned to the tattered awning that now marked the entryway to the restaurant.

Shit, it was Ku'Sox.

Twenty-five

Frightened, I stood amid a smattering of exclamations. Some were against me, but most were protesting Ku'Sox's presence. Clearly he wasn't much liked, but there was far less anger than I'd expect from a demon they had imprisoned in the next reality over, even if the demons at the informal bar fire were enthusiastically exchanging bets. The drums had stopped, and loud conversation had taken its place. I was scared, but Newt was smiling deviously as she stood my bench upright from where it had been, pushed over when I'd found my feet.

In the flickering oil light, Dali took a dramatic step back, his sleeves dropping to his elbows when he held his hands up in placation. "Calm down, or I'll sling all your asses out of here!" he bellowed, and the noise was cut by about half. "I agree that the question of her status should be settled." He smiled cattily at Al. "Isn't that why you're here?"

Newt toasted me to show her support as Dali smiled at me with false benevolence. My eyes closed as I finally understood what was going on. My standing was in question and needed to be settled before a gathering of my peers. If I wasn't a demon, I was a familiar. And if I was a familiar, I was in deep shit.

And there I'd been, saying I wasn't a demon.

Ku'Sox shoved his way through the camels and bales of cloth until he stood with the rough-hewn table between us. His steel gray hair was slicked back and he was wearing a masculine reflection of my attire. Beads clicking, he looked me up and down, his expression one of disgust, not a flicker of concern that I'd almost burned him alive in Margaritaville. My pulse raced as I recognized the barely leashed hatred from both Al and Newt as Ku'Sox started in on a harsh harangue aimed at me. He wouldn't be tucking me under his arm and popping out—unless he thought he could get away with it—so I was safe. Sort of. Demons were wimps, more inclined to take their rivals down with red tape than a physical approach. They only beat up people they knew couldn't fight back.

Trent wanted me to curse him. *Why should I risk it?* I thought as Ku'Sox started demeaning Al's reputation, bringing up events that had happened thousands of years ago and still made Al red with anger. Why should I curse Ku'Sox to be stuck in the same reality I was in now? But then I hesitated, tuning out Ku'Sox as I thought a little more deeply. If I shifted the curse to him, as Trent thought I could, then I wouldn't be stuck here at all. I'd still be shunned in reality, but there were ways around that. Right? Right?

Regaining my ability to be in reality, even in snatches, was a small thing, but after having imagined living in the ever-after without ever seeing the sun, Jenks, or Ivy again, I fastened on it like a lifeline. My foot twitched, and Newt slid her black-eyed gaze to me, nodding at the look of desperate thought I must now be wearing. Everyone else was focused on Ku'Sox, raving about purity and half-breeds polluting the genetic pool.

My eyes fell from Newt to the hard-packed earth, and I lightly tapped a line, glad my oiled hair wouldn't float and give me away. The barest hint of ever-after seeped into me, not enough to be noticed by anyone, but I was sure Newt felt it. She was jiggling her bejeweled foot, black eyes edged in kohl sliding from me to Ku'Sox, the barest hint of a wicked smile replacing her anger.

My knees were wobbling, and an odd feeling was sifting through me, almost a ringing in my ears or soul. Slowly I searched my theoretical self, surprised when I could feel the curse Trent had put on me. It hadn't been with me very long, and the alien, greasy feel of the elven aftertaste made it easy to sense, like a faint ache. Even odder was that the curse seemed as if it lay in my chi like shavings of iron, all of them aligning themselves to orient on Ku'Sox, like a flower to the sun. It had been created for him, like the focus had been created for the Weres. It wanted to go back to him.

Damn, I might be able to do this.

My shoulders stiffened, and I scrambled to remember the words Trent had used to tap into the communal collective and set the curse. One phrase to transfer it, one to sever the bond and prevent it from coming back. Something about deserving punishment?

Newt was watching me as Ku'Sox grandstanded, gesturing as he maligned my mother, my father, and Al all in the same breath. I gathered the curse together in my chi—every last bit—and held it in my fist, the pressure of it aching and throbbing like I was holding an exploded bomb.

Si peccabas, poenam meres. That was the invocation phrase. I knew it. I could do this!

"That is not a demon!" Ku'Sox shouted as if in finale, spinning in a flamboyant circle, making his purple robe furl. "And it should be destroyed!"

"Prove it!" I shouted, lunging. The curse glowed like black fire in my hand, and I jumped at him, right across the table.

Newt grabbed the plate of cheese and yanked it to safety. Al's wineglass wasn't so lucky, and the wine spilled like blood over the rough wood. The candle flared, and I hit the hanging lamp, sending flaming oil splattering on the watching demons. A cry of alarm went up and the sound of sliding benches and the sudden pulls on ley lines spun through me like threads of glass.

Ku'Sox's eyes widened, and then I had him, my hand around his throat as we crashed to the floor.

Si peccabas, poenam meres! I thought desperately, seeing my freedom in Ku'Sox's shocked expression.

Elation filled me as I felt the painful sensation of pinpricks in reverse as the curse left me. It was working, and I writhed as the curse soaked into Ku'Sox while he screamed.

"Get her off!" Ku'Sox shouted, and someone grabbed the back of my shirt, pulling me away. "Get her off me!"

"No!" I howled. I wasn't done yet. I hadn't fixed it into him! *Facilis descensus Tartaros!* I thought frantically, and my eyes widened as I felt the curse stretch between us like a rubber band. But with a snap that made Newt jump, it pulled from Ku'Sox, even as it had wanted to stay, cleaving to me instead. I'd done something wrong. It hadn't worked!

"No, no, no!" I raged as the rising imbalance ebbed to nothing and the surrounding demons laughed, thinking I was simply trying to scratch Ku'Sox's eyes out. "Let me go, you idiots!" I'd done it wrong! I'd done something wrong or it would have worked and I would have had him!

Al had an arm around my middle, physically holding me against him as my feet slipped on the reed mats while I struggled for purchase. "No fighting in Dalliance, Rachel," he crooned, and I shoved his hand off me as soon as I got my weight over my feet again.

"You see me!" I shouted at Ku'Sox, glad I'd finally gotten rid of that headdress thing, now broken on the floor. "If you *ever* touch me again, I'll *lay you out*!" I threatened him, almost spitting in frustration.

They only laughed. Except for Al, standing nervously beside me, and Newt, who had felt what I had tried to do. Dali was at the outskirts, knowing something had happened but not what. And Ku'Sox, of course, who was sallow faced, clearly knowing how close it had been. Why hadn't it worked?

Slowly Ku'Sox regained his pompous air as he shook off the good-natured offers of assistance, but he would meet my eyes only in quick glances, equal amounts of caution and loathing in him. But I'd seen him screaming like a little girl, and I knew he'd been terrified.

He ought to be afraid. I'd almost had the perv. Now it would be harder. He was warned, and I'd lost my easy chance. "You dare to call me less of a demon than you?" I exclaimed, pissed as I shook in anger with nothing between us but air. "*I'm* not the one doing the bidding of a lame-ass elf!" I said, pointing at him. "You owe your freedom to an elf! One that I let go!"

The surrounding jeers and calls from the watching demons rose high, and Ku'Sox frowned as the helping hands fell away. In the distance, I heard a fox bark, and the puddle of light grew when someone stilled the wildly swinging lamp and relit it with a tweak on a line.

"An elf?" Dali was leaning casually against a support pole. "Ku'Sox, you owe your freedom to Rachel's castoffs?"

It wasn't the angle I'd been going for, but it made Ku'Sox angry, his eyes squinting as he bent to beat the dust from his robes. "That *thing* is a witch," he said, pointing at me. "A stunted double X that Algaliarept is dressing up like a demon to further his pathetic attempt at familiar procurement."

"Pathetic?" Al drawled as he sat down, leaving me standing alone. "You've been gone too long, you little zit pus. I'm more of a snag artist than you'll ever be, and I know talent when I see it. Rachel may be born from a witch, but she *is* a demon as much as you are a pain in the ass with the social skills of a dog. Still eating souls, Ku'Sox? That's like eating God's shit."

"You know nothing!" Ku'Sox shouted, red faced as the surrounding demons laughed. "I'm stronger than all of you! I can take this world and destroy it! Open a hole to reality and drain this world to nothing until you're bumping around in a universe the size of a closet and you *all* get sucked into oblivion!"

The conversations stilled, and Dali cleared his throat in the sudden silence. Ku'Sox stopped, the hem of his robe swinging as he dared anyone to comment, his chin high and a defiant gleam in his blue, goat-slitted eyes. Every demon in the place wore hatred and fear on his shadowed, candlelit, ruddy face. And that, of course, was why they didn't kill him. If they tried and failed, he might destroy the ever-after, laughing all the way to the sunny side of reality and his survival. Their prodigal son was fucking insane.

"You're not stronger than me," Newt said into the quiet, and Ku'Sox's eyes narrowed.

"Aren't you dead yet, you old hag?" he grumbled.

The demons started to whisper, and Dali's slippers were a soft hush on the reeds as he came forward. He was looking at me with speculation, and now I knew why. *Is she the one? Is it her?* What he meant was, am I a demon? Can I kill Ku'Sox?

"Test-tube brat," Al said as he stood his empty wineglass upright with a thump. "DNA degenerate. Magical mistake. You're picking on Rachel because she might be a better demon than you."

"Her?" Ku'Sox exclaimed, and Al simpered at him. "*I'm* the way back to our rebirth, and you will respect that! Me! Not her! She's born from a witch. A stunted, damaged witch!"

Newt shifted coyly on her cushion, the only one who hadn't left her seat throughout the entire scene. "No, poor boy, you are a mistake we loved too much to put down. I still think you would have turned out fine if Dali hadn't dropped you when you were but a blastocyst."

"You are deluding yourselves," Ku'Sox said, frowning. "I am your rebirth."

"My dame's ashes," Al muttered. "The poor boy is going to go off now to brood about world domination."

A few of the demons sliding back to their tables laughed, and Ku'Sox flushed in anger.

"Something is wrong with you, my lovely little boy," Newt continued, the silver goblet of wine in her hand as demons drifted away and the tension eased. "In your head. Even demons do not eat souls. Is it because you're worried that you don't have one?"

"I have a soul," Ku'Sox said with a scowl, but I wondered.

"Of course you do. Otherwise, you wouldn't have an aura," Newt said brightly. "Come sit with us."

Oh, there's a good idea, I thought, sitting down between Al and Newt, leaving Ku'Sox to stand by himself.

"That," he said, pointing at me again, "isn't a demon. I need proof. We all do." He looked over the assembled demons. There were more people now than there were tables. They must have been coming in all this time, filling the Mesopotamian darkness with soft mutters and speculation. "It takes more than being able to invoke demon magic to be one," Ku'Sox said. "Do something demonic."

This last had been aimed at me, and my hands clenched in my lap. "Like rip your heart out? Come a little closer."

"Rachel . . . ," Al said as he reached across the table and patted my shoulder a little too hard. God, I felt like I was one of two little kids on a playground.

From her cushion, Newt cleared her throat. "Rachel should make us a new memory."

The surrounding demons exhaled, the sound rising like a sigh of excitement. I turned to her, surprised. *You want me to do what?*

"Be reasonable, Newt," Al protested, his face suddenly pale. "She's only a few hours old. I haven't had time to teach her anything yet."

"Doesn't matter," Newt said as she ate a grape with an odd precision. "If she's a demon, she can do it."

Al looked deathly worried, and I watched Dali energetically stride to the jukebox and press his hands to it, invoking who knew what as it glowed a hazed black. "Splendid idea," he was muttering. "Rachel, what do you want to call it?"

"Call it?" At a loss, I looked around the table, seeing worry on Al's face and satisfaction on Ku'Sox's. "Call what?"

"Give us a memory," Newt prompted, the beads in her hair clicking. "Only a demon has the mental fortitude to channel enough energy to make a tulpa construct this size. One that anyone can share."

Oh. My. God. I looked at the fake restaurant, the fire, the stars, the smells. "You want me to make something like this?" I squeaked. "Are you nuts? I don't know how to do that!"

"She admits she's not a demon," Ku'Sox proclaimed, and Al's grip on his wineglass became white-knuckled as he hunched against the raised voices around us.

"Lacking a skill doesn't translate into a lack of ability," he growled, but the demons were rearranging the tables, making an open space of sorts, wanting me to try.

Newt's eyes narrowed. "Only a demoness can make a free-existing tulpa, and only a male demon can fix it into reality. I say it's a fair test. Al, put your money where your mouth is. Or should I say where your student is."

I looked wildly from one end of the midnight Mesopotamia to the other, despairing as I realized why Newt had "apologized." She had killed everyone who could do this—except herself. I could not make this! It was immense!

"Of course you can," Newt said as she leaned toward me, almost as if having read my mind. "Making a construct is easy. Every one in that box there was made by my sisters, and they weren't nearly as clever as you." Newt raised her goblet in salute. "That's why I could kill them, you see."

My heart pounded and I sat down before I passed out. "Uh, maybe I shouldn't do it then."

Ku'Sox laughed, but Newt poured her wine into my glass. "That's not why I killed them. But that's why Ku'Sox tricked me into it. To make a lasting tulpa, one that can be stored and lived in, one must have the ability to safely hold more than one's own soul. Demons can't do it. A demoness can. It's on that little extra bit of X gene that they don't have."

I listened to crickets that had turned to dust thousands of years ago on a continent I'd never set foot on. "You're able to hold a soul so you can gestate a baby," I guessed, and she nodded, solemn.

"Ku'Sox is a fool, but he's right. You need to prove yourself, and now is as good a time as any. I will not have your standing in doubt. Don't you agree, Al?" she added lightly.

Al looked sick. "She's rather stupid yet."

"I am not!" I exclaimed, and he pointed at me.

"There, see? She is."

Newt waved a hand at Dali, still standing by the jukebox. "Even a dunce can have a baby. All it needs is stamina and a little imagination. Rachel?"

"I am not stupid!" I said again.

"Shut up," Al hissed as Ku'Sox gleefully ate someone else's cheese. "You don't know what you're doing."

"So teach me," I hissed right back. "Thanks to you, I can't be a witch anymore. I may as well be a demon."

My heart was pounding. God, what was I doing? I only knew that I had to be somewhere, and right now, this was it.

Al stared at me, hope dying in his eyes. "I can't teach you this."

"I can," Newt said, and my breath came fast.

Crap on toast.

"I will," she added, and I swallowed hard. "I will teach you, you will make one, and Al will fix it to reality. I don't have the balls to do that part. Literally."

No one was even whispering. All eyes were on me, the tables full of demons in robes and a small crowd bunched outside, trying to listen in. I hadn't counted on this. I mean, Al I sort of trusted. At least I trusted that he needed me alive and reasonably well. But Newt? She looked sane, and that was worrisome.

"Come here," she prompted. "You want to do this, yes?"

Not really. Taking a slow breath, I stood, feeling weird in these clothes with the green rocks sewn into them. They clinked as I came around the table, Ku'Sox moving in agitation as he stood, looking young next to Dali's tired jadedness. Al's hands were in fists on the table. A bead of sweat trickled down his neck.

"Sit before me, Rachel," Newt prompted, her voice oily, and

I wondered if this was how she'd killed her sisters, lulling them. She shifted on her cushion to sit cross-legged, pointing for me to take the tiny bit of padding right in front of her. "Back to me."

Better and better.

My gut was so tight I thought I was going to vomit, and my arms felt like sticks. Everyone was watching as I gingerly sat, pebbles clinking as I tugged a bit of cloth to cover my bare legs. "That's a love," she murmured, and I jumped when she touched my hair.

Someone laughed, and I whipped my head around to see who it had been, but Newt was there, rubbing my forehead from behind, trying to be soothing but only making it worse.

"She's not even going to be able to make a picture on the wall," Ku'Sox predicted.

Al stood, nervous. "Shut up, Ku'Sox, or I'll close your throat for you."

Ku'Sox grinned, pointing to the camels groaning at the outskirts. "Would you like to step outside, old man? I beat your sorry ass before, and I can do it again."

"Ku'Sox, shut up," I said, not liking anyone talking to Al that way, then wondered where my loyalty had come from. But a thread of fear was in Al's motions, so subtle that I didn't know if anyone but perhaps Newt and Dali had noticed.

"He has a right to be afraid," Newt said, leaning forward to whisper in my ear, and I shivered, hardly breathing. "If you can't do this, then you will be a familiar and I will buy you from Al. But I think you can."

"No pressure," I grumbled, and her fingers touching my forehead lifted briefly as she laughed. It sounded weird, her laugh, and I saw more than a few demons grimace.

"Close your eyes, tap a line, and find the collective," Newt said gently.

I took a last look at the faces ringing me, Al with his false confidence, Dali busy calculating the odds, the expressions of hope and doubt on demons I'd never met. I didn't know why they cared one way or the other. Maybe they had a bet going. Maybe they were bored.

"I said," Newt prompted, mildly ticked, "close your eyes."

I closed them, immediately feeling claustrophobic. I tapped a line, wondering what demon had made it, and if he was watching me or dead and turned to dust. I settled myself, plunging into the thick morass of collective thoughts, reeling when I found no one there.

Well, almost no one.

I kicked them out, Newt thought, and I gasped, almost flinging myself out again, but she grabbed my consciousness with a soft thought and hauled me back. *You don't want them here, seeing your soul,* she explained, and I got the impression of her swimming naked in a sea of stars, enjoying the solitude of a moment alone in her infinity.

My soul? I mused, alarmed, but she only seemed to twine her consciousness around mine, keeping us separate but close, rubbing her energies across me, old and jumbled, like a West Coast ley line.

You don't want the entire collective to see you helpless and vulnerable, she explained, giving me the impression of half-lidded eyes and a sultry whisper. *Having Gally see you as such will be punishment enough for almost killing him, I imagine.*

Whoa, Al? I thought, worried, and she swam closer, making me nervous as I remembered him pinning me to the bookcase and spilling ley-line energy into me. And then me, slamming his theoretical dick in a drawer. *Why him?*

Al, she reiterated, seeming bothered she'd forgotten his name again. *You want Dali to peel the memory from your thoughts instead? He's likely more skilled at it, and it's often easier for strangers to see us naked than . . . just what is Gally to you, anyway?*

I shook my head, or at least I would have if I had one. *I don't know.*

Well, when you're done, bring Gally in to separate your

construct from your conscious thought. Let him in, Rachel. Ignore the fact that he will see everything. Moment by moment, every little desire and hate you have, your soul sifting through his fingers as he pulls the construct free. What he doesn't see might be left here, so let him entirely in, she thought, and I had a moment of perfect panic. *It's rather more intimate than pinning you to the wall for a kiss,* she mocked.

I didn't like this, but what choice did I have? It wasn't as if Al hadn't been in my thoughts before. *Wait! I don't know what to do!* I thought as I felt her start to distance herself.

Newt's consciousness swooped and dipped about mine, making me dizzy. *Creating a collective thought real enough to touch is to prove you have the ability to shelter another soul within yours without absorbing it or accidentally changing what should not be changed.* I felt a wave of melancholy come from her, dimming the stars. *Do you know why demons are born able to twist curses? Their mothers curse them while still in the womb so they can defend themselves from birth. But it takes finesse to lay a curse within another's soul while you're sheltering it within your own. Making a tulpa and allowing another to exist freely in it is the same. It's also why Algaliarept can't remember what he looks like under all that prettiness he shows the world. He can't pick out what is rightfully his and what his mother added. Beautiful, beautiful baby. I never had any, but if I had, I'd have made her look just like you.*

It was starting to make sense. Making a construct would show I was fit to be a mother—a mother to demon children I would never have. *So . . . what do I do?* I asked, wondering if the demon who had helped Newt make that memory of an upscale bar was still alive, or if she'd killed him. Maybe it had been Minias.

Newt swam in circles around me, sending out ripples to the edge of the empty collective. *I do so like it when no one is here. Quiet.*

Newt? I prompted, and she returned.

Remember a place. Make it real in your mind. Fill the void here, and Al will separate it from you and make it real. That's their part. All you have to do is let him in.

I had to trust him. Damn it! How did I get here? *Just think of a place?*

In my mind, it was as if I could see her bobbing in the water before me, silver stars running down her face like water drops. *What do you miss the most? Now that you're here forever?*

What do I miss? I echoed, thinking immediately of Jenks, Ivy, and my church, but sharing that with the demons wasn't going to happen. My garden in the sun. The sun I would never see again.

Heartache seemed to double me over. *The sun.* I was going to miss the sun. That was what I could show them. Not the sun in my garden, but somewhere else, where the sun ruled everything, not just now, but for all the past and all the future. I would give the demons a forest so old and dead that only stones remained. I'd give them that, and nothing more.

With a ping that hurt my soul, I felt the memory of the desert rise in me, carrying all the lonely, empty desperation I'd felt when I thought I'd lost Jenks. I hunched, my eyes pinched tightly shut as my heart ached, resonating with the reality that I'd lost everything. Empty. Everything was empty, and the echo of space washed through my skull.

Heat soaked into me like an internal blanket, first frightening, then soothing. The hint of the abandoned ley lines in the desert seemed to glow, dead and gone and useless. From the inside of my eyelids came a reflection of them, etching through the collective like girders bracketing time. And from there, everything built upon itself, the entire desert melting back into existence. The chirp of insects; the soft click of a beetle; the wind pushing against me, oily and slippery, not recognizing me as I stood in the middle of a lost field of power and begged for a miracle.

The memory resonated in me, pulsing from me like a wave. It cascaded over my mental landscape, coloring everything, making it deeper, solid, real. I had been helpless then, and I was helpless now, and I held back a sob, refusing to cry. The scent of rock rose, strong, ancient air that dinosaurs breathed, finally loosed by a rockslide—once frozen by chance but now free to move again. I felt the immensity of my loneliness, and it hurt.

Open your eyes, little demon, Newt whispered in my thoughts.

I opened my eyes, blinking at the glare.

"Oh my God," I said, my lips drying out in the sun that existed in my thoughts. I was in the desert. Almost high noon. I was wearing dusty sneakers, and a short-sleeved shirt clung to me from a sweat that barely existed before the dry air stripped it from me. Grit ground under my feet as I turned, taking it in, hearing the emptiness, feeling the space. I knew it wasn't real, but it *felt* real.

I stood on a paved road, my shadow small under me. Behind me was my mother's car. Before me spilled the world, so vast that my eyes defined the edges with their very failure to comprehend. The sun was high, savagely baking the pinks, purples, and oranges out of the rock. The ground fell from my feet like a mountain turned inside out. A wind I knew existed only in my thoughts pushed on me with the affronted force of a god being asked to stop.

And I had made this.

Shocked, I turned to Newt, beside me. She was dressed in tight capri jeans and a brightly colored top. Dark sunglasses hid her eyes, and a ribbon of moisture ran beside her nose. A silk scarf covering her hair made her look like a fifties movie star out on location. I think she had dressed me, because I certainly hadn't.

"Is it real?" I asked. "Is it done?" The sky was so blue. I might never see it again, but I had it here—in my memory.

She smiled, her lips too red and an overabundance of blush on her cheeks. "Let Al in. Only Al. This needs to be remembered. They all need to remember this."

I had no idea what she meant, but I thought of Al.

A quiver went through me and the world seemed to hiccup. In a cascading wash, he spilled into my mind as if he had been there waiting, and when I opened the door, he fell in. He stood beside me in his Mesopotamia robes, his mouth open and his pupils so small his eyes were like pools of blood. Shock poured from him as he saw what I had done—and fear, but if it was because of what I had done or because now he had to peel it out of my brain, I didn't know.

"My God," he whispered, taking it in. "She even has the old ley lines."

"Al?" I warbled, scared, and it was as if he caught my soul as he grabbed my shoulder when my knees gave out. He hoisted me into his arms, trying to see my construct and search my eyes at the same time.

"Take it, Al," Newt said softly. "Before she loses consciousness."

Al took a frightened breath, his eyes fixing on mine. It hurt, almost, and I wanted it out of me.

"Let me in," he said, seeing the pain in me, and I closed my eyes, unable to refuse.

I started to cry as he took my soul and lifted me out of the collective, leaving only the memory of the afternoon at the Petrified Forest. Carefully he peeled back bits and pieces of the construct, freeing little parts I hadn't known were attached to it, the shape of a rock that I'd seen before on the beach, the color that was akin to a sunset when I was ten, the caw of a rook that sent shivers down my spine—I'd heard it before at camp. Al carefully drew the associated memories back, taking my soul from the construct to leave something that could be made real.

Slowly the pain lifted as I was made whole, and still he looked, making sure nothing was left. "I think," Al whispered, "I think I got all of her. I've not done this before. Oh God, I hope I got all of her." I felt him turn. "Newt. The word to fix it—" And then his voice cracked. *"Memoranda,"* he croaked out, and I felt a ping through me as the thought severed completely.

Things that must be remembered, I translated silently, waiting for the rising crest of imbalance, but nothing came.

And then, though my eyes were shut, I knew that every single demon who had been in Dalliance was with us. I hadn't brought them in; Al had moved my memory to them. It was fixed. It was *real.*

As one, the demons cowered, crying out as the cool night of Mesopotamia vanished and was replaced in a blink with the hot reality of the Arizona desert in June. "My God!" I heard one say, but most were silent with awe.

"Dali!" Al shouted, his thick-fingered hand cupping my head as he held me to him. "Did it take? Did I do it right?"

"We're here, aren't we?" the older demon called back, and I blearily looked, seeing the jukebox standing beside the memory of my mother's blue Buick. The trunk was open, and there was a picnic basket inside. I hadn't thought of the basket. Someone else had. I'd made something that the demons could twist to their own reality. I'd done it.

"A picnic," Newt said, snapping a red-and-white-checkered blanket out right there on the side of the road. "What a splendid idea. Dali, you must remember to give Rachel royalties every time someone uses this, seeing that she's still alive. I'll be watching your books. Us demonesses must stick together."

Demoness. I'd done it. I was a demon. Yay me.

My head fell onto Al's chest, and I whimpered, my hands balled up as I tried to keep my eyes open. At the outskirts of my vision, I could see the demons standing on the edge of the drop-off, throwing rocks to see how far the illusion went. Fists on his hips, Dali stood between me and Newt, gazing at clouds that somehow never seemed to cover the sun. Newt had sat upon the blanket with a bucket of fried chicken and a wineglass.

Al jiggled me up into a more comfortable posture. "She's not well. I'm taking her home. Anyone still think she's not a demon?"

"I'm fine," I slurred, clearly not.

"No!" Ku'Sox shouted, and my pulse hiccupped. "It was Newt! Newt made it!"

My eyes opened, then squinted. "Screw you. I'm a demon. Deal with it." *Oh God. I'm a demon.*

"Don't be tiresome," Newt said coyly. "I don't remember the sun. Or colors . . . like this."

She had cried. The tears were gone now, but she had cried when we'd been alone. I think she did remember, and it made her crazy. Was I going to go crazy, too?

"Al?" I warbled, feeling it all come down on me. "I don't feel so good."

Immediately he held me closer, his warmth doing nothing to stop my shaking.

"Take her home," Newt said, having left her blanket to shade me with her own body. "Her construct stretches the entire breadth of the collective. It's only hampered now by the size of Dalliance."

"She filled the entire collective . . ." Dali breathed.

"The whole thing. You could walk for most of a day and not run into the wall. I'd suggest we make this our new wallpaper, even as bright as it is. At least we could all fit in it."

"Al," I whispered, feeling the world start to spin. Shit, I couldn't go back. This was for real. I was going to spend the rest of my life here. Under the ground. Away from the sun. Every day exactly the same, surrounded by beings who had lived too long, trapped in their own hell. *If I turned around fast, would there be barren wall behind me?*

I was passing out. I felt it happen as if in slow motion, parts of my brain turning off, the horizon growing dark, and noises becoming dull. There were congratulations to Al even as he struggled to put space enough between us and them to jump out. Ku'Sox raged until someone shoved him in the trunk. The last thing I remembered was someone, Dali, I think, kissing the top of my hand as I slumped in Al's arms.

"Welcome home, Rachel Mariana Morgan," he said, his goat-slitted eyes holding a new, dangerous light. "It's a pleasure to finally meet you."

Twenty-six

The dry hush of sliding coals woke me, and I jerked, clutching to me a black blanket smelling of Brimstone. I didn't sit up since I was warm and comfortable, a hazy lassitude still heavy on me as I lay against the gently curving bench surrounding the central fire in Al's kitchen. I'd fallen asleep here before, but this felt different.

A dim light glowed on a new honey-colored slate table set before the smaller hearth. Al sat before it, his back to me as he chanted. At least I thought it was Al. It didn't look like him, but it didn't look like Pierce, either.

Al had been in my head. He'd made my thoughts real. He'd seen me down to my soul, and I'd seen nothing of his . . . and he's . . . humming?

The masculine figure was taller than Al by quite a bit but narrower, lacking the wide shoulders that I was familiar with. Short red hair pretty much covered him in a curly pelt where it showed past a lightweight black shirt and trousers. Muscles were well defined, with a long strength rather than heavy bulk. A shiny ebony hardness just above his ears might have been horns, and by God, I think he had that same prehensile tail I'd seen before when he'd threatened Treble.

"Al?" I croaked, putting a hand to my throat when the sound came out rusty.

The gravelly chantlike words cut off, and he spun, a ley-line doodad clattering until it fell off the table and he caught it with a long-fingered, double-jointed hand. A wash of black ever-after coated him, falling away to reveal the more familiar vision of Al, though he still wore that pair of casual jammies and had a surprised look in his red, goat-slitted eyes. The mirror he'd been looking into he slammed to the table, facedown, covering up the pentagram and glyphs he had scribed on the new slate table.

"You're awake!" he said, and I cowered when his voice seemed to boom inside my head.

"Yeah," I gasped, hands over my ears. I cracked an eyelid, seeing him muttering another curse and a new wash of ever-after falling from him. *What is he doing in here while I'm sleeping?* "I don't feel so good," I said as I sat up. "What are you doing in here?"

"Trying to remember what I look like," he muttered, his skin turning red from embarrassment, not a curse or a charm. He touched the mirror, and it vanished.

Grimacing, I looked over the candlelit room, missing the sun already. I felt like I'd been working out all day and gone to bed cold. It had to have been from making that construct. I hadn't taken the smut for it, and I wondered who had. Al? "You said I reset your DNA. Can't you just . . . plug and play?" I asked.

"Plug and play . . . ," Al drawled, his wide back to me as he put the ley-line stuff in a tall cupboard and locked the door with a key, not a spell that could be tampered with. "Such a way with words you have. Yes, my DNA has been reset, but not all the genes a person has are expressed. I have to decide which ones to turn on."

Like the one with curly red hair. "Oh," I said simply, slumping where I sat. Jeez, I was tired, and I stretched my legs out from under the black blanket, feeling everything ache. I was still wearing the short-sleeved shirt and jeans Newt had put me in at the edge of the desert, but at least Al had taken my sneakers off—and only my sneakers.

I was silent, thinking about that curly red fur he had been covered with. And the tail. "I kinda like you the way you are right now," I said, feeling my muscles ache as I swung my feet to the floor and touched my toes to the cold floor. "Where's Pierce?"

"I don't know."

My next words vanished in surprise. He didn't know? The way he said it was more like he didn't care. It wasn't like Al to let profit slip from him, and I wondered what was up. Shifting my aching shoulders, I mumbled, "I don't like you in here when I'm sleeping. It gives me the creeps."

"Yes, well, it was easier for me to work quietly here than to move you to my room." He stood, a handful of ley-line charms in his thick hands. "Now that you're awake, you'll be moving in there."

My arms ached, and I rubbed them. Then I stopped. *Moving in there?* "Whoa, whoa, whoa," I said, waking up fast. "Okay, I let you in my head and everything, but that doesn't translate into me moving into your bed!" I stood, wobbling, and suddenly he was there, holding my elbow.

"Let go!" I yelled, yanking out of his grip and falling back into the soft warmth of the blanket. My heart pounded, and I felt weak, surprising me. "I may be a demon!" I exclaimed, feeling my eyes start to warm as it all sank in. "But I'm not your girlfriend, wife, or anything. Anything!" I shouted, shaking as I drew my feet up and held my shins to me. "I'm not sharing your room, your bed, or your life. I can sleep just fine right here!"

"Rachel, Rachel, Rachel," he said, very still and unmoving. "Always jumping to the wrong conclusion. You're like a frog, you know." Looking nothing like himself, Al retreated to the smaller hearth. Slowly my knees dropped from my chin, leaving me embarrassed. Sheesh, I'd huddled up like a scared little girl.

"Wrong conclusion," I said bitterly. "What's not to understand? Move into your room? Sounds plain enough to me."

Al spun his chair at the table to face me, his back to the smaller hearth. He sat, looking disheveled and rumpled until he made an effort to sit up straight. "You can't continue to sleep in the kitchen," he said, looking discomfited. "Before you yell at me again," he said as I took a breath, "I'll sleep in the library. *You* get the bedroom."

My held breath exploded out of me. *Huh?*

Al sent his gaze over the shadowy workroom. "It's not safe for you here. Too many things might get out." His goat-slitted eyes met mine, and I shivered, my skin prickling as I remembered the tapestry that seemed to move on its own and had bled and cried. Or the bottle of soul that had almost taken me over, just sitting on a shelf waiting to fall over and break.

"Or in," he added with a little shoulder lift, his eyes on the ceiling, and I held my blanket closer, my thoughts going to the dark spot on his pantry floor that seemed to pull at me every time I went down there alone—and only alone. "You don't have enough smut on your soul to hide you, and you're like a light, attracting things."

"Like moths?"

Al's eyes dropped from the ceiling, chilling me. "No. Ugly things in the dark attracted to power, and I'm not just talking about my associates. It didn't matter before, but . . ." Al winced. "I knew you were special, Rachel. And don't take this as me going soft or sentimental—"

"You didn't think I could do it." My heart was pounding, and I felt sick. I was a demon. Crap on toast, I was a demon, and there was no going back. Stuff had been turned on in my head, and it couldn't be turned off.

Head lowered, Al looked at his bare hands, folded in his lap. "I knew you could, otherwise I wouldn't have let you get into that position. But now everyone else knows it, too. I wasn't expecting how vulnerable you would be, and word gets around. It is too easy for . . ." He hesitated. "You're so damn helpless . . . ," he tried again, his words cutting off once more. "How am I supposed to keep them off you now that they know?"

My stomach cramped, and I felt my expression go blank. Other demons. I had gone from a curiosity to a real demon. They might want to take by stealth what they couldn't buy now that I was one of them and not just a maybe. And Al didn't know if he could prevent it?

"Never mind," he growled, seeing my fear. "The bedroom has safeguards that you can't get here."

"Al?" I questioned, and he stood, showing me his back as he faced the fire.

"I'll stay in the library," he said, and I shifted uncomfortably. "I would have moved you to my room immediately, but I didn't want you waking up in a strange place." He turned, his eyebrows raised in familiar, mocking amusement. "Jumping to conclusions. Yelling at me. Breaking my things . . ."

I shivered, pulling my knees to my chin again and not caring if it made me look scared. I was. Vulnerable. He'd called me vulnerable. I had proved myself stronger, and therefore somehow become weaker. "You were in my head," I whispered, remembering how it had hurt—my soul stretched over the entire collective until he lifted me from it. "You separated the tulpa from my thoughts. Thank you."

He was back at the table before the fireplace, wiping out both the circle and the laundry list in Latin beside it with a red cloth. "You're welcome."

His reponse was guarded, and my tension rose. "You saw my thoughts. More than usual."

"Yes." Scrubbing, still scrubbing.

"I couldn't see yours."

Smiling, he turned, his eyes looking almost normal in the dim light. His teeth glinted. "That's the nature of it, yes."

Uneasy, I counted the dirty dishes scattered around, making it look like a frat boy's dorm. It appeared as if he'd been here for days. Maybe he'd been hungry. I knew I was. "What did you see?" I asked, nervous.

The rag he'd used to clean the table went into the fire behind him. "I saw what you are," he said, "and I was ashamed. I saw what you expect from a person, and I'd call you a bitch except you demand it from yourself as well. I saw how you see me," he explained. "It wasn't anything I didn't already know, but it made me wonder at what I lack, what isn't there."

"Al," I interrupted, remembering that forced kiss and how it had felt.

But Al was shaking his head, looking ill. "I am *not* going to be the person who completes you," he said, glancing at me and turning away. "You are one messed-up bitch."

"Gee, thanks," I muttered as I held my cold toes, glad that he wasn't going to try to change our relationship now that I was stuck here.

Al's expression shifted, became ugly, angry with himself. "I saw what we had become. Soft, ineffective, laughable," he said, his hand forming a fist.

"You still scare the hell out of me," I interrupted.

"Accepting our exile and making it comfortable instead of finding a way to go home. We are a joke."

Oh, that. I rubbed my feet, trying to warm them. "Sorry."

Al shook out a silver scarf that hadn't been there a moment ago and turned back to the table, running it lightly over the new slate as if erasing any electronic charge left behind. "I don't need your pity."

No, you need a good psychiatrist. My eyes went to his feet as they scuffed. *Slippers?* "Where's Ku'Sox?" I asked, wishing I could wake up again and start over. Having swum in my soul might have given Al the feeling that he could be casual with me, but it made me nervous. I had no idea what he was going to do next.

His shoulders moving slow and steady, Al wiped down the table again until even the last hints of what he'd written were gone. "Don't worry about Ku'Sox. You proved yourself." Becoming still, he looked at me, the candle and firelight making his eyes glow. "You have a place here."

Perhaps, but I didn't want it. I had things to do. I had to ask Trent what I'd done wrong with that curse. Then I had to find

Ku'Sox to give it to him so I could at least go home without being summoned. *Home* . . . "What time is it?" I asked, depressed.

Seeming to appreciate the change of conversation as much as me, Al squinted at the clock on the mantel, the lights getting brighter. "Noon?"

Great, I'd been out for hours. Ivy and Jenks were probably worried sick. Maybe come sundown they could summon me back for a couple of hours and we could strategize until the sun came up. I had to get out of here for a while. Al was scaring me.

I flung the covers off, then hesitated, putting a hand to my middle when I wasn't sure I could stand up yet. *Damn, I was dizzy.* "I passed out," I said needlessly, and Al sat back down in his chair to stare at me, one hand on the clean table, the other in his lap.

"Rachel, you made a construct large enough to land a jet in. Yes, you passed out."

I licked my lips, uneasy. "Thank you for taking the smut."

He frowned, almost growling. "I didn't take the smut. Newt did, and I'd give a lot to know why."

Newt had taken it? Was that good or bad? "I think it was because she wanted to be a part of it," I said, remembering that she had cried.

"Newt?" Al barked, shifting in his chair, appearing nervous. "I doubt that she wanted to be part of *that*. She doesn't like making constructs anymore. She doesn't trust anyone to watch her while she recovers. That, and she doesn't want anyone in her head." Al touched his chin, a nervous tic I'd never seen before. "How do you feel?"

How do I feel? I feel like crap. Hand to my middle, I tried to stand again, changing my mind and huddling under the blanket instead with my back to the large fire. Had that nervous tic been real when he'd asked me how I felt, or was that statement about not wanting me for a girlfriend bull and he was trying to seduce me? He knew everything. What turned me on, what turned me off. What lowered my defenses. What made me vulnerable. It was enough to make someone crazy. "Hungry," I finally said. "I can't believe I was out for half a day."

"Half a day?" Al drawled. "Try the better part of three."

"What!" This time, I managed to get up, wobbling until Al stood and steadied me, his grip a shade too tight on my elbow. "Three days? I couldn't have been unconscious for three days!" Crap on toast, I'd missed my brother's wedding!

"Slow," he said as I sat back down to get his hand off me. "Newt said you might be dizzy for a while. That's why I didn't leave. Can you tap a line yet?"

Yet? Head between my knees, I concentrated on breathing. I carefully reached for a line, just enough to know I could, then pulled back. I was starting to see the sense in this. Females thought up the construct, and a male lifted it from his friend's psyche and protected her until she recovered—and I say friend because no way was I Al's lover. But three days? Jenks and Ivy would be sick with worry. "Newt was here?" I was able to sense the mild disturbance in the energy surrounding Al that she always left the demon with.

I heard the creak of his chair as he sat back down. "After you didn't wake up the first day, yes, I asked her a few questions. Can you tap a line?"

I looked up at the worry in his voice, feeling something shift. "Yes. Thank you. For watching me."

"I had to force her to leave," he said, eyes everywhere but on mine. "She said I couldn't care for you. Bitch. I made sure you ate. Ran a brush-and-wash curse on you when you crapped yourself. Waited. Kept everything out until your aura recovered."

My aura? "Al?" I said, really scared as I firmly tapped the line to find no headache, no pain. I was okay. "You're kidding, right?"

His wandering eyes settled on me. "You'd rather I let you sit in your crap for three days?"

"No. I meant . . . Uh. Thank you. Just . . . Thank you." Holy fairy farts, I hadn't known making a construct would be so far-reaching.

Standing, Al pushed his chair back. "Damn lazy of you."

I could tell he was relieved as he stacked the plates and cups, sending them to the food kitchen all at once. He'd been watching me for three days? "Al. Thank you. I really mean it."

Turning, he took a breath to say something, sneezing instead.

"Bless you," I said, and he held up a hand in annoyance as he reached for his scrying mirror, tucked in among his books. Holding it out, he grimaced. "It's for you."

My eyebrows rose, and I stifled a shiver as the heavy, cold glass slipped onto my lap. "How do you know?"

"Because you touched a line, and they were waiting," he said. "You're going to have to make a new calling glyph. I'm not your bloody secretary."

What are you then, Al? "It wasn't like the coven gave me time to get my luggage before they banished me," I said, not wanting to put my hand on the more complex glyph that Al used. The lines practically glowed red, and the glass was so dark I couldn't see any reflection at all.

"So I buy you a looking glass and you make a new one," he said, and I smiled, glad to be back on familiar ground. "Answer it, will you?" he prompted, annoyed by my good humor.

Still smiling, I pulled my legs up to painfully sit cross-legged, resettling the heavy thing on my lap. "Couldn't make it any bigger, could you?"

"The boy with the biggest toy wins, love," he leered, and I looked down.

My hand was already placed, and I tentatively reached for a line, carefully tapping it until I was sure my head wouldn't explode. The line slipped in with a gentle smoothness, and I found the collective with ease. At least my aura was okay. I hadn't even known I'd damaged it.

Hello? I ventured. *Al's line.*

Rachel! boomed a thought in my head, and I cringed. *So glad I caught you and that you're feeling well, love.*

I glanced at Al, pretending to mess with the fire. *Yea-a-a-a-ah?* I hazarded. *Don't call me love. I have a name. By the way, I don't know yours.*

Absolutely. Absolutely, the demon fawned. *This is Strontanchaark. Two a's and an* rk. *You may not have noticed, but I was at Dalliance last week. Red feathers . . . silver headdress?*

Sorry, don't remember you, I thought, wondering if he was after a date. Not going to happen. No way. No how.

My call name is Tron, he added, and I sighed.

"Look, Tron," I said aloud so Al could hear some of it and maybe stop pretending to mess with the fire. "I'm kind of busy right now. Just woke up. Things to do, you know . . ."

Completely understandable, he gushed, focusing hard to keep me from breaking the connection. *But if you could wedge in a little time for me this week, I could make it worth your while. Do you think you could make me a replica of Rynn Cormel's pool?*

I blinked, trying to switch gears. He didn't want a date. He wanted a contractor. It made sense. They all had the same stuff they'd had for thousands of years, apart from what Newt could give them, and three days ago, I'd made a brand-new desert for them to play in.

"Rynn Cormel?" I stammered when Tron poked my thoughts to see if I was still there. "You're kidding, right? He doesn't even have a pool."

He does. It's in Washington, Tron insisted. *In the sun. The construct has to be in the sun.*

Feeling panicked, I waved for Al's attention, and he turned to me, a soft, secretive smile on his face. "Uh, I've never been to the White House," I stammered. And what was this about the sun? Didn't they know I'd been cursed?

So get over there and look at it.

My eyes pinched; I didn't like his attitude. "It's not that

easy," I offered, not wanting to get the reputation of being a bitch on my first conscious day.

But you can do it, Tron insisted, then hesitated. *How much?*

His thoughts were flat, and I felt a quiver of excitement. A demon was asking me what I wanted. My eyes flicked to Al, and he shrugged. "What do you want?" he said softly, his voice making me shiver.

Home was probably out. The next best thing would be a place of my own so I wasn't sleeping in Al's bedroom. I shifted on the cushioned bench before the central fire, making sure my hand didn't slip. There was no way I was ever going to see the White House pool in the sun, but maybe we could work something out. "How many extra rooms do you have?"

Rooms? Tron yelped, and I winced. *Putrid ash mother corn shucker, you want rooms? As in plural?*

Somehow his reaction emboldened me, and I gathered my courage, even as Al blinked at me in astonishment. "You don't think I'm going to just *give* you the sun, do you? Out of the goodness of my little demon heart? You want a full-blown tulpa with accurate artifacts and the sun? I'm going to have to get to reality and sneak into the White House estate in the daytime. Evade FIB and I.S. agents both."

Robbery! Highway robbery! Tron was wailing into my thoughts.

"Supply and demand, buddy," I said, preparing to break the connection. "Come on back when you're serious."

No, wait! I heard him think. *How about the car? The one in the desert. I can give you a gently used familiar, well broken in and skilled, if you can duplicate that car for me.*

You want my mom's car? I thought, then pulled my thoughts back to myself. "I live with Al," I said, glancing at him. "If I want a familiar, I go to the professional and get one, I don't take someone's castoff. You want an '89 Buick with leather seats and a tape player. I want a place to sleep. Call me back when you can give me a room. Unfurnished, if you don't mind. I don't like other people's junk."

Wait! he called again, and I grinned at Al, stifling my excitement lest Tron pick up on it. *If you can make it red and promise me an exclusive, I can cut out a closet for you.*

"A closet?" I exclaimed, and I felt Tron wince. "You think my mother's car is worth a lousy closet?"

A large walk-in, Tron added. *Thirty by fifteen by fifteen up. I can get the toys out of it, but the mess on the walls you're going to have to deal with. I want an exclusive, though. You don't make a car for anyone else.*

"No exclusive," I said aloud, watching Al for his opinion and seeing him shake his head and hold his hands out in a "bigger" gesture. He didn't even know how large the offer was, and he thought I could get one bigger. "Dude, if you want an exclusive, I want something twice as big as a lousy thirty by fifteen by fifteen. And the exclusive is only on that model." Tron groaned, and I added, "And I want it attached to Al's rooms."

Okay, okay! the demon said, and I got the feeling that he was agreeing before I added anything else. *It's a deal.*

"Done," I said, and Al sprang to his feet and almost ran down the narrow stone steps to the cellar below. "I can work you in before the end of the week," I said loudly so Al could still hear me. "I'm a little tired right now. Call back in about an hour." Al came back upstairs with a bottle and twin goblets in his hands. "Ah, make that two hours," I amended. "You can imagine that Al has me scheduled tightly with his tutorial," I said, and Al guffawed. "Actually, why don't you arrange the time with him for us to come over and put your car exactly where you want it. Soon as the room shows up and Al tells me it's safe for storing my shoes in."

Al? Tron thought, sounding disappointed. *I thought I'd fix the tulpa.*

"You?" I said, feeling a stab of alarm, having forgotten that little part. I'd wanted Al there as a buffer, but this was spiraling into something more complicated. "No, Al's fixing it into reality, er, the ever-after, not you."

I felt Tron sigh, making me wonder if half the reason he'd asked me to come over was for a chance to swim in my unconscious. Not happening, bud-*dy*. Al was opening the bottle with a soft pop, smiling. I couldn't meet his eyes. Who knew what I'd find there?

I'll have the room deeded to you in an hour, Tron thought somewhat disappointedly, and I broke the connection.

"The White House pool," I said with a snort, carefully setting Al's mirror to the side. "Is he nuts?" He was going to be in my head again, but it would be worth it. Right? At least Al wouldn't be sleeping in the library. I was embarrassed that I'd lost my ability to leave unless Ivy or Jenks summoned me, seeing as they knew my summoning name, but Al didn't seem upset. Actually, he was in a grand mood as he handed me a tarnished silver goblet in the shape of a champagne flute.

"And you doubt you're one of us," he said softly, pride and more than a hint of relief in his voice. "Well done, Rachel."

We clinked and I took a swallow, the unexpected honey-amber liquid flowing, feeling like heaven. "Wow!" I said when I came up for air. "I bet Rynn Cormel could get me the White House extended tour." It wasn't wine, but it was potent, and warmth tingled all the way to my toes. I had a room of my own, and a valuable service that no other demon besides Newt could provide. I was going to be okay.

I sobered at that. I was going to be okay. Just what did that mean—I was going to be okay? Was I going to be happy? And why wasn't I trying to get out of here?

Al grunted, seeming to know why my excitement had left me. "I started getting the calls yesterday when they figured out your scrying mirror was in reality," he said. "I had to put up a 'She's out' post, but you saw how long it took for the calls to resume when you tapped a line. They were waiting for you. Seems like you have a lucrative place here after all."

"With your help." I stared at the small hearth fire visible under the new slate table and remembered waking up and finding Al sitting there looking like . . . something else. "I'm making a car for him," I mused aloud. "And I'm getting a room out of it. You won't have to sleep in the library."

Al hesitated in his motion to top off my glass. "You're giving the room to me?" he asked as the liquid poured in and settled.

My eyes jerked to his at the hint of a question in his voice. "Actually," I said slowly, "I thought maybe I could have it so you could keep your room."

He took a breath, holding it for a moment before slowly letting it out. Hand shaking slightly, he set the amber bottle down between us. "You will be in my room. The safeguards are chiseled into the stone. But I would appreciate the chance to update my own décor." He took a sip, rocking on his feet. "I thought you would get that mark removed."

My gaze darted to my last remaining demon mark, the one on my wrist that had started our association. "Uh, I forgot," I stammered, embarrassed somehow. I sipped my drink, not knowing what it was but enjoying the mild buzz that was hitting me. "Al," I said, my tongue markedly looser. "You just tell me what you want, and I'll make it for you. I owe you big."

He looked at me, emotions hidden behind his silence, for so long I wondered if I'd said something wrong. The fire snapped in the center pit behind me, and when I shivered, Al absently tossed a chunk of polished wood on it, probably gleaned from a broken building at the surface somewhere.

"Um, Al?" I questioned, feeling more than a little uncomfortable, the honey and amber filling my head with a shiny clarity. "I do appreciate you saving my ass. If there's something I can do to show you that, you'll tell me, won't you?"

He turned to me, still no expression on his face. "I'm reasonably sure I had brown hair."

Oh God. I think I'd insulted him. "Al—"

Finally a shimmer of emotion crossed him. "Drink," he said as he tapped my glass with his. "It's a day to celebrate. You have come home."

I didn't know about the home part, but I lifted my glass, a

sneeze ripping through me as unexpectedly as a slamming door. My fingers shook, and a splat of liquid spotted Al's pretty black floor. Horrified, I met Al's demon-slitted red eyes, his first reaction of annoyance shifting to dread as he stared at me in what might be pity. I was sneezing, not him. And it didn't feel like an incoming call. It felt like a summons. And it was noon?

Ivy? Jenks?

"Rachel?" Al asked as the first gut-wrenching pain blossomed and I pushed the glass back into his hand.

"It's a summons," I muttered, jaw clenched and the good feeling from whatever I'd been drinking dying.

"But it's noon!" the demon exclaimed, gaze going to the clock to affirm it.

Ow. I hunched in on myself as the pull grew stronger. "Maybe Trent only cursed me to need a summons to be able to cross. Apparently I can still walk . . . in the sun. Ow!" I looked up, wincing. "I gotta go." *Day or night. Trent had said day or night.* Tron would be pleased. I could give him the White House pool in the sun after all.

I gasped as Al suddenly had my shirt front, yanking me up. "Who knows?" he snarled. "Who knows you can be summoned in the day?"

"Al, you're hurting me! It's probably just Ivy or my mom!"

His grip loosened, but he didn't let go. "I asked you, who knows your curse allows you to be summoned during day hours?" he demanded, and I pushed his hand off me, feeling the pain of an ignored summons.

"Everyone who was in the auditorium when Trent cursed me," I said. "Jeez Louise! I think you bruised me."

Al's eyes narrowed. "Trenton," he growled, thick hands clenching.

"If I'm lucky," I said, wondering if Trent even knew my summoning name. Probably. "I need to talk to him and get the Latin for sliding Ku'Sox's curse back onto him so I can walk free again. I did it wrong the last time."

I could almost see Al's understanding hit him when his expression went blank. "You tried to slide his original curse back onto him?" Al said in wonder. "At the restaurant? And I stopped you? Sweet mother pus bucket!" he exclaimed, and I swear, dust sifted from the ceiling. "Rachel, we have to work on this communication thing."

Hand around my middle, I bent almost double. "I gotta go," I panted. "Trent knows the curse. I have to talk to him. If I'm lucky, it's him."

Again Al touched me, but this time, his hand was gentle on my shoulder. "And if you're not, it's Ku'Sox. He knows you're too protected here, and you're a threat to him. He's summoning you. He's summoning you to where I can't follow. He's going to try to kill you!"

I panted, feeling my muscles shake as the pull worsened. God, I felt like I was being split in two. "Can't be him. He doesn't know my name."

"Trent does," Al said, his grip on me tightening into pain for an instant. "I told you to take that elf firmly in hand. Trent let Ku'Sox out. They're working together. They want you dead."

Holding my breath, I managed to look up, feeling a wash of betrayal. It couldn't be Trent. I'd just gotten the Latin wrong. Right? "I gotta go," I wheezed. "This is shitty, you know? How do you live like this?"

"Rachel!" he cried, but it was too late, and I let go of my hold on the world. The pain subsided, and the comforting gray of Al's kitchen vanished as I found myself yanked into the ley lines. Fear, hope, and anticipation rose high. If it was Ku'Sox, he was in for a nasty surprise. I was a self-proclaimed demon, and I should start acting like it.

But even as I thought it, my throat closed, and I felt a pang of homesickness. Ivy. Jenks. What would I tell them? Pierce, how could I explain what had happened? Trent . . . how would I kill him if he had betrayed me?

Okay, so it might not be all bad.

Twenty-seven

The discordant jangle of San Francisco's broken ley lines flooded my mind, and I watched as they all cycled down to one, foremost in my thoughts. I tried to listen to it without looking past the bubble of awareness that I was cocooned in, but without Bis to safely bring the sound in past my bubble, they all tasted the same.

I shivered as my lungs formed and the memory of my body rose, giving my soul something to reside in. With a pop of sound, I found myself almost exactly where I'd been not three days ago, in the dead center of the stage where I'd been cursed.

The lights were off, and it was dark but for the hiss of a kerosene lantern making a puddle of light on the stage. The circle imprisoning me took up most of it. Darkness made the huge room a cavern of black echoes from the drone of a generator in the distance. Acrid and sharp, the smell of broken cement tweaked my nose. Something had happened. The power was out.

"You see!" Pierce said, and I spun to see him standing between Oliver and Vivian. There was a fourth witch in coven robes huddled on the floor behind them. "If she was a true demon, she could not be summoned in the day. Let your claims go, Oliver."

Pierce! I thought, then anger slid through me. They'd circled me. Like the demon that I was. Sucking on my teeth, I looked at the three witches standing in a row staring at me, the fourth completely out of it and shaking behind them. I wished it had been Ivy or Jenks—or even Trent.

"Hi, Pierce," I said dryly. "This your idea?" I added, pinging the barrier with a finger and drawing back before it could burn me. How they knew my summoning name, my real summoning name, not Al's borrowed one, was a mystery, until I remembered that Pierce had probably been haunting me when I chose the stupid thing. *Great, I'm a demon for less than a week, and already I'm fielding calls.*

Expression pained and a little lost, Pierce strode forward, his full-length coat coated with dust. His hair was mussed, and his motions were quick. My flash of anger died. Tired. I was tired. For one brief moment in Trent's hotel, I had entertained the idea that even with our differences we might make a go of it. He loved me. I could love him, if I let myself be stupid. But I couldn't even pretend anymore that circumstances might change someday. He was coven, and I was a demon. What was wrong with me? Why was I attracted to the very things that could hurt me?

"Let her out, Oliver," Pierce said, squinting in anger at the stoic man holding the bubble, and my heart clenched in regret. "She's not a demon."

Yes, I am.

Oliver crossed his arms over his chest, the dim light catching the Möbius-strip pin on his lapel. His circle looked well drawn, and with a little effort I might have been able to break it. But the reality was, I just didn't care.

"Hi, Vivian," I said in greeting, not surprised that they were treating me like this. I'd saved her life, and here I was, circled like an animal. Hearing my bitter sarcasm, she dropped her gaze, ashamed. The last witch on the floor shivered, showing a masculine arm and blood-matted hair. The coven was down two witches. *What had happened?*

"Drop your circle before I throw you into it!" Pierce said stridently. "Rachel is not a demon!"

Again, Oliver made a grunt of negation, peering at me as if I were a bug, not a person he'd condemned three days ago. "No," he said, his voice rough, as if he'd been yelling. "If we let her out before she agrees to do what we want, she won't do it."

I couldn't help my snicker at that, and I shifted my weight to my other foot, wishing I had something on my feet other than socks. It was cold in here, and I wrapped my arms around my short-sleeved shirt. "I got news for you, Ollie," I said. "I'm not going to do what you want anyway."

Eyes wide, Pierce spun, making his coattails furl. "We are asking for help, not demanding it." His eyes shifted to mine, pleading for forgiveness. "I'm sorry. The circle was not my idea."

But you went along with it. "You think if you ask for my help, I'll give it for free?" I said, hearing my voice echo as my arms dropped to my sides. "After you let an elf curse me and label me a demon? In front of everyone?" *Oh yeah. I have to talk to Trent.* I looked at Oliver, seeing not a hint of guilt. "After you promised me a clean slate?"

Pierce dropped his head, hearing my rebuke. Hell, I knew it had been a slip of his tongue that had put me here and him working for the coven. It hadn't been intentional, but here I was, in a circle, and there he was, outside it. God, I was stupid. Tired, I was putting up a hand and glancing to the empty seats when a rumble echoed through the air. They all hunched, as if expecting the roof to come down, and the cowering witch shook, curling deeper into himself if that was at all possible. *Leon?*

"What happened? Where are the rest of you?" I asked, fatigue lapping about my ankles.

Vivian came forward into the light. Dressed in jeans and a sweater, she looked tired, as if she'd seen too much in too short a time. "We lost them," she said, her expression closed. "Ku'Sox . . ."

A pulse of adrenaline lit through me and my eye twitched

when her words cut off in heartache. *Ku'Sox. Why am I not surprised?*

"He killed them," Pierce said bluntly. "Ate them as they screamed for succor. Then he ate their souls as they watched. Consumed them. That was yesterday. It could have been averted if the rest of these lily-livered 'fraidycats had listened to me sooner."

They want me to fight Ku'Sox for them, I mused, seeing the power outage and the smell of cracked cement in an entirely new way. A thread of adrenaline-laced hope pulled through me, making me stand a little straighter. They wanted something from me. I wanted something from them. But first, I needed to talk to Trent.

I felt my lips curve up in a not-nice smile that made Oliver swear and Vivian swallow hard. Pierce alone seemed to have expected the nasty expression of confident, bitter satisfaction that I knew I was now wearing. I'd seen it on Al, and only now did I understand it. We were all fools. All of us.

"Ku'Sox tearing apart your reality isn't my problem," I said as I eyed my nails and wished I knew how to change my clothes into something suitably overbearing and sexy. "Who wants to banish me? Send me *home*?"

I hit the last word hard with sarcasm, and Pierce gave Oliver a dark look that said to shut up and stop his muttering about demons. "Rachel, please," he asked. "He's destroying everything, killing people. You beat him before."

"Yeah?" I said, and Pierce lowered his eyes. "That was when I was a witch. Where are Ivy and Jenks?"

All bluster and overdone emotion, Oliver strode forward until the hissing kerosene light made harsh shadows on his face. "You filthy demon. You're in my circle, and you'll do what I say!"

I tapped the barrier between us to make his aura run from the dimple of impact. It held firm, even if only Oliver was holding it. He looked old. Tired. Not a surprise if he'd been fighting Ku'Sox for three days. "It doesn't work that way," I said lightly. "The thing about demons is they can say no, and *I don't like you*." Smiling wickedly, I leaned close, the barrier humming a complaint. "It's called *Let's Make a Deal* for a reason. You shunned me, sent fairies to burn my church, tried to kill me and my friends. Then you made me drag my sorry ass clear across the continent chasing a promise of forgiveness that I won from you *fair and square,* only to have you curse me and call me a demon. And now, when you're in trouble, you have the balls to ask for my help?" I shook my head, not believing that Trent had anticipated all of this and prepared for it.

"What on *earth* might you have that I want . . . hmmmm, I wonder," I mused sarcastically, glancing at each of them in turn, Oliver in hate, Vivian in disappointment, and Pierce . . . well, he looked too tired to be sorry, but I could see his guilt.

"I can't begin to make reparation for this," Pierce said, his old-world accent ringing clear. "And I'm prepared to make amends any way you see possible. I wasn't of a mind that me winning the coven seat would put you in such straits. This was never my intent. It simply . . . happened."

It simply happened. The story of my life, and I slumped.

The three coven witches watched me with varying degrees of hope, shame, and disgust, and I licked my lips. Three days ago, I would have said, "Give me my citizenship, and I'll take Ku'Sox on," but after having spent three days sleeping under Al's protection because he thought I was *vulnerable,* I was having second, third, and fourth thoughts.

But the chance to walk away from the ever-after was irresistible.

Shifting my weight to my other foot, I cocked my hip, heart pounding. "You want me to get rid of Ku'Sox? Just what are you willing to give—Ollie? Or maybe I should say whom?"

Oliver's eyes widened. "Me?" he stammered, and I almost laughed.

"You?" I said derisively as Vivian steeled her expression back to neutrality. "You're not good for anything but bussing tables. What I want is all charges on me and my team dropped, every hint of my shunning exonerated, and I want you to publicly apologize to me and my family while standing in Fountain Square," I said, looking straight at Oliver. "I want what you promised me last year, and I want you to kiss my lily. White. Ass."

"Never," he whispered, and the slump of cloth in the shadows scrambled to life.

"Give her what she wants!" Leon shrieked, launching himself at Oliver. "You promised it would be okay!" As they went down, Leon straddled him and his hands thumped Oliver's head into the stage floor. "You said to vote with you, and it would be okay, and now Wyatt and Amanda are dead! They are *dead,* Oliver! *He ate them!*"

"Leon! Stop!" Vivian cried, grabbing the hysterical man and pulling him away. Oliver's foot hit the circle, and it fell with a tingling wash. Immediately I stepped over the line, back and away from them and into the shadows. No one but Pierce saw. Everyone else was focused on Oliver, who was getting to his feet and holding his face where Leon had hit his head on the floor, his eyes dark and venomous.

"You promised!" Leon raged, huddled again and looking like a feral beast. "I trusted you. We all trusted you. And now we're all dead!"

In the distance, the sound of falling rock grew and died, and the earth trembled.

"Where's my team?" I asked, missing Jenks's wiseass comments and Ivy's steady support. "But most of all," I said, free of the circle, "where is Trent Kalamack?"

Oliver blanched, his next words choked back when he realized I was free. "You want him? You want us to give him to you? My God, you are a demon."

Pierce bowed his head, but I didn't care what he thought. I didn't want Trent for a familiar, I wanted five minutes alone with him to find out what I'd done wrong with that curse . . . or punch him in the mouth. It depended on what came out of it when I saw him. Give Ku'Sox the curse, he says. You're the only one who can, he says. Stupid elf.

Oliver started in on his overdone theatrics—something about getting me in a circle or they would all die—and Vivian left Leon looking at his blood-caked fingernails and mumbling to himself to argue with Oliver about morality and reality. I didn't see what the big deal was if I was in a circle or not. They were probably all going to die if Ku'Sox was eating witches. That was just nasty.

"She's not going to drag us into the ever-after. Get a grip!" Vivian shouted, and Oliver finally shut up. "And get off your holier-than-thou pedestal! One person for an entire civilization? One person sacrificed for an entire world saved is cheap as far as I'm concerned!" she exclaimed, her face red in shame. "He's the one who cursed her. What did you expect? We'll give the elf a medal posthumously and put his daughter through college. Case closed. Life goes back to normal, and in twenty years, no one cares!"

"You are as black as Pierce!" Oliver shouted, his face red in the hissing kerosene light, and the two of them started a loud, angry argument that I decided not to listen to anymore. The sad part was Vivian was right. That didn't make me feel any better, though. They were ready to give me a *person* because they saw me as a way out. My God, who did we put our trust in?

My anger fanned to life, and I frowned. "You think I want Trent as a familiar?" I said over their raised voices. "Take him into the ever-after with me and make him twist curses? Punish him for the curse he put on me? I just wanted to talk to the man. Funny how you all thought I wanted to drag him back with me or kill him outright. Thanks a hell of a lot. I appreciate that."

Oliver's pudgy cheeks quivered. As his broken-voiced harangue echoed into nothing, he turned. Vivian, too, stopped yelling, and I crossed my arms over my middle and frowned, wondering what they'd do if I simply walked out of here.

Would I be pulled back to the ever-after when the sun went down? I honestly didn't know. When Trent cursed me, he hadn't said anything about being pulled back. Since I was out of the circle, maybe I could stay?

His head down, Pierce edged away from them, his shoes grinding the grit from the ceiling reminding me of the salt on my kitchen floor. "I never thought you were going to take Kalamack," he said softly, and as his gaze darted from me to them, he asked, "You have a plan? You need Trent for it? I can find him."

I stifled a quiver at a surge of adrenaline. "I have an idea," I admitted, "but Ivy's the planner. Where is she?"

Oliver and Vivian looked at each other, then me.

"If you can get rid of Ku'Sox, you will be reinstated as a white witch," Vivian said, not answering my question. "You'll be pardoned for the black magic you have done up to and including what you perform to get rid of Ku'Sox," she added. "The coven will leave you and your family alone. We don't know the magic to get the demon curse lifted from you."

"Trent does," I said, seeing no need to tell them that I knew how to get rid of it myself. Mostly. The Turn take it, I hoped I wasn't being stupid again. I didn't mind being stupid once, but twice with the same person was getting old. "But I'm not a white witch," I said, forcing my teeth not to clench. "I am a demon, and I want it to be official. Other than that, we have a deal. Oh, and I don't want to be responsible for the damage I do trying to get rid of him. Okay?"

Vivian looked scared, but Oliver gestured with a sarcastic motion that it was okay with him. Pierce closed his eyes as if pained. The arrangement wasn't anything I could hold them to, and I didn't expect them to honor it. Right now, all I wanted was a shot at getting the curse shifted from me back to Ku'Sox.

"So where is the little genetic designer dump of a demon?" I said, liking the insulting moniker that Al had given Ku'Sox. I had no idea how I was going to do this, but knowing where he was would be a start.

Vivian looked to the closed, locked double doors. "Just follow the screaming."

A quick breath slipped in and out. "And Ivy and Jenks? I'm going to need their help."

No one said anything. My heart seemed to stop when they both looked at Pierce.

"Ku'Sox has them," he said, and I quivered, fear sliding through me. "I opine he's not killed them outright, but is keeping them intact to call you out."

Twenty-eight

The vivid maroons and contrasting golds of the carpet had dulled to a gray smudge under the choking dust from broken concrete. It didn't help that the light was almost nonexistent as I strode through the hotel lobby, the ambient sun not able to reach deep enough into the large building to make a difference. Everywhere around me, people were quietly crying, whispering, or staring blankly as they huddled under yellow blankets pulled from hotel rooms, sitting against the walls or in informal groups in the middle of the floor. It was quiet. There were no more decisions to be made. They were down to just existing, shocked into a blank state, their minds as dull as the carpet, coated with the remnants of destruction. It stank of cracked rock and terror that had lost its ability to motivate.

But as I headed for the sun past the glass doors, a head lifted, awareness seeping in to show their individual fears and thoughts, like my feet pulling the dust from the carpet, leaving a bright and shiny trail of where I'd been. My jaw set and my arms swung a little harder. *Demon witch.* Clearly I'd been recognized, and I squared my shoulders. So I was a demon. Suck it up and deal with it. I was going to save their asses.

"Don't pay them any mind," Pierce said as he paced beside me, his dusty coat almost the same color as the carpet, the sooty gray fading as it rose until it regained its original brown at his shoulders. "They're scared."

"So am I," I admitted, staring straight ahead. I was scared and angry that Ku'Sox had been holding Ivy and Jenks for three days, hurting them to ensure I'd come to him. At least my mother was okay, having been in jail when Ku'Sox destroyed a huge chunk of San Francisco. She was still there, thank God, but at least now she knew I was back in reality. For a while.

Al, too, knew what I was up to. I don't know why I made them give me my scrying mirror so I could tell him I was okay, except that he had seemed worried, and that was a new emotion from him—at least where my welfare was concerned. I had sneezed for five solid minutes after I told him I wasn't waiting until dark to confront Ku'Sox and hung up on him, but that had been an hour ago, and he'd given up.

My scrying mirror was now in Vivian's care, but my magnetic chalk was tucked in my jeans pocket along with a couple of zip strips. I also had one of the coven's splat guns, its hopper full of charms I doubted would work at the beach we were headed to, but maybe Ku'Sox ducking them might buy me some time. Other than that, I didn't have much, having turned down the bits and bobs that Oliver grudgingly laid out for me. I didn't need his magic. Didn't trust it. Ku'Sox could take everything Oliver had and bathe in it. My intent wasn't to kill Ku'Sox. My intent was to hold on to him long enough to shift the curse. And survive. I wanted to survive, too.

My jaw ached, and I forced my teeth to unclench as I headed for the bright doors. Behind me, Vivian and Oliver trailed, creating a wake of whispers of their own. Why they were coming was obvious, but they were going to be little help other than as cannon fodder. I didn't care about Oliver, but I didn't want to be responsible for Vivian.

Pierce hustled to open the door ahead of me, but I stiff-armed the panel next to it. The door flung open, and a blast of sunshine hit me. It was like a smack, and I stood there, blinded, almost crying. The sun. I could hear sirens in the distance, and helicopters thumping, but I turned to the sky and smiled, blinding myself. Why had I ever wanted sunglasses to block this out? It had been only three days. Only a few hours if you considered that most of that time I'd been unconscious. But the warmth soaked into me as if I'd been in prison for years.

My gaze came down, and I knew I was still carrying my smile when Pierce stared at me, standing beside a black van with an I.S. logo on it, its side door open and waiting. Vivian and Oliver were already inside, arguing over who got the two forward-facing seats. Another black car with lights on it waited ahead, a third vehicle behind. The street was pretty much empty apart from the chunks of stray concrete and bits of paper. We were to have an escort to the drop zone. I looked up again, seeing three gulls gliding to the bay.

"Rachel?"

I pulled my eyes from the sky when a dark building hid the birds. Heart heavy, I trudged to the van, not a charm or spell in my possession. Not looking at anyone, I stepped in. Vivian and Oliver had taken the seats facing backward, so I took the one across from Vivian. It was next to a wide, square window, and I sat pressed up against the cold wall of the van, again searching the sky for the birds.

The thump of the door closing sent a shock through me, and the wonderful smell of redwood grew thick as Pierce sat close, leaving a wide gap between him and the door. "Let's move," Oliver said sourly, and the van inched forward. Through the big front window, I watched as the lights began to flash on the lead car, and we pulled out, quiet and peaceful—like a death march.

I sat and stared out the window. The gulls had reappeared from behind the building, and I propped the window open to watch them. Oliver complained; no one listened. The birds were beautiful, their stark white and black cutting across the blue as they screamed at one another, their voices echoing among the silent, broken buildings. It was quiet, the hush spoiled as the van's tires popped and crunched over the scattered debris.

Pierce touched my hand, trying to get my attention, but I didn't look away from the birds.

Ku'Sox held my friends hostage. I had nothing to fight him with except a curse I didn't know how to twist. Vivian and Oliver weren't going to be a help. Pierce might be, but I wasn't going to count on it.

The birds vanished behind another building, and I turned to Pierce when he squeezed my hand. He seemed different, older, tired, dirty. His hand atop mine was scraped from moving rocks, his fingernails split and knuckles gashed. His hair was gray from the dust. His youthful, never-say-die determination was wearing thin. And yet, as his hand gripped mine, his first words were "Are you okay?"

Anger flashed, but his grip tightened on me when I tried to pull away. "My friends are bait in a trap for me, I've been unconscious for three days in Al's kitchen, the city that cursed me is asking for my help, and you want to know if I'm okay?"

"Al hurt you?" Pierce asked, his eyes flashing, and I shook my head.

"He . . ." I hesitated. "He kept me safe after I proved to the collective that I was a demon," I said, not looking as Vivian gasped and Oliver harrumphed as if he'd known it all along. I didn't like the fact that the driver was hearing this, too, but there it was.

Pierce thought about that, his brow wrinkling even more until he smoothed it when he turned to face me squarely. "And you're okay?" he asked again, and I didn't say anything. No, I wasn't okay. Fine maybe. Yeah, I was fine. Fucked in Extreme, as Ivy would say.

The car swerved to avoid another stalled vehicle, and I reached to steady myself so I wouldn't lean into Pierce, reclaiming my hand in the process. The blue Land Rover had been abandoned when a two-ton chunk of someone's living room had fallen on the hood. Bet that had been a nasty surprise.

We were heading down to the bay, and I caught a glimpse of it, sparkling in the quiet sun. My lungs filled and emptied. The blank faces at the hotel nudged into my thoughts. They'd called for my blood, chanted to give Trent the collective strength to slide Ku'Sox's curse off on to me. *The collective . . .*

Crap, I thought, almost groaning as I figured it out. Could I be any more stupid? I'd forgotten the collective! That's why the curse hadn't stuck! The Latin was right; the implementation was flawed. I'd tried to shift the curse alone, and something that far-reaching needed a collective to make it adhere! I needed a witches' collective. I needed the strength only a group of witches could give me.

My eyes narrowed, and my chest tightened. Yeah. Like they would help me now? But it was worth a shot.

"Rachel?"

I started, almost shocked to see Pierce sitting beside me, concern in the slant of his eyes. From the beginnings of hope, I found a smile. "You have dirt on your nose," I said, reaching to wipe it away. I hadn't touched anyone in three days, and at the feel of his warm skin against my fingers, an unexpected welling up of tears threatened. I didn't love him, but I could have, if things had been different.

"It will be okay," Pierce said softly, his hand coming up to cradle mine, between us. His grip on me was solid, real, and I felt guilty that I was reaching out for his support when I knew he loved me and I didn't love him. But I felt so alone; I couldn't let go.

"Tomorrow the sun will rise. He's just a demon," Pierce said, making things worse.

A demon who held my friends hostage. Sniffing, I glanced out the window at the sun. Empty streets. The boats at the docks with their SEE THE WHALES signs flashed past. "Do I stink?" I whispered, and his grip on my hand twitched. I looked away, not needing his answer. I figured as much. With everything else that was going on, I was worried about how I smelled? But it mattered.

"I pay it no mind. You've been in the ever-after. I hardly notice it anymore."

Why was he being so nice to me? I didn't deserve it. But I needed it. Taking a breath, I softly said, "Thank you for helping me." I looked up, encompassing Vivian and Oliver. "All of you."

Oliver snorted. "If we could do anything, we wouldn't have summoned you," he said. "I'm here only to make sure you don't run away."

Vivian frowned at him to be quiet. "What do you need?" she asked, taking her cell phone out of an inner coat pocket. "Anything at all."

The car turned, and the new coven pin on Pierce's lapel caught the sun, sending little gleams of light about the car like the flashes of Jenks's wings. I looked at Vivian's phone as she waited for my answer. My heart clenched in pain. Her phone was so small, all black and silver with tiny little buttons that would do everything but make you a smoothie. Ivy would love it.

I closed my eyes as I tried not to cry. Damn it, demons didn't cry, even when their friends were being held by a psychotic nutcase.

When my eyes opened, they landed on the driver's in the rearview mirror. I was sure he was some I.S. goon they'd dug up somewhere and that he'd go back to his boss with whatever I said. Just as well. I wanted them to hear this, too. "Trent gave me a curse," I started, and Pierce smiled.

"I was there," he said, trying for a light air and failing. In his eyes was his remembered anger at how they had made him helpless. "It's of no never mind."

I licked my lips, glancing past Vivian and Oliver to the driver. "He gave it to me to give to Ku'Sox so I can banish him to the ever-after for good, but I need a collective to make it stick."

Vivian's gaze became sharp on mine. "He planned this? Then why did he leave?"

Trent was gone? Crap, maybe I was wrong.

"Ku'Sox must be killed, not banished," Pierce said tightly.

"The elven bastard will simply summon him again. I'm of a mind that the double-crossing scoundrel is the one summoning him now."

"We're not clearing your name if the demon can come back!" Oliver blustered.

"I don't think I *can* kill Ku'Sox," I said, glaring at Pierce. "And second, Ku'Sox is here on his own, unsummoned. He's special, created after the ever-after and not bound to it or to the pull of the sun. The demons don't want him, which was why he was banished here by using the same curse Trent gave me. Trent figured you wouldn't hold to our agreement at the FIB last spring. That's why he freed Ku'Sox. Trent thinks I can best him. Slide the curse onto the insane nutcase." My eyes went to Oliver, holding his. "After you promised me my citizenship, of course. This whole thing is your fault, Oliver."

Oliver took a breath. "Kalamack freed Ku'Sox!"

"You stupid . . . political . . . bastard!" Vivian exclaimed.

I shrugged, looking out the window to see that we were down by the waterfront and the tourist traps. When Trent wanted something, he didn't care who got hurt to get it. "He freed Ku'Sox because he knew Oliver wouldn't keep his promise unless forced to," I said, not sure how I felt about it. "Trent promised me my freedom, and Ku'Sox is his leverage."

"You can't make this my fault," Oliver protested, and Vivian rounded on him.

"Shut up, you oversexed, flabby warlock!" she shouted, and the driver glanced back at us through the rearview mirror. "This is your doing! All of it! If you'd just kept to what you promised her instead of trying to soothe your ego by bringing her down, half the city wouldn't be destroyed, Leon wouldn't need therapy, and Wyatt and Amanda would still be alive!"

"You cannot blame this on me!" Oliver exclaimed, and Vivian glared at him.

"I do," she growled, "and if any of us survive, I'm bringing you down. Count on it." Breathing fast, she looked back at me, flushed. Oliver gaped like a fish, shocked. And Pierce snickered. "Thousands of lives," Pierce said, his voice soft. "And the free world left in jeopardy if you should fail. Trent must believe most powerfully that you can put Ku'Sox back in his place." The young-looking but wise witch glanced at Oliver. "And by that you win your freedom, no matter what they call you, Rachel."

My breath slipped from me in a puff of sound. It was hard not to be flattered. All of this to make good on his promise to me? Trent was still a murdering drug lord, but he had honor. Not to mention a huge disrespect for innocent lives.

"If I can curse Ku'Sox and dump him in the ever-after, then we can all go back to being who we want to be," I said, then mentally added, *Sort of.* I'd still be a day-walking demon, but at least I would be in reality again. Vivian's expression eased, and I added, "I'm tired of being nice, though. If you *ever* screw me over again or piss me off, I'm letting him out."

"That's blackmail!" Oliver exclaimed.

Stiffening, Pierce turned to him, but before he could say anything, the van stopped with a tight squeal of brakes. My hand went out to stop my momentum, but Pierce was faster, holding me back from falling on Vivian. As one, we all looked to the front.

The unassuming-looking driver had unbuckled his seat belt and turned to us. His face was thin, and his expression from under his straggly brown hair severe. And his eyes . . . had gone vampire black. I shivered, feeling an ancient force take over the car, vampire incense filling me to overflowing. I stifled a shiver, a hand against my neck. Shit, this guy wasn't a driver. This guy was I.S. Inderland Security.

"Oliver," the man said, his voice causing ripples of sensation across my skin, "we at the I.S. think you've fucked this up far enough. If Rachel permanently eliminates the threat of this day-walking demon, no one will care if she's the queen of the damned and eats live kittens for breakfast in front of kindergarteners. You will leave her alone, or you will find yourself disgraced."

"Who the hell are you?" Oliver spouted, red faced, but he was scared. So was I.

Vivian flicked her eyes from Oliver to the driver, inching away from Oliver. Pierce, too, was staring with openmouthed awe. I just wanted to get out of this car before the vampire toxins sunk in my neck had me throwing myself at the guy. He was a living vampire, seeing as the sun was still up, but he was channeling a dead one. A really powerful, really old dead one.

"I'm your downfall, Oliver," the man said, and I shivered. "If you push, I will be on you with bodies in your pool and satanic symbols etched into your children's foreheads. But if all you put your faith in is titles, then I am the acting head of the I.S. west of the Mississippi, and as it stands, your coven is useless." His eyes went to mine, and a small sound slipped out. "You need to replace them with people not afraid to get dirty for the greater good."

I didn't think he was talking about the rock dust, and I smiled, letting it fade when he glanced at me.

"We're as close as we dare get," he said, and my pulse pounded when he leaned between Oliver and Vivian to take my unresisting hand in his. Pierce bristled, and amusement danced in the man's black eyes. "We at the I.S. wish you luck, demon. Letting you wallow amid mediocrity was our error." He looked at Oliver, then back to me. "Our grave error. Good hunting, Rachel."

It took me three times, but I stammered, "Th-thank you." Oh God. If I could pull this off, the I.S. would be . . . well, they'd probably not be on my side, but I'd probably not be on their hit list anymore. They'd grant me respect, maybe? Oh crap. Did I want their respect? They'd probably want me to do stuff for them.

The vampire kissed the top of my hand—and a thrill of desire spiraled through me, pulled into existence by a slip of teeth and the scent of incense. And then . . . he was gone, his door thumping shut behind him and his quickly moving figure getting into the first car. It drove away fast, the car behind us following. Silence crept in my open window, and fresh air coming right off the bay. We'd passed the chocolate factory on the way in, and I thought I could smell it.

"I'm not getting out of this van," Oliver said.

Vivian's brow furrowed. "Got that right," she said tightly, and then I gasped when she hauled off and hit him square in the jaw.

Pierce cried out, but it was over and the man had slumped to the door, out cold. Vivian was wringing her hand, eyes tearing as she held her red knuckles. A charm must have been involved because she hadn't hit him hard enough to knock him unconscious. "That hurt," she gasped, smiling. "Damn, I'm going to pay for that when the charm wears off, but it felt really good. He's such a prick."

Just three of us, then, I thought, glad of it. Oliver would have messed it up.

A quiver went through me. It was time.

Twenty-nine

The rasp of the side door opening was loud, and heart pounding, I slid across the seat and followed Pierce out. We were at a sloping park where the streetcars turned around. The grass was cut and the bushes were manicured. Across the street, where the beach was, there was a small stone building that might once have been a public bathroom but was now boarded up. The wind was brisk by the water, and I sniffed, not bothering to tap a line.

It figured that Ku'Sox would be down here. Regular magic wouldn't work well. Demon magic would, though, and I smiled grimly, feeling like a cupcake on a sparkling white plate. *Here I am, Ku'Sox. Come take a bite.*

My shoes hit the pavement, and I looked at them, wondering how they had found me a pair so fast when the city had come to a standstill. They weren't new.

"Rachel, you said you had something for us to do?"

I forced the worry out of my eyes as I turned to Pierce. "Keep me alive when it's over?" I said weakly, and he took my hand. It was a horribly romantic gesture, and it only made me feel worse. Things were clearer to me than they had ever been, and yet I gave his fingers a squeeze before I pulled away and turned to Vivian. There was a radio playing somewhere, and she was squinting up into the distant buildings, trying to place the sound. Otherwise, it was silent, rubble strewn about the edge of the shore. On the bay, it was beautiful, not a car on the bridge or a boat running out to Alcatraz. *Hi, Mary. Eat your toast and kill your magic. It's not worth it.*

I didn't understand this. My entire life would be decided in the next five minutes, the lives of Ivy and Jenks, the safety of all good people, and here I was delighting in the smell of the seaweed and how the sun shone on the tiny little bugs darting on the hard-packed shore.

"Vivian," I said, forcing myself to look back to her. "Oh, Vivian," I said, softer when I saw her fear.

"I'm fine," she asserted, her voice shaking. "Trent isn't answering his phone. I'm sorry. I'll keep trying. I think he flew back to Cincinnati with his little girl. What else can I do? I want to help."

The woman was terrified, and my heart went out to her. She had fought Ku'Sox for three days, seen two of her peers *eaten alive*. And yet she stood by me, ready to fight to the last. I didn't want her here. I needed her in the city finding me a collective.

My hair lifted in the wind off the bay, and I smiled at the feeling. *Focus, Rachel, focus.* "Will you go back to the city for me?" I said, figuring the I.S. "driver" had left the keys.

"L-leave you?" she stammered, and I took her arm, leading her back to the van. "I can help!"

"I'm counting on it," I said. "I need you to go back. Stop at every church you can find. There are people there, right? Get them to ring the bells for me."

She stared, her blue eyes going wide. "For a collective," she said breathily, realizing what I was asking. A city-wide collective hadn't happened since the Turn. It was both a warning and a gathering. An act of trust. I didn't know if they would help or not, but if they didn't, then I would fail and they would suffer.

"I'll do it," she said, her voice trembling. "Rachel, if I have to light a fire in the middle of San Francisco, I will get you a collective. I promise."

Somehow I managed a smile, and I stumbled when she gave me a quick hug. Her eyes were brimming when she stepped back.

I blinked fast, trying not to tear up. "Thanks," I said, and her dusty shoes with the little bows scraped as she started to drift backward. "Don't take too long."

Nodding, she turned and went back to the van. The door creaked as it opened, and her slight figure made the jump inside. "At least there won't be any traffic," she said, and the door thumped closed.

The rumble of the van echoed against the abandoned buildings as the engine turned over. I felt Pierce's presence beside me, and together we watched her pull away. The sound of the van quickly vanished, and we were alone. Sort of. Ku'Sox was here somewhere.

Nervous, I rubbed my palms together and breathed in the last of the exhaust fumes. "You don't think they dropped us off at the wrong beach, do you?" I asked, and Pierce took my shoulders and turned our backs on the bay to look up to the hills of San Francisco. From here, everything looked normal, if a shade quiet and with the air markedly clean. If I had to do this with someone, I could do far worse than Pierce.

"Rachel," Pierce said, the depth of the emotion in his voice stopping me cold. He was going to say something, overcompensating for his part in getting me cursed. But I was a demon and he had devoted his life to killing them. I didn't want to hear it.

"Wait," I interrupted, turning to find that he was too close. I didn't move as he reached to steady me, his hand not falling when I found my balance. His dusty hair was all over, making him look endearing as he squinted from the wind off the bay. The slant to his eyes was determined, and I knew he had the strength to back up whatever he deemed a worthy task. He thought he loved me, even forgiving me for having prevented him from killing Al, and it was breaking my heart.

And I will cry when I go because I could love you forever.

I couldn't love him. It would destroy him slowly, and I didn't want that.

I leaned toward him, wishing I didn't stink of the ever-after and demons. He blinked as he saw my intention, and his hands moved, one sliding behind my neck and the other holding firmly to my fingers. My head tilted and my lips opened. They met his in a shock of ley line, and I quivered.

I felt a tear slip out as Pierce held me, space between us as we kissed, leaving me aching when our lips parted. I didn't know why I'd done it, except that I might die today. At least I'd die in the sun.

"Pierce," I said softly, our kiss ended but our foreheads still touching. "I can't—"

We shifted apart, and he put a finger to my lips. I could taste his salt, and I blinked fast.

"I know," he said, his eyes flicking behind me to the water for a moment as if unable to hold my gaze. "Don't say it," he asked. "Wait until the sun sets tonight, and if we are both here to see it, then my heart will break knowing you are safe and yet not to be mine. If you are gone, then my heart will break knowing that God has taken you home, because there is no way in hell that that demon Ku'Sox is going to kill you. I won't allow it."

There was a lump in my throat, and I wiped my eyes, only to get the grit of sand in them.

"No," I said, taking a step back until his hands fell from me. "Pierce, I don't love you." His lips twitched, hearing a lie that wasn't there, and I took his hands. "I don't love you," I said again, my throat closing up. "I loved the idea of you and me together, and from that, maybe someday love could have come, but that isn't going to happen. Ever. I am a demon."

He took a breath to protest, his eyes wild and his denial obvious. "You are not."

My eyes dropped to his hands holding mine, seeing his calluses and strength. "I am. I did something no witch, no male demon can do, and all the demons agree. There's no way around it. It's not like I wanted this." My voice had gotten squeaky, and I looked up, seeing panic in him.

"It's okay," I whispered, sniffing back a tear before it showed. "It doesn't mean I'm bad, but it does mean that there is no way that . . ." I stopped. It was too hard to say.

His grip on mine tightened, but I felt dead inside. "I'm not afraid." Pierce's hand drew me closer, and I resisted until he eased his pull.

"I'd never hurt you," I protested, remembering him standing before Ku'Sox, fighting for my safety, risking his life for me. What person wouldn't be humbled by that? Grateful?

His gaze jumped to mine, his anger lighting his eyes. "I meant I'm not afraid of love being difficult. If it was easy, then everyone would find it. But have it your way."

He turned away, and I reached after him, saying nothing as my hand dropped. It was better this way. "Perhaps you should call him out," Pierce suggested, angrily looking at the hills.

I nodded, even as my stomach clenched. I'd told him I didn't love him, and he didn't seem to care. I'd told him I was a demon, and he'd said so what? Then told me love was hard. I knew that, but it shouldn't be impossible.

Shoes silent on the pavement, I walked across the street to the beach, stepping up onto the cement bench next to the boarded-up restrooms. It was covered in gang runes, and my feet spread wide, I cupped my hands around my mouth. Damn it, why couldn't I have a normal life?

"Ku'Sox!" I shouted up into the park, my frustration giving my voice some anger. "You have something that belongs to me!"

The radio, I realized, was playing bouncy beach music. With a sudden snap, it vanished. My pulse hammered, and I glanced at Pierce. He was standing with his hands clasped, ready to fight for me, even after I'd told him I didn't love him. Why?

"Just a minute!" Ku'Sox shouted back, and my lips parted. I did not believe this. Just a minute? Had he really told me to wait?

Pierce shrugged, and I jumped from the bench. "You might want to put some space between us if you want to stay alive," I suggested, forcing myself not to touch my splat gun.

Pierce put his hands on his hips, flicking his duster back. "You might want to put yourself in a bubble to do the same."

What was I thinking, taking Ku'Sox on without Al? But he had Ivy and Jenks, and I wasn't going to wait.

A soft scrape of boot on stone pulled my head around and I felt the blood drain from my face. It was Ku'Sox, his arm around Ivy's neck and his other hand twisting her arm painfully behind her as he forced her down the park steps.

"Let me go, you freak!" I heard her sputter as she strained to break his grip, but it was useless. One of her eyes was black, and she had a split lip.

"Jenks!" I shouted as they reached the bottom, and I pulled out the splat gun, my grip sweaty and the ley line I was connected to seeming to jump in me. "Where's Jenks?"

Ku'Sox stopped in the middle of the street, his steel gray hair close to his head, shining in the sun like raven wings. Looking as if he was enjoying himself, he tugged Ivy around to be his shield. "Tell her what happened to the pixy," he said softly, whispering it into her ear as his eyes bored into mine and the wind played with his hair.

My heart almost stopped. *Jenks . . .*

"He's okay!" Ivy said, Ku'Sox's hand going white-knuckled as he gripped her throat. "Short dick here had to lock him in a box. Jenks kept slicing his ear off."

Ku'Sox bore down on her, and she choked, falling to one knee.

"Hey!" I shouted, taking a step forward, splat gun raised. "Let her go. It's me you want." God, I felt as if I were in a western. *Hand over the little lady there, partner, and we'll settle this like men.* I was so screwed.

Ku'Sox grinned, showing his small white teeth. "Does it bother you?" he asked, yanking her up and dragging her through the rubble that littered the street. Her foot got wedged between two rocks, and he yanked her free. My face went blank at her muffled grunt of pain.

Fingers shifting on the butt of my weapon, I said, "Let her go, and come over here. I'll whisper in your ear how bothered I am."

Confident and sure of himself, Ku'Sox stopped at the curb. His hand opened, and Ivy fell, her elbow slicing open on a chunk of ragged concrete. Head down so her hair hid her face, she pulled herself together, lashing out with her good foot, making Ku'Sox dance sideways.

I shot at him as he was distracted, but he raised a bubble, absorbing it.

Ivy, though, was free, and my heart quickened. I slowly continued to draw that broken energy into me, pulling it from the jagged lines and trying to organize it.

"I only snapped every bone in her body and mended it to get you to come face me," he said, mocking me as he grabbed her shoulder and pinned her where she sat. "It took me a day before I realized you were unconscious and not simply afraid, but I thought, why stop now? I was bored, so she got a little more. We had fun, didn't we, Ivy girl?"

I seethed, my hands in fists, as Ivy didn't look up.

"It was only play," Ku'Sox was saying. "Nothing permanent. I—"

In a smooth motion, I pushed the energy from my chi into my hand. Grunting, I threw it. There was probably little besides eating her that Ku'Sox could do to Ivy that Piscary hadn't done already, but something in me had snapped.

Ivy screamed defiantly, kicking his feet out from under him and rolling away before the demon could direct my energy into her. Ku'Sox fell, arms flailing. My ball of unfocused energy arched to him.

"Celero inanio!" I shouted, exploding it right above him.

He cowered, a dark sheet of ever-after snapping over him. I knew such a common spell wouldn't hurt him, but it shut him up.

Ivy had staggered to her feet and was limping fast to Pierce, not me. Wise woman. I needed room to work, and I shifted my stance for better purchase.

"Oh, really. Grow up, will you?" Ku'Sox muttered as he got to his feet and his bubble flickered out of existence.

There was a tweak on my awareness as he pulled heavily on a line. Not trusting anything but a well-drawn circle, I dove to the side, landing with my back to that squat building between Ku'Sox and me. I watched his black ball of nastiness thump into the sand at the edge of the sidewalk. Water and grit sprayed up, a tiny crater hissing as it cooled to a green, milky glass.

"That's how the big boys do it," he said with satisfaction, but I couldn't see him. Crap, I had to get away from this building before he simply blew it up around me.

"Ivy?" I called, praying as I hurriedly sketched a circle around me. He'd simply break through it, but there were no bells ringing yet. I had to stall him.

"I'm good!" came back, and I crab-walked to the edge of the building and looked, seeing her with Pierce, crouched beside a broken bench. They were both inside an uninvoked circle, relatively safe.

"Keep her alive," I mouthed, and he nodded, even as Ivy read my lips and grimaced.

The clink of sliding rubble jerked my attention back to the beach where a black, oily smoke drifted from the person-size crater.

"I can hear you . . . Rachel," Ku'Sox mocked, his voice coming closer as I edged back to my circle. "I hear you breathing."

I couldn't help it, and I held my breath, sitting with my back against the building. My heart pounded, and sweat made clean tracks in the dust on my arms. I listened for the sound of church bells, hearing nothing. *Come on, Vivian . . .*

"How sweet of you to have come back, thinking you could best me," he said, a rock clinking closer. "It took six demons to shove me under that rock they built the arch over, and I killed one of them in the process. Almost got Newt, too. Sweet little Newt, more trusting than you, even after I had convinced her to kill all her sisters. You should have waited until dark. Al can't help you, but at least you wouldn't die alone."

"I don't need Al's help to squish a bug like you," I said, teeth gritted as I attempted to figure out where he was by his voice. Trying to be quiet, I pulled away from the building, an odd sort of pain drifting through me as the curse made for him felt him and started to align itself. Pieces of me that didn't fit, chunks of Ku'Sox's curse. Slowly I gathered them together in my chi, praying for bells. Just one. But there was nothing.

"Don't need Al's help?" he said, and with a sideways step, the demon appeared from behind the side of the old bathroom, cocky and sure of himself with the sun in his hair and his lips curved up in amusement. Crap, he was almost on top of me. "You're stupider than I thought," he finished, smiling.

Pain exploded from nowhere inside. My concentration shattered, and the bits of the curse I'd pulled from myself sprang back into place with a twang. My knees gave way and I hit the pavement beside the building, burning in agony. It felt like my lungs were exploding. Teeth clenched, I lifted my head to find Ku'Sox standing beside the building, a bundle of cloth in his hands. Great, he had a focusing object. He didn't have to throw charms at me. He could just wish on a star.

"Oh God," I moaned, feeling the cramping slither across my heart and wend its way to my gut. Panting, I tried to inch my fingers to my scribed circle, but I couldn't focus long enough to even find a ley line. I took a gasping breath as I realized that there was a pair of black slippers in front of me. He'd moved, and I hadn't even noticed. But in all fairness, it was hard to see around the pain.

"That was so easy, it wasn't any fun at all." Ku'Sox pouted.

I looked up, squinting at the doll with red hair and leather boots, and I got a clean, albeit ragged, breath as his fingers loosened on it. "Wanna play dolls?" he asked me, and pursed his lips, exhaling.

I flung myself backward, landing against the building. My lungs were suddenly overflowing with air, feeling as if they were going to burst even as the hot, moist breath lacking any oxygen at all filled them. I was suffocating, though I heaved for air. One hand on my throat, the other on the ground scrabbling for the circle, I saw a movement behind Ku'Sox, a soft ghost of gray. I tried not to look, but Ku'Sox noticed my eyes, turning in time to see Pierce winding up with a black ball of hurt dripping in his hand.

"Compages!" Ku'Sox shouted, and a shimmering protection bubble flashed into existence, breathtaking in its utter sordidness. This was true smut, making the black shimmer on my own aura look like a drop of oil in the ocean. Pierce's curse hit Ku'Sox's protective bubble and bounced right back at Pierce.

It was a beautiful bit of defensive magic, but it cost Ku'Sox his concentration. The pain in my chest vanished. My head came up, and I took in a huge gulp of air. In an instant, I read the strength Pierce's thrown curse had absorbed from Ku'Sox's bubble, knowing that the ill-made, green-tinted circle Pierce had taken refuge in wasn't going to hold against it. The curse had Pierce's aura and would go right through.

My eyes narrowed, and still on the ground, I whispered, *"Rhombus."*

The rusty, broken West Coast ley line limped into me, and I wrestled with it, trying to get some semblance of order, but it was thin, ragged. My circle was huge, me at its center, as all theoretical, undrawn circles are, the edge of it just shy of Pierce and Ivy. They were outside my circle, but Ku'Sox and the deadly curse he had bounced back at Pierce were inside.

I grunted when Pierce's curse hit the inside of my bubble, absorbing most of the energy from his magic as it tore through my circle and hit Pierce square on, having passed right through his bubble as if it didn't exist.

"No!" I cried out as the curse struck Pierce and he fell, mouth open in a silent scream. "God, no!" I called again, struggling to get up as the curse spread to Ivy, and they both collapsed under a green-tinted wash of ever-after.

Mouth agape, Ku'Sox spun to me, his shock clear. "You . . . ," he managed, and then I saw Pierce move, his chest rising and falling as he lay stunned by his own magic. They were alive. They were out cold, but they were alive. Thank you, God, they were alive!

"Clever," Ku'Sox managed, clearly peeved that I'd managed to save them, and I kicked him with all the force I had.

Yelping, he fell back. I sprang at him, my hands reaching for that doll, but he vanished an instant before I touched him, and I fell right through the space he'd been in, landing hard against the sidewalk, my curled-in fingers taking much of the impact.

"Ow," I huffed, then rolled, instinct and too many fights telling me to move.

I was too slow to escape everything, and the toe of Ku'Sox's boot helped me over, bruising my ribs instead of breaking them.

"Mother of a dog whore!" Ku'Sox shouted, following me with his foot swinging, and I rolled the other way, right into him.

He wasn't expecting that, and he fell forward over me, hitting the sidewalk with an *oof* of surprise. Immediately I reversed my motion, almost crawling across him as he lay facedown on the sidewalk. Inside, a part of me was shrieking with laughter. Here we were, two demons in the sun, down to kicking and punching.

"You're scum, Ku'Sox." I breathed heavily, straddling his back as I found his arm and yanked it backward, almost breaking it as I smashed his face back down onto the sidewalk, but he only started to laugh, his cheek against the cement and unable to see me. He was starting to piss me off, and I gave a little pull, cutting his mirth short.

"Rachel, what do you hope to accomplish?" he said, clearly

feeling the pain of the position but not taking it seriously. "I can jump to a line from under you. Burn every last thought from you as I lie here."

Maybe, but he hadn't. Grimacing, I shoved his wrist into his back and lifted his bent elbow, making him yelp. "Then why haven't you?" I asked. I let up, but just a little. The hills of San Francisco were silent, not a single bell ringing. *Please, Vivian . . .*

"Because this is sort of nice," he said, and I pulled up on his elbow, making him laugh more even though his face started to show the strain. He was getting a kick out of this, the bastard.

"Nice?" I leaned closer to his ear. "You should see me when I get warmed up. I'm like a hemi, baby. Run all night."

"Maybe we got off on the wrong foot," Ku'Sox said, and I eased up a smidge. "I heard you almost killed Al. You made a damn fine construct for the collective. I walked it while you languished in Al's tiny kitchen, trying to survive its creation. I can admit I was wrong. You're a demon. A damn fine one. I don't care if you came from witches and the genetic engineering of elves. I myself am born from tinkering, and I'll admit that my abhorrence might have originated from my own shame."

"I'm not ashamed of where I come from," I snarled softly, my worry growing as I glanced at Pierce and Ivy, still not moving.

"I'm even impressed with how you tried to slide that curse into me," he added, eyes roving to find mine. "You forgot to include the collective, though. Good luck finding one. The demons won't help you. They want me even less than your pitiful coven does. No, you're down to one choice, and that's me."

Vivian would find me a collective. She would. I had to believe it. "You?" I said as I leaned in, my shadow covering his eyes, and he winced, his gaze finding mine at last. A grimace grew on my face as I pinned him to the cement. Ku'Sox was an ass; he was getting turned on by this. I could tell.

"I told you I liked red hair, yes?" he murmured, sand stuck

to his face. "I could get to like you," he said, and I forced myself to smile back at him. "We could enjoy each other, enjoy the best of the ever-after and this world both. Just you. And me. The hell with the rest of them."

Keep him talking, I thought, feeling a weird sort of energy starting to slip from him to me. Damn it, was he trying to do a power pull? But the memory of him eating a pixy, the warrior struggling to pierce Ku'Sox's throat even as he gulped him down intruded. *As if.* "What about Ivy?" I asked breathlessly, glancing at her.

"Bring her along," he said. "Variety is the spice of life."

"I meant," I said in his ear, "you hurt her."

"I didn't do anything permanent." His voice betrayed his bewilderment. "You want to know the way to keep her soul after she dies, right?"

Shock quivered through me. "You know how to do that?" I warbled.

I couldn't help it. My grip eased, and Ku'Sox drew his arm to his chest, laughing low as he shifted out from under me, sitting up and turning to face me. Streaks of dirt had turned his black shirt gray, and he felt his shoulder before wiping the sand from his face and arranging his hair.

"That's better," he said, gaze taking in my rumpled body, eyes cataloging the curves and lines of my face all the way down to my borrowed shoes. "This is what you really look like?"

"You can return Ivy's soul to her when she dies?" I prompted breathlessly.

"No. I just wanted you to let go."

My jaw dropped. "You son of a bitch." I swung at him, my wrist bursting into pain when he caught my hand, inches from his face.

"Find something new to call me," he said, yanking me to him. My hand curled into a claw, and I panted through the pain. I was kneeling before him, and he pulled me closer, almost into his lap.

"I've been alone a long time," he said, his hand gripping my wrist painfully, promising me even more hurt if I struggled. "Lots of time to think of how to pleasure myself with a woman who wouldn't die at her first orgasm. Lots of time to imagine what it could be." His groping hand reached, taking the chalk from my pocket and throwing it away. "Lots of time to lose what few inhibitions I might have had."

My splat gun was next, and I struggled as he found it, slipped in the small of my back, and threw it into the nearby ocean.

"I can shift the smallest mote of energy," he said, a new depravity in his eyes, as if he wanted to strip me of everything else. "Make it dance in you."

"Promises, promises," I said, listening for the bells, but still there was nothing but the *shush* of the water and the crying of the gulls. It wasn't going to happen. They were too afraid, and my hope began slipping from me, leaving the sour taste of burnt amber on my soul.

"I don't want to fight you," he said, sounding reasonable as the wind moved the ends of his hair. "I'm not even asking you to submit. Simply . . . let me be."

Let me be. It was what I wanted. "Let you be?" I said, my gaze darting to the chalk, well out of reach.

He nodded, and my hand hurt when he let go and the blood flowed again. "You aren't wanted here," he said, his eyes lifting from me as I leaned back, the deathly silent hills watching us. "They hate you. Why are you trying to save them? This is your playground. Play! Play with me."

He was smiling, looking as beautiful as only a satisfied demon could, knowing the world was his and nothing could stop him. I felt my wrist, looking for a way out and not finding one. There was no collective to help me move the curse, no white knight in the guise of a city-wide outflowing of goodwill. They had turned their backs on me, not trusting me. The hurt part of me said screw them, but I'd been afraid before and I couldn't fault them. They were scared, and no one should die because they were scared. Not when someone else had the courage to say no.

"This isn't my playground, this is my home," I said, seeing my reflection in his eyes, my hair mussed, face flushed, and a heady hatred in my eyes. "And if you don't leave, I'm going to kick your ass out."

His head tilted and he laughed, beautiful in the sun with the ocean behind him. "Oh, Rachel, we could have had so much fun," he said when he looked back at me, the last remnants of his mirth still lingering at the corners of his mouth. "I wish I could make you last, but truly, you are too close to being a threat to survive. Right now you are alone, with absolutely no curses, vulnerable. But someday you'll be better than me. And I don't trust you."

Vulnerable. That's what Al had said. But I hadn't listened, and now all I had was what God had given me and what Trent's father had enabled me to survive with. And as I squinted at Ku'Sox, hating that he thought he had power over me simply because he was stronger, my will solidified. I didn't need the damn collective. I was a coven-damned demoness.

Unaware of my thoughts, Ku'Sox reached out and snatched my wrist again, delighted as I struggled when he pulled me closer. "What, no long monologues?" I taunted him, and his expression became more domineering yet.

"No," he said, rising to keep the weight advantage. "When I see a snake, I cut off its head and have done with it. After I suck out its poison for myself, of course."

I twisted, trying to avoid his reaching hand, and he splayed his fingers. They were coated in his black aura, sparkling at the edges, and I did *not* want that touching me. But with a grunt of satisfaction, he thrust his hand against my face and shoved his will into mine.

I gasped as he was suddenly in my head with me, more oppressive and heavier than Al had ever hinted at. My heart pounded, and every thought of fighting vanished. Power. He had it. He was it. He had no morals. His soul was empty. He was content with what he was, confident that none could stop him. He was a day-walking demon who, like me, hadn't been born a slave to the ever-after. He could see the sun, and it gave him strength. And he wanted me dead.

Except, I wasn't a demon, I was a demoness, and that last little bit of X chromosome was going to save my ass.

You stupid son of a bitch, I thought, and then grabbed his thin soul by the short hairs, yanking it completely into mine with callous disregard.

No! Ku'Sox's aggressive sexual heat flashed into fear. His power suddenly meant nothing as my soul swallowed his, cutting him off from everything but the memory of existence.

Si peccabas, poenam meres! I thought, holding him within me as the pinpricks of the curse lifted from me, arrowing into him like flakes of iron to a magnet. And as he howled in fury, I screamed over him, *I curse you, Ku'Sox, to be fixed to the ever-after, cursed be it day or night, forever bound as a demon! Facilis descensus Tartaros!*

I'll kill you, you damned succubus! Ku'Sox shouted as he felt the curse lift from me and settle into him. I was a demoness, and I could hold another soul, even if it was as disgusting as Ku'Sox's. And once there, I could give him a curse, collective or not. Fix it into his very DNA so that even should he transform, it would go with him. Forever.

A heavy mallet smashed into me, and I fell off him, the connection between us breaking. The cement slammed into my back, and the sun blinded me. I blinked, trying to figure out what had happened. I was on my back, looking up at the sun. And my mouth hurt.

"Take it back! Take it back!" Ku'Sox demanded, and I propped myself up on an elbow to see him standing before me, stiff with fear.

I looked at the blood on my hand, then back to him, the sun in his face and the ocean behind him, the sky full of birds. "You lose, Ku'Sox," I said, panting as I started to smile. "I banish you. Get out of my reality."

"No!" he screamed, lunging at me.

My hands came up to fend him off, and just as his weight fell on me, I felt the line take us. He was taking me with him!

Shit, I thought, floundering as I reoriented myself, then clenched in pain as my bubble snapped into place around us. His hot anger made clouds of agony and hate rise from his mind, like the choking stink of decay. He gripped my consciousness, dragging me with him, and I felt my soul shiver in pain at the fire he poured into me.

Take it back! he demanded. *Or I'll kill you here!*

Try, I thought, then screamed as he began to shred my memories. I caught glimpses of my life as he burned them, taking them as his own. A blue-eyed tiger at the zoo, pacing to me as if he could walk right through the glass—and it was gone. A birthday at the hospital, him standing in the background as I blew out the candles and wished for a day without weakness—gone. One by one, Ku'Sox found my most happy thoughts and ate them, ate my soul.

Take it back, he seethed, shredding me, cutting me down to the bare bones of myself. *Take it back or we'll die here together.*

Gentleman's choice, I thought grimly, then punched a hole right through my protective bubble.

Infinity screamed in at us, and he let go of my mind, pushing me away as we floundered. Pain like no other crippled our thoughts. It was as exquisite an agony as angels singing the beginnings of the world, exploding the idea of infinity into reality, stripping my aura from me in sheets, scouring it layer by layer. I struggled to keep myself together.

The howling of the demons lost in the lines before us echoed, their voices caught in the moment of death forever. *Out!* Ku'Sox's soul shrieked, and I clutched it, a point of common ground amid the absence of anything but pain. He was struggling to keep his aura, failing. He couldn't get out of the line and was already dead. For all his strength, he didn't love, couldn't manage to tune his aura to another's, giving all, trusting. And suddenly it struck me that only the demons who knew how to love had survived.

Al, I thought, shocked to find it was a strong enough connection. A glimmer of light pierced the black pain, and Ku'Sox clawed at it, gouging my soul until memories leaked from me like tears. *I'm opening the line,* I thought, and Ku'Sox struggled, striving to get through the hole, failing as he ran into a barrier he couldn't see.

I'm opening the line! I thought more stridently. *I'm saving your life, Ku'Sox. Remember that!*

I'll kill you! he screamed, a vow to fulfill. *You are dead. Dead!*

Dead to you, I agreed. *You will leave me and those I love alone forever!* I demanded, bits of me drifting off, motes of thought sparkling in the nothing. *Promise or I'll let you die here!*

You are dead, he sobbed, the words becoming a promise, not a threat, capitulating as his soul began to burn. *You are dead to me. You and yours are safe.*

I started to shift his aura to match Al's, hard though the sound-never-heard beat at us, and the colors no one had seen blinding me. *Good,* I thought savagely. *Because if you ever touch anyone I care about again, I'll find you. And then I'll dropkick you back in here to die with the rest of them.*

A pinprick of an opening began, and he slipped from me, darting through it and closing it behind him like a trap.

He was gone. Alone, I writhed in pain, trying to scrape together enough memories to tune my own aura. I had to get out before I was shredded to nothing. I wasn't going to go to Al, who was now playing patty-cake with Ku'Sox.

The memories of those who meant the most to me flashed through my mind: Memories of Jenks, smirking at me, his hands on his hips as the sun lit his hair. The soft smile Ivy would allow herself when she thought no one could see. Trent, his face showing love as he held his daughter—and then his powerful grace when he sat atop a horse, the hounds baying and the moon lording over it all. And Pierce, a single wistful thought of a touch I'd never feel again, the soft sound of another's breathing against mine. I couldn't have him, and he loved me anyway.

One by one, I fastened on them as a way out, and one by one, my memories were ripped away by the energy screaming through me, burning until I realized that my aura was gone. There was nothing left for the line to recognize. I couldn't think fast enough, and I was going to die here amid the screeching of unbalanced energies and the forgotten souls of demons who couldn't love. In utter agony, I curled my memories around what was left and tried to see past the pain, to form another thought to prove that I wasn't dead yet. But it was too late, and terror struck me when my thoughts gave a hiccup, vanishing for an instant, then returning weaker than before.

Ms. Morgan! a panicked thought touched mine, and recoiled, leaving the scent of rock chips in the sun.

Bis? Mindless from the pain, I felt my soul start to burn. The sensation of dry grit and the sharp feel of ion-charged water grew stronger. I felt him wrap his soul around me, and yet I still burned.

Help me, Bis, I managed, and then with a ping, the shattered remnants of my soul shifted.

Thirty

I screamed, raw and pained, and it was real. My agony was joined by a woman's startled cry and the sudden wailing of a baby. My face plowed into a tile floor, and my arms and legs went askew. Flat on my stomach, I lay on cold tile and burned, the salt-laden air cauterizing my skin. Above me, the drafts from Bis's wing beats burned across my shoulders, and I moaned. *Make it stop. Please.*

"Help her!" the gargoyle cried out, and I sobbed with relief when he settled beside me and it was only the salt in the air that burned my skin. I was on fire, and I tried to move, the slippery sheen sliding under me.

"My God. Rachel?"

It was Trent, and I started to cry. *Bis had found me and taken me to Trent.* I couldn't get up. Every breath hurt. Someone was having hysterics, and Lucy—it had to be Lucy—was crying at the top of her lungs, frightened by the noise.

"She's burned!" Bis was saying, and my body started to shake as I curled into a ball. "She was in the lines. I felt her burning, and it woke me up. I found her. Got her out. Please pick her up. She needs help."

I sucked in the air in giant heaves, recognizing the sound of surf over the unmistakable commotion of a frightened woman being ushered out. I was with Trent. *Where were we?*

"Ms. Morgan!" Bis babbled, and a spasm shook me when his clawed hand touched me and the broken lines of San Francisco exploded in me.

"Bis! Don't touch her!" Trent shouted, and a door shut. The crying baby and the woman were gone.

"Her aura is gone," Bis said, and I sobbed in relief when his fingers fell away. *Oh God, it hurt.* "Someone needs to hold her, give her an aura. That's why I brought her to you. I saw your aura in the kitchen. It's the same as hers. Her mind might not know the difference. She really hurts, Mr. Kalamack. Please!"

I slowly began to realize that I was out of the lines. Bis had found me and pulled me out. But I was raw. My soul was leaking. I had no aura to protect it. I was dying. But at least I was in the sun. *I was in the sun? With Bis?*

I tried to open my eyes a crack, seeing green tile and the soft movement of a white curtain. Bis had found me when no one else knew I was in danger. He was awake in the sun. And as I lay on the floor of the seaside patio, my heart seemed to break. He'd bonded with me, and now I was going to die. It was so unfair.

The air shifted, and the breath in me hissed over my teeth as the salt in it burned. My sweat had gone cold, and I shivered as Trent's black slippers scuffed to a halt and he dropped to his knees before me, his hands outstretched but afraid to touch me. There was a bloody stick beside me, and horror trickled through me as I realized it was my arm. I wasn't soaking in sweat but blood.

"Please make it stop hurting," I whispered, then gasped when Trent turned me over and lifted me into his arms. The twin sensations of fire and ice flashed like a cracked whip over my skin, and I clenched my body, gasping as his aura—Trent's aura, golden and hazy—came between me and the world.

The burning eased, and I looked up at him, lungs heaving. The air hurt, but I couldn't get enough in me. Ku'Sox was going to win. I was going to die. I felt it.

"Is she going to be okay?" Bis said, and I smelled cinnamon and wine, warm from the sun. Trent's aura wasn't enough, and I felt bits of me flaking off, but it gave me enough relief so that I could breathe. "It's better, right, Ms. Morgan?" the gargoyle asked, shifting from foot to foot just inside my narrow range of vision. His red eyes turned to Trent. "Can you fix her?"

"I don't know." The arms under me shifted, and a blissful coolness sifted over me like shaded sand. I hissed at the scraping sensation, my eyes closing. He smelled like hot wine, and all my muscles relaxed. I was leaking more than blood. My thoughts and memories were flaking from me every time the wind blew.

"But you have to," Bis said, and I heard a bird crying far away. My eyes were burning, and the trails of tears were like fire on my cheeks. "You simply have to. That's why I brought her here."

Trent shifted, and I stifled a groan. "She's lost a lot of it," he said. "Mine can't keep her alive until she starts to make her own again."

It. He meant my aura, and I began shuddering in earnest, unable to stop. My muscles were seizing, and everything was going cold, even the fire licking what was left of my soul. My body was shutting down. I couldn't stop it.

"But you made her do this!" Bis exclaimed. "You made her believe she could! You can't just let her die!"

There was silence, and I felt Trent's grip on me tighten.

"Rachel? Rachel!"

It was the silence that got my attention, and I managed to open an eye a bit. "What?" I breathed, glad the pain had eased. No one should die in pain. The blessing of angels.

Trent looked worried, a smear of blood on his face. I almost smiled. He was worried about me.

He grimaced, and my vision narrowed to almost nothing. "Hold on," he said, his voice sounding like he was in cotton. "I have to set you down for a second. I'll be right back."

The beautiful haze I was in vanished and agony split between my thought and reason. I gasped as he shifted me to the floor. He was leaving, and my heart thudded wildly. Eyes open, I frantically looked for him, seeing Bis staring down at me, his eyes as big as saucers. His wings and ears were pinned back. His tail was wrapped around his clawed feet, and he was as black as midnight, scared to death. I smiled at him, and he turned to Trent, fear in his eyes.

"Mr. Kalamack!" he exclaimed, and then Trent was back, frowning as he knelt beside me. I could feel his aura, and I wanted to roll into it, but I couldn't make anything move.

"Foolish witch," Trent was muttering as he kneeled by me. There was a little cap on his head, and he was arranging a thin ribbon to drape around his neck and down his front. He was wearing an odd shirt, red in front, white in back—very unlike him. And then I realized it wasn't red—it was soaked in my blood. "Why didn't you just give him the curse and banish him?" he finished.

"I did." My hand stretched out, and though it burned as if a dog was chewing on it, I managed to edge it into his aura. Bliss slipped into my fingers, and I started to cry. I wanted it, and it was so close, smelling of cinnamon and the shadows under trees. "He dragged me into a line with him," I said, the tears burning me. "He was eating my soul." *Pick me up. Oh God, just pick me up again.*

"That would account for its shredded look."

The soggy warmth under me was getting cold, and I moaned in relief as Trent gathered me back to him, pulling me into his lap and setting my back to his front, almost covering my entire body with his aura. My eyes opened a bit, and I felt my heart slowing as his aura lapped about me. He was reading from something, his lips moving. I could feel elven magic seeping out of the earth and into me, but it didn't matter. It was too late.

"What did you want to be when you grew up?" I asked. We were innocent once. How could it have gone so bad?

Trent's attention flicked to me, his worried frown becoming

one of shock. "A tailor. They were the only men who could order my father around. Rachel, listen to me."

"I think I'm dying," I whispered, and Trent shifted my weight closer to him.

"You are," he said, no emotion at all in his words.

Heavy and hot, the tears slid down my face. "I know," I said. For all the agony, for all the heartache, I wasn't ready to go yet. But I couldn't stop it. There was just nothing left to hold me together. Trent's aura wasn't enough.

"I'm sorry," Trent was saying, but I wasn't really listening, I was trying to blink the tears away enough so that I could see the wind moving the fabric of the sun shelter hanging between me and the sky. "I can't fix you. Not like this. Your soul isn't sending out enough of an aura to convince your mind that you are still alive, and mine isn't making enough of an impression. Your body is shutting down."

"Yeah, I know," I said breathily, staring up at the blue and white. My God, it was beautiful, those colors up there.

Bis was crying, I could hear him, and I pulled my attention from the sky, wanting to tell him it was okay. My gaze found Trent's instead, and he grimaced, grabbing my chin with a hand and forcing me to look at him when my focus slid away. "Pay attention," he said, and I thought it rather rude. "I'm going to put your soul in a bottle until it heals."

Bis's sobs hesitated, and I blinked. With that little hat and ribbon around his neck, Trent looked vulnerable and scholarly. Like a priest and a rabbi all mixed up and all the better for it. It was kind of cute. "Whhaaat?" I slurred, and then fear hit me as his words took on meaning. He wanted to put my soul in a bottle. Like the one Al had. The soul had been in there so long, it had gone insane. Elves could do that, too? Why not? They would have to be smart to survive a war with the demons, even if they were almost extinct. The demons were on the verge of extinction themselves.

Trent turned away, watching his hand as he dumped the milk out of a nearby baby bottle. His head lifted as the door opened. Someone gasped, and Trent's lips pressed into a thin line. "Get out!" he shouted, then, "Wait! Call 911. Tell them she's gone into cardiac arrest and isn't breathing."

"Yes, sir," the cool, masculine voice said, and the door shut. A baby was crying in the distance. Or maybe that was me. At least the burning had stopped. I couldn't feel a thing.

"But I'm still breathing," I said. It was taking forever for anything to make sense.

I winced as Trent shifted me farther up into his arms so he could see the little book he was holding in front of us. "You won't be in a minute," he said, and Bis took a breath in alarm. "As soon as your soul leaves it, your body is going to shut down."

I thought about that as Trent started to hum, the sound going deep into my psyche and setting my blood to slow. Elven magic stirred, rising like fog in a dusky meadow, tingling and heavy. It didn't hurt like the ley lines did, and my muscles grew slack. Suddenly my eyes opened wide. "You're going to kill me!" I exclaimed, and the magic faltered as Trent's humming cut off.

"I'll keep it alive. Get it on life support. Your soul needs to regain its strength. It can do that in a bottle, and when it does, I'll put it back in."

He began humming again, rocking me. The prick of wild magic tingled across me, heady and slow. Until a thought pinged against the muzzy softness and shredded it into pinpricks. "You can do that?" I asked, and the magic broke. "You want to put me in a baby bottle?"

The humming stopped. "You're going to have to trust me. I've been practicing this, but I need your consent. I'm not good enough to do this without it."

I blinked up at him, trying to understand. My breath came in and out, and Trent waited, impatience in his eyes. "How many times have you done this?" I asked.

"And had it work? Never. But I've only tried it with birds, and they are rather stupid. Be quiet. I've got to concentrate."

I felt like I was floating. "You want my permission to kill me?"

He sighed, and Bis shifted his wings nervously. "Yes," Trent said.

I was numb, his magic already having taken hold. It was either that or I was dying in his arms. "Okay," I said, closing my eyes, and he sighed again, but it was different—as if he finally believed I trusted him. The world got spongy and black as the humming evolved into words I couldn't understand, the vowels deep in his throat and the pitch rising and falling in unexpected beauty. It was the wind in the leaves given voice, and the movement of the stars in the heavens, and I started to cry again as I remembered the elf under the arch singing me to sleep.

"Tislan, tislan. Ta na shay, cooreen na da," he sang, the words circling, going around and around in my head, pulling energy into existence from his soul, not a ley line, and giving my thoughts something to hide behind from the pain. His voice coated me in soothing darkness. My heart slowed until it decided to stop, but I didn't care. I didn't hurt anymore, and Trent's aura was warm.

So very warm.

Thirty-one

I looked at my hands as they pressed the cookie cutter into the dough, realizing that I'd been making cookies for quite a while—but not consciously aware of it. It was as if I'd been sleepwalking. Maybe I still was. A pleasant sense of lassitude lay heavily on me, and I used a pancake turner to carefully set the cut cookie, smelling like milk, onto the baking tray. I was making trees, but it didn't feel like the solstice. It was too warm.

Setting the cutter down, I shifted a second cookie to the tray, then hesitated. The one I'd just put there was gone. My head came up, and I calmly looked at the sink. The light beyond the window was too bright to see anything. The ceiling, too, was a hazy white, as well as the floor. I didn't see my feet down there, but it didn't bother me.

"How odd," I said, going to look out the window, but it was as if the sun had washed out the world. I turned, unafraid as I realized that the wall against which Ivy had her big farm table pushed was gone, too. The table was there, but the wall was a hazy white mist.

That didn't bother me, either. It had been like that for a long time—I'd just now noticed, was all. Even the sight of the unmarked circle of cookie dough and the empty cookie tray was okay. I'd been making cookies forever. Unconcerned, I went to the center counter and cut out another. It didn't matter.

I hummed as I moved cookies to an empty tray, the same tune going around and around in my head. *Ta na shay, cooreen na da.* It spun over and over, and I moved to it, feeling good with it in my head. I didn't know what it meant, but it didn't hurt, and not hurting was good.

It was awfully quiet for my kitchen, though, so often full of pixy chatter, and after setting another cookie on the empty tray, I looked back at the hazy wall. There was a dark spot on it, about eight inches tall, a few inches wide, at chest height. I squinted, trying to decide if it was getting closer.

Kisten? I thought, and it took on a masculine outline, wavering like a heat mirage, but the shoulders weren't broad enough for him.

Maybe it was Jenks? But there was no sparkle of pixy dust. And besides, Jenks wasn't that tall. The figure's arms moved as it paced forward, becoming my size. Taking on a sudden flash of color, it stepped into my kitchen.

"Trent?" I said in surprise as he shook off the mist, looking refreshed and collected in a pair of black slacks and a lightweight short-sleeved shirt, clean and bright and well pressed.

"Not really," he said, and I wiped the flour from my hands on an apron I hadn't realized I was wearing. "Well, sort of?" he amended, then shrugged. "You tell me. I'm your subconscious."

My lips parted, and I looked again at the floor that wasn't there and the ceiling that wasn't there, either. "You put my soul in a bottle," I said, surprised I wasn't scared.

Trent sat on Ivy's table and leaned forward to snatch a bit of cookie dough from the perfect circle waiting to be cut. "I didn't. I'm just a figment of your imagination. Your mind, not me, is creating all of this to cushion itself."

Frowning, I focused on him. "So I could imagine Ivy standing there instead?" I said, thinking of her, and Trent chuckled, licking the last of the sweetness from his fingers.

"No. *Trent* is trying to reach you. That's why I'm here. Bits of him are getting through, just not enough."

But I already knew that, seeing as he was simply a part of my subconscious, voicing what I was figuring out the instant I was realizing it. It was a weird way to have a conversation.

Trent slid from the table and came around to me. His hands were outstretched, and I backed up when he got too close. "What the hell are you doing?" I said, giving him a shove, and Trent rocked back, his arms dropping.

"Trying to kiss you," he said.

"Why?" I said, peeved. God, dreams were weird.

"Trent is trying to get your soul back in your body," Trent said, looking mildly embarrassed. "He can't do it unless you agree."

Oh yeah. Elven magic. It worked by persuasion and trickery. Sounded about right. "And a kiss is the only way to show agreement?" I mocked, putting the center counter between us. The floor had shown up, looking faded and scratched. My soul was starting to put things together. "Hey, how long have I been in here?" I asked, and Trent shrugged. Apparently my subconscious didn't know.

Looking unconcerned, Trent picked up the cookie cutter. "You want to leave, right?"

I eyed him standing in my kitchen, and I wondered if he really looked that good or if my subconscious was adding to his sex appeal. "Yes," I said, coming closer.

He handed me the spatula. "We have to work together."

I figured he meant more than making cookies, but I slid the spatula under the cut dough and moved it to the tray. "I want to leave. Isn't that enough?"

A second cookie joined the first, and my eyebrows rose. The first one hadn't vanished this time. "Now you're getting it," Trent said, then seemed to shudder. "You've been in here three days," he said, his visage losing its clean, pressed look and becoming haggard. His hand working the cookie cutter was swollen, and he was missing two digits on his right hand, a very white bandage hiding the damage. I hadn't imagined him looking like that. It was something outside—impinging on me.

"Trent?" I said, backing up in alarm, and his posture slumped. His eyes were red rimmed and tired, and his hair was limp and straggly. He was still wearing his black slacks and black shirt, but they were wrinkled, as if he'd been wearing them for days.

"Yes," he said, his gaze rising to the ceiling. "It's me."

I didn't think I was talking to my subconscious anymore, and I set the spatula down, my alarm turned into fear. "What's happening?"

His eyes landed on me, and I clasped my arms around my middle. "I'm trying to get you out, but I've run into an unexpected snag."

"You said you could do this!" I exclaimed, and he took a breath, his expression a mix of irritation and embarrassment. "Oh my God, is my body dead?" I squeaked, and he shook his head, raising a hand in protest.

"Your body is fine," he said, looking at his hand and the missing digits. "It's in a private room and I'm sitting right next to it. It's just . . ."

My foreboding grew deeper. "What?" I said flatly.

He looked up, grimacing as if in distaste. "It's a very old charm," he said. "I didn't have much choice. You were *dying*. All I had with me was one very stressed young gargoyle and the ancient texts I'd been playing with. I've been studying them for the last six months, trying to find the truth in the, uh, fairy tale."

"What is the problem, Trent?" I said. I could smell him now, sort of a sour wine, maybe vinegar scent.

"Ah, I think it would help if you kissed me," he said, not embarrassed, but irritated.

I dropped back a step. "Excuse me?"

He turned away and cut out another cookie. "You know . . . the kiss that breaks the spell and wakes the, uh, girl? It's elven magic. There's no figuring these things out."

"Whoa! Hold up!" I exclaimed as it suddenly made sense.

"You mean like love's first kiss? That isn't going to happen! I don't love you!"

He frowned, seeing that the cookie *he* had moved onto the tray had vanished. The two I'd placed were still there, though. "It doesn't have to be love's first kiss," he said. "That was someone trying to write a good story. But it does have to be an honest one." Almost angry, he spun back to me, the pancake turner in his new, awkward grip. "My God, Rachel. Am I so distasteful to you that you can't tolerate one kiss to save your life?"

"No," I said, taken aback. "But I don't love you, and I couldn't fake that." *Did I?* No, I didn't. I was really sure about that.

He took a breath and held it as he thought about that for all of three seconds. "Good," he said, handing me the spatula. "Good. So if you just kiss me, we can get you out of here."

I took the spatula as he held it out, edging closer to move a third cookie to the tray. "Kiss you, huh?" I said, and he sighed.

"Here in your subconscious," he said. "No one will ever know. Except us." His eyes met mine, and a small smirk started. "You've been doing it in your dreams since you were ten."

I frowned, setting a fourth cookie on the tray. "Have not. Grow up."

He set the cookie cutter down, facing me in expectation, and a nervous thrill spun through me. Kiss Trent? Okay, maybe the thought had occurred to me once or twice, but not as anything that I'd ever do apart from curiosity maybe. Because he looked good, maybe more so with the stubble and the heavy weariness on him. There was no way . . . I mean, he was Trent, and I hated him. Okay, not hated anymore, but a kiss?

Stop it, Rachel, I thought, wiping my hands on my apron and turning to him.

He was too close, and I shivered when his hands slid around my waist. "I suppose a peck on the cheek won't do?" I said as he started to lean in. He was just a shade taller than me, and I was suddenly a hundred times more nervous. He practiced wild magic, and he could sing his enemies to death or my soul into a bottle. He was dangerous now, tantalizingly dangerous, whereas before he'd been simply annoying, and my pulse increased.

I stiffened, and his motion toward me hesitated. "Sorry," he said, and he pulled me close. I was as nervous as all hell, and I didn't know what to do with my hands. They felt funny at his hips, but I left them there—the best of a bad situation. My eyes closed when he got too close, and the smell of cinnamon and wine hit me.

It pulled my head up, and with a startled brush, our lips met.

His touch was light on mine, as if afraid or, more likely, reluctant. A bare hint of pressure, and then he leaned in, his hands on me, pulling me to him. His lips moved against mine, and I still stood there, my heart pounding as I tasted him— oak and leaf, sun on moving water. The prick of wild magic raced over my skin like a shimmer of electricity, enticing, warning me even as I felt it pull a response from me. Breath held, I relaxed my grip on him, finding my hands moving, shaping to him, becoming natural.

Okay, this wasn't so bad.

Encouraged, my head tilted, pulling away from him with the unsaid language of lovers that demanded he follow. And he did, spinning a thrill through me from his lips to my toes. My pulse jumped, and I pushed against him, my body molding itself to him. Breath catching, he responded, his good hand lifted to touch my face, his fingers light on my jaw, but hinting for more. A slip of tongue touched mine, and a thought rose like a bubble.

Oh my God. I'm kissing Trent.

Making a small noise, I pulled back, heart pounding as I looked at him. "This isn't working," I said, my lips cool where he had been. I was tingling everywhere, and wild magic was making his eyes flash in anger.

"Because I'm the one doing everything here," he said, reaching forward.

"Hey!" I yelped, but he'd grabbed my arm and pulled me back to him.

"It's like the cookies," he said as his bandaged hand encircled my waist. "You're not helping. Give me something back to show your agreement."

"What the hell do I have to do? Rip your clothes off?" I snapped, then gasped as he yanked my hip right into him. "Trent!" I protested, but the word was muffled as he found my mouth. Wild magic lit through me, burning not with fire but warmth. It raced like flash paper, flowing to my chi, overflowing and tingling to my fingertips.

"Oh my God," I mumbled, and my hands, once splayed behind me for balance, reached to find his hair. I wanted to touch its silky smoothness. I'd been dying to do so for years. His body was against my entire length, and I pushed from the counter, slamming his back into the fridge.

Our lips parted upon impact, and my eyes opened. He was inches away, watching me, daring me. He'd pulled passion from me, and now I'd have to own up to it.

"No one will know?" I said, and blood pounded through me when he nodded.

"I won't tell anyone," he said, a smile lifting his lips.

Why the hell not? I thought, and then I tilted my head and kissed him back. Giving in, I pressed into him, my hands feeling his outline, his stubble rough against me as our breaths found a rhythm both slow and building. Memories flitted through me, of him in that silly hat as he held me while I died. His white face when he realized he'd summoned Ku'Sox to kill the pixies and I'd already taken care of the problem. His fear in Carew Tower's elevator when it opened and he saw me standing there with Al. His terror at camp as he leaned over me and begged me to breathe after I'd knocked the air out of myself and he thought I was dying.

His tongue touched mine, and this time, I pushed forward,

pulling him closer. My leg went around his, and I demanded more, running my hands through his hair, enjoying its silky softness, enjoying the feel of his hands on my body, tingles arcing through me.

Slowly I let go of the last of my reservations, feeling his energy spill into my chi, kindling it back to brightness. He started to pull away, but I wouldn't let him, reaching out and pulling him back. I wanted more. He could have everything, just give me . . . a little more.

"Tink's pink dildo, all that money and he can kiss, too," came a high-pitched, sarcastic voice and the clatter of pixy wings.

My breath caught, and I felt myself drop into nothing. My lips on Trent's stopped moving, and I realized I could smell disinfectant. My eyes flew open.

I was sitting upright in a hospital bed, my arms wrapped around Trent as he sat beside me. My hands were buried in his hair and his hands were curved around me, holding my backside—rather tightly.

"You little prick!" I shouted, smacking him. Trent sucked in his breath and fell back. The sharp crack was startling, and Jenks laughed merrily, dripping a bright silver dust as he flew backward to Ivy, sitting calmly in a nearby chair. Damn it, she was smiling at me, her eyes bright with unshed tears. She was okay! They both were! My face flamed as I realized they had seen me . . . enjoying myself. Enjoying Trent. But they were okay, and a knot of fear loosened.

"You said it was only in my imagination!" I exclaimed, turning back to Trent as he stood up and the bed shifted. "You said no one would know!" My eyes darted to the cold feel of metal around my wrist. "And what is this!" There was a band of charmed silver on me. No wonder my head hurt. I was cut off from the ley lines.

"Don't take it off!" Jenks shrilled as I tried to push it over my wrist, and I let go of it, frightened by his fervor. Maybe my aura wasn't healed enough to tap a line.

Looking unruffled, Trent tugged his shirt straight, the bright imprint of my hand on his stubbled face. There was a large bruise on the other side, spreading up under his hairline, looking ugly. His right hand was bandaged, and my anger dissolved when I saw that he was missing two fingers, just like in my dream. *What had happened?*

"Would you have kissed me if you had known it was real?" he asked, and when I simply stared at him, my face flaming, he turned on his heel. "Ivy, Jenks," he said, looking stiff as he reached for a cane. "It's been a pleasure."

My jaw dropped when his pace was awkward, and then I saw his foot, in a cast. "Trent, wait!" I called, but he kept walking, his back stiff and his neck red. Jenks and Ivy exchanged a heavy look, and I tried to get up, failing. "Trent, I'm sorry for slapping you! Come back. Please! Thank you for getting me out of there. Don't make me crawl after you. I'm sorry! Damn it, I'm sorry!"

He stopped, his arm stiffly holding open the wide hospital door. The hall noise slipped in, both familiar and hated, and then . . . he let the door shut and turned back around. I exhaled, falling back against the raised bed, shaking in exhaustion.

"Hey, Rache!" Jenks buzzed close. "What's it like being dead?"

"A lot like being a sixties housewife. What happened?" Trent said I'd been out for three days. Three days? Where was Pierce? And Bis?

My attention shot to the top of the wardrobe, and a new fear joined the rest when I found him there. The gargoyle was sleeping, an exhausted pale gray with a baby bottle in his tight grip. But what scared me was that I'd known where he was. Even though I was cut off from the ley lines, my eyes had gone right to him. Bis had saved me. Our fates were bound together, and there was nothing I could do about it. He'd chosen me, and now I was responsible for him. For life.

Ivy stood, and I wasn't surprised when she leaned over the

bed and gave me a hug, shocking me from my thoughts. The spicy scent of vampire soaked into me, better than a calming spell. I smiled up at her warmth, feeling loved. "Welcome back," she whispered, and then she pulled away, her eyes black and tearful. "I have to go, but I'll come back when your dinner tray is here."

"You're leaving?" I said, not liking how my voice wobbled. My gaze darted between her and Bis. "Why?"

"Jenks and I have something to do," she said, giving the pixy a pointed look.

Jenks hovered between us, spilling a red dust. His hands were on his hips in his best Peter Pan pose. "Like what?" he shot at her. "We've done nothing but sit here for three days while you've moaned and pissed over Rachel, and now that she's awake, you want to leave?"

My gaze went to Trent, standing by the window, his back to us.

"Yes," Ivy said, and I jumped when she gathered my blankets and pulled them up around me, hiding my arms. They were pink, as if I had a sunburn. Ivy and Jenks looked okay, but Trent was a mess. Bis looked kind of gaunt, too. I was afraid to look in a mirror. I had been bleeding from my pores. And Trent had saved me. Maybe twice. Maybe three times.

Seeing my worry, Ivy started to drift back.

"See you around, Rache," Jenks said, humming loudly as Ivy gave me a last touch on the shoulder and walked out, her boots clattering confidently on the tile. I remembered hearing them in my dreams, their cadence frightened and hesitant. The noise from the hall grew loud, then soft, then silent.

My eyes went to my band of charmed silver, rising to find Trent when the memory of that kiss made my face warm— until my gaze dropped to his cast, then rose to take in his hand. He was missing two fingers. I was missing three days.

"Thank you," I whispered, but what I wanted to say was, what happened?

Trent's silhouette stiffened, his back still to me. "You said that," he said softly.

I tried to shift my weight farther up the pillow, and the blanket that Ivy had tucked around me fell down. "I'm sorry for slapping you," I added.

Still he didn't turn. "You said that, too."

His voice was low and soft, and I remembered him singing to me in words I didn't understand, holding my soul together. Grimacing, I tried again. "Uh, you're a good kisser. It was nice."

His bandaged hand shifted behind his back as he turned to me, wonder in his expression. "Is that why you asked me to stay?"

I managed a thin smile. "No, but I figured you'd turn around if I said it." He frowned, his thoughts somewhere else, and I added, "You're supposed to say I'm a good kisser, too."

At that, he chuckled, but his smile faded fast. Awkward, he moved to an empty chair, one not as close to me as Ivy's was, but here nevertheless. His eyes flicked to Bis as he sat down, and then a heavy sigh escaped him, a world of hurt in the sound. "You want to know what happened," he said flatly, more of a statement than a question.

I fingered the band of braided silver around my wrist. It was heavy, more substantial than the one I'd had on in Alcatraz. A faint tingling came from it, not ley line in origin. Wild, elven magic. I flushed again, remembering the kiss, remembering letting his magic flow through me, kindling my chi back to life.

My gaze went to Bis, wishing he would wake up. He looked so sad up there, holding that bottle that had once held my soul. "I remember you singing my soul into that bottle," I said. "I don't remember you being hurt."

A shudder lifted through him. "The sun went down. Al came." His eyes met mine, the green of them almost gray in the light. "He saw you brain-dead. He was . . . upset."

Guilt went through me. "Oh." Upset, hell, I'd be willing to

bet he was furious and looking for someone to take it out on. Damn, Trent was lucky to be alive.

Trent leaned back, his hands going to cradle his knee as he crossed his legs. "I'd go as far as to say he was very upset," he said, looking at his hand. "It was my fault, naturally. I was the one who freed Ku'Sox. And because he couldn't take me to the ever-after, he decided to take me apart and move me there bit by bit."

"My God," I whispered, seeing his missing fingers in a new way.

"Vivian tried to stop him—"

Worry pulled my heartbeat into a faster pace. "No . . ."

"She's in intensive care," Trent said, and I eased back into the pillow, not relieved, but not as frightened. "She'll be okay," he added, his eyes on the floor, undoubtedly reliving it.

"I'm sorry."

Trent wiped his face in an unusual show of agitation, and I remembered the feel of his bristles on me. "You were brain-dead. He never noticed the bottle. Bis took you, your soul, and hid it away. As far as Al knows, you are still dead."

He was looking at my sunburned arms and the band of charmed silver, and I saw it in a new way. Al thought I was dead? "You bested him," I said, and Trent gave a bark of laughter. It was a bitter, angry sound, and it struck through me cold.

"Bested him?" he said, uncrossing his legs. "We survived. And that was because of Pierce."

Again fear took me. Trent had said Al thought I was dead. Al was still alive. "Where is Pierce?" I asked, already knowing the answer.

Trent stood, turning to the window. I couldn't read his tells. I was afraid to. "Pierce knew you were alive in the bottle," he said softly, the hospital noise coming in faintly. "He also knew that I was the only one who could get you safely out. If I died, you would die." Trent turned, his head bowed, looking nothing like himself in his wrinkled clothes and with his hair unstyled. "Pierce doesn't like me much, but he took the blame. Said he was the one who caused your death by his failure to protect you and keep Ku'Sox from taking you into the lines. Al dropped me and took him instead."

My face lost its expression. Pierce had sacrificed himself. To save me.

Panicked, I sat up, swinging my feet to get out of bed and coming to a frustrated halt. Damn it, I had a catheter. "Where's my mirror?" I asked, knowing he wouldn't have it. I started pulling at the silver around my wrist again. "I have to talk to Al."

Trent's face was empty of emotion when he turned back to me. "He did it because he loves you. I pity him."

"Al won't kill him," I said frantically, not knowing if it was true. "He'll be okay."

Shaking his head, Trent smiled sadly. "I don't pity him because he's a demon familiar. I pity him because he loves you."

I took a breath to say something but couldn't exhale. Damn it, he'd sacrificed himself so that I would live. He knew I didn't love him, and he'd done it anyway. "I-I . . . ," I stammered, fingering the band of silver around my wrist. It was humming with wild magic, slumbering deep within it. I could feel it. I looked up at Trent, confused.

"Al saw you comatose," Trent said. "He told the demon collective. Perhaps you should keep it that way. This is why I gave you the charmed silver. It was a chance for me to . . ." He hesitated, sighing as he sat back down. His head was bowed over his knees, and his eyes were on his hands—his beautiful hands, now broken and marred. He might never be able to work some of the finer ley-line charms again, and I shivered.

"My father made you into a tool to save the elven race," he said softly, his voice pained. "It saved your life but took it from you at the same time by making you into something that most people would deem too dangerous to live." His head came up, and he met my gaze squarely. "I don't know why, but I feel responsible. For everything. You weren't given a choice, and I'm sorry for that."

"You didn't do anything," I said, my mouth dry. "And your father saved my life."

"By twisting it to his own ends, without asking your permission." Trent exhaled. "I wanted to give you your choice back. That's all."

I followed his gaze to the band of silver around my wrist. That's all? That was everything.

"It's not a normal zip strip," Trent said as he straightened up from his hunch over his knees. "It doesn't simply cut off your contact to the lines but to the demon collective as well. Otherwise, they would know you were alive, even if you shunned the lines for the rest of your life."

My lips parted in understanding. If Al had seen me comatose and I was cut off from the collective, then I was as good as dead. Free?

"You can do earth magic still, and ley-line magic will work on you like any human, but demon magic won't if it goes through the collective," Trent said, and I brought my wandering thoughts back to him.

"Curses won't touch me," I said, and he nodded, his expression more earnest and open than I'd ever seen it. It was as if he was down to his bare essence, too tired and beaten to hide it.

"I didn't do it to protect you. I did it because my father made you into something, and unless you choose to be that person, then you are nothing but a tool. You are not a tool, Rachel," he said earnestly, almost frighteningly. "You are a person. You can stay as you are and be, well, not normal, but as close as you can get to it seeing that the coven has denounced you as a day-walking demon. Or you can take the charmed silver off and be who you really are. It's up to you. It's your choice."

He was silent and still now, and I looked at the band, circling it around and around my red wrist. I was a day-walking demon who couldn't do magic. But I could feel wild magic in me, simmering. Was it coming from the band of silver? Or had it been there all the time, and I only now noticed it, now that my contact with the ley lines was utterly and absolutely cut off?

"Isn't that what you wanted?" Trent said, not understanding my silence. "A choice?"

I took a deep breath, pulling my gaze up as I gathered my thoughts.

"Yes. Yes it is," I said, and he smiled weakly. "Thank you."

It was what I wanted. What I had always wanted. So why did it feel so empty?

Thirty-two

Trent's long black car pulled up to the curb, a soft hush in the dark. In an instant, Ivy was reaching for the handle. The front passenger's door opened, and she was standing in the street, her eyes on the church's steeple. Looking back in, she glanced first at Quen, then at Trent, sitting in the back with me and Bis, Lucy in her car seat between us.

"Thanks for the ride, Trent. Quen," she said, her voice low but sincere. And then she was gone, boot heels clicking on the night-cooled pavement, visibly shaking off being too far from home for too long. Vampires truly were the homebodies of Inderland society, and it had been hard on her in ways I could never imagine. That Trent had chartered a specially designed, low-flying jet to get us home in hours, not days, had been a godsend.

"Tell your pilot his pressure control still sucks," Jenks said through the open window in parting, and then darted to join Ivy. Giving me a toothy grin, Bis hopped to the open sunroof, and launched himself after them and into the dark.

I held a hand to my head to keep my hair from flying around in the draft from his wings, and Lucy frowned in her sleep, her hand flashing out as if she was falling. Together, Jenks, Ivy, and Bis ascended the stairs in the dark, pulling the heavy oak doors open to let out a flood of light and pixies. I glanced at the headache-inducing cloud of silk and gossamer, then settled back in the soft leather, reluctant to get out—even as glad as I was to get home.

A flash of liquid light turned into Jenks darting to the steeple as he checked in with the pixy on sentry duty. I heard a sharp wing chirp and a high-pitched harangue start. Jenks wasn't happy about something. More reason to just sit for a moment.

With the sound of clicking metal, Quen undid his seat belt and got out. There were kids shouting somewhere in the next street over, and the revving of a car engine. The trunk whined open, and I shifted my new shoulder bag onto my lap. I didn't know what had happened to my old one. My phone was gone, but at least Vivian had given me my scrying mirror—for what it was worth. "Thanks for the ride home," I said to Trent softly, so as not to wake Lucy. "Don't mind Jenks. The pressure was fine."

Smiling, Trent tucked a blanket with the Disney logo under Lucy's chin. She squirmed, but didn't wake. "It was my pleasure. The honey seemed to do the trick."

"Yup." Ivy was yelling at Jenks, who had dropped back down into the church by the sound of it—something about leaving his kids alone and that they'd done okay. Angels and ass seemed to figure into the conversation. Sighing, I looked at the light spilling from the church. I was tired, and getting out of the car only meant more work.

"I know I've said it before, but thank you. For Lucy," Trent said.

I turned to Trent, then smiled at her, pouting in her sleep. My gaze flicked back to him, and I studied his love for her, honest and irrefutable on his face. He was different, less confident, softer. Or maybe I was just seeing him that way. "She's beautiful," I said, readjusting her blanket.

The thumps from the trunk were obvious, and I reached for the door.

"Ceri is due any day now," Trent said, and I wondered if he

was trying to get me to stay a moment longer. "But with Lucy there first, Ceri's baby will be the second born."

I slumped back, curious. "Lucy is the ranking elf of the next generation? Not Ceri's baby?"

His new softness vanished, and he eyed me steadily. "I meant it when I said you'd have a say in it."

Tugging my new jacket closer, I tried to make light of it. "You mean, like I have to babysit or something?"

"I was thinking more like godmother."

My nervous mirth changed to alarm. Oh jeez, a demonic godmother. Feeling ill, I glanced at him. "Okay. Yes. I'd like that. Thank you. It's an honor," I said, not sure this was a good idea but gratified nevertheless. I had Trent's trust, and it was apparently an all-or-nothing affair. And I guess . . . he had mine.

I jumped when my door opened, Quen standing ready with my two suitcases and garment bag at the curb. They had canceled my brother's wedding since my mom had been stuck in jail while San Francisco rocked and rolled. Robbie was never going to forgive me, and I wasn't invited to the new wedding next month.

Giving Trent a last smile and Lucy a fond touch on her toes, I got out. Quen helped me arrange one suitcase over my shoulder and handed me my garment bag, never unzipped the entire trip. "Thanks, Quen," I said when his pockmarked, weathered face curled up in a smile. "Tell Ceri I said hi." Leaning in, I whispered, "And sorry about the ranking elf-baby thing."

He laughed, making the dark street seem comforting. "She doesn't care," he said. "The two of them are to be raised as sisters, though they don't share a drop of common blood." Hesitating, he looked to the church's open door as a stream of noise flowed out. "Would you like some help getting this in?"

Thinking Trent had to be anxious to get home, I shook my head. "I got it. Thanks." Leaning down, I grinned at Trent through the window, surprised he'd shifted seats and was now in mine. "Thanks for everything." I raised a hand, the circle of charmed silver catching the light. "You're, uh, a lifesaver."

Oh God. I'd said it. And what's more, I think I meant it.

Trent flushed in the dim light of the car's interior. "Thank you. I appreciate that." Then, as if he'd been waiting for the apology, he reached into an inner coat pocket and extended an envelope.

I looked at it suspiciously, shifting the weight of my small carry-on. "What is it?"

"If you don't want it—" he said, and I snatched it. Sometimes Trent's envelopes had money in them. "It's from the Withons," he said as I tore it open and saw a check. A nice check. Six months' worth of check. Damn, it would pay for a new car to replace the one I'd cracked up on the bridge and then some.

"It's restitution for the trouble they put you through," Trent said, bringing my attention up to see him smiling in a rather devious way, and I tucked the money in my back pocket. This would help a lot. Not to mention that it would be the only monetary recompense I was likely going to get for ridding San Francisco of Ku'Sox. 'Course, the demon had destroyed a huge chunk of the Tenderloin, but that area could use a little sprucing up.

"Did you make them do this?" I asked, wincing at the shrill pixy harangue filtering out. *Ahhhh, it's good to be home.*

Trent's expression went from sly to gratified. "You did good," he said, fingers resting gently on Lucy. "Have you given any more thought—"

"What, you still want me to work for you? I'm pretty much useless," I said, feeling the charmed silver heavy on my wrist.

"That?" Trent said, his eyes flicking to the braided bit of charmed silver. "I told you it was a choice. Just say the word, and I'll tell you the charm to break it. We can talk at Lucy's birthday party. You like clowns?"

My mouth dropped open, and Quen edged away from me. "You are not subjecting that sweet little girl to clowns!" I exclaimed.

Chuckling, Trent settled back in the car. "Take care, Rachel," he said as the window started to go up. "Don't be afraid to call me. We can teach Lucy how to ride."

Riding. Right. "You take care, too . . . Trent," I said, not knowing if it felt odder saying it or meaning it. The last ten days had been educational. The man was clever, intelligent, and utterly lacking in someone he could just . . . talk to. He was never himself, even with Ceri. It had to be a lonely way to live.

But it wasn't my problem, and I gave Quen a small wave and turned to the church. I didn't wait for them to leave, just picked up my suitcases and headed for the stairs. Jenks met me halfway up. "Fairies!" he shrilled. "In the garden!"

"Now?" I stammered, heart pounding.

"Yes! I mean, no!" he shouted, flying backward as I hesitated on the steps. "They attacked two days ago!"

"Is everyone okay?" I asked, my gaze going to the steeple, seeing Bis there now, the glint of his red eyes and his relaxed posture telling me everything was fine.

Trent's window rolled down, and leaning out, he asked, "Is there a problem?"

Concerned, I said, "Jenks says we were attacked two days ago."

Quen paused with his hand on the door, exchanging a look with Trent. Was the coven still at it? They'd pardoned me, and even though they were mad at Trent for having released Ku'Sox, they weren't going to do anything about it lest Trent retaliate with something worse.

"I was eating Tink-blasted cotton candy while fairies were attacking my children!" Jenks said, dripping a red dust.

A faint smile touched Quen's face, and giving me a nod, he got in the car. Trent, though, was still leaning out the window. "Perhaps Quen should look over your security before we go," he said, then ducked back into the car.

Quen met my startled gaze, sitting behind the wheel but with the door still open. "Sa'han?"

Jenks was a bright ball of irritation. "My security is fine," he snarled.

But Trent was talking to Quen over the seat. "It wouldn't hurt to look around," I heard him say faintly. "I'll come in in a minute. Lucy needs attention."

He wants to come in? But Quen was getting out of the car, his body language not confused but perhaps . . . indulgent, and it wouldn't hurt to have Quen look under my bed. "Okay. Sure. I don't care," I said, and Jenks rose up, appalled.

"Rache!" he shrilled.

"We've been gone for almost two weeks," I said as I started up the steps again. "What can it hurt?" But what I was thinking was, *What does Trent want?*

Quen's door thumped shut, and I waited on the threshold for him, yanking the door shut behind us and dropping the suitcase in the dark foyer. Ivy was casually standing at the pool table sorting almost two weeks' worth of mail, and I relaxed. Something felt like it was missing, though. *Pierce.*

"We are all fine," Jenks was saying as I breathed in the scent of Quen, seeming all the stronger for the foyer being dark. "We don't need your help."

Quen flashed a bright smile. "Mr. Kalamack would like me to inspect the grounds." His gaze shifted to Ivy as if for permission. Wise man. "Is that all right with you, ladies?"

Ivy didn't even look up from the mail. "Knock yourself out. Stay out of my room."

Quen turned to me next, and when Jenks buzzed off in annoyance, I asked him, "What is he really looking for?"

Again, he smiled, but it was softer this time. "An excuse, I think."

Great. Just friggin' great.

Quen brushed past me, a shredded wisp of cinnamon and wine lingering in his wake. "I'm telling you, we're fine!" came Jenks's irate shout as he followed him into the hallway, and then the pixy darted back, dripping a bright silver dust. "Rachel!" he whined at me, his long hair getting in his eyes. There wasn't a single pixy kid in the church, not unusual if their dad was on the warpath.

I trudged forward with my stuff. "Go with him if you want."

Jenks rose up and down indecisively as if on a string, but when he heard the back door open and shut, he darted to me, flying backward as he fumed.

"What does he want?" Ivy asked mildly as I passed her.

"I've no idea." I had none whatsoever, but I imagined that his claim of tending to Lucy was an excuse so I wouldn't see him taking the steps in his cast. He could make it all right, but he lacked his usual grace, and I knew it bothered him.

"What happened?" I asked Jenks as I smacked my luggage into the wall in the hallway.

"The kids fought them off," Jenks admitted, his dust finally starting to dampen as he followed me to my room. "Them and that *fairy girl*."

He had almost spat out the last, and I elbowed my light switch on to see his face screwed up in a nasty expression. "Belle?" I asked, remembering that Sidereal's daughter had remained behind to watch me. It smelled stale in my room, and leaving my garment bag and overnight case on the bed, I propped the narrow stained-glass window open. Night sounds, the scent of marigolds, and the singing of pixies seeped in. Hands on my hips, I sighed, glad to be home.

"She has a name? You knew she was here?" Jenks yelped, a burst of dust lighting my perfumes.

"Well, yeah." I took off my jacket and hung it on my bedpost. "Didn't you? Jeez, Jenks. She's been here for months."

He fumed, his wings drooping and his tiny features cross as I needled him. Relenting, I tugged my closet door open and hung up my garment bag. Unzipping it, the smell of clean fabric spilled out. "Everyone is okay, right?" I prompted, wondering if I should be more concerned.

"Yeah . . . ," he admitted. "But . . ."

"Then relax." I pulled the beautiful dress from the bag and hung it at the back. "Bis!" I shouted, sensing him up on the steeple. He probably couldn't hear me, but he'd come anyway.

"You don't care!" Jenks exclaimed, twin pixies rising in my dresser's mirror. "We were attacked and you don't care!"

"Of course I care," I said, then shut the closet door hard enough to make his dust shake. "But I've been trapped in a plane with you for five solid hours. No one is hurt, and you need to chill!" He was scowling at me, and I lowered my voice. "Let me catch my breath, okay?" I pleaded.

A small scraping at the lintel brought my attention to the ceiling. It was Bis, his ears pricked and expectant. He hadn't been his usual self during the few days we'd spent recovering on the coast before flying home. There was a hesitancy between us that hadn't been there before, a feeling out of new responsibilities and expectations.

Neither of us knew what being bonded meant, but I sensed where he was most of the time, and he knew where I was. And since we couldn't ask Al or Pierce what my responsibilities were to Bis and his to me, we'd just have to figure it out as we went along. Him teaching me how to line jump wasn't an issue anymore, so maybe the question was moot.

"Hi, Bis," I said as Jenks fumed on my dresser. "You want your shirt?"

Immediately he perked up, slithering into my room and dropping onto my bedside table, wings flat to his back. "I was just going to ask you for it," he said, sending a sliver of concern through me. "Can you put it on me? I want to show the kids."

He wanted to show the kids. Subtle phrasing, but significant. He was seeing himself as less of a kid and more of an adult. I'd seen it on the jet when he settled into a watchful mode with a magazine, and how he kept an eye on the people in the airport instead of being distracted by the jets or the people staring at him. Growing up wasn't bad, but I kind of missed the old Bis and his wonder at everything. He still had that inquisitive good nature, but now it was tempered with the knowledge that life wasn't fair and that bad things happened, even if you watched for them.

"You bet," I said, opening the snaps of my overnight case. Still in a huff, Jenks landed on the open lid. We had spent a day at Disneyland before coming home, and Jenks had gone a little nuts, buying out a gift shop and generally acting like a chipmunk on Brimstone. Bis had contented himself with a tourist T-shirt, but Ivy and I sat on a curb for almost an hour waiting for Jenks to come out of the Tink history exhibit. Since then, there hadn't been a single swear word using the "Inderlander pioneer," as he now called her.

I pulled Bis's tank top out, carefully folding the brightly patterned bag with Tinkerbell on it after Jenks started making tiny, pained noises when I crumpled it up. I couldn't help but wonder if we had a little crush going. Finally I snapped the bright red shirt to get out the wrinkles and held it up to Bis. "I don't think we're going to have to make wing slits for you," I said, seeing a glimpse of his old self in his delight at the screened picture of characters in the latest gargoyle flick.

"Too cool," he said, holding his arms up, and I settled the soft cotton tank top over his head, tugging gently to get it around his ears. I tried to imagine him my size but failed. He was still a kid—and my responsibility. Damn, how had my mom done this?

"Belle says the battle was Sunday," Bis said, his voice muffled. "After I left."

"Yeah?" Jenks barked, his wings moving but not lifting him at all.

"Wings," I prompted, and Bis lifted them high so I could work the tank top around them.

"She said a passing clan thought that Jenks had died, so they attacked," Bis said, his red eyes glowing. "They didn't know what to do. The kids, I mean. Jih was across the street, and it was noon. But Belle was awake, and she saw them. Raised the alarm. They would have taken the garden and killed everyone if not for Belle."

I dropped back, thinking the shirt was perfect—even if it looked odd on him. There was the faint click of the front door opening, and Ivy's soft murmur followed by the thunking of Trent's cast on the old oak. My tension spiked. Trent was in my church. *Why?*

"*She* saved the garden," Bis said as he looked at himself in my dresser mirror. My perfumes were scattered about his feet, and he didn't hit one as he shifted and turned. "Took over the fight. Told everyone what to do. Kept the lines from breaking until Jih could help. No one got hurt except Belle. She took an arrow in the leg."

Alarmed, I turned to Jenks. "I thought you said no one was hurt!"

"A fairy?" he said in disbelief. "Since when are you worried about a fairy?"

"When one saves the lives of your children," I said, and Trent thumped to a halt at my door. My eyes fell from Trent's, and I slammed my suitcase shut. "Jenks, you're ugly when you talk like that," I said, then turned to Bis, hesitating at the sight of him in a bright red shirt. "Where's Belle?" I asked, imagining her broken and bleeding somewhere in the garden.

"Uh, the kitchen," he said, glancing at Jenks as if the pixy was going to protest.

A last hard look at Jenks, and I started for the hallway. Trent was standing in the doorway with Lucy, smelling of fresh baby powder and baby wipes, and his injured hand gently patted her as he rocked. I jerked to a stop when he didn't get out of my way fast enough, my eyes dropping to the floor as I flushed. "Come on in," I said softly. "I don't think we have anything but water, but you're welcome to it."

He awkwardly edged back, and I breathed easier. "Ivy?" I called as I strode to the kitchen. "Belle's been hurt!"

"Belle?" came from her room. "Is she okay?"

"I think so. I'll let you know in a minute."

Jenks's wings were clattering, and Bis was a bright spot as he crawled along the ceiling to get there before me. His expression worried, Jenks dusted at my shoulder, not coming to rest there like he might have otherwise. "Ivy knew, too?" he asked, and I realized his somber mood wasn't because he felt bad but because he was the last to know.

I flipped the bright kitchen lights on, squinting. Bis had said he'd talked to her; she had to be awake. "Jenks, if a fairy can hide in your garden for three months, then have the grace to help your kids survive an attack, don't you think you should rethink your attitude?" I turned to him, and his defiance faltered. "You're going to live to be forty years old. You're going to have to grow up. It's a small world after all, or didn't you go on that ride?"

Wings silent, Jenks hovered dead center in the doorway, at a complete loss. Trent edged in around him, taking in the kitchen as he stood between Ivy's farm table and the center counter. My annoyance at Jenks vanished in a flash of memory: a memory of Trent standing in my unreal kitchen, confused, irritated, and attractive as all hell as he tried to save my soul with a kiss. And then the kiss itself, burning its way through me, kindling my chi back to life. I'd been mortified when I'd woken up and discovered that the kiss had been real—which didn't negate how good it had felt, but did lead me back to Trent standing with Lucy in his arms, his eyes roving over my kitchen as if comparing it to his memory.

Flustered, I turned, seeing the chrysalis trapped under the brandy snifter where my Mr. Fish had once been. My beta was still in the ever-after with Al, and I hoped the demon would remember to feed him. Maybe Pierce would do it—if he was still alive.

With a surprising jolt, my eyes started to swim and I spun before Trent could see, hiding my tears by opening the window behind me wider and letting in the night air and the sound of pixies. Someone was mowing his lawn at half-past midnight. They don't sell lawn tractors with headlights for nothing. I didn't know if my sudden emotion was relief that I was home—really home—or that I'd said good-bye to everything in the ever-after for good.

A small touch on my shoulder shocked me, and I stiffened

to find Bis standing beside the sink, his eyes wide in concern as something he had no control over had set me to shaking. But even his worry did nothing to help; he was touching me, and I couldn't feel a thing. There was nothing in my mind, nothing but a faint hum of elven magic coming from my wrist. And I missed the ley lines, even as I relished the freedom I now had.

"I'm fine," I whispered to him, then squared my shoulders and turned slowly on my heel. "Belle?" I warbled, and Jenks stared at me like I'd gone nuts when I wiped the back of my hand over my eye. Trent made no comment, but he gingerly sat on the edge of Ivy's chair, his foot in the cast tucked under it.

A ping at the rack over the center counter drew all our attention up, and Jenks flushed, swearing and dusting an embarrassed red when a tiny white-haired head showed over my smallest spell pot, the one with the dent in it. I still didn't know how it had gotten there. The dent, not the pot.

"Welcome back, Rachel" came Belle's curious hissing accent, sounding like crickets. "Have a good vacation?"

My eyes darted to Trent, thinking of the wingless fairies he now had in his garden. If he hadn't known they'd come from me, he soon would. "I've had better," I said, head craning. "Are you okay? Jenks said there was a fight."

Jenks made a small sound as a thin line dropped from the bowl and Belle snaked down it. She looked odd in a bright pink pixy dress that was too short for her, and I glanced at Jenks on the spigot, his arms crossed and standing almost sideways so he wouldn't have to face her.

"I'm fine," she said, smacking her bare leg and the bandage there. "It's going to take a few more days before I can pull my longbow with any strength, but I'll mend. If I live or die, doesn't matter. We held our territory." Her eyes went to Bis on top of the fridge, and she smiled. "I like the shirt."

"Thanks."

I did a double take at the soft shyness in his voice. Jenks had heard it, too, and cleared his throat, making Bis blush a deep black.

"Your territory," Belle amended, thinking that's what Jenks had taken offense to. I wasn't so sure.

Wings clattering, Jenks landed beside her. His eyes went to her bandage, then her face. She looked like a long-armed, sinewy Amazon next to him. "Uh, thank you," he said grudgingly, glancing nervously at Trent, but the man was more interested in the spell pots over the counter, his hand gently patting Lucy as she slept. "I should have said that first off." Belle's sparse eyebrows rose, and he added, "Thanks for telling them what to do. They're good kids, but—" He tried again. "You saved their lives. Please . . . stay in *my* garden. If you like."

Even as hesitant and possessive as that had been, I looked at Bis in wonder. The gargoyle was grinning, accepting Jenks's change of heart with a quickness only a kid could possess. I'd be a little more hesitant, but Jenks wouldn't say anything unless he meant it.

Belle's long features were pale and out of place with the pixy colors on her. "Your hair is getting long," she said shortly, her tone giving nothing away.

Jenks's hand went up to touch it. "Yeah, well, I don't have anyone to cut it anymore."

I wondered how these two warriors were going to find a way to exist together. Belle finally nodded her acceptance of his apology but clearly was withholding complete judgment.

Feeling awkward, I opened the fridge and cringed. Yep, we were down to water, ketchup, and a tub of butter. Maybe I could make Trent a virgin Bloody Mary; we had some Worcestershire sauce, too. "Anyone want to order pizza?" I said softly, wondering how long it would take for Quen to check out the graveyard.

"I do!" Bis chimed out, and I ducked when Jenks's kids swarmed in from the garden and hallway, shouting out their toppings. Their high-pitched voices woke up Lucy, and she began to wail, frightened. Bis pinned his ears to his skull and made the jump to the top of the fridge. Trent frowned as he tried to calm Lucy, but the pixy girls were humming over her and scaring her even more. Clearly they had been eavesdropping, and the lure of pizza had overridden their fear of their dad. *Nasturtium blossoms?*

"Jenks!" I exclaimed as I shut the fridge door, and he shrugged.

Belle, too, had sat down, her bored expression clearly saying that it wasn't her problem. "You've had nothing but pizza for a week," she complained, her voice loud to be heard over the noise. "I would have thought you'd be tired of it by now."

"Pizza?" Jenks exclaimed. "What about all the good food I put aside . . ." His voice faltered. "Never mind," he finished, scowling at Bis, and the gargoyle went three shades darker in embarrassment. "I want you all out!" he shouted, and the noise was cut by about half, leaving only Lucy crying. "Out and watching that elf in the garden!"

"But, Papa," one of his younger daughters complained, "he's only sitting in the car."

That figured, and I gave Trent a sidelong glance. *Check out my property, huh? Make sure everything is safe, eh? What do you want, Trent?* I sighed as it struck me that this was the way I'd begun this mess, standing in my kitchen and wondering what Trent wanted.

"Go! All of you!" Jenks said, pointing, and they flowed from the kitchen, a mix of complaints and shouted topping requests. "Asleep when the garden was invaded! You'd all be *dead* if not for Belle. What have you been doing all week? Watching TV?" Jenks crabbed as the last of them left.

Lucy's blanket was almost slipping from her, and I wanted to go tuck it back around her. Trent had given her a pacifier, and Lucy was wide-eyed in his arms, quiet but sucking on it with a vengeance, angry almost. It brought a smile to my face.

The sound of Ivy's boots was loud as she came in, having changed into lots of leather. Hand on her hip and posture screaming sexual domination, she gave Trent the once-over as he sat in *her* chair. The angry, frustrated baby on his lap seemed to grant him some immunity, and she turned away with only the slightest widening of her pupils. "I'm going out. You going to be okay?" she asked.

Across the kitchen, Trent's posture seemed to relax, which only tightened mine. He wanted to talk to me alone. Great. We had just spent five hours in a little tin can flying through the air. Couldn't he have brought it up then?

"Go." I wiggled my fingers for the pizza coupons stuck to the fridge, and she handed them to me.

"If you're sure," she prompted, and my eyes met hers, sending a shock of realization through me. We were home, and though everything had changed, we were still solid. Better, even.

"You really want to stay for pizza?" I asked, and she took a backward step to the hallway, smiling as well to tell me she knew it too.

"No. See you after sunup. Bye, Trent," she called over her shoulder when she reached the hallway, then louder, "Jenks! Can I talk to you for a moment about our security?"

A knot in me unraveled. We were okay. Grinning at me, Jenks rose up. "Coming, Mother!" he mocked.

Her boots clunked into the sanctuary, and I watched Belle snake down to the floor, sword ready as she braved Jenks's cat to go outside.

"I'm glad you're home, Ms. Rachel," Bis said shyly, taking his shirt off and leaving it on top of the fridge before he jumped to the ceiling and crawled out after Belle. There was a faint scrape of nail on stone, and I figured he'd slithered out through the flue in the back living room instead of using the smaller cat door.

Yes, it was a weird life, but it was mine, and I wouldn't trade it for anything.

Trent scuffed his foot cast against the floor, and my anxiety came flowing back. Ignoring him, I wiped the dust from the phone and scooted up onto the counter as I tried to remember what he liked on his pizza. Just in case he was staying.

The bracelet on my wrist jingled, and I breathed deeply for the faint scent of burnt amber still clinging to me. The band of silver around my wrist seemed to send sparkles into me, and I shivered. I could hear the pixies playing in the night, the near and far-off sounds of life in motion. Exhaling, I remembered the glory of the collective rolling through my mind, the power at my fingertips, and the knowledge that I could create something from nothing. It was gone. Forever.

"You could have all this, too, Trent," I said, hearing the dissatisfaction in my voice. "All you have to do is quit your job, piss off the vampires, the Weres, a stupid human who knows black magic, and let a demon loose on a major metropolitan area. Oh wait, you did that."

He laughed, but his smile faded fast. "You don't have to keep it," Trent said suddenly, his gaze going to my wrist. "I gave it to you so you'd have a choice, not to hide from them."

I cringed inside, not liking that I'd telegraphed so much. "I already made my choice," I said, but I couldn't meet his eyes.

He was silent, buying time by tucking Lucy's blanket up as she willfully kicked it off. "It was an awful lot of power to give up," he said, and a flash of anger lit and died in me.

"It was an awful lot of trouble it caused," I answered, uncomfortable as I looked over the coupons. They were expired, but the delivery guys didn't care if you tipped them enough.

"I don't know if I could make myself that vulnerable after making so many enemies," he said, his gaze on the smudged counter where we'd cut out cookies.

I looked up, wondering if he was going to offer me protection, and if I could get Lucy away from him before I smacked him in the bahoogies. "Enemies are nothing new," I said calmly. "At least no one is gunning for me. And I can still do earth magic." He looked to the dusty bowls overhead. "Maybe I can relax for a while. Rescue some familiars out of trees for a change."

His expression smoothed, almost becoming a smile. "I do believe that's why you quit the I.S., remember? Boring runs?"

I snorted, nodding as I scanned the coupons. Everything was for Alfredo pizza as they tried to curry the favor of humans. "Be careful what you wish for."

"Because you might get it." Trent gazed at the dark square of night past the window.

The memory of that kiss we shared rose up in my thoughts, and I grimaced. "I'll be fine," I said softly.

"I'm not so confident," Trent said, and he raised a hand. It was the one with the missing fingers, and I hesitated. "You're not helpless," he added, "but I've had my lawyers look into your situation, and it's not as clear cut as you want it to be."

"My situation," I scoffed. Agitated, I slid from the counter to throw the coupons away. Pizza had the appeal of cardboard right now. "There aren't any laws for demons," I said, fidgeting. "And if there aren't any laws for demons, I can't break them. I don't need a license to practice magic. I'm not shunned. I can sell stuff now. People can sell to me."

"But will they?" he asked, his brow furrowed as he gave voice to my real worry.

Probably not. "The I.S. is off my case, and the vamps. Jeez, Trent. For the first time, there is no one gunning for me, including you!" I protested.

"I'll give you that." Trent was smiling, Lucy drowsing on his lap. "But along with no legislation on the books for demons and their magic, there are no laws protecting you, either. If Rynn Cormel wanted, he could drive over here, shove you in his trunk, and drive away."

I leaned back against the counter and crossed my arms over my middle. "That's the last thing he is going to do," I said, not sure I believed it.

"Probably, but he could." Trent was looking at Lucy, but talking to me. "Anyone could. A stray dog has more legal protection than you." His eyes met mine, and I stifled a shiver, knowing he was right. "That band of silver around your wrist makes you almost helpless, and anyone with enough smarts will know it. There are no laws that pertain directly to demons, and until there are, you are vulnerable."

"Vulnerable." There was that word again, and it rang through me like a warning bell. The stronger I got, the more vulnerable I was.

"You take favors from me," he said, "but you are not on my payroll. You claim to be protected by a master vampire, but you have no ties of blood, and you saw how deep Cormel's word went when he was confronted by the coven. Ivy can't protect you from everything, either. You're the alpha female of a Were pack, but you don't live with David and refuse to take a tattoo to show affiliation."

"What if I get the tattoo?" I said, hearing the truth in his words. "I didn't before because it wouldn't last through a transformation curse, but I don't have to worry about that now."

"A tattoo isn't going to fix this," he said, his eyes intently on mine. "You are a demon, but you can't perform the magic to back yourself up. I'm not telling you that you need to take that charmed silver off to survive, but I'm asking you to stay out of trouble for a while. Lay low for about six months. I'm trying to get some legislation protecting you pushed through, but it's going to take a while."

Stunned, I looked at him sitting in my kitchen with a baby on his lap, his dress pants wrinkled and his shirt almost untucked. I didn't know what to say. He was helping me? For nothing? "Why?" I asked, and he stood, agitated as he began to pace with a sleeping Lucy.

"Just six months," he said, not answering me. "David and I can't keep slapping Band-Aids on the chaos you leave behind. The lawsuits alone—"

"Lawsuits?" I asked, my arms untwisting from my middle. "Who?"

"Who doesn't matter . . . ," he said evasively.

"Who?" I said loudly. "I want to know who tried to sue me," I said softer when Lucy's hand rose, startled by my voice.

Shifting Lucy to his shoulder, he began to rock without moving his feet, a movement new to him but as old as fire and having the grace of a thousand years. "There was one from a woman about dog theft," he said calmly. "And a couple from my wedding. That's how I got involved. Someone on a bus thought you hexed them with bad luck. Two people sued when you crashed your car into the bridge."

Hands clenched, I turned to the window, wanting to hide how disturbed I was. I owed David a big thank-you. I knew he'd been paying my lawyer, but I hadn't realized I'd been keeping him so busy. And how did Trent figure into it?

"The one concerning the Rays' fish went away when I brought it up at a party," Trent continued, answering my unasked question. "The harassment lawsuit from the Howlers for magicking their field . . . That was harder. That woman doesn't like me."

I shrugged. "They weren't going to pay me," I muttered.

Trent sighed. "You getting your five-hundred-dollar fee cost David several thousand," he said, still rocking, his damaged hand pressing into Lucy, holding her close. "He's not begrudging it, but it supports what I'm saying. I've got my people working on getting some laws on the books for you, but until they do, you have all the drawbacks of being a noncitizen and none of the protection. And that's not even bringing up the fact that for every person looking for monetary compensation, there will be at least two looking to take you on for the notoriety."

My head came up. "What?"

He shrugged, Lucy on his shoulder. "A demon with no magic? You are irresistible, and there will be idiots lining up to prove they're stronger than the great Rachel Morgan, demon banisher and savior of San Francisco."

I didn't like his mocking tone, but what could I say? "I understand," I managed flatly, not knowing how I was going to iron out this new wrinkle. Six months. I could do nothing for six months.

Trent relaxed, his rocking easing. "Good. Thank you. I appreciate that."

"What choice do I have?" I said, eying my charmed silver. "The check from the Withons?" I guessed, and he nodded.

"And if you ever do want to come work for me—" he started, ruining the moment.

I exhaled, now realizing why he had been blocking the lawsuits. He *still* wanted me to work for him.

"Shut up, Trent, before I smash your face," I said lightly, not a whisper of threat in my voice. "Do you want to stay for pizza?"

Trent sucked in his breath, and an alarmed expression filled his face. "Good God, no," he said, making me laugh.

He was tidying Lucy's blanket, showing all the signs of getting ready to leave, and all of a sudden, I didn't want him to. "Thanks," I said, standing forlornly next to the sink, not knowing what to do with my hands. "For everything." He looked at me from under his bangs, and I made a weak gesture. "I suppose I could have done without you releasing Ku'Sox, but thanks for picking up the pieces and putting me back together."

Trent was drifting to the door, moving slowly because of his cast. "You're welcome. Uh, about that kiss," he said, his voice hesitant.

I froze, wanting to ignore it. "Forget it," I said. "I am."

He hesitated a bare instant. "I was just going to say I was sorry for misleading you." Turning away, he headed for the hallway, Lucy in his arms and his head bowed. "Good night."

That was *not* what he was going to say, and I licked my lips in a flash of understanding as I again saw his loneliness, the space he kept between himself and the rest of the world. I knew he would love Lucy, but even then, he would hold himself apart. I'd seen him afraid. I'd seen him vulnerable and down to his last option. He had risked not just my life but his to give me a *choice*. And it bothered me that he was going to be so . . . alone. *He had wanted to be a tailor when he grew up, because they had been stronger than his dad to his young-boy eyes.*

"Trent?"

The word was out of my mouth before I even knew I was going to say it, and he stopped in the threshold, spinning quickly back to me.

"Yes?"

It was hopeful, and my heart beat strongly. But fear shot through me, chased by adrenaline. "Never mind," I whispered. "Have a good night."

He turned, but not fast enough to hide the light in his eyes, dimming, and it scared me even more. "You, too," he said again, his voice precise and controlled again. "I'll let myself out."

He walked stiffly into the hallway, and I swallowed hard, feeling unreal. "Bye, Trent," I said, my fingers trembling slightly as I felt my way around the center counter to sit in my chair and stare at the table. There was a new feeling trickling through me, making my breath come fast and my heart thump. It was more than having Trent off my case. The witches, too, and the I.S. if that conversation in the van was any indication. True, I was a day-walking demon and I couldn't leave Ohio or Kentucky without notifying the I.S., but the legislation would go through soon, and I wasn't shunned anymore. It wasn't the satisfaction of saving San Francisco from Ku'Sox, or having finally freed myself from Al and the rest of them, or even that I'd become a demon godmother to Trent's daughter and gotten my Saturdays back, too.

The mix of fear and exhilaration filling me grew from the undeniable fact that Trent had liked that kiss we had shared. Not only liked it but had hoped that I liked it, too.

And that was very fine information to have indeed.

Don't miss the continuing
Hollows adventures of Rachel Morgan with
A PERFECT BLOOD
by Kim Harrison
Coming March 2012

The woman across from me barely sniffed when I slammed the pen down on the counter. She didn't care that I was furious, that I'd been standing in this stupid line for over an hour, that I couldn't get my license renewed or my car registered in my name. I was tired of doing everything through Jenks or Ivy, but DEMON wasn't a species option on the form. Friday morning at the DMV office. God! What had I been thinking?

"Look," I said, waving a faded photocopied piece of paper. "I have my birth certificate, my high school diploma, my old license, and a library card. I'm standing right in front of you. I am a person, and I need a new driver's license and to get my car registered!"

The woman gestured for the next guy in line, her bedraggled graying hair and lack of makeup only adding to her bored disinterest. I glared at the tidy Were in a business suit who had moved to stand too close behind me, and nervous, he dropped back.

The clerk looked at me over her glasses and sucked at her teeth. "I'm sorry," she finally said, tapping at her keyboard and bringing up a new screen. "You're not in the system under witch or even other." She squinted at me. "You're listed as dead. You're not dead, are you?"

Crap on toast, can this get any worse? Frustrated, I tugged my shoulder bag up higher. "No, but can I get a dead-vamp sticker and get on with my life?" I asked, and the Were behind me cleared his throat impatiently.

She pushed her thick glasses back where they belonged. "*Are* you a vampire?" she asked dryly, and I slumped.

No, I was obviously not a vampire. For all accounts, I looked like a witch. Long frizzy red hair, average build, average height, with a propensity to wear leather when the situation demanded it and sometimes when it didn't. Until a few months ago I'd called myself a witch, too, but when the choice was becoming a lobotomized witch or free demon . . . I took the demon status. I didn't know they were going to take everything else, too. Demons were legal non-entities this side of the ley lines. God help me if I should land in jail for jay-walking—I apparently had fewer rights than a pixy, and I was tired of it.

"I can't help you, Ms. Morgan," the woman said, beckoning the man behind me forward, and he shoved me aside as he handed her his form and old driver's license.

"Please!" I said as she ignored me, leaning toward her screen. Beside me, the man grew nervous, the spicy scent of agitated Were rising high.

"I just bought the car," I said, but it was obvious the date was over. "I need to get it registered. And my license renewed. I gotta drive home!"

I didn't—I had Wayde for that—but the lie wouldn't hurt anyone.

The woman eyed me with a bored expression as the man took a moment to write his check. "You are listed as dead, Ms. Morgan. You need to go down to the social security office and straighten it out there. I can't help you here."

"I tried that." My teeth clenched, and the man in front of the counter fidgeted as we both vied for the scrap of worn carpet. "They told me I needed a valid driver's license from you, a certified copy of life from my insurance company, and a court-documented form of species status before they'd even talk to me, and the courts won't let me make an appointment because I'm listed as dead!" I was shouting, and I lowered my voice.

"I can't help you," she said as the man pushed me out of his space. "Come back when you have the right forms."

Shoved to the side, I closed my eyes and counted to ten, very conscious of Wayde sitting at the faded orange plastic chairs under the windows as he waited for me to realize the inevitable. The twenty-something Were was one of Takata's security people, having more muscles than tattoos showing from around his casual jeans and black T-shirt, and the small, stocky man had a lot of tattoos. He'd shown up on my doorstep the last week of July, moving into the belfry despite my protests, a "birthday gift" from my mom and birthfather/pop-star dad. Apparently they didn't think I could keep myself safe anymore—which bothered me. He'd been on my mom's payroll for nearly four months, and the anger had dulled.

My eyes opened, and seeing that I was still in this nightmare, I gave up. Head down, I gripped my birth certificate tighter and stomped to the bank of orange plastic chairs. Sure enough, Wayde was carefully staring at the ceiling, his feet spread wide and his arms over his chest as he snapped his gum and waited. He looked like a biker dude with his short, carefully trimmed orange-red beard and no mustache. Wayde hadn't told me this was a lost cause, but his opinion was obvious. The man got paid whether he was playing chauffeur for me or camped out in the church's belfry talking to the pixies.

Seeing me approach, Wayde smiled infuriatingly, his biceps bulging as his arms crossed over his deep chest. "No good?" he asked in his Midwest accent, as if he hadn't heard the entire painful conversation.

Silently, I cocked my hip and fumed as I wondered how the woman could treat me like I was just some jerk-ass nobody. I was a demon, damn it! I could flatten this place with one curse, burn it to nothing, give her warts, or turn her dog inside out. If . . .

Hands clenched in a fist, my gaze slid to the decorative band of charmed silver on my wrist glinted in the electric light like a pretty bauble. If . . . If I hadn't wanted to cut all contact with my adopted kin. If I wasn't such a good person to begin with. If I wanted to act like a demon in truth. I'd devoted my life to fighting injustice, and being jerked around like this wasn't fair! But no one messes with a civil servant. Not even a demon.

"No good," I echoed him as I tried and failed to get rid of my tension. Wayde took a deep breath as he stood. He was small for a man, but big for a Were, coming to my five-foot-eight exactly, with a thin waist, wide shoulders, and small feet. I hadn't seen him as a wolf yet, but I bet he made a big one.

"You mind driving home?" I asked, handing him my keys. Crap, I'd had them in my hand for only the hour it had taken to get to the front of the line. I'd never get to legally drive my car.

Introspective, Wayde fingered the lucky rabbit's foot key chain, the metal clinking softly. There wasn't much on it these days—just the key to a car I couldn't drive and the key to Ivy's lockbox. "I'm sorry, Rachel," he said, and I looked up at his low, sincere voice. "Maybe your dad can fix something."

I knew he meant Takata, not the man who had actually raised me, and I grimaced. I was tired of going to people for help. Hands in the pockets of my little red-leather jacket, I turned to the door, and Wayde slipped ahead of me to open the milky glass. I'd get the car registered to Jenks tomorrow. Maybe Glenn could help get my license pushed through—they liked me down there at the human-run Federal Inderland Bureau.

"Ms. Morgan?" crackled and popped over the ancient PA, and I turned, a stab of hope rising in me even as I wondered at the hint of worry in the woman's voice. "Please come to window G."

I glanced at Wayde, who'd frozen with his hand on the door. His brown eyes were scanning the room behind me, and his usually easy-going expression was professionally wary. The switch surprised me. I hadn't seen it before, but then, it had been pretty quiet around the church since I'd officially switched species to demon. Very few people knew the band of silver around my wrist truncated about half my magic arsenal. It was basically a Mobius strip, the charm's invocation phrase never ending, never beginning, holding the spell, and therefore me, in an in-between space where it was real yet not completely invoked and barred any contact with the demon collective. Long story short, it hid me from demons. My inability to do ley-line magic was an unfortunate side effect.

"Ms. Morgan, window G?" the worried voice came again.

We turned our backs on the bright, windy day beyond the cloudy glass. "Maybe they found another form," I said, and he slid into my personal space, making me stifle a shiver.

"If you'd give the I.S. and the FIB the lists they want, you'd get your citizenship faster," he said, and I frowned. This didn't feel good. There was way too much whispering behind the counter between the no-longer bored clerks. People were looking at us, and not in a good way.

"I'm not going to write out every single demon curse so they can decide which ones are legal and which ones aren't," I said as I found the hand-lettered, dilapidated G hanging over a small window at the end of the room. "Talk about a waste of time."

"And this morning wasn't?" he asked dryly.

I ignored that, hopeful as I approached the woman waiting for me in front of window G. She was dressed like a supervisor, and the flush on her face ratcheted my worry tighter. "Ah, I'm Rachel Morgan," I said, but she was already lifting the counter to let me into the back area.

Eyes bright, she glanced at Wayde. "If you could come with me, Ms. Morgan. Both of you if you like. Someone would like to speak to you."

"If it's about—" I started.

"Just please come back," she said, standing aside and ushering me through in excitement.

My lips pressed, but I wasn't helpless, even lacking half my magic, and Wayde was with me. Again my eyes touched on the band of charmed silver. I didn't like being without ley-line magic, but I'd rather that than the demons knowing I was alive. I'd made a few mistakes the last year, the least of which caused a leak in the ever-after. The entire alternate reality was shrinking, and as soon as the demons realized it, they'd probably take turns at me.

The woman sighed in relief as she closed the partition behind us, her low heels clacking fast as she led us to the back offices. An elated, frazzled living vampire in a black dress suit sat behind a cluttered desk in one, her face flushed and her eyes bright. She was young, professional, and probably bored out of her mind with working in an office day in and day out, if the photos of her skydiving and running zip lines that were posted to her three-by-two calendar on the wall meant anything. Her office was overflowing with stacked folders and files in a weird mix of organized clutter as she probably took on more than she could handle. Trying to prove herself at the office, maybe as she clearly liked doing on her weekends?

I'd guess her human heritage was Hispanic, with her long dark hair pulled back in a simple clip and her dusky complexion, dark eyes, oval face, very red lips, white teeth, and pretty eyelashes. Her fingers tucking in her blah-brown blouse were long and slender, her nails painted a dull red. I could sense her confidence as she looked up at our entrance, a strong thread of self that ran through her. She was a living vampire, but clearly not high on her master's favorite list. I though it odd that the more favored a living vampire was, the more emotionally damaged they were. This woman was clearly one of the forgotten. Lucky her. Being forgotten meant you lived longer, and having been forgotten, she'd probably lack most of the darker abilities that Ivy, my roommate, had developed in order to survive.

"Nina," the supervisor said, and the young woman stood, not interested in me by all appearances as she stacked the papers on her desk in a vain attempt to tidy. "This is Ms. Morgan, and, ah . . ."

Wayde stepped into the hesitation, extending his hand as he moved both him and myself into the small, cluttered room. "Mr. Benson," the Were said. "I'm Ms. Morgan's security. Pleasure to meet you, Ms. Ninotchka, Romana, Ledesma."

The elaborate name rolled off his lips as if he'd grown up in the south of Spain, and surprised, I looked at the nameplate on the desk and decided I'd stick to Nina.

Nina blinked, her gaze going from him to me as if seeing

me for the first time. "Ah, good to meet you," she said as she confidently shook Wayde's hand. She turned to me, hesitating as she saw my hands deep in my pockets of my red coat. "Sit if you want."

I glanced at Wayde. Nina was excited, yes, but not about us. *Was someone else coming*? I thought, looking at the only open chair in the cramped office.

"Uh," I started, blinking when Nina shifted her bra strap and took a peek down to make sure everything was where it was supposed to be. "Do we need another chair?"

"No," she said abruptly as the woman who had brought us back here left, closing the door behind her. "Unless your security wants one. But don't they usually stand?"

"I'm fine," Wayde said as he took up a position just inside the closed door. "Ma'am, just what is it you want with Ms. Morgan?"

Tense, the young woman ran a hand down her hips and sat behind her desk, making her hands into fists when she noticed her fingers trembling. "*I* don't want anything. It's not me, it's *him*," she said, and the tang of excited vampire reached out and smacked me. God, she smelled good, and I felt a tingle from the vampire bites under my perfect skin. "I've never done this before. I didn't even know he knew I was alive, and now this!"

"Ah, all I want is my license renewed and my car registered in my own name," I said, a bit shaken from the surge of pheromones. I'd been right. She was lacking in control, but if she had been forgotten, it didn't matter much. "If you can't help me, I'm leaving."

Alarm flashed over the living vampire, and she almost stood. "Someone in the I.S. would like to talk to you," she said, her eyes wide. "I'm the only one here he wants to work through. My cousin is in the I.S., and well . . ." Flashing me a nervous smile, she suddenly looked scared. "It's an honor to be asked to channel a master."

I felt for the chair behind me and sat down. "A dead vamp

wants to talk to me?" I gingerly perched myself on the edge of the seat. Sure, it was daylight, but the dead ones were still awake, deep underground. Apparently one wanted to talk to me, one so old that slipping into an unfamiliar living vampire was possible. *Not good.* But maybe they could get my car registered for me. . . .

Uneasy, I glanced at Wayde. He shrugged and fell into a parade rest. "Fine," I said. "But make it quick. I've got to ask Jenks to register my car since you won't do it through me."

Ignoring my sarcasm, she shivered violently, jerking once as her eyes became unfocused and she reached for the stability of the desk with a white-knuckled strength. Her breath came in with a slow, sensual sound, her hair falling forward as her head bowed. She sighed, her red lips closing and her gaze sharpening on her hands gripping the edge of the desk. Slowly her fingers let go and her hands dropped into her lap. She seemed to grow taller as she pulled herself straight and looked at me—smiling to show her little pointy canines. I shivered at the new glint in her pupil-black eyes. I couldn't help it, and her smile grew wider still as she took in the shape of my face in a decidedly masculine fashion. It wasn't Nina anymore.

I stiffened as she breathed deeply, shifting her shoulders back as she tasted my unease, something Nina probably wasn't skilled enough to read on the air currents. The slight grimace as she looked down at her clothes made me wonder if she was uncomfortable with being in a dress, or because of the cheap fabric. Her confidence before had been within herself. Now it was the assurance that she could do anything she wanted and no one would think twice. From the door, Wayde whistled, his arms lose at his sides.

"You've never seen this before?" I asked, and he shook his head. I watched "Nina" look over the room, placing herself, hearing things I could only guess at, sensing things I'd seen on the way in. "I once saw Piscary take over Kisten," I said softly. "Ivy hated it when Piscary took over her."

Across from me, Nina smiled. "She enjoyed it," she said,

her voice sounding deeper, richer, more sophisticated. "Don't doubt it."

Realizing I had crossed my knees submissively, I put my feet square on the floor and leaned back in my chair as if relaxed—but I wasn't. This was eerie, seeing a man in a woman's body, and I was sure the undead vamp was a man. Someone's phone was vibrating, probably mine, and I ignored it.

Nina stood, gracefully catching her balance and frowning down at the scuffed heels she was wearing. Her hand came out to me in invitation, and I cursed myself when I found my hand rising to hers against my will, shivering as she breathed deeply over it, sensing what he/she was doing to me. "It's good to see you again, Ms. Morgan," she said slyly, and I reclaimed my hand before she tried to kiss it. God, I hated dealing with the old ones.

I glanced at Wayde, standing stiffly by the door. "You were the driver in San Francisco," I guessed, remembering the driver had been channeling an undead vamp of some importance, eavesdropping on coven business as he drove me out to take care of someone they couldn't.

Smiling to hide her teeth, Nina inclined her head, looking devilish and seductive both as she took up a slightly wide-footed stance. It was really weird. That was not the flustered vampire that had been here when I'd walked in. And it wasn't what Nina would become when she died her first death. It was someone else entirely, someone old.

"I don't like not knowing who I'm talking with," I said, trying for annoyed but hearing it come out as petulant.

"Today, I look like Nina," she said, settling back in her chair and grimacing at the dirty corners of the office and lack of a window. "You may call me that."

"Who *are* you?" I said more firmly, and she just smiled, steepling her fingers.

"Someone who can help you," she said, and I rolled my eyes as Wayde coughed. From my bag on the floor, a tiny ping told me someone had left a voicemail. "If you're willing to make an effort, that is," Nina continued, ignoring him. "We failed in recognizing you. We let you slip from us. You've done well, but you could do even better—with a little . . . structure."

"I'm not coming back to the Inderland Security," I interrupted, flushing. Crap, if that's what this was about, I might be in trouble. Saying no to them could shorten your lifespan. But all Nina did was send her pupil-black eyes to a form on her desk. It was a copy of my license. Under it was a blank registration. I sighed, remembering the world we lived in. Damn it, my phone was ringing again, too, but anyone important like Ivy or Jenks would know to call Wayde.

"I might work a job for you, though," I added grudgingly. Still Nina said nothing, her black eyes making me fidget. If the dead vampire had really been here, he could have made me do anything, but Nina was a young forgotten vampire, and she didn't have the right hormones turned on for the vampire she was channeling to use. Yet.

"What is the job?" I prompted, wanting to get out of here before I asked to have her baby.

The light in her eyes speaking of a possessive strength, Nina smiled, showing enough teeth to make me stifle a shiver. "Right to the point," she said as if it pleased her, and I stared when she tried to put a foot on one knee, checking her motion at the last moment when her skirt caught. She reclined instead to look even more masculine, more in control, not caring she was showing a healthy portion of leg. "You do know the only reason I didn't notice you was because Piscary saw you first?"

Piscary was dead now, but I liked this even less. "What do you want?"

Nina tilted her head, dangerously suave as she eyed me from under her thick eyelashes. Ivy had given me that look before, and I stifled a flash of libido, knowing it was coming from the pheromones Nina was kicking out.

"I want you and Ivy Tamwood to help us find a group of Inderlanders doing demon-like crimes in and around the Cincinnati area. We have three sites to look at."

I sat up, shocked. "Three! How long has this been going on?" There'd been nothing in the papers, but then, if the I.S. didn't want it in the news, it wouldn't be.

"Several weeks," Nina said in regret, her gaze falling from mine for the first time, "which would be evident once you looked at the data, so listen as I tell you what you won't find there."

My eyes squinted. She was ticking me off. Anger was better than being turned on, though. "You should have come to me right away," I said. "It will be harder now."

"We thought it was *you*, Ms. Morgan. We had to make sure it wasn't. Now that we know for sure, we wish to engage your services."

Engage my services. How old is this guy? "You've been following me," I said, remembering that itchy feeling between my shoulder blades whenever I was out: the grocery store, the shoe mall, the movies. I thought it was Wayde, but maybe not. Crap, how long had they been shadowing me?

"Three weeks," Wayde said, answering my unspoken question. "I didn't know it was the I.S., or I would have told you."

I turned to look at him, appalled. "You knew someone was following me, and didn't think I needed to know? Isn't that your job?" I snapped, and Nina chuckled.

His expression closed, Wayde looked first at Nina, then me. "It's *my* job, and *my* call."

"We believe there's more than one person responsible for the crimes," Nina broke in, and my attention was recaptured by his/her silken, aged voice. It was still Nina's, but the self-assurance was mesmerizing. "There seems to be two modes of operation, harvesting and dumping. Witches. All the bodies were witches."

My expression twisted. I didn't like the sound of that. "Harvesting? That's ugly."

Nina took a deep breath, almost as if she'd forgotten to breathe—which was a distinct possibility. "It's the dumping that's disturbing us the most. Nina will escort you through the newest site, and by the time you're done, a courier will have delivered the information we have on the earlier crimes to your church. I'd rather you not come into the I.S. tower, if you don't mind."

"Not a problem," I said softly, thinking it over. Demon-like crime, not demon crime. I didn't want to risk the demons knowing that I was still alive. But if it was truly demonic work, it would be all over the airways. Demons are not subtle. No, it was likely a group of wannabe witches dabbling in black magic, giving demons a bad name. Taking them out would not only make me feel good, but it might help me get my citizenship pushed through.

"Okay," I said softly, and her soft, pleased sigh slipped over my skin like a silk scarf, raising gooseflesh. "I have to make a call. And that's even assuming I take the job. What does it pay?"

Nina reclined in her chair as if she owned the entire building. "What do you want?" she asked, her slim fingers gesturing gracefully, the red-painted nails catching the light. "Money?"

The word held a badly-hidden disdain, but no, I didn't need money. My purse was plenty fat. Literally. My credit cards had been canceled, my bank account, my phone plan, everything. I was unwillingly off the grid and carrying cash thanks to the money Trent Kalamack had given me, money originally from the Withons, a small (by his standards, not mine) token amount he demanded as an apology for them trying to kill him. Good thing I had a bodyguard.

"A valid driver's license would be nice," I said, fighting not to look at the form on the desk. With that, I might get my bank account back. "And my car registered in my name." The independence would do wonders for my self-esteem.

Leaning forward with a masculine huff of air, Nina brushed her long fingers through the forms between us, making me wonder what it would feel like to have those sensitive fingertips on me, and I shivered again. It wasn't her/him, it was the vamp pheromones rising in here, and I leaned past Wayde to crack the door. Office chatter, loud and excited, drifted in, and the undead vampire smiled, knowing why I had cracked it though Nina wouldn't have a clue.

"I'd appreciate a list of the curses and how they're performed so we can decide which are legal and which are not," she said, and I caught back a bitter laugh.

"You have a library card, right?" I said flippantly. "It's all in there."

Nina cocked her head and eyed me from around her long, beautiful eyelashes to make my heart thump. "Not all of it," she said softly, her words like an old jazz song down my spine.

I licked my lips and sat straighter, knees pressed together and hands clasped in my lap. "I don't deal with my legal kin—Nina," I said tightly, not liking the undead playing on my libido, and not through a young, innocent woman. Raising my hand, I jiggled the band of silver preventing me from tapping a line. He knew I had it. They all did. "I'm a limited-magic demon. Give me my car and my license, and I'll find them for you. That's my offer."

"Done," Nina said so quickly that I wished I'd asked for more.

Nina leaned forward, her long hand extended. I took it, and as we shook, the undead vampire left and I was suddenly shaking Nina the DMV worker's hand.

Nina's eyes widened as she gasped and pulled away. The scent of sweat rose thick, and she fell back into her chair, her head lolling as her legs splayed awkwardly under the desk. "Wow," she breathed to the ceiling, her lungs heaving as she struggled to catch up on the air her guest had probably forgotten to take in. Her face was pale and her fingers were trembling, but her eyes were so bright it was as if electricity was arching through her. "My God, what a rush!"

I looked at Wayde, who seemed nonplused, and Nina suddenly sat up as if remembering that we were still in here. "Ah, thank you, Ms. Morgan," she said, rising to her feet, full of energy. "I'll get your registration started and give you the address to the cemetery. I'd take you there myself, but I have to do something for him first and will meet you there. I have to go." Eyes wide, her breath caught, and I swear I saw her shiver.

The paper was a soft rustle as she darted for the door, her speed edging into that eerie vampire quickness that Ivy, at least, took great pains to hide from me. I jerked, staring at Wayde as Nina's exuberant voice echoed in the outer offices. "My God! I could hear everything!"

Exhaling, I unclenched my fists. Track down some bad witches. I could do that. Like *Nina* had said. All it would take would be some detective work—which I sucked at—and some earth charms—which I could still do. "I should call Ivy," I said softly.

Looking uncomfortable, Wayde handed me my bag, and I slipped a hand inside to find my cell phone. My eyebrows rose at the missed-call number. *Trent? What does he want?*

"That's probably a good idea, Ms. Morgan," Wayde said, leaning to look out the office door, but I was having second, third, and fourth thoughts.

Good idea? Right. That was the last thing this was.

At Avon Books, we know your passion for romance—once you finish one of our novels, you find yourself wanting more.

May we tempt you with . . .

- **Excerpts** from our upcoming releases.

- Entertaining **extras**, including authors' personal photo albums and book lists.

- Behind-the-scenes **scoop** on your favorite characters and series.

- **Sweepstakes** for the chance to win free books, romantic getaways, and other fun prizes.

- Writing **tips** from our authors and editors.

- **Blog** with our authors and find out why they love to write romance.

- **Exclusive content** that's not contained within the pages of our novels.

Join us at
www.avonbooks.com

AVON

An Imprint of HarperCollins*Publishers*
www.avonromance.com

Available wherever books are sold or please call 1-800-331-3761 to order.